Victor Davion returned to his desk and dropped into the chair. Tapping the screen of his computer, he looked up at Curaitis.

"I know you'll advise against this next thing, but I want it done. Send the assassin to Solaris. Put him in a safehouse."

Curaitis' head came up, but his face betrayed no emotion. "Is it not premature to kill Ryan Steiner?"

"You and I know he killed my mother. We don't have the smoking gun yet, but I want the assassin in position for when we get it. He will make a mistake. I'm certain of it." Victor curled both hands into fists and rammed them together. "And when he does, I will have him dead."

BATTLETECH®

ASSUMPTION
OF RISK

Michael A. Stackpole

A ROC BOOK

ROC
Published by the Penguin Group
Penguin Books USA Inc., 375 Hudson Street,
New York, New York 10014, U.S.A.
Penguin Books Ltd, 27 Wrights Lane,
London W8 5TZ, England
Penguin Books Australia Ltd, Ringwood,
Victoria, Australia
Penguin Books Canada Ltd, 10 Alcorn Avenue,
Toronto, Canada M4V 3B2
Penguin Books (N.Z.) Ltd, 182-190 Wairau Road,
Auckland 10, New Zealand

Penguin Books Ltd, Registered Offices:
Harmondsworth, Middlesex, England

First published by Roc, an imprint of Dutton Signet,
a division of Penguin Books USA Inc.

First ROC Printing, September, 1993
10 9 8 7 6 5 4 3 2 1

Series Editor: Donna Ippolito
Cover: Boris Vallejo
Interior Illustrations: Liz Danforth
Mechanical Drawings: Duane Loose
Copyright © FASA Corporation, 1993
All rights reserved

 REGISTERED TRADEMARK—MARCA REGISTRADA

To William Cox, John Watts, Sr., and John Watts, Jr.
for helping three guys who never
assumed the risk
but got saddled with it anyway

The author would like to thank the following people who by intent or accident contributed to this book:

Patrick Stackpole for his weapons' expertise; J. Ward Stackpole for medical advice; Kerin Stackpole for the title; Chris Hussey and Fredrick Coff for keeping me honest with Kai; Sam Lewis for editorial advice; Donna Ippolito for making me write in English; John-Allen Price for a Cox; Liz Danforth for tolerating me as it all came together; Scott Jenkins for fact checking; Larry Acuff, Keith Smith, and Craig Harris for the loans of characters; and the GEnie Computer Network over which this novel and its revisions passed from the author's computer straight to FASA.

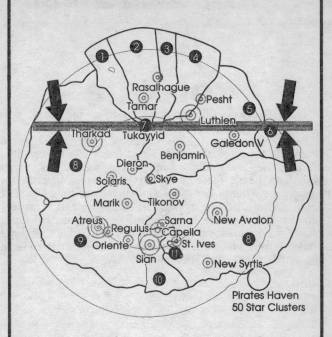

MAP OF THE SUCCESSOR STATES
CLAN TRUCE LINE

1 • Jade Falcon/Steel Viper, 2 • Wolf Clan, 3 • Ghost Bear,
4 • Smoke Jaguars - Nova Cats, 5 • Draconis Combine,
6 • Outworlds Alliance, 7 • Free Rasalhague Republic,
8 • Federated Commonwealth, 9 • Free Worlds League,
10 • Capellan Confederation, 11 • St. Ives Compact

Map Compiled by COMSTAR.
From information provided by the COMSTAR EXPLORER SERVICE
and the STAR LEAGUE ARCHIVES on Terra.

Prologue

New Avalon
Crucis March, Federated Suns
17 January 3037

Justin Allard watched his six-year-old son march into his study like a soldier reporting for disciplinary action. The blue blazer, white shirt, striped tie, and short pants made it easy to view his stiff strides as a childish parody of martial precision, but Justin knew his quiet boy was not playing. *The boy has begun his own punishment.*

Kai came to a stop at the left side of Justin's chair, well within striking range of the metal forearm and hand Justin had worn since losing the real thing in service to the Federated Suns. The boy's face did not betray the fear he had to be feeling, but the hushed tone of his whisper implied both remorse and personal mortification.

"I have done something wrong, Father."

Having spoken to the headmaster before sending a car to collect his son, Justin knew what had happened at the school, but he wanted to hear it in Kai's words. "What was it, Kai?"

The little boy pressed his lips together into a flat line, then swallowed hard. He held himself together with a self-discipline that belied his years—a self-discipline Justin had at times found lacking in MechWarriors six times the boy's age. It frightened him to see his son so rigid, yet that level of maturity also fed his paternal pride. He knew his son could still be a boy and run and play with other boys, acting his age, but when he had to deal with adult matters, he could handle them in an adult way.

"Some of the other boys at the school watched a holovid of a 'Mech fight from Slaris."

"That is Solaris, Kai."

"Solaris, yes, sir." Kai's gray eyes flicked down and color rose to his cheeks. "They said you were in that fight and that you killed a man. They said you had killed many men. That made you a hero. Then I got into a fight with Jimmy Kefaveur. He said his father could beat you up. I said you could *kill* his father. That made him cry." Kai's confession ended in a strained whisper filled with pain.

Justin nodded slowly. "It's time we had a talk." He left his chair and took his son's left hand in his flesh and blood right hand. Father led son to the brown leather couch on one side of the room where they faced the dark holovid monitor. Justin draped his right arm over his son's shoulders, and filled his mechanical left hand with the holovid remote control.

"Kai, six centuries ago—a very long time, before even your grandfather Quintus was born—some very smart men created BattleMechs. They made them big, taller than two or three of our houses stacked upon one another. They filled them with powerful weapons—lasers and particle projection cannons and missiles and guns—and put armor on them. They made them very strong and, just like in ancient times, BattleMechs ruled war the way knights in shining armor once did."

"Like King Arthur or Charlemagne?"

Justin caressed his son's head. "Yes, just like them. In combat the BattleMechs were frightful machines, and everyone in the Inner Sphere fought each other until they decided to unite and live in peace under the Star League. Then three hundred years ago . . ."

"Before grandpa was born?"

Justin chuckled quietly. "Yes, before my father was born, a very bad man named Stefan Amaris destroyed the Star League and wars have been waged ever since by people trying to put it back together."

"You got your metal arm in the war."

"I got it just before the last one, Kai, but that's not the point." Justin hit a button on the remote control and brought a picture to life on the screen. He killed the sound on the holovid with the punch of another button. "That's Solaris VII,

Kai. It's called the Game World because people go there to play at war. They engage in fights and all the fighters want to become Champion. Back before the last war Hanse Davion asked me to go to Solaris and fight to become Champion. Because he is my ruler, I did as he asked."

Kai's head turned toward the screen and Justin felt a jolt run through the boy. "This is the fight."

The holovid, which had been edited and broadcast throughout the Inner Sphere almost ten years earlier, showed Justin in a *Centurion* pitted against an equally humanoid *Griffin*. Because the fight took place in an arena called The Factory, with everything in scale to the thirty-meter-tall BattleMechs, the holovid could have been seen as a fight between two men in exoskeletons.

The lack of sound made the whole battle eerily surreal. "The man in the *Griffin* was Peter Armstrong. He was a brave man, but he trusted a very bad man. The bad man talked Peter into doing something very stupid."

The holovid showed Justin's *Centurion* stepping out from hiding within the debris in The Factory and aiming the muzzle that replaced the 'Mech's right hand at the *Griffin*. The *Griffin*, in turn, opened its arms wide. *Armstrong wanted me to take the first shot because he thought I had a light autocannon in that arm.*

Fire blossomed from the muzzle, and armor exploded on the *Griffin's* chest. The *Griffin* staggered, then fired back with its weapons. Missiles shot out from the launch canister on its right shoulder and peppered the *Centurion's* chest. The PPC in its right hand came up, but the azure rope of artificial lighting shot wide of its target. Through the swirling smoke from the missile launches, the extensive damage to the *Griffin* could be seen. Any MechWarrior could tell that a 'Mech with so little armor left on its chest was bound to go down.

"Peter Armstrong thought I was a coward. He wanted to kill me, but I didn't want to kill him. I tried to end the fight quickly."

Justin felt his throat constrict as the screen showed the *Centurion* again pouring fire into the *Griffin*. The autocannon's second burst blasted away the armor on the *Griffin's* right arm. It ate into the myomer fibers of the hand and forearm, devouring it as if the artificial muscles were succulent meat served to half-starved dogs. The pistol-like PPC dropped from the crippled hand, then exploded as the autocannon's shells tore through it.

The *Centurion's* medium laser drove a ruby energy spike through the heart of the *Griffin*. Compounding the damage done by the first autocannon burst, it burned away the fusion engine's shielding and ignited a fire that would consume the 'Mech's heart.

The faceplate on the *Griffin* exploded outward and Justin wished that just this once the outcome would be different than in the countless nightmares he'd had since the day of that fight. He wanted to see Peter Armstrong sailing out of the cockpit on his ejection seat, but where a man should have been, he saw only flames. The *Griffin* began to fall backward, a votive fire burning where its face had once been, now robbed it of all humanity.

Justin froze the frame. "Kai, Peter Armstrong died in that 'Mech. I didn't want him to die. I wanted him to live. For all I know he had a family, a son or a daughter, children like you and your sisters and brother. He could have had a wife, like I have your mother, and sisters and brothers of his own like your aunts and uncles. His mother and father could have been crying when he died."

He saw the boy's lower lip begin to tremble and Justin hugged him. "Remember this, Kai, remember it always: Killing a man is not easy, and never should be. Once you've done it, it's something that never goes away. This is the first time I've watched the holovid of this fight, but I relive that battle in nightmares. Peter Armstrong did not have to die and only did so because Philip Capet made him believe that punching out from a 'Mech was a cowardly thing to do."

Kai looked up at his father and nodded. "Killing is not easy, and never should be. I'll never kill anyone, father."

Justin again hugged his son. "It may happen that someday, in a war, you will be forced to kill. As long as you take responsibility for what you do, as long as you don't kill without reason, you will do well, my son."

The proud smile slowly vanished from the face of the elder Allard. "Now you hurt another boy's feelings. How will you take responsibility for that?"

Kai's brow knotted with concentration. Justin knew his

son would impose a punishment more harsh than his father ever would. *And thereby a lesson will be learned.*

"I should apologize. I should give him something to say I'm sorry."

"What do you think that should be?"

"My favorite book disk?" Kai offered it as a question, then took on a look of grim determination when his father nodded. "I will give him *Owl Moon.*"

"I think you have made a wise choice, Kai."

The boy looked up fearfully. "You don't hate me?"

Justin killed the picture on the monitor, then pulled his son into his lap. Once again he wished his metal limb could feel so he could enfold the boy in a proper hug. "Kai, you're my son. No matter what you do, I will always love you. I may be disappointed in you, but I will always love you."

"I love you too, Father."

Justin held his son close, then looked down at him. "You're a very special boy, Kai."

"Can I ask you a question?"

"By all means."

The boy's face again screwed up with concentration. "The boys said you became Champion of Solaris. They said that made you the best."

"Yes, I became Champion of Solaris."

"Why did you stop?"

Justin hesitated for a moment as he searched for an answer—not just one that a six-year-old could understand, but one he could understand as well. "Solaris is a world of make-believe, Kai, where men fight battles for no reason. Many people go there to hide. I could not. I went there, and I left there, because the real world needed me."

1

The slight breeze brushed the lazy drizzle lightly over Kai Allard-Liao's clean-shaven face. *It is right that the world weeps this day.* Unconsciously he hunched his shoulders, less in reaction to the chill air than to the chill of standing graveside watching a casket being slowly lowered into the dark ground. He pulled at the two ends of the belt holding his black trench coat closed, tightening the knot that imitated the one in his stomach.

The priest standing at the head of the grave smoothed down the page of his prayer book. "Salome Kell, into this earth we commit your earthly body, returning it again to the dust from which all men are made. We are confident you now dwell in heaven with our Lord, and will remain there for all eternity, forever and ever, amen."

"Amen," Kai echoed, crossing himself as the others did, but not moving away as the rest of the mourners departed one by one. He remained there alone, staring down at the casket but with his thoughts far away. Time passed unnoticed, and it was only the touch of a hand on his shoulder that brought Kai back from his reverie.

"Kai, thank you for coming." Phelan Ward, clad in Clan Wolf leathers as gray as the storm clouds overhead, gave Kai a tight-lipped smile that died almost before it was born. Phelan, who had been born on Arc-Royal, but who had been captured by the Clans and risen to the rank of Khan among the powerful Wolves, did not look nearly as strong or terrifying as legend would paint him. *Grief at the loss of a parent humbles even the greatest of warriors,* Kai thought.

He looked up, then nodded slowly. "Thank you for permitting me to attend."

"You do us great honor, coming here as a representative of the St. Ives Compact, my lord." Morgan Kell moved stiffly forward to stand beside his son. He offered his left hand, which Kai shook firmly, painfully aware that Morgan's empty right sleeve was pinned up in place at the shoulder. "Your mother and your nation have been most fair in their dealings with us."

Kai nodded, suppressing the shiver that the sight of Morgan Kell threatened to produce. He had first met the mercenary commander on Outreach, during the year of special training he had undergone in preparation for battle against the invading Clans. Morgan had been a powerful and charismatic presence there—and the fact that he had survived the bomb blast that killed both his wife and Archon Melissa Steiner Davion attested to his vitality. Still, the bomb that had taken his arm had also stripped away his veneer of invulnerability; at the moment Morgan looked drawn and weak.

Kai felt a lump rising in his throat and swallowed it back down again. "I have done my best to stay out of state business, accepting its obligations only when I must. Coming to Arc-Royal has been a painful duty, and your grief is my grief. I must confess, though, that I am not here only because my family honors you. I am afraid I usurped a bit of this service for my own ends."

Morgan looked him in the eyes and Kai felt an electric tingle run through his soul. "Of course, for your father. I understand, and I am yet more honored."

Phelan frowned, obviously confused by his father's statement. "Your father died years ago, *quiaff?*"

Kai ignored the Clanism in Phelan's question. "He died during the time that I was trapped on Alyina, trying to escape from ComStar and your Clan Jade Falcon. Afterward I did make a pilgrimage—though visit is probably the more correct word—to his grave on Kestrel."

Morgan Kell nodded solemnly. "I knew your father. What he endured, the sacrifices he made in the war against the Capellan Confederation, make him worthy of such reverence. In fact, you owe your existence to what he did in the service of Hanse Davion."

The comment brought a quick smile to Kai's face. "True. Had he not been in place on Sian, working for Maximilian Liao as a double agent for Davion, he and my mother might never have married, and St. Ives would still be part of the Capellan Confederation." His face darkened a bit. "Even though I visited his grave, I never really had a chance ... the funeral was held while I was away ... I ..."

Morgan reached out with his left hand and squeezed Kai's right shoulder with more strength than the younger man would have thought possible. "I understand. None of us begrudge you the opportunity to say goodbye." He looked up and around at the newly turned mounds of earth dotting the green bowl of the graveyard. "We've been saying goodbye to many of our dead, both recent and long departed."

Kai again felt his throat thicken. "My father and I, we understood each other—or, at least, he understood me. I always thought he put on a brave face for me, telling me he was proud of me without really believing it inside." Kai tapped the fingers of one hand against his own chest. "After Alyina and all I did there, I thought I would finally make him truly proud, but then ..."

Phelan's eyes half-closed and his face tightened. "I'm sure he *would* have been proud. I recently had reason to visit Alyina. The Jade Flacons and the Wolves are rivals and treat each other with barely concealed contempt. When I met Taman Malthus, the leader of the garrison on Alyina, I discovered that using your name helped make it possible to deal with him. In return for your Uncle Daniel's promise not to attack, Malthus gave us what we needed. He gave in out of respect for you, purely and simply. Whatever you did on Alyina, it impressed him mightily."

"Taman Malthus is a good man. I would and did entrust my life to him there, and he didn't let me down." Kai looked from Phelan to the elder Kell. "But my actions on Alyina or in the rest of the Clan war were really nothing compared to the miracles my father accomplished twenty-five years ago. I think, though, that he would have been pleased."

"Fathers take pride in all manner of things their sons do, Kai. I know I do." Morgan patted Phelan on the shoulder. "I think your father would have smiled at your adventures on

Alyina, and I think he would have been equally proud of your successes on Solaris. You've managed to eclipse his old mark there, and I understand his stable, under your leadership, has chalked up an impressive number of victories."

Kai nodded respectfully to the older man. *My father would have been pleased with what I've done, but would he have been proud of my using Solaris as a hiding place?* "The war against the Clans made for many changes. I'd like to think the changes in me were for the best, but it's hard to know."

Phelan's expression eased, but Kai felt him withdrawing. "War brings change and brings regrets. Because of the war I am cut off from my family. Just coming here to attend my mother's funeral required that Prince Victor Davion send a request for my presence as a representative of Clan Wolf to the Precentor Martial of ComStar, who approved it and then relayed it back to the ilKhan for his consideration. I would wish it different, but I acknowledge that it cannot be so. I am certain you have similar regrets."

"Comrades dead and friends lost, yes." Kai hesitated for a moment as, unbidden, the image of the dark-haired Deirdre Lear came into focus in his mind's eye. "There are times when learning the lessons that war teaches us about ourselves drives us apart from those we love. Deny the truth of the lesson and we can live in a kind of peace, but the truth will lurk in us and fester, erupting to destroy our lives without warning."

A curious look passed over Phelan's face for a heartbeat, then he nodded. "As much as we would like it, Kai, we can never again be the people we were before the war, nor should we want to. War stripped us down to our cores. It revealed to us what we are, what we were born to be. We cannot turn from it, because if we do, someone else will find a way to use it against us."

Returning Phelan's steady gaze, Kai felt the unspoken bond of similarity between them, yet knew how different was the way of life each one must follow in order to be who he must. Phelan, living within a culture that prized martial skill and daring above all else, could indulge and profit from his warrior's soul. *My world is not like yours, Phelan. I can only play at being a warrior.*

"It has been a long time since I have heard grim young

warriors philosophizing." Morgan glanced at the grave into which his wife had been laid, then shrugged wearily. "I have seen too much of war in my lifetime, but what I have seen reminds me that life continues after it. In adversity we find facets of ourselves that we never suspected. We form new relationships and draw new insights from the time in the crucible."

He nodded toward his son. "I thought Phelan lost to me, but he returns a Clan Khan and with a wonderful woman at his side. In the midst of death and destruction he found a key reason for living."

Again Deirdre's face flashed through Kai's mind. "Your son is most fortunate." Kai looked up, past both father and son, to where a small knot of people waited quietly at the edge of the valley of tombstones. All four people were dressed for mourning, three in black and one in white. "If the holovision broadcasts I saw as I came into Arc-Royal are even half true, it looks as though Galen Cox and Victor's sister Katrina have become an item. That's surely a meeting that be blamed on the war."

The Kells glanced back at the group behind them and nodded slowly, leaving Kai no doubt that their thoughts paralleled his own. The woman in white, Omi Kurita, had been sent by the Draconis Combine to represent her realm at the funeral. She and Victor Steiner-Davion had fallen in love when the war had forced their two nations—bitter enemies with a long history of grievances against each other—to work together to defeat the Clan threat.

Phelan shook his head slightly, his black forelock becoming pasted against his forehead by the mist. "I understand why Victor loves her, but I pity them. They can never be together, never."

"Never is a word that often turns out otherwise, Phelan." Morgan Kell smiled slyly. "It would once have been said that the Draconis Combine would never acknowledge its expatriate fighters on Solaris, but that too seems to be changing." He looked over at Kai. "I understand the DropShip *Taizai* will be taking Omi-*san* to Solaris itself as a gesture of rapprochement with the Combine community there."

Kai's jaw dropped open. "Is that possible? I mean, it's not that I doubt your word, Colonel Kell, but the Coordinator is sending his only daughter to Solaris? That's unprecedented."

"As will be your seventh defense of the Champion title in just over a year. I was asked to speed clearance of her DropShip so it could continue on its way. I've also arranged for the *Taizai* to run the same route and through the same connections taking you back to Solaris."

Kai recovered himself and nodded. "It will be quicker than any commercial route and saves the difficulty of having Combine JumpShips passing anywhere near the Isle of Skye. Ryan Steiner's propaganda factory has already spread a lot of dirty lies about Victor abandoning me on Alyina and stories about him having a rift with Galen Cox over Katrina. All he needs is another rumor about Combine ships operating in the Commonwealth."

"Precisely my thoughts, hence my caution. Luckily, Ryan's pathological hatred of the Clans has him preoccupied with Phelan's visit. He seems not to have noticed Omi's presence here, and I wish to maintain that illusion." As Morgan spoke, Kai saw fire return to his eyes and knew that despite his crippling injuries, Morgan Kell would always be a staunch defender of the Steiner bloodline and the Federated Commonwealth.

Morgan cast a weather eye at the descending clouds, then turned and started the long walk up the slope toward where Katrina, Galen, Omi, and his daughter Caitlin waited patiently. "Come with me, gentlemen. We have buried our dead and talked of wars and of enemies old and enemies still living. Let us set all that aside for a moment. Let us go and make a toast to the living and celebrate the memories of those we love and those we have let go before us."

Kai paused for one last instant at the grave and bowed his head. "When you see my father," he murmured, "tell him his son still loves him." He crossed himself again, then trailed after Morgan and his son, never looking back as the thickening mist fell over the graveyard like a shroud.

2

Tharkad
District of Donegal, Federated Commonwealth
19 December 3055

Standing there alone, before his mother's grave, Prince Victor Ian Steiner-Davion felt ensnared by the layers of interpretation people gave to his every action. Many would see the fact that he had come alone, banning press and aides alike, as a devoted son's desire to grieve for his mother in private. Countless multitudes of people living in his empire, which spanned more than a thousand light years, would accept that judgment. He also knew that most of those multitudes lived within the borders of his father's old realm, the Federated Suns.

The diminutive prince dropped to one knee, ignoring the icy wind that bit at his skin and whipped across the snow-blanketed cemetery. He unfastened the lower buttons of his gray woolen longcoat, then doffed his cap. The wind tore at his sandy blond hair, and the sting of icy snowflakes made him squint.

The eternal flame burning at the base of his mother's memorial hissed and snapped, instantly melting any snowflake that passed too near. The water on the stone surrounding it became solid or liquid depending upon which element—air or fire—held sway over it at the moment.

Victor dug with gloved hands at the snow near the base of the memorial. It came away in uneven clumps as if the crust were a puzzle he had sprung apart. The wind carried away the lighter snow-crumbs, leaving heavy kernels of ice still to be dug out by hand. He did so, carefully piling the snow on the other side of the long box he had carried with him from the waiting hovercar.

Victor knew that somewhere, well out of his sight, some journalist would be capturing his image, digitizing and even editing it so the universe could have a record of what Victor Steiner-Davion, Prince of the Federated Commonwealth, was doing. He knew that the scandal vids might label his actions as a desperate attempt to disinter his mother or to cover up telltale clues that would prove, beyond a shadow of a doubt, that his mother had not been killed in a bomb blast, six months to the day of his visit. He knew he could do nothing about what anyone would make of his visit and he tried to find comfort in his sister Katherine's admonition, "There is no such thing as bad publicity, Victor."

"Ah, but there is, Katherine, there is." Victor shivered, adamant in his refusal to bestow his grandmother's name on his sister even though almost everyone else in the realm now called her Katrina. "There *is* such a thing as bad publicity, and Ryan Steiner orchestrates it with damnable skill."

Victor let his anger at Ryan fuel him as he dug deeper into the snow and exposed the words carved into the memorial's granite base. "Melissa Steiner Davion, devoted wife, beloved mother, and beneficent monarch." He smiled, reading again the words he had read many times before. "You would have been happy, I know, Mother, to be remembered that way."

The prince hesitated, wondering suddenly if he should be talking aloud to the woman buried beneath stone and ice. In his heart it seemed so natural and normal to speak this way to his mother, but it didn't take much to realize how his mumbling at his mother's grave might be used against him. At even the merest hint of it, Ryan Steiner and his toadies would manufacture a network of lies that turned Victor into a superstitious fool who consulted with ghosts before making his decisions.

In his fury at the thought Victor almost slammed his right fist down into the stone, then smiled ever so slightly to himself when he did not give in to the impulse. The old Victor would have given vent to his anger right then and there. While the scandal vids would have played the story to the hilt, Ryan would have been turning Victor into a lunatic and ungrateful son railing against the woman who had given him life.

Victor had felt the sting of just that sort of vicious lie when his sister Katherine decided that it would be a mockery of their mother's dignity and beauty to permit her bomb-torn remains to lie in state. Katherine, acting in accord with Victor's admonition to use her best judgment in that matter, had ordered the funeral held quickly. Of all Melissa's children, Victor had been the only one who failed to attend the funeral.

Ryan quickly built that fact into a story suggesting that Victor hated his mother and might even have had a hand in her death. Katherine's immediate and passionate denials managed to blunt the damage done, but there were those within the Federated Commonwealth who clung to the vile myth like ivy to stone. Even though Victor had been raised and schooled on Tharkad, some considered him a traitor to the Steiner half of his heritage and would have been more than happy to support a rival who might return to traditional Steiner values.

Just the role Ryan covets for himself. Victor took in a deep breath, letting the cold air dry his throat and make his teeth ache. Ryan played the game of politics very well, but with Katherine's help, Victor had learned a thing or two that had helped him regain lost ground. It was true that although he cherished the chance to visit his mother's grave, and did come to offer a prayer and his respects, he knew the act could and would be turned to his advantage to erode some of Ryan's influence.

Victor forced political concerns from his mind and picked up the box he had brought with him. Tharkad's weather was so unpredictable that even in the supposedly seasonable portion of the year it could occasionally become bizarre. Some doomsayers suggested that a cold snap coming at the six-month anniversary of his mother's death proved that God was angry and that the world would end on Christmas. The prince believed nothing of the sort and felt secretly pleased that the inclement weather would make it miserable for anyone out to spy on him.

He smiled as he opened the box. He had anticipated the chaotic twists of climate when, two months previously, he had made his plans to visit Melissa's resting place on the same day the Kell Hounds buried their dead on far Arc-Royal. As much as he loved and mourned his mother, he regretted not being able to go there personally to thank the mercenaries for performing a mission that had saved the Inner Sphere from again being locked in a brutal war with the Clans. Because image became substance in the media, he could not attend and had sent Katherine along with his aide Galen Cox to represent him on Arc-Royal.

He opened the box and delicately withdrew a perfectly crafted crystal flower. Fashioned after the rare *mycosia* blossom his mother had so loved, the simulacrum had been shaped and polished until its beauty rivaled the real thing. The artisan who created it had been paid handsomely. Examining it again now, Victor resolved to reward the man still further.

Each leaf and petal had been formed from a holograph. The leaves on the stem contained the images of such lifelong friends of Melissa as Misha Auburn or her cousins, Morgan and Patrick Kell. The broad twin leaves that protected the blossom held rainbow portraits of her parents, Katrina Steiner and Arthur Luvon. Each of the flower's five petals was devoted to a different child, while in the center sat a wedding holograph of Melissa with Hanse Davion.

Victor wanted to say something, but his throat closed up on him. He gently laid the glass flower on the icy ground at the foot of his mother's memorial obelisk, then slowly stood. Keeping his head bowed, he offered a brief prayer, then stooped to recover his hat and the box he had used to transport the flower. Then he crunched his way back through the snow to the waiting aircar.

As he approached, a tall man climbed out the back door of the black limousine. After sweeping the cemetery with his gaze, the man held the car door open for the prince, his long black coat unbuttoned and his right hand free to draw the submachine gun holstered under his left arm.

Victor knew better than to smile at him or do more than grunt until he was safely ensconced in the car. Curaitis had opposed the solitaire visit to the cemetery, only demurring after Victor agreed to having the area placed under surveillance for the previous seventy-two hours and to letting no one but Victor enter it for the past eight. *That, I'm sure, won't make me popular with Curaitis' colleagues in the In-*

*telligence Secretariat, especially the ones who had the duty
of watching the place.*

Victor settled in to the wide seat in the back of the limo,
discarding the box and unbuttoning his coat as Curaitis
climbed in and closed the door. The big, dark-haired man
tapped lightly on the bulletproof glass between the passenger
compartment and the driver's seat. "Go."

The prince sank down into the seat as the hovercar's tur-
bine started, lifting the vehicle on a cushion of air. Snow bil-
lowed up and around as if a blizzard had suddenly arisen
outside, but the car's forward momentum carried it free of
the cloud. Victor glanced out at the desolate field of neat,
even rows of gravestones in the Triad National Cemetery. He
wondered if he, too, would someday be buried there with the
other Steiners who had ruled the Lyran Commonwealth or
its successor, the Federated Commonwealth.

Curaitis, perched on the jump seat beside the door, also
looked silently out the window. Victor knew the man would
say nothing unless asked to speak, but he nursed no illusion
that Curaitis behaved so out of deference or respect for Victor or his office. If the security agent thought Victor should
know something, he would tell him. If Victor requested information, Curaitis might just tell him more.

"Report?"

Curaitis pressed his hand to his ear, then nodded. "Our
teams found three holovideographers watching you and two
other remote recording devices. We have identified two of
the vidders—stringers for scandal vids. We're watching
them but have not detained them. The third is someone new,
but looks to be a journalism student trying to get images to
complete a semester project at the University of Tharkad.
We'll keep her under wraps until we can verify her identity,
but the prelim check has turned up negative."

"What about the two remote devices?"

"One belongs to one of the stringers, the other is still un-
identified. We're watching it." Curaitis frowned slightly as
the hovercar took a corner rather wide. "If no one comes to
pick it up in the next two days, we'll bring it in."

Victor nodded, pulling off his black leather gloves. "Anything in the realm of good news?"

Curaitis shrugged somewhat indifferently. "Peter presided
over the reintroduction of the Lyons gold panther into the

glades of the Dordogne Wetlands Preserve. Environmentalist and sportsman-hunter groups both applauded the move, which is probably the first time in history those two groups have ever agreed."

The prince smiled broadly. "That *is* good news. Is Peter settling in there?"

"Perhaps. Your brother still hates being stationed in a backwater like Lyons, but he endures it. His 'Mech company seems to like him, and though they're quite green, Leftenant General Gardner reports your brother is an able warrior whose influence is rubbing off on his people. He also gets on well with the locals, and the way he brought both sides of the panther dispute together did a lot of good because there are some influential folks on either side of that issue."

"Are the people calming down, or is Ryan still organizing protest marches."

"The only protests are mild and are coming out of the Bellerive religious community."

Victor shook his head. "Are they still claiming that I'm the anti-Christ?"

"Yes, with Peter as your apostle." The security man shrugged. "We can find no connection between them and Ryan, but we're prepared to act if they decide to do more than pray for the both of you."

"I'll take all the prayer we can get at this point. I need Ryan hobbled, and having Peter winning us friends in the Isle of Skye is one pebble for Ryan's shoe."

"You may, in fact, have another."

"How so?"

Curaitis' expression lightened, dulling the intensity in his eyes by the merest fraction. "When your sister and Galen Cox diverted to Ginestra to investigate the earthquake disaster, they gained a lot of notoriety by pitching in and working with the relief effort. The scandal vids linked them immediately, of course, but the more legitimate press began to run with the story as well. Katherine praised Galen as the one who suggested they divert, and his service record with you is getting good play. Because he's from the Isle of Skye and Katherine seems taken with him, some anti-Ryan forces have begun to champion Galen as a rival to you. There are also rumors that he befriended Ragnar Magnusson during the time you all trained together on Outreach, which has raised his stock in the eyes of the Rasalhague exiles in Skye."

Victor pressed his fingers together, unconsciously tapping the index fingers against one another. He didn't know which bit of that news he liked better: Galen being touted as an antidote to Ryan or Galen and his sister becoming linked in the scandal vids. He had expected that to happen—he and Galen had even joked about it when Victor asked his friend to escort Katherine to Arc-Royal. Galen's becoming a thorn in Ryan's side was an unexpected benefit, which Victor liked all the more.

"Are the stories about Galen and my sister all smoke, or is there fire there?"

Shadow hooded Curaitis' eyes as the limo descended a ramp beneath the Triad. "They have not slept together, if that's what you mean."

The prince stiffened for a second as his sense of family honor and any possible breach of it warred with his liking for Galen. "That does not surprise me. Galen is a gentleman and Katherine has a good head on her shoulders." *Besides, I wouldn't want to deny them the happiness Omi and I have yet to know.* "Frankly, if they do want to bed each other, I don't want to know about it. What I do want to know is whether or not they're interested in each other?"

For the first time since Victor had met Curaitis, the security agent seemed at a loss. "Ask me if a man is a murderer, Highness, and I can tell you. Ask me if a man would make a good agent—and Cox would—and I can answer that. Don't ask me about affairs of the heart. All I can say is that I've not received any reports of a romance from the field agents assigned to their security, but those people aren't trained to notice or quantify that sort of thing, either. There have been no public displays of affection in the media coverage, but beyond that I have no way of answering your question."

Victor smiled, then allowed himself a laugh. "There are few men I would welcome as brothers-in-law, but having one who could be used to undercut Ryan's base of support in Skye, well, that would be special indeed. Let me know if anything does seem to be blossoming there."

"As you wish, Highness."

"Oh, and I assume, because of your silence on the matter,

that the rumored lead on a payout to the man who killed my mother did not check out?"

Curaitis shook his head. "Working it backward led to a dead end, and our intelligence assets around Ryan haven't been able to produce any link to it."

"Dammit! I'd hoped we would finally have the smoking gun and be able to prove he gave the order to have my mother killed." Victor's left hand knotted into a fist. "I can't believe Ryan managed to have her assassinated without making a mistake somewhere along the line."

"We don't know that he didn't, Highness, we just know we haven't found it yet." The larger man flexed his hands as the hovercar slid into its parking place and slowly settled to the ground beneath the palace. "He is arrogant and believes himself invulnerable. One day he'll slip up somewhere and we'll have him."

Victor nodded. *And then I'll kill him with the same assassin the used to kill my mother.* "Very good. Keep me . . ." Victor let his voice trail off as Curaitis pressed a hand to his earpiece again. "What is it?"

Curaitis shook his head. "The student holovideographer checks out clean. We'll release her."

"No, wait."

"Highness?"

I think even Katherine would appreciate the way I'm going to handle this one! Victor smiled confidently. "She wanted images for a school project, correct?"

Curaitis nodded.

"Very good. Have your people bring her and her equipment here. Giving her an interview is the least I can do to make up for her inconvenience, isn't it? It should earn me points with the journalistic community and the education lobby." Victor shrugged slightly. "At least I can hope so. You're frowning, what is it?"

"Arranging the meeting will be simple, but it will mean you have to put off the envoy from Tormano Liao."

Victor groaned. His father had supported Tormano Liao and his Free Capella movement because that operation had helped to distract Romano Liao's paranoid attention. With Ryan's meddling in the Isle of Skye and the Clan War's devastating effect on the Federated Commonwealth economy, Victor had been forced to cut back on funding to Free Capella. In a compromise to get the Estates General to approve other legislation, he had agreed to put off a new appropriations bill until the second quarter of next year.

"Just thinking about having Karla Hsing haranguing me about funding cuts is enough to make me want to hand the whole F-C over to Ryan." The prince frowned. "Have someone in Foreign Affairs put her off and suggest that my patience, like my treasury, is not bottomless. As one runs out, so will the other. Diplomatically, of course."

"Of course."

"Tormano doesn't realize that he's really just a toothless old war hound, and his growls are not worth what they were in his sister's day." Victor shivered. "I wish Tormano would retire and persuade Kai to take his place. Then Free Capella would have a strong leader and one with whom I could deal."

"I would say that Tormano would be pleased to have Kai succeed him at the head of Free Capella. It's Kai who seems reluctant."

"Kai has more sense than most." Victor smiled in recollection of his friend. "So, then, we will have Hsing dealt with, yes?"

"As you wish, my lord. You're learning well how to play the political game." Curaitis shook his head. "My job is to protect you from harm, but Victor Davion the distant military leader was much easier to safeguard than Prince Victor the politician."

"There's the rub, Curaitis. My job is to keep the Federated Commonwealth alive. To do that I've got to become a politician as well as a soldier." Victor gave the other man a smile. "But don't worry, we both hate our new jobs."

Curaitis nodded. "But we'll do them anyway."

"That we will, Agent Curaitis, that we will."

═══ 3 ═══

DropShip **Taizai**, *Recharging and Transfer Station*
Tetersen, District of Donegal
Federated Commonwealth
24 December 3055

Zero gravity allowed Kai to grab the rungs of the transit ladder and propel himself along through the docking tube that connected his DropShip Zhanshi with the JumpShip that would be hauling it, the *Taizai,* and four other DropShips from Tetersen to Colinas and on to Solaris. The JumpShip's movement forward to the charging station had provided the illusion of gravity, but the illusion evaporated when the ship became stationary, its giant sail unfurled to collect solar energy to fuel the hyperdrive. Without gravity, anything not hitched down would float away if inertia could be overcome, and Kai did just that by shooting himself further along into the heart of the JumpShip.

He passed through a short corridor and entered another docking tube. Grabbing a stanchion, he brought himself down to the deck and used the guide rail to pull himself forward. Doing so cut his transit speed, but the dark-haired young man willingly made that sacrifice. Though he was traveling to the Kurita DropShip at the invitation of a friend, the invitation had been worded formally, requesting his presence not as the Champion of Solaris, but as the Duke-Designate to the throne of the St. Ives Compact.

Rounding the corner of the docking tube he caught his first glimpse of the Combine's Internal Security Force troopers guarding the airlock leading into the *Taizai.* The face of one of them resembled Kai's, with dark, almond-shaped eyes and the yellow skin tones of an ancient Asian ancestry. The other guard also had sharpened eyes, but his darker skin and kinky black hair suggested that he had inherited a strong dose of African blood.

Kai proceeded down the corridor until he stood two meters or so from them, then tightened his grip on the guide rail to stop himself. Planting his feet on the deck and holding himself down in place through pressure on the rail, Kai carefully executed a deep bow.

"Konnichi-wa," he said, then straightened slowly. He kept the expression on his face neutral and hid the exertion it took to keep himself planted on the deck.

Both ISF men, clad in loose-fitting black fatigues, returned the gesture, but then had to hop slightly in order to wrestle themselves back to the decking.

"Konnichi-wa, Kai-sama," the younger guard said with a nod, earning his darker partner's disapproving glare.

Kai assumed that the older man's frown was not because of the familiarity of address his partner had used. Allard-Liao was a mouthful, too packed with Ls and Rs to be easy for native Japanese speakers. He actually preferred being addressed by his first name as it reduced some of the anxiety within the Combine community on Solaris. What had even greater significance in this instance was the use of the title of "Kai-*sama,*" which revealed that the two ISF men were on different sides of a current split within the Draconis Combine.

Solaris, the Game World, attracted MechWarriors from all the star empires of the Inner Sphere. Solaris City, the capital, was divided into five major districts, each one identified with one of the ruling Great Houses of the Inner Sphere. The warriors from the various states tended to live among their own people in their own sectors of the city and to fight in local arenas. Aside from Terra, which boasted a neutrality established and administered by ComStar, Solaris was one of the few worlds in all the vastness of human space where people from different nations could mingle.

Though most warriors enjoyed a strong following in their native nation through packaging and rebroadcast of fights, those from the Combine were different. The Kurita rulers had never permitted legal distribution of fight holovids, and they treated contraband versions the same way they did forbidden weapons, explosives, or drugs. Even holovids in the possession of private citizens could be confiscated when the individual entered Combine space. To salve a visitor's bruised feelings, he was usually mollified with the fiction that the items would be returned at the time of his departure from Combine space.

The reasons for such harsh treatment were, Kai decided, justified if viewed from the perspective of the Combine's dominant Japanese culture. It harkened back to the medieval code of bushido, or the way of the warrior. Their mores dictated that all citizens were, ultimately, chattel of the ruling Coordinator and that their every action must be conducted with honor, compassion, and duty to each other, in accordance with the wishes of their masters. Those masters, in turn, drew their power from obedience to the wishes of their own masters and so on until everything led back to the Coordinator of the Draconis Combine.

The Combine warriors who fought on Solaris were not bold samurai like their homebound brethren, but were ronin. For millennia the masterless ronin had been both revered and castigated within Japanese culture. Like modern Robin Hoods they were admired for their courage, yet at the same time viewed as being honorless because they acknowledged no lord. With the reemergence of bushido in the Combine's culture over the last four centuries, ronin warriors had become more scorned than revered; indeed, any interest in the games on Solaris was officially viewed as something shameful, akin to a taste for pornography in other states.

"Kai-*sama*" was a title Kai had been given when he bested the Combine's best fighter, Theodore Gross, on his way to the top. Before the battle, Gross had boasted and postured about his skill and invincibility, while the promoters cast the fight as a contest between a seasoned arena fighter and a bored dilettante who needed to be taught a lesson. No one ever mentioned the fact that Kai was conceding his opponent twenty tons' worth of BattleMech, and when Kai took Gross down within thirty seconds of their first exchange, his quiet commitment to getting the job done immediately won him fans within the Combine.

And enemies, not the least of whom was Thomas DeLon, the stable owner for whom Gross fought.

Kai smiled politely. "I have come at the invitation of Kurita Omi-*sama*."

The elder man nodded. "We were informed of your coming. This way, my lord."

Kai followed him, vaguely amused and distracted by the way his starched and pressed tunic and trousers hung stiffly and allowed him to move within them. The guard said nothing as he conducted Kai into the DropShip, but the lack of other people moving through the corridor suggested to Kai that their passage was being monitored and his presence here being kept strictly confidential.

The invitation had come through normal diplomatic channels, which were anything but direct or overt. Omi's request for his visit had actually been relayed from the *Taizai* to the ComStar relay station on Tetersen, then sent on to Kai on the *Zhangshi* by the Ministry of State office of that planet. This made Kai think that keeping his visit secret was not so much for the universe at large, but for the slice of the Combine in the DropShip—which made a certain amount of sense.

Given that the Combine, by and large, firmly believed that the Solaris games and their devotees were a disreputable lot, permitting Kai to openly visit the ship would have been a dishonor. The fact that Omi was bound for Solaris must have caused no end of inner conflict for those assigned to take her there, because, on the face of it, to be assigned such duty was a disgrace. Yet Kai doubted that she had been given the mission as some form of punishment for a transgression against her father Theodore Kurita, but he also realized he did not know the Coordinator's mind.

But I do know Omi and she would never burden me with any part of her disgrace. In that single fact Kai took some comfort and had to kill the hint of a smile as the ISF guard pulled up at the mouth of a corridor walled with paper and wood-lattice *shoji* panels. "You will wait in here for her Highness."

Kai nodded and stripped off the rubber-soled shoes he had worn in transit. The guard pulled an elasticized pair of shoelets from a small niche in the wall, and handed them to Kai. The tongue of the shoes was so exaggerated and elongated that it ran up the front of his shin to cap his knee. He pulled the right one on, then fastened the elastic band in place around his knee by fitting the two velcro ends together.

As he tugged the second shoe into place he noticed two things about them. First was what anyone but people in the Combine would have considered a minor point: the color of the shoelets. The gray matched his eyes and coordinated well with the emerald green of his trousers. The same people watching his arrival and clearing the way must have made sure his shoelets and their color would not embarrass him or his hostess.

The second thing he noticed was that the front of the shoelet had the hard polymer hooks of the velcro used to secure the strap around his knee. He knew from practical experience that the velcro teeth could bite against bare flesh; the shoelets were not designed primarily as a fashion accessory. These thoughts vanished within a moment, however, exactly the amount of time it took the guard to slide a *shoji* panel open and wave Kai into the small room beyond.

If not for the subtle hint of the nearly invisible fuzzy stripes running across the *tatami* mats on the chamber floor, Kai would have thought himself in a small tea house. Barely three meters square, the room felt cozy the moment he pulled his knees up under his body and floated in. The low ceiling would have hit him in the head had he entered standing up. He gently pushed off it, then cushioned his landing on the mats. Touching down in a kneeling position, he firmly placed his knees and toes against the fuzzy stripes.

Immediately he bowed to the room's other occupant. "*Konnichi-wa*, Kurita Omi-*sama*." Kai touched his head to the mat, then carefully levered himself back into a sitting position.

Omi Kurita smiled at him before she bowed. Tall and slender, long black hair gathered at her neck with a thick red bow, she was dressed in a silk kimono edged at the sleeves, neck, and hem with wide emerald-green ribbon. The gown itself was ivory, with beautiful green herons woven into the silk. A green sash encircled her waist, and Kai had to assume that she had chosen the kimono specifically to harmonize with the clothing he was wearing to their meeting. Her ivory shoelets did not mar its beauty.

"It is very good to see you again, Kai Allard-Liao." Omi

tripped over none of the difficult sounds in Kai's name. "I am honored by your visit."

"As was I by your invitation." Kai caught a caution in her blue eyes, but could not place it until another panel slid open in the wall facing them. The individual kneeling beyond it kept his eyes downcast and moved with a stiffness that Kai marked as extreme formality. *What little we have already said is a breach of etiquette. We are not ourselves in this, but representatives of our nations.*

Kai set himself with his hands resting flat and palm-down on his thighs, mirroring Omi's position, as the third person gently pulled a long, slender casket into the room. The old man, bent as much by age as deference, pressed the mahogany box to the mats and let it settle into place. He fumbled at one of the three brass latches holding the lid shut, but Kai sensed that it was a deliberate mistake instead of a true miscue. This surprised him because he caught no horror for the action in the man's whispered *"Sumimasen."*

A frown flashed across Kai's face. *You are thinking too much like your father, and not enough like your mother.* The Asian cultures of China and Japan somewhat united the Combine, the St. Ives Compact, and the Capellan Confederation. Though Kai had been born to Candace Liao, Grand Duchess of the St. Ives Compact and one-time heir to the Celestial Throne of the Capellan Confederation, he had been raised within the confines of the Federated Commonwealth. He understood and took pride in his Asian heritage, but more often defaulted to the less elegant and less subtle logic of occidental philosophy when seeking guidance for his life.

As if reading his mind, Omi nodded slightly in the direction of the old man. "Jiro Ishiyama is a tea master who has served the Coordinator since before the time of my grandfather."

Kai absorbed that information and felt himself relax. *A* cha-no-yu, *and in zero gravity no less! Omi honors me, or her nation honors mine, beyond anything that has gone before.* He allowed himself the barest ghost of a smile, which he killed before Omi could be certain she had seen it but which, because of the ties that bound their cultures, she would have glimpsed.

Forcing himself to watch through Asian eyes as the tea master set up, Kai began to notice subtle nuances that would have escaped him otherwise. The paper of he *shoji* panels, for example, had a watermark that looked like a dragon. And the old man's robe was shiny at the elbows and knees, an indication of how long he must have been using it. The fact that Kai could see the man's knees meant the tea master was not wearing velcro, and his ability to remain in place told Kai why the man had maintained his rank for so long.

Kai had never actually attended a tea ceremony before, but those he had seen in holovid dramas or documentaries had not been held in zero gravity. In all those he had seen the ceremony centered around a table, but this room did not contain one. *How is he going to lay out his tools?*

The tea master pulled two bright blue bowls from the chest and set each one out as if placing them on an invisible table. When he withdrew his gnarled, age-spotted hands, the bowls remained floating in the air ten centimeters or so above the *tatami* while he turned back to the chest. The bowls remained in place, wobbling only slightly and out of sync with each other in a pattern that Kai found almost hypnotic.

The trance imploded when Ishiyama freed the next item from the chest, handling the thick glass sphere as if it were a fragile soap bubble. Kai noticed that two sealed openings marred the ball's perfection, but at the same time he marveled at how nearly perfect an item produced by the hand of man could be. One opening on the ball appeared as a black dot chased with stainless steel appro꞉imately a quarter of the circumference from the larger latched opening. The second opening actually appeared to be a section of the ball connected to a clear cylinder that reached to the center of the sphere.

This, too, the tea master brought out of the chest and left hanging in the air. It hovered above the two bowls, and as Kai watched it slowly rotate, he saw that what he had taken for one thick wall of glass actually was two, with an open space between them. *Insulated, like a Thermos bottle.* He suppressed a smile. *That, then, is where the tea will be brewed.*

Ishiyama turned to the casket one last time and withdrew a small tea chest and a silver cylinder with a needle-shaped nozzle at the upper end. The tea chest was pressed into place on the floor, while the silver cylinder hung in space like a

blimp. Ishiyama grasped it firmly, twisted the bottom, and then pushed it up toward the top. The cylinder contracted about three centimeters and Kai heard a faint crunch.

The tea master released the cylinder with it hanging perpendicular to the floor. Turning his attention to the tea chest he pulled the top off the little octagonal box with more force than was really necessary. That formed a vacuum, and small pieces of dried tea leaves began to shoot into the air as he lifted the lid up and away from the chest. If not for the understated grace and gravity of Ishiyama's movements, Kai might have assumed he'd made a mistake.

He had not. With a feather-light touch, the old man flipped open the latch on the brewing sphere, then sent it spinning up to drift along the line of the escaping tea particles. As if the opening were the southern pole of some planet, the sphere positioned itself perfectly to accept the tea leaves. Slowly and delicately, fluttering against each other as they filled the glass cylinder, the tea leaves fell upward and were trapped.

Almost playfully Ishiyama watched the glass sphere out of the corner of his eye. He brought the lid back down onto the tea chest, then with a flick of his wrist summoned just a pinch more tea. It flew upward, faster than the rest had, but still remaining on target. Kai did not doubt that all of it made it into the receptacle—the white *shoji* panels would not have hidden a single particle of any that might escape— and he felt no need to dishonor the tea master by looking for errors in his ritual.

The older man snapped the tea sphere shut, then recapped the tea chest. The latter he returned to the casket while the glass ball slowly drifted down toward the *tatami* mats. Before it could hit, the tea master firmly grasped the cylinder and inserted the needle into the small nipple on the sphere. With a touch to the lever at the needle's base, he sent steaming water spraying into the sphere.

Kai smiled. *That must have been a chemical heating tab. It heated up the water, which expanded and created the pressure needed to propel itself into the sphere.* It occurred to him that he should probably have been able to figure out the whole procedure from the nature of the teapot itself, but Kai set those thoughts aside. *That's science. This is art.*

The hot water collected in the bottom of the sphere and

fountained up inside as more water shot in. Satisfied that he had filled it sufficiently, Ishiyama pulled the cylinder free of the sphere and returned it to the casket. Holding the sphere in both hands, he began to gently swirl the water so that it collected on the walls of the sphere. The tea had been moistened by the water spraying into the sphere, giving the transparent liquid just the hint of color.

Once the water covered the interior of the globe, Ishiyama immediately rotated the sphere ninety degrees. Turbulence whipped silvery highlights through the water. Impact with the tea-leaf cylinder created a froth that came away a pale green. As the water washed over it, the liquid became darker and darker.

Whenever the water's motion began to slow, Ishiyama tipped the globe or gave it a spin. Each time he changed the sphere's attitude and position, the water broke in new and wonderful patterns. Kai found himself seeing symbols and creatures in it, the faces of old friends and fragments of long-forgotten nightmares. He made no attempt to catalog what he saw, but instead lost himself in the experience of seeing.

After a time that seemed too brief and yet like forever, Ishiyama let the water slow. Through a gentle and controlled rocking cradling motion, the tea master collected the water in the bottom of the sphere and turned the globe so the nipple stood at the north pole. Like a magician, the tea master suddenly produced another object from the sleeve of his kimono; a slender silver needle nearly thirty centimeters long and containing a fat plastic cylinder with a spring in one end. He inserted the needle into the nipple, sinking its far end into the green tea.

Ishiyama grasped the first blue bowl and pressed it down on the plastic cylinder. His right hand steadying the globe against the floor, he used his left hand to gently push the bowl down. Kai heard the hiss of liquid and saw steam form and pour out of the bowl, but he remained far enough from the tea master that he could not see down into the bowl to figure out what he was doing.

The tea master pressed down twice, then waited and pressed down twice more. He freed the first bowl and, bowing deeply, extended it to Omi. She accepted it with a bow of the head, then held the drinking bowl as if it were fragile enough to crumble at a moment's notice. The tea master then repeated his double pumps and presented the other bowl to Kai.

He accepted it as gingerly as if someone were handing him a live grenade with the pin pulled. In truth, it could have been just that, he decided. Only the very adventurous or curious would try to drink freestanding liquid in zero gravity. He found it remarkable enough that the tea master had managed to brew and serve the tea without any globules floating free. Drinking it could prove more difficult than his last championship defense.

Ishiyama bowed deeply to Omi and Kai, then reached into the casket one last time. From out of the box he lifted a white rose. He shielded the blossom with his hand as if it were a candle flame, then let it drift out from his hand and float between them. As it did so, heading out blossom-first, the air pressure stripped away the petals one by one. They spun away in the flower's wake. Kai watched it go, then turned back to nod his appreciation to the tea master, only to find that Ishiyama had silently left the chamber.

Kai glanced down at his tea bowl, feeling the warmth bleed out through the sides, and he smiled. Sitting in the bottom was something that looked like a small ceramic mushroom. Through it the tea had been pumped up into the cup through countless little holes in the stem and under the cap. Around the interior of the cup, about a third of the way up—roughly the level of the top of the mushroom—a little ledge kept the tea from rolling up and out over the sides of the bowl. Extending up from the ledge in a flowing clockwise spiral was a little tube that emerged near the lip of the cup.

Using as little movement as possible, he started the tea flowing clockwise, then raised the cup to his mouth just in time for the warm liquid to flow into his mouth. Its warmth and the sweet taste took him back to his childhood and to simpler times before the coming of the Clans, the death of his father, and his flight to Solaris. *It is good to have the memories because I can never go back, can I?*

He pressed his tongue against the tube opening, then swirled the bowl counterclockwise to evacuate the tube. He smiled and lowered the bowl. Across from him, returning his smile through a thin screen of rose petals, Omi likewise lowered her bowl.

"You are quite perceptive, Kai. Very often the tea will jet into the air when one has not done this before."

"I would rather die than spoil this ceremony." Kai blinked as a white petal brushed near his right eye. "It was beautiful. *Domo arigato*."

"You are welcome. It is my gift to you, on this eve of your Christmas."

Kai hesitated for a moment and felt the heat rising to his cheeks. "You are most gracious. Forgive me, but I had not thought ... I mean I have nothing for you ..."

Omi dismissed his concerns with a slight shake of her head. "Do not feel embarrassed, for I am the one playing at deceit here. I have trapped you and I have no desire to do this. You are a friend."

"As are you. Perhaps the nations we represent have a need to lay traps for each other, but you have merely to ask and if it is within my power, I would grant anything you desire."

Omi's expression lightened. "You know, of course, that I am bound for Solaris."

"I do."

"And you are doubtless aware of the Combine's general view of the warriors who fight on Solaris."

Kai nodded. "I am."

"And you can imagine the dishonor attendant to being sent there by the Coordinator."

The MechWarrior's eyes narrowed. *Are you in trouble? Some rift between you and your father?* "You are a friend, Omi-*sama*. What others might see as dishonor I would not."

She smiled. "Good, then you should have no problem granting my request."

Kai raised an eyebrow.

"I wish, Kai Allard-Liao, to be seen in your box when you defend your title."

Kai's jaw shot open. "Gladly, Omi, happily. Had you not asked I would have demanded it." He recovered himself and frowned. "But why? You know as well as I do that holovids of that fight will be bootlegged throughout the Combine. If your visit to Solaris is a dishonor back home, you are guaranteeing that trillions of people will witness the disgrace."

"That I know, Kai, and only too well—better than you, in fact." Omi smiled cautiously. "You see, this fight of yours is the first that will ever be permitted for viewing across the whole of the Combine."

"What?" Kai shook his head in amazement. "I don't understand."

"It is simple. This mission to Solaris is one I suggested to my father." Omi dropped her gaze, staring unseeing into the depths of her bowl. "If it fails, all blame will be mine and, as befits a crime of some magnitude, I will be destroyed."

4

Porrima
Isle of Skye, Federated Commonwealth
24 December 3055

Duke Ryan Steiner never thought of anger as a hot emotion. For him it was always something else, an iciness, a calm, cool clarity. Revenge is a dish best served cold, he often mused.

He knew that many of his subordinates—and even his wife—found his bloodlessness in matters political and personal disturbing. For him heat was synonymous with disaster because of his days as a fighter pilot for the Lyran Commonwealth. Any pilot who let his aerospace fighter overheat would surely die in space or by crashing into the planet. Hot-blooded passions, so common among the fighter jocks he'd known, often led to fights and the needless injury or death of others.

Emotions make for mistakes. As that thought echoed through his brain with the force of a biblical commandment, he clamped down hard on lingering traces of irritation that threatened to raise his emotional temperature. He tensed his jaw, glancing again at the glowing green neon numbers hovering in the air above his desk, then beyond them at the two advisors in his office.

"You are correct, gentleman, and I commend your vision. It does appear that the Isle of Skye news media is increasing its coverage of people who are less than sympathetic to *our* goals." Ryan stabbed a slender finger at the numbers reporting the expanding coverage of Peter Davion. "The slope of Peter's rise is rather steep, is it not? Reasons?"

David Hanau, the shorter, stockier of the two advisors, shrugged uneasily. "Peter forged an alliance between hunting and conservation groups that got the Lyons gold panther reintroduced to its natural habitat. As he has done for years, he is supporting the breeding, conservation, and reintroduction of wild animals to worlds where war has depopulated them."

Ryan impatiently beckoned with his right hand, coaxing Hanau on to make his point. "Which means?"

Hanau hesitated. "Bluntly put, my lord, fuzzy animals are cute and, therefore, popular. Pictures of Peter out on a conservation photo safari or petting panther kittens make for good media material. Peter knows it and he thrives in the spotlight. He spends so much time with the conservation forces that he seems to have no time for women."

A frown knitted Sven Newmark's bushy blond eyebrows together. "Is he homosexual?"

Hanau blushed at the question.

Ryan raised an eyebrow. "Is he?"

Hanau's mouth opened, then closed, then opened again. "I have no indication of that. I mean, I did a search for any possible illegitimate children he may have sired. I found a number of women he'd escorted while at the New Avalon Military Academy. None claimed to have borne him a child out of wedlock, but most were vehement concerning his heterosexual . . . uh . . . abilities."

Ryan patted his blond hair into place, suppressing a shudder as his fingers passed over the growing bald spot on his crown. "An illegitimate child would be better than a same-sex scandal, in any event. People will do more for children than even for lovers—doubtless a genetic imperative of some sort."

The duke pressed his hands together, fingertip to fingertip. "We have decent assets on Lyons, do we not?"

"Ja," Newmark said. "But no one in the Lyons militia. Davion's Intelligence Secretariat transferred out all questionable individuals when Peter accepted assignment to that unit. They had to transfer in so many new soldiers to fill out the ranks that the overall experience level of the unit dropped to the point the Federated Commonwealth Armed Forces now considers it a green unit. But unless something drastic happens, like a new invasion by the Clans, it's unlikely the

Lyons Militia will be doing anything but training. I have people assigned to keep an eye on him, of course."

"Of course." Ryan gave Newmark a smile. The man was one of a number of Rasalhague refugees whose flight from the Clans had led them to sanctuary in the Isle of Skye. Newmark had come to the duke's attention and into his personal service after the refugee press had published some of the man's articles highly critical of Prince Victor and his handling of the Rasalhague question.

Ryan's dark eyes flicked up to another number in the analysis chart hovering before him. "Galen Cox's media coverage is growing at a more controlled rate, it seems."

Newmark nodded appreciatively. "He has attracted their attention because of a number of coincidences. First and foremost, of course, is the fact that he is traveling with Katrina Steiner."

"She does know how to manipulate the media, doesn't she?"

"Yes, my lord. She attracts a great deal of attention, and everyone's curiosity about her transforms into curiosity about anyone near her. Kommandant Cox had been quite close-mouthed about their association, however. The news-hounds have been trying to dig up the facts about him and it turns out he's a wonderful subject. Born in the Isle of Skye. Orphaned during the War of Thirty Thirty-Nine. Later on he attended the War College on Tamar. In fact, it was you, Excellency, who conferred on him the Gallantry Award in the graduation ceremony for his class."

Ryan tried to think back, for he recalled the ceremony, but not the details. To him it had been a data point, an opportunity to impress people with his presence and existence. His wife, Morasha Kelswa, was heir to the throne of the Tamar Pact, and his goal at the time had been to convince Melissa Steiner and Hanse Davion to wrest those worlds back from the Free Rasalhague Republic. Speaking to the graduating class at Tamar had presented him the opportunity to inspire and recruit those young men to the urgency of accomplishing his goals.

Newmark continued his analysis. "Cox served with Victor Davion during the Clan wars, even saved his life on several occasions. He has been with Victor ever since, some saying he functions as Victor's conscience or reality anchor. That

Victor asked him to escort Katrina shows how utterly the prince trusts the man. In the promotions for reruns of those holovid dramas about Prince Victor, they've been playing up Galen's role in the story, even when it's only a minor one. That probably accounts for the rise in his numbers."

"I see. Do you think this is temporary?"

Newmark nodded emphatically. "I do."

Ryan shot a glance at Hanau. "I gather, from your frown, you do not agree?"

The dark-haired man shook his head. "No, my lord. Cox's media exposure comes in both news and entertainment coverage. In a number of markets the programs about him and Victor have been counterbroadcast against shows about you. Granting that the holodramas about your days as a fighter pilot are dated now, the shows featuring Cox are twice as popular. In addition, because the dramas feature Victor, news programs often place little promotional bits in with the advertisements, touting items about Victor, Katrina, Peter, or even about Kai Allard-Liao's latest fight. It's hard to say if this is a coordinated effort against you, my lord, but I would be negligent in not pointing out that Katrina's aptitude for media manipulation may have rubbed off on Victor and even Peter."

Hanau looked down. "As their numbers rise, so do Victor's, while yours decline."

Ryan smiled at the touch of panic elevating the pitch of Hanau's voice. "Well, then, it seems we'll have to work at severing that connection between Victor and the others." The duke smiled carefully. "Mr. Hanau, you will begin placing the rumor that the rift between Katrina and Victor over the disposition of their mother's body has never truly healed. Cox, in attempting to reconcile the two, has become a close personal friend of Katrina. Hint at intimacy, but back away from any confirmation of it. As a result of this, Victor has become disgusted with Cox, and *that* is the reason Cox was sent off with Katrina. It is not that Victor trusts the man, but that he does *not* trust him, and for that reason sent him away."

Newmark smiled appreciatively. "If we promote Galen Cox as a loyal son of Skye and heighten the rumors of Victor's rejection of him ..."

"Exactly, we use Galen's rising popularity to force a

wedge between Victor and Skye." Ryan nodded his congratulations to the blond man. "Any attempts by Victor or Galen to deny this rumor can be construed as their effort to cover up public knowledge of how bad things are going."

The duke looked at Hanau as the man tapped away on the keyboard of his comp pad. "Your point about my dramas being out-of-date is well taken. I need to expand my profile to get coverage in more areas. Your mention of Kai Allard-Liao also reminds me that I invested in a stable of fighters on Solaris some time back."

Newmark nodded. "Oonthrax Stables. Vito Oonthrax's wife is a distant cousin of your wife. Her family had a claim to the ownership of Laurent, and he needed money to rebuild his stable. The initial return on your investment—ownership of fifteen percent of the stable—was good, but has fallen in the last few years."

Ryan waved a hand through the financial data that suddenly appeared before him. "It was never about money, that deal, but politics. Laurent is gone—the Wolf Clan took it, and good riddance to it. Buy the stables outright. Fire Vito and put someone else in his place. Change the name to Skye Tigers and announce that I have become the owner. I will be traveling there in time for Kai Allard-Liao's next defense of his title. It's not against one of my fighters, is it?"

Hanau shook his head. "No, he'll be fighting Wu Deng Tang, one of Tandrek Stables' rising stars. It's being billed as a war for the Liao throne, since Ling is a Liao fighter."

"Good, that should attract plenty of attention." Ryan smiled. "Being there will garner me a fair share of it."

Newmark frowned. "Backing up for a moment, what do you think Katrina will do in response to our attempt to drive a wedge between Prince Victor and Galen Cox?"

"Nothing." Ryan interlaced his fingers and let his hands rest on the desk. "Katrina and I understand each other. She will undermine neither Victor nor me. To undermine her brother would be foolish because he could isolate her. To go against me, well, that would be equally foolish."

The Rasalhague expatriate nodded. "I see. What about Peter?"

"Peter's greatest weakness is his temper. He is on his way to conquering it, but he has still not done so. We must test him, to see how stable he really is." The duke closed his eyes for a moment. "The militia is the only armed force on Lyons, correct?"

"Yes, my lord," Hanau replied quickly.

"Good. Tell our people there we want an increase in political unrest. Just civil disobedience at this point. Anti-Davion rallies focusing on the refugee problem and the general sluggishness of the economy. Also have them establish connections with any pro-violence anarchist cells."

Hanau looked up, surprise spreading over his face. "Those groups hate you as much as they hate the Davions."

"True, but they can and do have their uses." Ryan took comfort in Hanau's shudder. "If it's true that Peter is learning to control himself, one of those fanatics could be just what we need to eliminate him altogether."

5

DropShip Zhangshi, *Jump Orbit L3*
Tetersen, District of Donegal
Federated Commonwealth
25 December 3055

Kai Allard-Liao bowed deeply as Omi Kurita stepped into the dining salon of his DropShip. "I am glad you were able to join me on such short notice."

She nodded to him. "And I am glad of the invitation to come here." Her long black hair, which she wore loose, hung down over the shoulders of her silken dress. Though the garment resembled the chic style seen on countless worlds of the Federated Commonwealth, Kai could tell from the subtle pattern of threads woven through the sky blue fabric that the dress had been manufactured in the Draconis Combine. *If they go so far as to provide Omi with a FedCom wardrobe for visiting a FedCom world, her mission must be vital indeed.*

Omi looked distractedly around the room. Its deep mahogany paneling and brightly polished brass fittings contrasted with the ferrosteel and ceramics of the ship's construction. The room's furnishings were also in a style more suited to a splendor of ages long past, as if this were a cabin on the kind of luxury liner that used to ply terrestrial oceans more than a millennium ago.

Her face brightened as she crossed to the small artificial evergreen tree set up in the corner and strung with lights. "A Christmas tree? I have heard of such things, but never actually seen one."

Kai shrugged. "I'm afraid this one is very poorly appointed. Normally we would have tinsel and ornaments, but with our occasional drops to zero gravity, the tinsel would be a tangle and the ornaments would float off and smash when we started moving again."

The Coordinator's daughter laughed softly. "And that is the reason why you have no mistletoe hanging from the ceiling?"

Kai blushed, the reaction surprising him. "Ah, I'm afraid I've no one I want to kiss."

Omi raised an eyebrow. "No one?"

He hesitated, betraying himself, then laughed. "Aboard the *Zhangshi*, no." *Nor elsewhere either.* Kai did not let his heartache show on his face. "I am currently, as is said in polite company, unattached."

"I understand."

Kai arched an eyebrow. "You know, Victor could have asked me that question himself. I would have answered him."

Color rose to Omi's cheeks as she sat down on the leather couch beside the small tree. "Denial would be fruitless and would devalue the concern he feels for you. It was not lurid curiosity that prompted the question. Victor respects you and only wishes to know whether you are happy."

"I appreciate that more than you know. And I appreciate your willingness to act as a go-between for us. I owe you for yet one more thing than the ceremony yesterday. That was exquisite." Kai sat down in a chair across from her, tugging at the creases in his black trousers as he did so. "I'm glad you two manage to exchange messages. We send things back and forth, too, but Victor is very busy."

"True, though he very much values the fights you dedicate to him. He often tells me of them and your great skill." Omi sat back on the couch. "Of course, I recall the simulator battle in which you and Phelan Ward killed each other. You are very skilled—as evidenced by your holding the title."

"I am very lucky." He looked up at her. "I will grant your request to be in my box during the defense of my title, of course. However, I am not anxious to play any part in your destruction."

Kai picked up a small plastic box from the table beside his chair and pushed a red button on it. The button glowed with a red light that did not waver. "The room is now secure. What we say to each other will not go beyond these four walls. Why are you being sent to Solaris? Given the Combine's cultural bias against Solaris and anything associated with it, it's political suicide."

"I know, Kai, from what you have just said, and what you have left unsaid, that you understand the situation very well. My father, even before he became the Coordinator of the Draconis Combine, had introduced reforms into the military. Those reforms encouraged flexibility and a loosening of the stiff codes that bound the military and the whole culture together. The feudal ideal of placing all trust in one's superior worked well while the world was still a primitive place where only the nobles had the education sufficient to make decisions."

The MechWarrior nodded. "Terra outgrew that sort of government in the twentieth century, but lapsed back into it as the vast distances and harsh conditions involved in the colonization of space required local authority with strong ties to the worlds left behind. Even so, most of the Inner Sphere nations have liberalized their governments to allow for increasing growth and development.

"All except for us. Four and a half centuries ago, Urizen Kurita, my ancestor, reinstituted the code of bushido." She smiled in an almost embarrassed way. "He kept our culture strong and used it to bind us together. It was this that allowed the Draconis Combine to survive the centuries of Succession Wars after the collapse of the Star League. It would have stood us in very good stead had men of vision like Hanse Davion not come along.

"In the War of Thirty Twenty-eight his strategies showed us our weaknesses. By thirty thirty-nine my father had changed enough things to be able to strike back and show Hanse Davion that we were capable of new tactics, too. Then the Clans came and we discovered that our tactics were not new or innovative enough. We needed to do more, and that meant more change."

Omi had a gift for understatement. The Clans—super warriors in superior BattleMechs—had carved great chunks from the Federated Commonwealth and Draconis Combine, as well as all but totally swallowing up the Free Rasalhague Republic. The Combine, being smaller than the Federated Commonwealth, had taken a severe beating that included the near loss of its capital world of Luthien. Units fighting in the traditional methods of the Combine had been slaughtered, while newer units had adapted much more readily to fighting the Clans.

Omi chewed her lower lip before continuing. "The people of the Combine are proud and, because of past policies, insulated and isolated from the harsher realities of life within the Inner Sphere. Your propagandists say that is the price of not having a free press, but we would like to think that saving our people from the scourge of scandal vids is worth the selective news policy we employ."

"I have no problem with the ban on scandal vids, but I cannot sanction having a misinformed public."

"Not misinformed, Kai, but *underinformed*. They know what they need to know, but events have outstripped our constraints. We could not isolate them from news of the Clan conquests. Because our people have for so long been suckled by stories of our military invincibility, this comes as a great blow." Omi glanced at the evergreen beside her. "It is akin to being told there is no Santa Claus."

"There isn't?" Kai allowed himself to look stricken, then softened his face with a smile. "Sorry, old joke. You were saying . . ."

"The blow to the Combine's morale is worse than you could ever imagine. Our military tradition, the way of the warrior, is the foundation for our society. Defeat calls all that we are into question. If we are not invincible, one must wonder how we will know if we are honorable, how we will know if we are civilized, and how we will know if we are true to all that has gone before."

Kai nodded. "On Alyina, during my time there, I felt an earthquake. It wasn't much of one, maybe a five on the Richter scale, but the ground actually moved. I'd never experienced that before, and it made me realize that I took for granted that the earth would always remain solid and stable under my feet. The fact that it didn't still wakes me in a cold sweat from time to time."

"Yes, it is a fundamental betrayal of trust. In your case it was reality betraying you. In the Combine the people wonder if their culture has betrayed them. It is very unsettling."

"I can imagine."

"My father knows that more changes must be made in the

Combine. We cannot and will not abandon bushido, because it forms the ligaments and tendons that bind our society together. This is a difficult decision to make because the samurai who help define the whole system have been discredited. And if not for help from the mercenary Wolf's Dragoons and Kell Hounds, we would have lost Luthien. Because our culture holds mercenaries in such low regard, that was an even greater blow to our honor—despite the rescue of Luthien."

Kai smiled as he began to realize where she was headed. "The ronin on Solaris have not been discredited in any substantial way. The bootleg copies of their fights have made them heroes among your people. They are like outlaws who refuse to conform within a society that demands conformity, and watching them is a safe form of rebellion in a community that badly needs a safety valve to relieve pressure."

"It is believed we can use them and their exploits to introduce to our people the idea of surviving defeat to fight yet again. The Draconis Combine Mustered Soldiery will still be the pinnacle of bushido in our country, but the ronin will allow people to have heroes akin to your Robin Hood. This is actually in keeping with some of our heroic legends, and can be used to provide confidence and even distraction as we prepare for the resumption of the Clan war."

Kai found himself marveling at Omi and her command of the situation within her nation. The Combine rarely permitted its women anything beyond traditional, domestic roles as career choices. Though he knew nothing could ever have kept Omi so confined, her traveling to worlds outside the Combine was largely unprecedented in Kurita history. He had no doubt that the plan to use Solaris as a tool for rebuilding her nation originated with her, and that her willingness to act on it and risk everything showed the depth of her commitment.

From Victor he had heard the story of how the Tenth Lyran Guards had been given the assignment of rescuing Hohiro Kurita, Omi's brother and heir to the throne of the Dragon, from the Clan-occupied world of Teniente. Omi had proposed asking Victor's unit to make the rescue and her father had permitted her to do so, but only on the condition that she agree to sever all contact with Victor after her request was sent. She agreed to the condition and informed

Victor of it in the message asking his help for Hohiro. As much as it pained her, she kept her part of the bargain until Takashi Kurita, her grandfather and the Coordinator before her father, released her from it in gratitude for Hohiro's rescue.

"Bringing the battles from Solaris to your nation is a bold gamble, Omi. They may bring with them more than stories to fire the imagination of your people."

Her head came up serenely. "Yes?"

Kai nodded. "I have no doubt that your father will welcome the fact that Solaris fights generally feature a wide range of unorthodox—at least to Kurita traditionalists— tactics and plans. Allowing people to learn to take pride in initiative will promote the flexibility he needs in his troops if they are to defeat the Clans.

"More important, though, your people will no longer be isolated from the rest of the Inner Sphere. Even if you screened all fights and showed only those in which one of your ronin won in an honorable and overwhelming manner, people would begin to be curious about other fighters. You are opening a Pandora's box that will give your people a clue to where they stand in the universe."

"We will not be editing fights." Omi kept her voice flat. "Our people will see what can be seen in the St. Ives Compact or the Federated Commonwealth."

"Including advertisements?"

"No government would refuse lucrative payments such as are offered for their broadcast."

A shiver worked its way up Kai's spine. "Ah, I begin to see the problem. The flexibility, the de-emphasizing of the rigid military, the promotion of contacts, and the introduction of advertisements for commercial products, all these things can help your father and his drive to reform the Combine. In the eyes of the hard-line traditionalists, however, this is very dangerous."

"Yet because I propose it and execute it, they see it as merely the fantasy of a woman. In their eyes that means it is doomed to failure, so they take no steps to prevent its success."

"And if it fails, it was the fantasy of a woman." Kai shook his head. "You are already questionable in their eyes because of your relationship with Victor, and they believe you can be sacrificed with no political cost to your father or brother. Still, your celebrity status in the eyes of the people gives your enterprise a good chance of taking root before forces move to destroy it."

"You are wasted as a fighter on Solaris, Kai Allard-Liao. Your grasp of the political is instinctive and correct."

Kai held up a hand. "Politics is one thing I want to avoid at all costs. To escape politics is exactly the reason I went to Solaris." He saw something flash through her eyes, but any words she meant to speak were cut off by a mechanical tone echoing through the DropShip.

Kai reached down into the padding of the chair and came up with the two ends of a safety harness. He belted it across his lap, while Omi did the same with the restraining belt built into the couch. He leaned back in his chair, letting his hands rest on the padded arms.

The tone sounded again as the JumpShip prepared to leave Tetersen. In the blink of an eye the Kearny-Fuchida jump drive created a displacement field around the JumpShip and all the DropShips attached to its docking arms. When the field reached stability, the ship was instantaneously transported a distance of up to thirty light years.

At least Kai had been told the jump was instantaneous. His subjective observations were of no help in the matter because, to him, the world slowed to the point in which each of his thoughts took a lifetime to develop. The Christmas tree seemed to grow out of all control, piercing the bubble of reality defined by the salon's walls. It vanished into the hole it had opened in the ceiling, then everything else in the room stretched out and followed the tree, including Kai himself.

He felt no pain as his legs whirled out and up into the black hole. For an instant it felt disturbingly like he'd been turned inside out, but that abruptly ended when the universe slammed down around him like a mold being used to cast him anew. He felt intense pressure, then it let up and only the new constellations glowing outside the porthole in this cabin wall told him that anything had changed.

"We should be at Thuban. We'll lose two DropShips, pick up one more, and be on our way." He frowned when he saw Omi looking at him curiously. "Did I say something wrong?"

She shook her head. "It is a remnant of my thoughts before the jump. The war has changed you greatly."

That surprised him. "It changed us all, Omi."

"True, though it has affected you in a most interesting way."

"How so?"

She smiled. "I remember you on Outreach. You were your harshest critic. Victor commented on it often. Had the Kai from Outreach been engaged in that conversation with me, all the analysis would have been couched in conditional statements. You would have offered everything as the wildest and most improbable conclusions that could possibly be drawn from the fact."

She is right. Kai looked down at his hands. "The war changed me." He hesitated because what had happened on Alyina was known only to him. He had not even told Victor, possibly because he could not have abided the validation his friend would have given him. But then, Victor would have validated Kai no matter what—Victor's loyalty was given unconditionally to those who had earned it.

"On Alyina, I intervened when I thought the Clans were going to kill Victor. Because of that, I ended up being trapped there."

Omi's blue eyes filled with compassion. "Because of what you did on Alyina, Victor escaped the Clans and was able to rescue my brother."

"No one else could have done it." Kai saw her nod, and blushed. "Save Hohiro, that is."

"You survived for six months alone on a Clan-held planet and helped the Clans take it back from ComStar. That is no mean achievement."

"I wasn't alone. I had help. The Clans would have killed me. Star Colonel Taman Malthus would have done it if ComStar had not interfered with our fight." A twinge of pain in his chest reminded him of the injuries he'd suffered at the hands of Clan Elementals while on the run on Alyina. "You are correct, though, that I learned something about myself on Alyina. A friend told me that I had held myself to so high a standard that I did not realize what my special gifts really were. Malthus and the other Elementals agreed. Their efforts have helped me build greater confidence."

"Your friend was very perceptive." Omi smiled gently.

"He must have been special himself to make you realize what your family and superiors could not."

Kai nodded. "She was." He saw Omi waiting for elaboration, but he declined the silent invitation to supply it. *I trust you, Omi, but I'm not certain I would trust myself in discussing Deirdre Lear.* "Because of her I came to Solaris, to find out just how special I am."

Omi nodded politely. "Your championship should be an answer. Your friend must be proud."

"I doubt it. She hates fighting, especially the ones on Solaris." He shrugged. "We lost touch with each other after I left Alyina. It's been almost three and a half years."

The look on Omi's face told him she sensed his discomfort with the talk. "Your invitation to dine said you would be serving a traditional holiday meal. Am I permitted to ask what that might be?"

Thank you, Omi, for understanding. "Ah, a great number of utterly wonderful things." Kai flipped the lock plate on his restraining belt and freed himself from the chair. "Most of them defy description, so I won't even try. I think it best if we just proceed to the galley and let you experience everything firsthand."

He offered her his arm, and Omi deftly slipped her left hand through it. "Merry Christmas, Kai Allard-Liao. May the spirit of the season be in your heart always."

"I wish the same for you, Omi Kurita," he said forcing a smile. *And to you, too. Deirdre Lear. Especially to you.*

6

Deirdre Lear could see by the tears brimming in her mother's eyes that this wasn't going to be easy. "Mom, I love you—you and Dad both—but I can't stay here. Living on Odell is killing me." She shrugged helplessly and looked up at her stepfather. "You understand, don't you, Dad?"

Roy Lear stood behind his wife, his stocky body wide enough to show on either side of her. "I understand, Deirdre." He rested his hands on his wife's shoulders and pulled her back toward him. "Why don't we go into the living room to discuss this? Standing here in the kitchen . . ."

Deirdre took the hint gladly and left them alone for a moment as she walked through the arched doorway into the dining room, then beyond it and the foyer to the living room. The tall ceiling and arched window set high in the front wall made the room feel more like a cathedral than part of a home. Deirdre recognized that sensation as a remnant of her childhood, when the living room had been reserved for use with guests.

The plush ivory carpeting felt good beneath her bare feet as she walked toward the center of the room. Skirting a low table, she selected a tall chair that faced the cream-colored couch where she knew her parents would sit. She sat down, hugging her arms around her knees, suddenly embarrassed by her blue work shirt and ragged jeans. The contrast with the subtle elegance of the room only underscored her inability to return to the life she had known before the coming of the Clans.

Roy Lear followed her into the room and perched on the arm of the couch. "Your mother will join us in a minute, Deirdre, but I want to say that if there's anything . . . wait a second, let me finish . . . anything I can do with the practice to make it easier for you, let me know. More money, different hours, more subspecialty work."

Deirdre shook her head. "You've done more than you know, Dad. Taking me in, giving me part of the practice, permitting me extended leave, all that. You've been great and you mustn't think I'm doing this to hurt you in any way. You couldn't have been more generous, more understanding, really."

A smile widened Dr. Lear's beefy face. "I know I'm not your real father . . ."

"But you are. That's one of the things I learned out there, on Alyina." *One of the things Kai made me realize.* "Everything I am today, now, I am because of you."

Roy scratched at the tip of his nose. "Look, Deirdre, you've made me prouder than any biological daughter could. When you took up medicine, well, I thought my heart would burst with pride and happiness. And when you came back and joined me in the practice . . . even your going away again can't rob me of the joy of that. And you know, of course, that you can come back any time. The door will always be open. You know that."

Deirdre nodded, unable to speak past the lump in her throat.

Her stepfather's voice dropped to low tones. "When we were notified that you were missing in action on Alyina, well, your mother took it very hard. Your mother, she's a strong woman, but her emotions run deep and the thought that she had outlived her only child was devastating. When you came back, we both thought it was a miracle. Sure, you were down and had to work through the stress, but at least you were alive and well. Then David came along and you entered the practice and everything looked fairy-tale perfect."

"But it wasn't, Dad." Deirdre leaned forward, clasping her hands together and resting her elbows on her knees. "Being out there on Alyina, dealing with people having a hard time satisfying their basic human needs, it did something to me inside . . . I admire you more than you'll ever know because your skills have saved countless lives and helped so many people." She sat back, opening her arms to take in the opulence of the room. "And I also appreciate everything your skill and knowledge have provided us. Without it I could never have become the person I am now. And yet that person now feels uncomfortable living in splendor knowing there are so many people lacking even the most basic medical care on so many worlds out there. I can't live with that, and I need to do something . . . anything."

Roy Lear's face softened with a smile. "I understand, I really do. I don't know if you remember it very well, but I met your mother after I had come home from doing my stint with the forces that took half the Capellan Confederation. I've seen the conditions you're talking about, and I tried to do everything I could to help when I had the chance. I never got to the world of Zurich, but I can imagine the kind of difficult living conditions you're talking about. And I agree that it's unforgivable."

He held up a hand to forestall her comment. "You and I, we have an understanding of what it's like in other parts of space. It's no slight to your mother that she's only known life on Bell and then here on Odell. She hasn't seen what we've seen. She's a good woman—the finest—and she's afraid of losing her daughter a second time."

"I know, but it won't happen. Zurich isn't a war zone."

Roy's face darkened. "It's close enough to both the Capellan Confederation and the Free Worlds League borders to be a target at any time. There are even reports of pro-Liao guerrillas working against the government. Terrorists often attack civilians, and you would be a prime target."

"But I'm a doctor. A noncombatant. I'm going to be working for the Tristar Foundation and we're neutral. I'll treat whomever I have to treat, which means that no one will want me dead." She smiled at her stepfather. "I'll be fine."

"What about David?" Marylyn Lear came in and stood beside her husband, stiffly refusing to sit. "Have you thought about him."

"Marylyn, that was uncalled for." Roy forced his hand into his wife's closed fist. "Of course she's thought about David."

Marylyn Lear remained rigid, and Deirdre braced for a

searing lecture. "What sort of life will he have on Zurich? You, you've known the best and you've endured the worst there on Alyina, but what of him? He was born here. This is the only life he's known. What will he do when you end up in some village with no running water, no sanitation, no . . . ?"

"He'll adapt, mother. We've talked about it. He understands where we're going."

"Does he? He's only three years old, Deirdre. He lives in a world of fantasy centered around you. This is a big adventure for him, and will remain so for the first two or three months, then he'll tire of it." Marylyn sat, but remained tense and stabbed her finger across the table at her daughter. "What will you do when he says he wants to go home?"

"He'll learn. He's coming with me." Deirdre blue eyes sparked hotly. "There's no choice."

Her mother's expression sharpened. "He can stay here."

"No! Absolutely not!"

"Why not, dear?" Her mother's voice shifted from steelshod to compassionately curious. "This is your adventure, not his. Let him stay."

"No!" Deirdre tried to keep anger from her voice, but it slipped through and shocked her mother. "Tearing us apart is the sort of thing the Clans would do. I won't have it."

A shriek of delight sliced through the house as David Roy Lear came careening around the corner and into the living room at a dead run. In his right hand, swooping through the air, he held an airplane he had cobbled together out of the brightly colored plastic building blocks he'd gotten for Christmas. "Mom, lookit."

Her anger burning away like fog in the presence of David's sunny disposition, Deirdre grasped the boy under the arms and set him in her lap. "Did you make that yourself?"

The dark-haired child nodded emphatically. "Ah Chen only helped a little."

Deirdre looked up as the elderly amah came to stand in the archway. "Forgive me. He is quick."

"I understand, Ah Chen. He'll be fine, now." She smiled at the old woman who cared for her son, noting not for the first time that David's slightly sharpened eyes and skin coloring made Ah Chen look more like his grandmother than the woman seated on the couch across from her. "I'll call for you if I need help."

David squirmed slightly in her lap. "Gram looks sad." The boy twisted and slid down from his mother's lap, then walked around the table and set his toy plane in front of Marylyn Lear. "Mom says you need to take a plane to go to where we're going. Now you can visit us."

Marylyn's lower lip quivered, then she gathered her grandson up in a fierce hug. Tears streamed down her face and Deirdre had to look away to keep back her own tears.

She appealed to her stepfather. "You understand why I can't leave David behind."

Roy rubbed his wife's back with his right hand. "Intellectually? Sure. You saw the Clans up close. You understand what kind of people their program of genetic breeding and raising children without parents creates . . ."

Deirdre sensed his hesitation. "But?"

"But if you hold that view so strongly, why haven't you communicated with the boy's father?" Roy held his hands up as Deirdre slackened back into the chair. "You might think that cruel of me, and God knows I've loved every minute as Davy's surrogate father, but I'm not enough."

Kai! Deirdre felt a sudden chill at the question, a chill that nothing could warm. It was as if she knew two Kai Allard-Liaos. One was the man who'd helped her survive on Alyina. He was brave and compassionate, smart and relentless. He had fought for her and saved her, then worked with his enemies to win a planet back from the people who had betrayed them all. He was a hero, yet never arrogant or prepossessing.

At the time they had parted on Alyina—*when I drove him away from me*—she had seen his true nature. Kai was everything a world, a nation, the universe needed in a leader. He had vision and heart. He could forge alliances with and command respect from men who had hunted him like an animal. He was big enough to learn from his enemies and his mistakes. His loyalty to friends and his willingness to accept responsibility for his actions marked him as a man destined for greatness.

The challenge of remaining with someone like that frightened her. She had imagined Kai leaving Alyina and becoming for Victor Davion what his father had been to Hanse

Davion. With Kai tempering Victor's impulsiveness and setting a standard for fealty, the Federated Commonwealth would become even stronger than before the Clans' coming. And that would lead to more wars against the Clans, more fighting and more killing. Sanctioning such actions by the man she loved—even knowing that the slaughter would be worse if led by someone lesser than Kai—was something Deirdre did not believe she could face.

She had become a doctor to reverse the harm that warriors do. Her biological father, Peter Armstrong, had died senselessly while fighting in a BattleMech. She wanted to do anything possible to combat the insanity that made men think they could kill for ideals or material gains or, worst of all, for the sheer sport of it. She knew Kai understood that—he had helped her identify that piece of herself—but she feared compromising her goals if and when they came in conflict with Kai's duty.

So she had driven him away. Deirdre hadn't been sure, when last she'd seen Kai, that she was carrying his child, but she'd had reason to suspect it. But she'd have made the same decision even if she'd known for sure. She didn't want to drag Kai down and force him to subordinate his greatness to her idea of dedicating her life in service to humanity. She had freed him so he could attain the greatness she'd seen in him.

He had, in return, humiliated her. Instead of using his gifts to help Victor guide the Federated Commonwealth through a difficult period of transition, he had fled to Solaris, where he'd followed in his father's footsteps. It took him longer to become Champion of Solaris than it had Justin Allard a quarter century before, and Kai had done it without killing anyone in his fights, but it was all such a waste.

And a vengeful waste at that. Kai knew that his own father had killed Deirdre's biological father in a duel on the Game World. Kai had told her that his father regretted it deeply, but all the regret in the world wouldn't bring Peter Armstrong back to life. Kai's decision to go to Solaris did validate his skills as a warrior—skills for which Taman Malthus and the other Jade Falcon Elementals had praised him—but it mocked her loss and magnified her pain.

I cannot let my son know that Kai is his father. She looked over at David. *And I cannot allow Kai to taint him.*

Almost at once a shiver passed through her again. Once again the part of her hurt by Kai's going to Solaris warred with memories of him on Alyina. She could not imagine the two men being the same person unless something had changed him radically. She knew that upon leaving Alyina, Kai had learned of his father's death. Perhaps it was that which drew him to Solaris, but would he have become a different person?

The only thing that could have changed him so is my rejection of him. Deirdre almost laughed at the arrogance of the thought, but deep down she knew it was the truth. She had told Kai that she couldn't weigh herself down with someone who was locked in a military mindset. That could only have undermined his budding self-confidence and made him want to prove himself in the giant martial playground of Solaris—and to spite her.

She looked up at her stepfather. "What the Clans do is train children to become killers of other men. I will not have my son learn such lessons. War is a terrible, terrible thing. I don't want him placed where he has to accept it or glory in it."

Roy nodded. "I understand your position, but how can you shield him from violence? You're arguing that lack of exposure to a disease is the same as immunity to a disease, and we both know that's a fallacy."

"Your point is well taken, but you're missing one thing," Deirdre said firmly. "Where I'm going I can teach David how to fight violence with peace, how to heal instead of injure. Not only will that make him immune, it will also make him able to cure violence. That's a lesson I wish all men could learn."

Roy Lear leaned back against the couch, and shook his head wonderingly. "You and your mother are so alike. You both hold your passions tightly and let them energize you to accomplish whatever you want. But those passions blind you to the times when you're going to lose your fights. Marylyn, this is one of those times for you. Deirdre and Davy are going to leave, and that's that."

Marylyn sniffed as she released David from her embrace and stroked his hair. "I guess there's nothing left for me to do."

"Sure there is, dear." Roy patted her hand gently. "Turn

your passion into making their last four days here a happy remembrance. An experience that will bring them back soon."

Marylyn forced a smile and swiped at her tears with both hands. "I shall do that, then." She held her right hand out to David. "Want to help your Gram make some cookies?"

The boy nodded emphatically and let Marylyn lead him out of the room.

Deirdre smiled. "Mom and I were lucky she met you."

"Not as lucky as I was. I was in a lot of turmoil back then, and your mother helped straighten me out. It's true she doesn't want to lose you, but she really has your best interests at heart."

"I know, but sometimes it's hard to see it." Deirdre paused, then looked her stepfather in the eyes. "So, do *you* think my going to Zurich is a mistake to which my passions have blinded me?"

Roy Lear shrugged his shoulders and stood up, extending a hand out to her palm up. "I don't know, Deirdre, I really don't. I hope not."

Deirdre smiled and took her stepfather's hand as she rose. "Me, too." She gave him a kiss on the cheek.

Roy squeezed her hand. "Just remember that no matter what happens, you'll always have a home with us. No reservations, no recriminations, no questions."

=== 7 ===

Solaris City, Solaris VII
Tamarind March, Federated Commonwealth
10 January 3056

Tormano Liao sat alone and undisturbed in the Emerald Lounge of the Solaris City starport. He greatly detested having to travel from his mansion in the Cathay sector of the city to this high hill in the Davion quarter. Radical shifts in architecture marked the border between the Black Hills and Cathay sectors, with the Davion buildings lacking anything even approaching a soul. Tormano hated the sharp, square Davion architecture, and its lack of color merely served to make the gray world of Solaris City even more bleak.

The two tall, slender men standing behind him kept people away from him. They also kept other people from enjoying the spectacular view offered by this quite rare clear day in winter. Tormano didn't care that he was monopolizing the view, nor did the scene particularly interest him aesthetically. Rather, he looked down on the city stretched out below as a vast and treacherous chessboard representing the universe in microcosm.

Directly north of the spaceport, across the Solaris River and covering half the gentle upward slope, the Kobe sector of the city seemed the most inviting. Islands of green alternated with beautifully crafted and constructed buildings that looked as if they had been rescued from Japan of a millennium and a half before. The low haze that usually shrouded the city had dissipated over Kobe first, making it seem like a model of what the rest of Solaris might possibly become.

Tormano shook his head, for he knew what a thin façade

that was. Pride was the only thing that kept the Combine sector of the city going, and that was quickly wearing thin. Until now the people of Kobe had lived almost entirely off the vast profits made in the black market for holovids of the Solaris fights. But now the Clans had hammered the Combine severely, swallowing a full third of their worlds. Kobe's golden-egg-laying goose was dead, brutally slain. The sector only looked as good as it did because its people spent their own money trying to keep it up—willfully denying that the foundations of their world were in danger of collapse.

Beyond Kobe, further east on the north shore of the river, Montenegro festered like Kobe's shadow. Built in what had once been Solaris City's industrial sector—before the whole planet had moved to a "service economy"—Montenegro was indeed a black mountain of rotting factories, tangled streets, and internecine wars. Represented here were every one of the dozen smaller provinces that made up the Free Worlds League, with the denizens of each fiercely guarding their own turf.

Across the river from Montenegro, the Lyran sector of Silesia lay gray and strangely clean. As with the people of Kobe, the Lyrans struggled to make their sector rise above the squalor that threatened to engulf Solaris City. Despite the unification of the Lyran Commonwealth and the Federated Suns into a single Federated Commonwealth, on Solaris the Lyran loyalists kept as much distance as possible from their counterparts in the Black Hills. Tensions had grown ever since the invasion by the Clans, which had gobbled up a hunk of the Lyran nation while leaving the Federated Suns intact and untouched.

Directly south of Kobe, the high hills of the Black Hills sector dominated the city. The orderly and formidable buildings stood as the only true reminder of the military considerations that had created the BattleMechs that warred in the arenas of Solaris City. As with everything connected with the Davions, the Black Hills quarter was overdone, as if a mere display of might could win battles in Solaris.

Between Silesia and the Black Hills, at a low point in the city, lay Cathay. A quarter of a century before it had been staunchly pro-Capellan, its people rallying around the brilliant fighting skill of Justin Xiang. Tormano vividly recalled placing bets from Sian on the fight between Xiang and his arch-rival, the Davion puppet Philip Capet. The victory had won him a fair sum, and was also the spur that had made Tormano's father, Maximilian Liao, bring Justin to Sian to work for him.

Justin Xiang, it had turned out, was operating as a double agent for Hanse Davion; while pretending to serve Maximilian, he had worked secretly to destroy the Capellan Confederation's ability to defend itself. Tormano himself had been captured on Algol by Davion troops. He had expected prison or execution, but instead the Davions had treated him as an ally. As peace fell over the newly conquered area now known as the Sarna March, Hanse Davion had begun funding Tormano as the leader of the resistance movement against Romano Liao, Tormano's sister and the new Capellan Chancellor.

His other sister, Candace, had her St. Ives Compact, and this tripartite split of the old Capellan realm was now reflected in Cathay. Down by the river and on up through a patch bordering Silesia, Capellans loyal to the current Chancellor, Sun-Tzu Liao, and the Capellan Confederation held sway. They were, by far, the most numerous group in Cathay, and produced most of the warriors who fought in the Liaoist stables.

The St. Ives section dominated the center of Cathay. The expression "Middle Kingdom" had originally been used to ridicule those who looked to Candace and her small nation for their identity, but it had proved to be prophetic. Untouched by the war, St. Ives had come over intact when Justin Xiang returned to Hanse Davion's service, bringing Candace with him. The St. Ives Compact made a fortune producing the goods needed by the newly conquered Sarna March, and that money had also gone into investment and support of kin in far Solaris, obtaining the best for people in the Middle Kingdom.

Free Capella clung to the border with the Davion Black Hills like a tick sucking blood from a hound. Trapped between the Middle Kingdom and the Davion sector, and denied access to the river front by Capellan loyalists, Tormano's little realm consisted of a luxurious core surrounded by slums. Those fortunate enough to escape the Davion invasion of the Capellan Confederation with their wealth intact had joined Tormano in building a grand island of prosperity on the highest hill of their section. Around them, decaying buildings and twisted, trash-strewn alleys were all the shelter available to the people whose labor created the fortunes accumulated by the wealthy.

Tormano acknowledged that their condition was piteous, but he knew the stubborn pride of those people and that they shared his goal. They were citizens of Free Capella and dedicated to overthrowing the illegitimate regime headed by Tormano's nephew, Sun-Tzu. They were patriots willing to sacrifice, awaiting the day when they could return to their ancestral homeland as liberators.

Tormano had told them and himself that he did indeed intend to free the rest of the Capellan Confederation from the cadet branch of the family that held it. He also knew that his true worth—a worth Hanse Davion had seen and exploited—was as a diversion for Chancellor Sun-Tzu and before him, Chancellor Romano. The Davions gave him just enough money to carry out raids and disinformation campaigns. They promised that "someday" they would marshal the forces needed to finish what the Fourth Succession War had started, but there was always some excuse for why they had yet to do that. Uprisings in Skye, the disastrous war of 3039, and most recently, the Clan invasion.

For a while Tormano had been complacent, content with the generous pension provided by Hanse Davion. In the meantime he had also managed to carry out a number of operations that vexed his sister Romano no end, raising his prestige among the people of Free Capella. He had even established various organizations to help the citizens of the Sarna March recover from the war, increasing his popularity among them and stimulating private donations to his cause.

During those years Tormano had told himself he was building up strength. His wife had borne him two children, a son and a daughter, but neither seemed to have the heart for the struggle to which their father was so totally committed. Hanya, his wife, had become thoroughly wrapped up in the social causes championed by Melissa Steiner-Davion, and become depressed and inconsolable since Melissa's assassination.

Now time was running out for his dream. Victor Davion had already cut funding to Free Capella, forcing Tormano to trim the rehabilitation programs he had set up. He noted

with pride that Kai had begun to funnel funds into those programs, picking up slack and then some, saving Tormano the
embarrassment of being forced to dismiss the staff he maintained at his estate on Equatus, the western continent of
Solaris.

Kai had come to dominate his thoughts more and more as
Tormano saw the universe and circumstance conspiring to
rob him of his dream. Had he been asked to custom-design
an heir to Free Capella, that person would have been a man
just like Kai. Not only was his nephew a warrior of unparalleled skill, but he was also a close friend of Victor Davion
and no great friend of Sun-Tzu Liao. Now, as the Champion
of Solaris, Kai had become well known throughout the Inner
Sphere.

Tormano's new aide, Nancy Bao Lee, came up from behind, clearing her throat politely. "Mandrinn, Aerospace
Traffic Control reports the *Leopard* Class DropShip *Zhangshi* is on final approach. It should be at the gate in ten minutes."

Tormano looked up at Nancy. "What do you think of our
Kai Allard?"

The tall, slender woman's dark eyes flickered briefly before she answered. "He is a masterful warrior, my lord. He
would be a great asset to our cause." She looked down, making her long black hair billow around her shoulders and
down over the bodice of her royal blue silk jacket. "Is that
what you wished to know?"

Kai's uncle smiled slyly. *What I wished to know, your eyes
have told me.* "Do you find him attractive?"

Again her mouth lied while her eyes spoke the truth. "I
can see how others would find him so. He is not hard to look
at, but I prefer more mature men, my lord."

Tormano nodded to her. "I am afraid you will have more
than your fill of such in my company, for the pack I run with
is filled with old men."

"You are not old, my lord. You are vital and look young
enough to be Kai Allard's brother." She gave him a worship-
ful smile. "Through all the difficulties of our cause and your
wife's infirmity, you have persevered. It is no wonder the
people call you Ironheart."

*Is your flattery meant to get you into my bed? And do you
think from there you will one day be able to plant yourself*

on the Celestial Throne of the Capellan Confederation?
"Yes, I am Ironheart, but Kai is Steelsoul and the people love him. His victory over Wu Deng Tang in defense of his title could strike a blow for our cause more potent than any made so far."

"That is so. Were he to publicly endorse Free Capella, or better yet, dedicate his victory to us as he has done for Victor Davion, we would benefit greatly."

"*If* Kai wins."

Nancy looked surprised. "Do you think he might not?"

"Wu Deng Tang is no fool. He grew up as a military brat, and his father has just won command of the Harloc Raiders. Wu Kang Kuo came up through House Imarra before becoming commander of this unit built from BattleMechs given Sun-Tzu by Thomas Marik."

Nancy frowned. "Those BattleMechs are supposed to be part of Isis Marik's dowry, are they not?"

Tormano laughed. "Yes, yes, indeed they are. It seems that Thomas would more willingly give away his realm in pieces to Sun-Tzu than actually give his daughter to the man in marriage. Thomas apparently still harbors hopes that Victor Davion's scientists can cure his son Joshua's leukemia so that the boy and not the daughter can inherit the throne. I must admit that it would suit me also, for it would destroy Sun-Tzu's chance of ruling the Free Worlds League—and without the firing of a single shot."

Tormano looked beyond Nancy at a dark speck in the uncharacteristically clear sky over Solaris City. "But, back to your question: no, I do not believe Kai will lose the fight. I am not above taking steps to assure that he wins, however. I want leverage on Wu Deng Tang. Check our files—I believe he has a paramour. It is my thought that she might enjoy a vacation at my estate on Equatus. Do you think you can arrange that?"

Nancy Bao Lee nodded. "As you wish, my lord."

The *Zhangshi*, an aerodynamically sound DropShip, swooped low toward the spaceport. The paired wheels beneath the stocky wings touched first in a puff of smoke, then the blunt nose came down and the front wheels also made contact with the ground. Decelerating quickly, the ship continued to speed out of Tormano's line of sight.

"You are correct, of course, Ms. Lee, that Kai would be a

great asset to our cause. I am thinking we might need leverage with him as well. We must learn his secrets so we can
entice him to become part of Free Capella." Tormano's eyes
half-closed. "If I required it of you, do you think you could
seduce him and become his confidante?"

"You would place a spy in your nephew's bed?"

"I have heard rumors that Quintus Allard placed a spy in
his son Justin's bed here on Solaris, at Hanse Davion's request. It is, therefore, something of a family tradition,
wouldn't you say?" He steepled his fingers and watched her
carefully. "Would you accept that mission?"

Nancy's head came up, her eyes glittering like chips of
ice. "You know what I have already done in the service of
Free Capella, my lord."

"Indeed I do, but reporting to me that your predecessor
had been recruited by Sun-Tzu's Maskirovka is one thing. I
am asking you to gather information for me on a man who
may be the most loyal son Free Capella has ever had. There
is an old adage: All that is required for the victory of evil is
that good men do nothing. Are you willing to be the instru-
ment that might force Kai Allard to do something?"

"I live to serve you in any capacity." She bowed her head.
"I assume you have a file on your nephew that I could study
in preparation?"

"Very good, Nancy, very good. I do." Tormano stood and
gently pressed a hand to the middle of her back. "You
should return to the office and begin your review of it. I will
go and greet my nephew on his return. I will arrange for you
two to meet when you are ready."

She smiled seductively at him. "I do what Free Capella
requires of me, and gladly, my lord."

"Free Capella will always need patriots like you,"
Tormano smiled. "We will continue to work together closely
and well, united by our cause, and tireless in its pursuit."

8

Solaris City, Solaris VII
Tamarind March, Federated Commonwealth
19 January 3056

Though weary and a little achy from the reentry into Solaris City, Kai Allard-Liao smiled heartily as he saw the trio of men waiting for him in the landing lounge. "I'm surprised your harsh taskmaster allowed you time off from work to come out here."

The eldest of the three bowed deeply, white strands of hair slipping out of place over the top of his bald head. "You are correct, of course, except in that our taskmaster is so fair that he allows us to leave the shop when the sun shines on Solaris."

Kai laughed. "That fair, is he, Fuh Teng? It's a wonder he's not fired a loyal retainer like you, being that fair."

The old man smiled in a grandfatherly way. "He is most gracious and ignores my grievous errors."

"He learned from his father that you seldom make errors and never are they grievous." Kai shook the old man's hand, then folded him in a hug. With Fuh Teng's help, Kai had been able to build Cenotaph Stables into a successful and highly profitable organization.

As good a manager as Fuh Teng was, however, the Clan Wars had hurt Cenotaph. Unlike other stables, Cenotaph had allowed and even encouraged the fighters it had under contract to go off and fight the Clans. The policy had earned the stable the good will of the Federated Commonwealth government, but it also succeeded in killing off much of Cenotaph's talent. When both Justin Allard and Kai were reported killed during the war, arena buffs on Solaris wrote the stable off.

But Kai had not died in the war. Combining his energy with Fuh Teng's knowledge and experience, they had rebuilt the stable. They were in agreement that MechWarriors who had faced the Clans had an edge over those who had not, and began a policy of hiring war veterans even when they had no name recognition on Solaris. This gave them a chance to earn far more with their martial skills than they were likely to make in peacetime jobs.

Many of the ex-soldiers who signed fought only long enough to make the kind of money that would ease the transition to civilian life and then left. Kai was neither surprised nor unprepared for this, but took great joy when some decided to remain with Cenotaph for the long haul. The second man Kai greeted now was just such a fighter. "I caught the holovid of your fight with Jason Block, Larry. Nice long-range slugging match."

The brown-haired man smiled, but with restraint, as if embarrassed by the praise. "Being in the Steiner Arena worked to his advantage. He's like a shark on a bleeding fish if your heat goes up. Next time—if there is one—I want Boreal Reach with a howling blizzard."

"It worked for Tanya O'Bannon against Bloch." Kai shook Larry Acuff's hand, then slapped him on the right shoulder. "And there will be a next time, count on it."

Kai turned to the third man. "Keith, I got your message coming in. So, Ryan Steiner has bought out Oonthrax?"

Keith Smith smiled as he shook Kai's hand. "Nothing official yet, but money is moving all around the Federated Commonwealth to snap up the Oonthrax debts and quietly buy out stockholders. Steiner's been trying to hide it, but they're working too quickly to hide their trail." The computer tech patted the left breast pocket of his tan jumpsuit. "I have the data here, encrypted and all, but I expect an announcement of the changeover within the week. I hear he plans to name the stable the Skye Tigers."

Kai frowned as he considered some of the implications of Ryan Steiner buying a stable on Solaris. At first the idea had struck him as foolish because running a stable would take the duke away from his seditious activities against the Federated Commonwealth. "Is Ryan coming here to take control, or is he going to be another absentee owner?"

Keith shrugged. "Not while his toy is still new. His personal DropShip left Porrima on the first of the year, and the traffic is right to get him here before your title defense. He might even make it in time for the announcement."

"That would be amusing." Kai nibbled on his lower lip, distracted. "Buying a stable means the deal will have to go before the Board of Owners. Perhaps it can be voted down."

Fuh Teng shook his head as he started the quartet heading down the long corridor toward the garage. "That's not likely. Ryan was already part-owner of the stable. All he's doing now is increasing his share. And no matter how well you argued against it, the owners wouldn't be likely to take your side in preventing Ryan from taking over."

Kai nodded. "If *I* argued against it, they'd vote in favor just to spite me."

Unlike his father, Kai had become Champion and then remained on Solaris to attend to the affairs of Cenotaph. Almost immediately he had begun to object to some of the common business practices. He thought the contracts for fighters who risked their lives in the arenas were little more than agreements to involuntary servitude, mainly because the yakuza and other organized crime forces had shattered all attempts by the Solaris warriors to form a union. The cooperatives formed by independent MechWarriors gave better deals to their owner-fighters, but the stable owners controlled booking access to the elite Class 5 arenas. The only way the cooperatives could get their fighters into those venues was to pay exorbitant booking fees that were little more than kickbacks.

Kai had immediately instituted reforms in the Cenotaph structure that marked an end to the Dark Ages on Solaris. Because of Fuh Teng's careful attention to developing a feeder system, Cenotaph had quality fighters for all levels of the games on Solaris, and the stable's fighters became the "local" champions on Solaris. By bringing in warriors who had fought against the Clans, Cenotaph also built up a solid following for its warriors throughout the Federated Commonwealth. That some of these fighters had been prisoners of war only added to their popularity. Larry Acuff was just such a one, having survived a prison camp on Alyina.

All this created a demand for Cenotaph fighters on fight bills, a demand that prevented the other owners from treating the stable like a giant cooperative and freezing them out. They would probably have turned to help from organized crime to break Cenotaph, but Kai's friendships with Victor Davion and Theodore Kurita's son Hohiro promised retribution if those groups began to play rough. Besides that, Kai himself was heir to the throne of St. Ives—a sovereign nation with its own army. And if that weren't enough, Kai could also call on his uncle Daniel Allard, who ran the crack mercenary unit, the Kell Hounds. None of the major stable owners truly considered violence against Kai and Cenotaph an option.

Having established a nearly unassailable foundation, Kai then began to raise the pay of his fighters. He gave them quick-cut contracts so they could fight, win some purses, and retire to another planet if they wished. The other owners assumed that Kai was losing money left and right, and would soon realize the error of his ways. In reality, Cenotaph lost very little money because of Fuh Teng's careful stewardship of the stable.

Then, in early 3054 Kai fought a stunning series of victories that reminded longtime fight fans of the run his father had made for the title in 3027. He scheduled himself for two fights a week, using his own money to double the purses offered. He started with Glenn Edenhoffer of Oonthrax Stables, at the time rated the number twenty fighter on Solaris, and worked his way up. In three months he had met and defeated each of the top twenty Solaris warriors. By the end of the year the Tournament of Champions seemed only a formality, and Kai officially won the title of Champion.

Though the title gave him unprecedented leverage, he used it only in tiny doses. Kai still intended to revamp the Solaris system to make it fairer to the men and women who risked their lives in the fights, but he also knew that salaries spiraling out of sight would destroy the Solaris games. The only way to walk that tightrope was to expand the market for the games, which would also increase profits for the owners.

Making his case to the other owners was difficult and had set off an ongoing war between them. But Kai had a secret weapon—Keith Smith's incredible ability to worm his way into the computer systems of the other stables. With Keith's help, Kai got hold of the kind of financial data needed to pinpoint and demolish resistance to his ideas. It also put him into position to exert pressure on the other owners if they balked and dug in their heels.

Up till now Kai had succeeded, to a certain extent, in arranging matters to his liking. The arrival of Ryan Steiner could upset all his careful planning. Solaris City was nothing if not a political place, and a sizable chunk of the population supplemented their income by being on the payroll of the various intelligence organizations in the Inner Sphere. The politics of the Game World seldom operated on the interstellar levels of power, however. In fact, Kai was in some ways the biggest dog in the pound because of his ties to Victor and St. Ives. Ryan, on the other hand, had an established power base as well as more years' practice at politics. He seemed to have a real taste for it.

And I have none of those things. Kai shook his head. "Keith, any word yet on whether or not Taman Malthus and his Elementals will be allowed to come to my title defense?"

"The same troop movements that slowed you down have made it really difficult to create a command circuit of ships from Jade Falcon territory to Solaris, but we're hoping things will improve."

"Good. Keep me informed on the logistics of it all. What's the word on the diplomatic clearances for the trip?"

"Mostly a lot of 'we're considering it.' The Federated Commonwealth government is willing to permit a diplomatic mission from the Jade Falcons to come here for the fight, but only because the request came through the St. Ives Compact government. ComStar, who has to approve it, is stalling. There's also a rumor that the ilKhan is willing to approve the journey, but the Free Worlds League is wary of having Clanfolk so close to their border. The real sticking point concerns Rules of Engagement. Everyone agrees the Clanners should be able to defend themselves if attacked, but ComStar and the Jade Falcons are arguing over what constitutes an attack."

He shook his head. "You had to go and befriend Clanners who consider sarcasm a breach of honor."

Kai shrugged. "I don't believe there are any Clanners who'd be terribly receptive to humor at their own expense."

Larry's head came up. "Speaking of the humorless," he managed in a stage whisper.

Kai glanced further along the corridor and saw a group of tall, strong, silent types wearing the dark suits, white turtlenecks, and dark glasses that his uncle required of his security men. Weariness from the long journey down washed over him anew. *This is all I need.*

Just rounding the corner behind his men was Tormano Liao, displaying the air of a busy man who was happy to have made time to greet his nephew. Smaller than Kai, yet still possessed of a wiry strength, Tormano ignored the phalanx of security men and quickened his step. "I am pleased to see that you weathered your journey well."

"*Zao, bofu.*" Kai bowed sharply and maintained the bow for a respectful number of heartbeats. "The journey was less taxing than the funeral. I offered your condolences, as you would have wished."

"I am in your debt."

Kai sensed Tormano's desire to trap him in a web of conversation that would eventually separate him from his friends and culminate in another recital of all the Free Capella efforts to unseat Sun-Tzu. Having neither the time nor the inclination to endure that, he decided to cut his uncle off before he could even begin. "It's good to run into you here, Uncle. I assume you were here on business and managed to slip away when you heard I was coming in?"

Tormano's eyes half-shut and his face lost its joyful animation. "Actually I came expressly to welcome you back to Solaris. I thought we could spend some time together, perhaps dine. You must be famished."

Without being prompted, Keith looked at his chronometer. "Forgive me for interrupting, sir, but we're running tight on that meeting."

Kai almost winced at Keith's use of such formality, but Tormano had accepted the charade of the subservient tone without suspicion. "Thank you, Mr. Smith. Perhaps if Mr. Acuff, Fuh Teng, and you will give me a moment, we can still make it."

His three companions moved further down the corridor and Tormano's security men turned to watch them as if they were serial murderers. Kai shook his head. "If I had known,

Uncle, I could have made time. I have been away far too long and there is business to which I must attend."

Tormano laid a gentle hand on Kai's left forearm. "I understand. My former secretary would have taken care of just such detail, but he is no longer with me."

"I heard he had been compromised by Sun-Tzu."

"Yes, but the attempt was clumsy. He was discovered and immediately confessed. We got his controller and have another Romaniac under surveillance." Tormano smiled coldly. "Sun-Tzu is dangerous, as well you know. He is not, however, invincible. He will fall."

"Of that I have no doubt, Uncle." Kai felt the conversation headed toward uncomfortable territory. "I've had my accountant shift money to some of the causes you're sponsoring, so they're covered. I will see what more I can do when this next match is over."

"Wu Deng Tang will be a formidable opponent." Tormano's voice dropped to a raspy whisper. "This is a fight you *must* win."

"And that is just what I intend to do." Kai patted the hand on his arm. "You will be a guest in my box, of course?"

"It would be my honor." Tormano nodded gratefully to his nephew. "I am planning to hold a reception for you and Wu a month or so before the fight. I have been told that Katrina Steiner and Galen Cox may be here then."

And winning influence with Katrina wouldn't hurt your cause, would it? Kai smiled. "Wonderful. I am certain Omi Kurita will enjoy seeing them again."

Tormano blinked. "The Coordinator's daughter is coming to Solaris?"

"The *Taizai* is no more than half a day behind the *Zhangshi.*" Kai wanted to laugh at the shocked look on his uncle's face, but he maintained control of himself. "I trust you will invite her to your reception as well."

"Yes, yes, of course."

Kai smiled innocently. "And I imagine you would not want to slight Ryan Steiner, either."

Tormano recovered himself with that suggestion. "Of course not."

So, you knew about Ryan Steiner buying a stable here. Your intelligence network isn't so bad after all. "Good."

Tormano's grip on Kai's arm tightened ever so slightly. "You *will* win this fight, Kai. And all your friends will be honored by your victory."

"Thank you for your confidence, Uncle." Kai bowed again, then slipped his arm free of the other man's hand. "Please, call my office and have them arrange for us to have dinner some time this week. Would that it could have been now . . ."

"Go to your meeting, I understand." Tormano gave him a bow. "Later this week, then."

Kai caught up with his friends in the underground garage. They had recovered his luggage from customs—a task made simple by the diplomatic tags—and had already loaded it into the boot of the stretch Feicui aircar. Keith Smith slid onto the bench seat, his back to the driver's seat, with Larry Acuff sitting beside him. Kai and Fuh Teng occupied the back seat, sunk deeply into the plush leather.

Fuh Teng hit a button that informed the driver—one of his grandnephews—that they were ready to be on their way. "Did your uncle have any news of import?"

"Not really. He knew about Ryan Steiner."

Keith frowned. "I'll do another sweep on our systems, but I don't think he pulled it from us."

"Don't worry about that." A chill ran down Kai's spine as he replayed the conversation with Tormano. "He seems to desperately want me to beat Wu Deng Tang. It would be just like him to do something sneaky to make sure I won."

"Like what? Making sure you got to use both hands for once?" Larry laughed.

Kai shook his head. "No, he's more likely to make a move against Wu. Put the word out, Fuh Teng. Let me know if anything strange is going on. Be sure folks know that Wu's safety is guaranteed by my honor. Keith, can you penetrate Tormano's computers?"

"Faster than you go through opponents." Keith's face darkened for a moment. "Tormano does keep an incredible amount of information off-line, but some quick passes through his stuff might pick up trace memos and notes. I'll see what I can do."

"Good." Kai settled back in his seat as the aircar emerged

from the garage and into the streets of the Black Hills. Overhead, the clouds had already begun to reclaim the sky, veiling the day in grayness. "Despite the gloom and double-dealing," he said, "it really is good to be home."

9

Deirdre Lear offered her hand to the man in the white lab coat. "I'm Deirdre Lear, Dr. Bradford. Pleased to meet you."

Bradford, a smallish man who looked rather haggard despite his youth, shook her hand with surprising vigor. "Not as pleased as I am to meet you, Dr. Lear." He looked beyond her at the two nurses who had arrived with Deirdre for orientation. "Ms. Thompson, Ms. Hanney, glad to have you with us." He straightened up from shaking their hands, then opened his arms wide. "Welcome to the Rencide Medical Center. It may not look like much, but it's the only thing most of these folks have."

Deirdre had to agree with the assessment, though she knew it was overly harsh, considering where they'd set the place up. The three-story building had been plunked down in the middle of a rain forest, and it was all but invisible until the last twenty-five meters of the approach up the bumpy road leading to the front entrance. Climbing out of the wheeled vehicle that had brought her, Deirdre noticed so many tracks leading up to the door that she guessed most patients came either on foot or carried on stretchers.

"We built the center here, away from Daosha, because we knew so many of the country people are too afraid to go to the city. We get our power from Daosha, but we have generators in case the power goes out." Rick Bradford pulled a handkerchief from his pocket and wiped sweat from his brow and upper lip. "We also have air conditioning most of the time, but it's down for repairs at the moment."

The cracked tile floors and dingy walls suggested other repairs that needed doing, but Deirdre ignored them. "You've got a hundred and fifty patient beds here?"

Bradford nodded and beckoned as he led deeper into the complex. "Fifty per floor. Bottom is pediatrics, which handles everything except surgical recovery. That's up on the top floor along with the intensive care unit and surgery. The middle floor is reserved for the adult wards and that's where we handle most communicable diseases and maternity— well-isolated from each other, of course."

"Of course." Deirdre smiled and Bradford responded in kind. "Oh, the emergency room is on the ground floor and we have one trauma surgery theater there. We've got triage rules, of course, but we don't need to rely on them very often."

Anne Thompson, her white uniform already beginning to wilt in the high humidity, tried to put a serious expression on her pudgy, apple-cheeked face. "Do you have a terminal illness hospice annex?"

Bradford shook his head as fatigue began to sap the animation he had so far displayed. "I know that dealing with the terminally ill is your specialty, but we haven't had the staff to set one up. I hope it's something you can do. Actually, I wanted the project further along by the time you arrived, but our funding got trimmed when the government started cutting back a year ago."

Cathy Hanney frowned, her pale eyebrows nearly meeting in the middle of her forehead. "I thought this clinic was independent of the government?"

"It is, it is." Bradford stopped in the middle of the corridor and folded his arms over his chest. "We're funded by private donations by and large, and they were plentiful until the Clan War. Now there's a new focus for most of the charity drives, and people of the Federated Commonwealth find it easier to give money to relocate Rasalhague refugees than to help folks who were conquered twenty years ago. Our largest contributor—our patron, if you will—has been Mandrinn Tormano Liao, but his resources only stretch so far. Luckily, CCI picked up the slack after a funding gap of four months, so we're back on track."

Cathy shook her head. "Victor Davion's money being laundered through Free Capella is still government money. I thought. . . ."

Deirdre reached out and laid her left hand on Cathy's right shoulder. "Look, you may have decided to come here as some sort of protest against things you don't like about Victor Davion. For all I know you think he had his mother killed—"

"He did, you know."

Deirdre and Rick exchanged quick glances, then she shook her head. "Well, that would probably be a good topic for discussion later on, *if* we have time for it. We may not have much leisure here, where so many people need our help. If I can give them that, I don't really care whose money is funding the medical center or paying for me to be here."

Cathy's blue eyes narrowed as she looked from Deirdre to Rick and back again. "It may be easier for you FedComs to accept Victor's money, but not me. His father let the Clans rape the Lyran Commonwealth, and he's no different. He ran from the Clans on Trellwan, and then again on Alyina."

Deirdre stiffened and the fire that flashed through her eyes made Anne blanch and stopped Cathy cold. "I will tell you this once and then I will not speak of it again. While you were graduating from secondary school, I was *on* Alyina. I ran a medical field station there, and boys and girls even younger than you are now came to me in bits and pieces, hoping I could put them back together again. Sometimes I could, but more often I could not. I had to watch them die, screaming in pain, praying for death but fearing it all the same."

Deirdre felt anger rising in her chest and she fought to keep it out of her words. "Whether they were natives of Alyina or soldiers who had traveled hundreds of light years to die on a world they couldn't have found on a star chart, they all bled bright red. They died so you'd get a chance to finish school and decide to come here or join the army or chuck it all and become an opposition politician. It didn't matter to them because they were fighting to keep the Clans from robbing you of your future."

"You were on Alyina?" Anne Thompson voiced her question in a whisper, willingly deflecting Deirdre from her ashen-faced companion. "You fought against the Clans?"

"I *ran* from the Clans." Deirdre reigned her temper back in. "When they tried to capture Prince Victor, they overran the sector where my hospital was located. We medivacced everyone we could, and the rest of us took off into the brush."

Rick shook his head. "You didn't stay with your patients?"

"Twycross showed me that the Jade Falcons considered battalion aid stations to be legitimate military targets." When she looked up, Deirdre saw all three of them staring at her. "Look, I was in both places because I'd joined the army and been assigned to the Tenth Lyran Guards."

Anne's face brightened a bit. "Were you with them when they rescued Hohiro Kurita on Teniente?" Her question ended on a high, hopeful note that trailed off when Deirdre shook her head.

"No. I spent the rest of the war on Alyina, running from the Clans."

"And?"

Deirdre forced a smile on her face for Anne's benefit. "No more story. We're here for orientation. We're here to learn how to help people." Seeing Anne's disappointed look, she relented slightly. "Yes, I've met Prince Victor and maybe, just maybe, on a slow shift I'll tell you about it over coffee."

Anne's face brightened and Cathy wanted to frown but seemed to lack the energy to do so. The blond woman scratched at the back of her neck. "I didn't mean to disparage what you did, Dr. Lear. I . . ."

Deirdre hugged the other woman. "I know you didn't, but maybe sometimes we get so wrapped up in our own ideas that we don't check out the other side of the story. At this point I think we'll be fine if we just concentrate on doing the best job we can here in the clinic instead of worrying too much about politics."

"Amen to that." Dr. Bradford pointed to a door a bit further on down the corridor. "That's the female staff lounge. You can go in and pick out a locker and stow whatever you want before we continue."

Deirdre hung back as she sensed her colleague wanting to talk to her. As the other two women disappeared through the door, she turned and smiled at him. "I apologize for that little tiff there."

Rick shrugged. "It's not the first time something like that has happened. Not everyone is happy about Tormano Liao financing us, because some consider him just another warlord waiting for his chance to strike. As far as I'm concerned, I'll spend his coins as fast as anyone else's as long as he's interested in improving the quality of life on Zurich. Now that we've got CCI, though, that's no longer a concern."

"How bad are things here?"

Bradford shrugged. "That's kind of hard to say. The average life span of someone in the Federated Commonwealth is ninety-seven point eight years, barring sex modifiers. Zurich is one of the worlds that lowers the average. The planet enjoyed a certain amount of development before the war—Maximilian Liao had a master-pet fixation on this planet, which is one of the reasons Tormano pays so much attention to it. All the people had to do was transfer their loyalty from Max to his son. And it's Tormano's interest in Zurich that has prompted Sun-Tzu to back the local dissident and revolutionary elements."

Deirdre held her hands up. "I've already had a bellyful of politics, Doctor. What interests me more are the kind of medical problems that are typical or problematic here. Most of the major diseases should have been eliminated."

"They have. We've got a nasty local flu that goes around and gets some of the old folks and kids, but we've been grinding away at the death toll on a regular basis. When flu season comes along, we actually buy ads on the holovid to get people in for vaccine. Other than that, it's mostly parasites and bacterial infections, cuts, and breaks—very rarely do we get rapes, and then it's usually a case of a local girl getting mixed up with a soldier or visitor to Daosha."

"From the way you say that I gather that the indigenous people keep quiet about rape among their own people?"

"Something like that. The man, when caught, has a choice of fates: If the woman isn't pregnant, he pays the restitution she demands of him and then, at her whim, is castrated or not. If he cannot pay, he is castrated and made her slave until he has performed tasks equal to the value of the restitution she demanded. Then he is killed."

"That's barbaric!" Deirdre blurted, knowing that her words reeked of ethnocentrism, but reacting instinctively.

"Not to the Zurs. If the woman is impregnated by the man, he's held until she's in labor, then killed. He provides the soul for the new child. It all makes sense in their cosmology."

"Why wouldn't a non-local be held and treated the same say, then?"

"The Zurs see us as an inferior people. They'd no more want us inhabiting one of their bodies than we'd want the spirit of a goat inhabiting one of ours." Bradford smiled. "Anyway, the incidence of rape is low in the indig culture."

"Not much chance of repeat offenders, I would imagine." Deirdre folded her arms. "How much violence?"

Rick hesitated. "Not that much, really. Fistfights sometimes, a knifing on the rare occasion. We do get gunshots every so often."

She nodded. "I see. Domestic violence, or something more organized?"

"The revolutionaries live out here in the jungle, but we don't have much to do with them. I've been here four years, and the only one I've seen was for an infected leg break. That's it. They do occasionally stage attacks against Daosha's police barracks or shoot a patrol going through the jungle, but they stay away from us. We're neutral ground."

Deirdre raised an eyebrow. "Is there another shoe to drop, Doctor? My son is in Daosha with my landlord's daughter. Is he safe?"

"I'm sure he is. The *Zhanzheng de guang* never hit civilian targets." Bradford smiled reassuringly. "But you can bring him here and keep him in our daycare facility if that would make you feel safer. We maintain it for the locals who are sick or who work for us. My wife runs it."

"I think I'll do that, thanks. I like seeing David during the day anyway."

"I understand." Rick glanced over as the two nurses came back into the corridor. "Well, let's continue our tour. Down here is emergency admitting . . ."

Lyons
Isle of Skye, Federated Commonwealth

Sitting with his teammates in the *Hart of Gold* tavern, Peter Davion focused beyond his friends and stared at the large-screen holovision unit in the near corner of the common room. His view of it was unobstructed because it rose above the rail isolating the booths in the back from the lower floor of the bar level. The screen showed the local news anchor all prim and pretty in a blue silk blouse and yellow wool jacket. Hovering over her left shoulder was a map of the Sarna March. Four of the worlds on it suddenly turned into multi-pointed explosions.

He held his hands up to quiet his two friends, who caught the gesture and immediately fell silent. " ... series of strikes which hit a number of garrison and police facilities in Zurich, Aldebaran, Styk, and Gan Singh. Pro-Liaoist War of Light factions have claimed responsibility for the attacks. They state that resistance to the illegitimate occupation government of Victor Davion would continue until the Sarna March was reunited with the Capellan Confederation. Federated Commonwealth officials claim the strikes are 'pathetic attempts by reactionary forces to deny what their fellow citizens had come to embrace and profit from.' "

Peter shook his head, then noticed that one of his two security watchdogs aped the motion from a table away. "Sun-Tzu is getting bold. Someone ought to explain to him that he can't turn back the clock."

Eric Crowe nodded in agreement as he poured the last of his Timbiqui Dark into his mug. "He's playing a game with his uncle. Tormano has been making noises for a long time about returning to take the throne. Now that your brother's decided to put Tormano's Free Capella movement on a diet, Sun-Tzu's decided to push to see how seriously that may have weakened his uncle."

The man across from Crowe scratched at his short blond hair. "Could be, Eric, or maybe it's that Sun-Tzu is probing to see how weak we've become on the Sarna border. With the Clans up here to occupy us, some of those worlds might look ripe for the taking."

"You could be right, Ben, except for the fact that Sun-Tzu hasn't got the military strength to take a world away from us." Peter snorted as he heard his words play back through his head. "Well, maybe I should say that he could conceivably *take* a world, but he couldn't hold it. We'd get it back, and he'd lose a lot of prestige in the exchange. Besides, it might make us mad enough to give him a pounding, and do what his uncle can't."

"But what if Sun-Tzu attacked from the Free Worlds League?" Ben leaned forward, setting Eric's empty beer bottle up and placing his half-full one across from it. "If he hit from the Free Worlds, then retreated back across the border, we wouldn't go after him."

Peter held his own beer bottle out at arm's length away from the table. "Thomas Marik won't allow that because his son is with the doctors on New Avalon. Even though we'd never do anything to harm young Joshua, Thomas can't be sure of that. Besides, if Joshua can't be cured of his leukemia, Thomas is stuck with Sun-Tzu marrying his daughter Isis and one day taking over his realm."

"That would make it the only time a Liao has taken over anything in the last couple of centuries." Eric lifted his bottle and waggled it in the air to signal the waiter. "Chances are this is a play to give Sun-Tzu some room to maneuver if Kai Allard-Liao beats Wu Deng Tang. Let me amend that: if Kai clobbers him as bad as all the bookies are predicting."

"He will." Peter took a swallow of beer, then smiled. "I was at NAMA when Kai was in the graduating class. He was the first person ever to defeat the La Mancha scenario. Anyone who can turn a no-win situation into a victory isn't going to be stopped by a single Liaoist in a BattleMech."

The three men laughed together for a moment, but then an angry shout from a patron seated at the bar drowned out their merriment. Peter looked up and saw the holovid viewer displaying a scene of police using watercannons on a crowd of protesters. He thought he'd become inured to such scenes, then felt a jolt run through him. *Wait, that's Freedom Square downtown. They must have cleared the streets before the game tonight! I didn't know there were protesters out there.*

"Yeah, we have freedom of speech, all right," the patron ranted. "As long as our name is Davion, that is."

"What do you expect from a whelp what killed his own mother!"

Peter saw the two security men move toward the back door to give him a way out. He stood and started toward them, having been trained to entrust his safety to his bodyguards. This time, though, one too many beers after playing a game of basketball slowed him down considerably.

"Victor's a vicious little pissant who throws temper tantrums when he can't get what he wants." The shouting patron looked around the room as others nodded in agreement. "See, there isn't a man-jack among you who will say different!"

Peter stepped forward, resting his hands on the railing. "I will."

"What?"

Holding his head up high, Peter saw the people below him transformed as they recognized his face. Some looked shocked, then smiled and whispered to their companions. A few became angry again and stared in hostility, but most grinned as they looked from Peter to the man at the bar and back again.

"I said I would dispute your claim. I doubt anyone here has better knowledge of Victor than I do." Peter felt exhilaration run through him as he took the anger burning his stomach and shunted it away. That brought a calm even more powerful than the anger. It filled him and made him aware of everything going on in the room.

More important, he didn't suffer all the mental static that usually accompanied his fury. Thinking clearly, Peter could feel the rhythm of the room and could orchestrate it. He smiled carefully, purposely letting his gray-eyed gaze touch as many pairs of eyes in the room as he could. "I will agree that my brother is small, but from my perspective there aren't many men who are not." He shrugged helplessly and laughter coursed through the crowd.

You were right, Katrina. After a recent basketball game against Kelswa-Aptos he'd received a holodisk recorded by his sister. In it she'd tried to tell him that he was only hurting himself when he let his temper get the better of him in sports or other unimportant settings. She went on to say that if he couldn't control himself in those harmless situations, no one would ever trust him with greater responsibilities.

Then she chided him for being about to pick up something to throw at the viewer. He'd put down the glass, and listened as she explained how he could use his celebrity and intelligence to great advantage if only he could conquer his temper. She suggested that he start while engaging in his pastime sports and it had worked. He learned to achieve a mental tranquility, which permitted him not only to excel in his performance but to become even more skilled than before.

The patron planted his hands on his hips. "Victor's still a pissant."

"Is he?" Peter arched an eyebrow and let the question sink in before shrugging nonchalantly. "Who really knows what a pissant is? I know what it sounds like, but I don't think I actually know what it means. Do you?"

The patron, an older man with a goatee and no more than a fringe of hair on his head, gaped for a moment. He opened his mouth to reply, then frowned and shut it again.

Peter didn't give him a chance to speak. "Anyone else have a guess?"

"A pissant is an annoying twit," someone shouted from the back.

"Hmmmm, annoying twit." Peter screwed his face into a frown. "Annoying, sure, Victor can be that. His idea of relaxation is to work on only two projects at once instead of his normal workload. Not much fun in doing that. Twit, on the other hand." He shook his head. "Twit always strikes me as a sort of inconsequential fellow, and I don't think anyone would call Victor that."

The patron snarled over the laughter Peter's comments had elicited. "He still murdered your mother!"

Peter let his face go blank as a new wave of anger raced through him before being transmuted into more cool calm. He straightened up, then clasped his hands staunchly at the small of his back. "Sir, I have no doubt that you *believe* you have evidence to back up that claim. If you do, I wish you would present it to me so I could act upon it."

"You wouldn't do nothing."

"If you knew who had murdered your mother, wouldn't you do something about it?" Peter said quietly.

"I'm not a Davion."

Peter held himself rock-still as he fought an inner battle. "Nor am I, sir. I am a *Steiner*-Davion. As are Victor and Katrina, Arthur and Yvonne. You mock us and what we felt for our mother. Moreover, you mock her if you imagine she could inspire love and admiration in the hearts of her countrymen and yet be unable to do the same in the hearts of her own children. You may insult my brother all you like, but do not insult my mother."

"And if I decide to insult you? You gonna have your police come in here and soak me down?"

"No. I'm like my brother Victor. I'd never ask others to do what I can do myself." Peter again leaned on the railing, letting his smile make his hulking form seem menacing and benign at the same time. "However, I think a better solution would be if I offered to buy you a drink . . ."

"I'll not drink with the likes of you to your brother's health."

"I offer the drink to my mother's memory." Peter let those words sink in and felt the mood of the room shift. Where there had been jocularity and high spirits, with everyone enjoying the exchange, a chill feeling seeped in, quieting the crowd. "If you'll not join me in a drink to my mother's memory, well, what more can I do to reach someone so cold? My offer stands, though, to you and everyone here. A round in her memory on me."

The first man tried to look defiant, but Peter had won the others over, isolating him. The man's fists knotted, then opened several times before he shrugged. "Be the first time I've gotten some of my taxes used for a purpose that benefitted me."

"No, my friend. To be contrary. *I* am buying out of my own militia salary." Peter held up his wallet and pulled out a handful of bills. "I hope you all enjoy this, for I'll not be drinking for a month because of it."

The people below him mouthed comments and laughed, and Peter laughed along with them even though he couldn't make out the remarks. His heart filled his ears with thunder, and he smiled broadly at the pure giddiness running through him. *This is incredible! Katrina is right, this is fantastic!* Peter gave out a whoop that the other drinkers echoed loudly enough to drown out his laughter. *As high as I feel now, I won't need another drink for the rest of my life!*

10

Solaris City, Solaris VII
Tamarind March, Federated Commonwealth
25 January 3056

Kai waited for the other stable owners to be seated in the Sesame Inn's handsomely appointed tower dining room before passing through the doors of the private elevator into the little mirror-walled lobby. The floor was carpeted in a black and red design that began as a chaotic tangle of color at the elevator, but resolved itself into twisting bands that scrolled around the perimeter of the large room. The black and red competed to create mythological creatures and to depict Chinese greetings and proverbs.

The lobby opened out into the dining room, replicating two copies of Kai that flanked him as he strode forward into a woodwork maze. Intricately carved lattices and delicate screens covered with rice-paper paintings separated the area into a series of discreetly concealed alcoves meant for private assignations. The low lights kept everything so half-hidden in shadow that only cinnabar highlights and the warm glow of burnished gold betrayed the alcoves as he walked through to the far side of the room.

The twined bodies of two dragons formed the arch over the threshold to his goal, their tails supporting the ceiling lost in shadow high overhead. At ground level the dragons snarled at each other across a three-meter gap. As Kai passed between them he heard a loud static hissing and felt a chill downdraft, but neither disturbed him. Both were part of a system designed to ensure that anything said within the

Dragon's Realm would go no further unless any of the participants recorded it from within.

Only on Solaris would this work. The interior of the Dragon's Realm was decorated with artificial rocks on three of the four walls. Little grottoes held Taoist and Buddhist shrines as well as candles and delicately displayed orchids. Other plants clung to the rocks, and little streams burbled down from the shadowed heights to dark pools lit by the flashes of enormous koi striking at the surface.

The fourth wall was made of glass and looked out over Solaris City. In any other city, where the sun could be counted on to shine at least occasionally during the day, the cavernous room would have been transformed into a rocky outcropping suitable for a school children's picnic. In Solaris, where the clouds trapped the city's garish lights, and where the city itself appeared to be a transparent body with neon blood pumping through it, the Dragon's Realm truly did become an Olympian hideaway for those who would style themselves masters of the world.

"Welcome, my friends." Kai smiled cautiously, well aware that the group around him presented more danger than any two foes he might face in any arena. Taking his place at the head of the stout ebony table, he never stopped smiling. "I trust you were not inconvenienced in coming here. As it is my turn to host our meeting, I thought perhaps you would enjoy trying a new place."

The petite woman seated to his left graciously returned his smile and set down her glass of what looked like plum wine. "This *is* different, Kai. I would have expected you to bring us to The Crane. It's supposed to be the best in Cathay."

"I think you will find that for atmosphere and cuisine, the Sesame Inn has no parallel, especially in its upper precinct." He pulled his chair out and sat. "George, the owner, is an old friend of the family. He lost his previous establishment on Sian and has relocated here."

"Another one of your charity cases, Liao?" The man sitting beyond Fiona Loudon scowled at Kai. "You take in more strays than the pound."

"I believe charity begins at home, Drew." It was no surprise to Kai that Drew Hasek-Davion and Fiona were sitting together. Both were from the Federated Commonwealth, though to call either one a Davion loyalist would have been a joke. Fiona, though shrewd—*or perhaps because of being shrewd*—avoided politics.

Drew used up her part of it and then some, having bought into the anti-Davion sentiment of his late uncle, Michael Hasek-Davion. Victor Davion often joked about Drew Hasek appropriating the Davion name as a suffix to his own surname. The prince said he let Hasek get away with it because it reminded people of Michael's fatal addiction to politics, thereby frustrating Drew's own his quest for power.

Thomas DeLon, Roger Tandrek, and Winslow Kindt completed the Compensation Committee of the Solaris Stable Owners Association. Kai had not met Kindt before, but he expected, at best, hostility from him since the man was acting in proxy for Duke Ryan Steiner. The fact that the man was talking so animatedly with Tandrek meant trouble for Kai; the Liaoist hated him and couldn't wait until Wu Deng Tang stomped Kai to blood and bones.

DeLon, sitting at the far end of the table, looked remarkably serene. That surprised Kai somewhat, because the man from the Draconis Combine had always been a focus of opposition to Kai and his policies. So far Kai had put it down to a misplaced sense of honor, in that fighters moving in and out of contracts amounted to mercantilism, not soldiery. *What have you got up your sleeve, Thomas?*

Kai signaled to George Yang and the staff began to serve dinner. Hot and sour spicy soup gave way to moo shu pork with plum sauce, sesame chicken, kung pao beef, and tangerine beef. Lychee nuts and brandy capped a meal in which the food was superior and the conversation a light overture to the discussions likely to begin once the meal was cleared away.

After the table had been cleared, Kai sat back in his chair and opened his hands. "I call this meeting of the SSOA Compensation Committee to order. We can waive viewing the minutes of the last meeting, I believe, unless Mr. Kindt has not had a chance to get caught up."

Winslow Kindt shook his head. He had a long face and a beanpole body that reminded Kai of what he'd felt like during one of the jumps on the way to Solaris. "I believe I am up to speed, both with what has gone on before and what Duke Ryan wants me to do."

"Good. Old business?" Kai glanced at Hasek-Davion. "Drew?"

"It's old business, though not really anything we can vote on, I suppose. Kai, do you really think it necessary to make public all the things that you do?" The portly man's face folded in on itself as he winced painfully. "There was no reason, for example, for you to go public about the counterfeit T-shirt deal. New Syrtis-Gap offered compensation in good faith, but then you went and exposed what they had done. Your announcement made them lose a lot of ground on the New Avalon Exchange."

Fiona laughed lightly. "Got our trust fund caught in a crack, eh, Drew?"

"It's not funny, Fiona. Stables are having to cut to the bone to make a profit, and I need my offworld investments to see me through lean times as well as the good. I've never had two simultaneous champions in my stable—none of us have except for you." Drew's dark eyes narrowed. "You really hurt them with the settlement you imposed."

"Good," said Kai, "because *they* really hurt the people with whom I had my licensing agreement. I saw NSGI offers for the right to distribute our logo and imageware throughout the Successor States, and I didn't like it. I had my people negotiate with local suppliers of sports apparel, and the expense for those negotiations came out of Cenotaph, not the SSOA. When NSGI started competing with my local people, it hurt them and hurt them bad. I hurt them back." Kai leaned forward on the table, his fingers interlaced. "And if I ever find out that the rumors about you getting kickbacks from NSGI are true, Drew, I'll go through your stable like a bullet through tofu."

"Oh, sure, Mr. Holier-than-thou! Who do you think you are?" Drew slammed a fist into the table, then pointed a finger at Kai. "You set up a charitable organization and then publicize the fact that a chunk of each purse you win goes to it. You also talk your opponents into contributing, which looks great for you, but makes the rest of us look like misers. You refuse to let NSGI sell off its inventory, and instead have that go to charity too. People down in the streets call you Steelsoul, and say it shields a heart of gold. Well, if you're so damned great, what the hell are you doing here in the ass-end of the universe?"

"Keeping you honest? It's a full-time job, you know."

"He has a point, Kai." Roger Tandrek leaned back in his chair, brushing the ends of his white mustache into place with one hand. "We applaud your efforts at charity, but publicizing it the way you do seems to cheapen it. Other owners have also commented to me about it, so it isn't only us. I know you think we're just a corrupt group of money-grubbing robber barons—"

Fiona patted Kai on the wrist. "I always knew you had twenty-twenty vision, Kai."

"—but not all of us are as affluent as you are." Tandrek shot Fiona a hard glance, but the diminutive redhead dismissed it with half-lowered eyelids.

"Roger, I understand fully and completely what you are. You look at Solaris and the games as a business. You look at profit and loss. In doing that you see fighters as the cost of training their replacements." Kai shook his head. "I don't."

"That is absurd. I know they are human beings and I treat them as such. Wynn Goddard is a personal friend."

Fiona smiled. "His preference for energy weapons does help that P and L bottom line when it comes to ammo expenses, doesn't it?"

"Fiona, I don't need your gibes." Tandrek's florid face deepened to an angry purple. "Kai, Wu Deng Tang is a good friend of mine. I get to know all my fighters and I treat them well. Yet, as much as I like them, I have to run the stable like a business. I have costs and I have investors to consider."

Kai shook his head. "I consider *people,* and my stable runs as profitably as any of yours—perhaps more so. I managed to find a solution to the training problem."

Drew snarled in frustration. "Sure, hiring veterans of the Clan War was smart."

"You could have done it."

"Yes, but then we would have had to match your salary offers to unproven fighters." Tandrek looked over at Kindt, then shook his head. "Your father would never have done business this way."

Kai laughed aloud. "If I were my father, I'd know even more about your operations than I do, and I'd own you all. What you don't realize is that the universe has changed, and changed drastically. For a long time Solaris was a stable source of entertainment and income. We pay taxes, those companies who market our merchandise pay taxes, and the people who buy our product pay taxes. We had a known quantity in our hands, something everyone wanted and we had no competition.

"Well, the Clans changed that. Our competition is raw footage shot by amateur cameramen during Clan raids on border worlds. The real thing competes with us. We no longer have it easy out there, so why should you have it easy in here?"

Kai looked over at Fiona. "She saw what was coming and planned ahead. Fiona's contracts with her fighters are iron-clad, and people sign them because they get a long-term benefit for good service. I think her contracts aren't much more than a step up from slavery, but the people who sign them are adults capable of making their own rational decisions."

"You do know how to flatter a woman, Kai."

"The rest of you treat your pilots like they were jockeys riding prize race horses, not warriors risking their lives every time they strap themselves in for a fight. I appreciate the risk they take because it's the same one I have to take. I want to see them justly compensated for their activity, and that's what I do. And that's what you'll have to do if you want to compete here."

Winslow Kindt shook his head. "I realize I'm the new boy, but I must say that I believe you to be in error, Mr. Allard-Liao. The SSOA Charter, to which Cenotaph is a signatory, clearly points out that you have violated the just compensation clause of our charter since your arrival here. I would suggest that this invalidates your membership in this committee and even calls for a full investigation of Cenotaph and forfeiture of your title to Victor Vandergriff of the Skye Tigers."

Roger Tandrek looked ready to explode, while Drew Hasek-Davion sat back, staring into space. Fiona swirled brandy around in her glass and laughed lightly. "Has the Achilles heel been found?"

"If the title is forfeit, it should go to Wu Deng Tang!"

"Oh, yes, very good." Drew's lips revealed yellow teeth in

a ratlike grin. "The compensation distribution formula, I like that."

Kai refused to let any emotion show on his face and slowly let his moment of panic bleed away. "Would you care to be more specific, Mr. Kindt?"

"By all means." Kindt steepled his fingers and leaned forward to place his elbows on the table. "As Drew suggests, it comes down to the language used in the fighter compensation formula. It specifies that *all* income from purses, endorsements, and other bonuses and optional compensation plans be factored in together to determine the compensation paid to the lower-echelon fighters within a stable."

Kai nodded. "I am familiar with the wording. It was put in place to guarantee that the warriors who don't rank interstellar media attention can still profit from the stables' compensation by the broadcasting networks. We use the formula, and Cenotaph is the only stable that publishes a complete public audit at the end of each fiscal year."

"Commendable, to be sure, Mr. Allard-Liao, but as you will recall, a top fighter's compensation is limited to no more than four thousand percent over the top fighter on the next-lowest echelon. Even so, *your* reported income was something in excess of twenty-seven thousand percent higher than your next fighter."

The young MechWarrior nodded. "Ah, so you took the income I made as the owner of Cenotaph and combined that with my winnings and compensation as Champion, correct?"

"I am afraid so," Kindt replied apologetically. "What is good for the gander will, in this case, cook the goose."

"The compensation formula was never meant to apply to ownership earnings." Kai frowned. "Of course, the formula went in when there were no owner/fighters, so it was never tested. An interesting point, Mr. Kindt, but something that is more appropriate to a proposed charter amendment at our next general meeting."

"I beg to differ, sir." Kindt tapped his two index fingers together. "This Committee has the power to suspend a stable's license if we find and verify corrupt activity relating to compensation of arena fighters. Even if this is an oversight, I feel constrained to make a formal motion to suspend Cenotaph's license . . ."

His words trailed off suggestively and Kai bowed his head

in the man's direction. Kindt had read the gathering well. He knew that Kai and Fiona would likely vote against the motion, but the other four would vote in favor, supplying the two-thirds majority needed to pass the suspension. The Championship would be forfeit until the next general meeting of the Owners Association in two months. Tandrek, Hasek-Davion, and the others would present an immediate plan for an interim tournament, which the Championship Committee would likely approve and then allow to take place before Kai would be off suspension. With no one in the Cenotaph stable eligible to fight, all his people would be hurt.

Unless . . . "What does Duke Ryan want from me?"

"Want from you? Just a chance to have a Champion, the same wish as any other owner. Your title defense is two months away. He proposes you fight against Victor Vandergriff a month from now. Given the schedule you met to attain the title, two fights in two months should not be that difficult."

There it is. Neatly packaged and nicely done. If Kai agreed to the request for the fight, Duke Ryan would make a small fortune on his half of the media rights, and that would help him recoup what he paid to buy out Oonthrax. In agreeing he would have Kindt's vote if one of the others brought up the motion, and the three-to-three deadlock would kill it. If he did not agree, he would lose the Championship and Cenotaph could be seriously hurt.

"It would be easy. I've beaten Vandergriff before." Kai thought a moment longer, then shook his head. "But the only thing I would hate worse than losing the Championship to political games is giving Duke Ryan Steiner the satisfaction of making me dance to his tune even for second. No deal. Consider your motion for sanctions made. Any seconds?"

"I second the motion." Drew bounced in his seat like a child attending his first 'Mecharama.

Kai nodded. "Sanction votes are verbal and shall be recorded. Mr. Kindt?"

"Aye."

"Mr. Tandrek?"

"Aye."

"Mr. Allard-Liao votes 'Nay.' Ms. Loudon?"

"Nay."

"Mr. Hasek-Davion."

"Aye."

Kai looked across the table at Thomas DeLon. "The deciding vote is to you, Thomas."

"Iie."

Kai knew what he had heard, but he couldn't believe it. "In English, please, for the record."

"Nay. I vote no." DeLon remained impassive, though Kai thought he saw a momentary mischievous glance at Fiona after the vote.

Drew, Tandrek, and Kindt looked stunned. "By my count the vote stands at three in favor and three against. The motion fails to carry the needed majority."

Fiona smiled at Kai. "I move we adjourn."

DeLon nodded. "I second the motion."

"All those in favor say 'Aye.' "

Tandrek switched sides from the previous vote and dissolved the meeting. Fiona led the trio of her defeated comrades out of the room, leaving Kai and DeLon at either end of the table.

Kai frowned. "I expected you to vote with Kindt. Hell, I thought you'd *engineered* his maneuver."

"It was his idea," De Lon said. "I found it clever and in the past would have supported it, even though I admired your courage at rejecting his deal."

"Why didn't you support it?"

DeLon smiled. "You are correct, Kai—the universe is changing. The Kobe sector has a visitor who has expressed a desire to sit in your box when you defend your title. She considers your granting her request a great honor."

Omi. Kai nodded. "I owe her my thanks."

DeLon stood and slid his chair back into place. "She is also impressed with your ideas for Solaris. Her opinion has opened my eyes to many things." He smiled. "Warring against opponents like Kindt and Hasek-Davion brings with it very little honor, but perhaps I will find some amusement in helping you accelerate the pace of the change on Solaris."

11

Zurich
Sarna March, Federated Commonwealth
4 February 3056

Deirdre Lear pulled the stethoscope from her ears, then draped the ear pieces around the back of her neck. She smiled at the little boy's mother and helped ease one of the four-year-old's arms through the correct hole in his T-shirt. "I think Jimmy will be fine. He has a little bit of a cold, maybe some allergies."

Deirdre glanced at the computer monitor built into the wall of the examining room. "Looks like he had a previous episode of this type of rhinitis last year and again six months ago. Do you ever notice his eyes watering or the runny nose starting when he gets near flowers or something else that's blooming?"

The Zur woman pulled her son into her arms and shook her head, though she never let her broad smile die. "Thank you, Doctor." She nodded her head, then hugged her child and repeated, "Thank you, Doctor."

Deirdre kept her own smile just as constant, then opened the examining room door. "Anne, have you got a minute?"

Anne Thompson immediately appeared in the doorway. "What do you need, Doc?"

"Your language skills. I think Jimmy Looduc here has allergic rhinitis. He had it last year and six months ago and I'll bet it's related to some local blossom, but I can't get details from his mother."

Anne nodded, her short brown hair bouncing in ringlets as she did so. "Okay, I can ask her that. Anything else?"

"The nasal discharges are clear, so I don't think we're dealing with sinusitis. If they get cloudy, she should bring him back for another check." Deirdre took a prescription pad from her pocket and wrote out a quick message. "This is for an antihistamine, Rondeka. Four times a day, with meals if possible. It's good for two weeks. If he's still got a runny nose after that, have her bring him back. Ditto if he develops an earache."

Anne smiled. "I know the drill."

"I know. Thanks."

Anne winked at her and guided Mrs. Looduc and her son out of the room. Deirdre waved at them, then leaned back against the door jamb of the examining room. Her legs hurt from standing all day and her eyes were burning. She had no doubt it was a reaction to the same sort of airborne pollen that was making Jimmy Looduc stuffy, but she also acknowledged a big slice of fatigue sitting on her plate.

"You look beat." Rick Bradford said over his shoulder as he bent to wash his hands in the sink across the hall from her. "Ghost plague days are really bad."

Deirdre arched an eyebrow at him. "Ghost plague?"

Bradford nodded as he dried his hands with some paper towels. "The locals have a fairly rigid theology by which they live. Ghosts and spirits play a big part in it."

"I gathered that from what you said about their treatment of rapists who get their victims pregnant." Deirdre slipped the stethoscope into the pocket of her white lab coat and crossed the hallway to wash her hands. "What's a Ghost plague?"

"Three days ago the *Zhansheng de Guang* hit a truck carrying some ammunition and fuel to some troops that are establishing a forward patrol base. Four men died in the truck, and reports put five terrorists down. I think you were off the night of the hit. We got two of the wounded troopers here. Nothing much, but the four guys in the truck were DOA. I don't know about the terrorists.

"Anyway, the Zurs believe that the ghosts of men who die violent deaths are determined to reenter a physical body to exact revenge upon their killers. They believe these ghosts travel through the world and are sufficiently powerful to pull the soul out of a living body so the ghost can take over.

They enter through any body orifice, and a fight can take place for dominance. A fever is a sure sign."

Deirdre finished washing her hands, then shut off the water with her elbows. "Runny nose, coughing, diarrhea, burning upon urination, or an infected cut would all be signs of possible ghost entry, right?" She pulled paper towels from a dispenser to dry her hands.

"You're catching on." Bradford glanced at the schedule on the wall and crossed off the patient he had just seen. "The Zurs consider us about the least spiritually oriented people in existence, so they bring possible ghost-hosts here for our medicine. They think our science is repellent to the ghosts. If our stuff doesn't work they will exorcise the ghost through traditional means. The ritual takes about a week and a half."

"The time it takes for a cold to run its course."

Bradford laughed. "Normally, men and women of science are skeptical because of that coincidence."

She shook her head. "I've practiced medicine on a half-dozen different worlds. I've seen diseases that would cause a panic on one world being treated like a cold on another. I've had patients with allergic reactions to plants and animals never seen on their world of birth, and I've heard of local cures for things that are a scourge on worlds hundreds of light years away. For all I know the Zurs may be right."

Deirdre crossed Jimmy Looduc off her schedule and smiled. "Looks like I'm done unless you want me to pick up one of your sickies."

Rick glanced at his schedule. "Nope. Boondao is likely a haunting and Langkuoki is a recheck on an otitis media. Go on, get out of here. If you take David off Carol's hands, that'll give us a fighting chance of getting home before we have to turn around and come back."

"Thanks, Rick." Deirdre cut through the records room to the small office she'd been assigned. She took off her lab coat and hung it on the rack beside the door, then went to her desk, fingering the mail and choosing a medical journal holodisk to review at home. She slipped it into her jacket pocket, looped her canvas carryall bag over her shoulder, and turned off the light.

Carol Bradford had created a wonderful daycare center from a suite of four rooms originally intended as on-site housing for the clinic's medical director. Huge murals featuring well-known holovid characters covered each wall in brightly colored splendor. On one the alphabet and Arabic numbers wound round the characters like a red ribbon, while on another approximately two hundred of the most basic characters in written Chinese provided the decoration.

Toys, desks, and other furnishings dominated two of the rooms. Mats covered the floor of the third, which served as the sleeping room. The fourth and smallest had been converted into Carol's office, but was really a room all overflowing with supplies, lost and found items, and a tiny desk. Carol was emerging from that room when Deirdre caught her eye and waved.

"Hi, Deirdre. David's got a surprise for you."

At the sound of his name, David got up from behind a wall of blocks and ran over to his mother. A big smile on his face, he held out his arms to her. *"Wan'an muqan!"* He laughed as Deirdre blinked. "It means 'Hi.' "

Deirdre smiled as she knew she should, both because David obviously wanted her to and because of Carol watching discreetly but expectantly. Deirdre slowly dropped to her haunches, letting her bag slip to the floor as she gave her son a hug. Then she held him out at arm's length, grasping the hem and right shoulder of his navy t-shirt trying to get a better look at the design on it.

The BattleMech emblazoned there had been romanticized to such a point by the artist that it looked as much like a cartoon as the man standing beside it. Deirdre instantly knew that the man had been drawn out of scale, for he stood half as tall as the war machine that would have towered over the whole clinic. She did not know who Larry Acuff was, but she recognized the 'Mech as a *Warhammer*. With a shudder she remembered the kind of destruction one of those could leave in its wake.

"Carol," she began cautiously, "where did David get this shirt?"

"We had an accident earlier and David's shirt got wet, so I lent him one from the last shipment that came from CCI." The brown-haired woman smiled easily. "David wanted a Yen-lo-wang shirt, but this was all we had in his size."

Deirdre felt her guts knotting up. *"Yen-lo-wang?"*

Carol nodded to reassure her that nothing was out of the

ordinary. "CCI had a lot of shirts and other clothes to distribute because of a lawsuit or something. A couple of our older kids were wearing the Yen-lo-wang shirt and David liked the design. I think he might be a budding artist, because that one is definitely the most colorful. Of course, the older kids like the shirt because it's the 'Mech Kai Allard-Liao pilots."

David's smile slowly died. "What's wrong, Mommy?"

"Nothing, honey." Deirdre frowned and enfolded him in another hug.

"Deirdre, are you all right?"

"Yeah, Carol, ah, I think so." She stood up, lifting David up with her. "Look, I appreciate what you did and I know you meant well. It's just that, well, I've tried to shield Davy from things."

Carol looked stricken. "Oh, God, you were in the war. Rick said that. I didn't think. I'm sorry."

"Don't worry, Carol. I know you had no way of anticipating my reaction. I think if we don't make a big thing of it, no harm's done." Deirdre fought to control her emotions so as not to lash out at Carol. "I'll, ah, I'll get the shirt washed and you can pass it on to someone who needs it more than Davy here. I'll also bring another one of his shirts tomorrow, a spare, in case we run into trouble again."

She forced a smile and actually started to feel a bit better. "The way Davy is growing, pretty soon you'll have all his old stuff to give away ... I mean, if you want that kind of donation."

"Yes, by all means, of course." Carol closed the gap between them and hugged Deirdre, then helped her slip the carryall back over her shoulder. "Look, I'm really, really sorry. We don't allow war toys in here, but I was thinking of the shirts as, well, shirts; not what they had silk-screened on them."

Deirdre nodded and patted Carol's arm. "Chances are Davy won't remember a thing about it tomorrow. Will you, honey?"

"I won't, promise."

The two women smiled at each other. "I'll see you tomorrow, Carol. I really appreciate your sensitivity about the war toys." Deirdre put David down, then took his right hand in her left. "I'd have thought CCI would be more sensitive about that sort of thing, too."

Carol looked surprised. "You would?"

"It's a charitable organization. I wouldn't think . . ." Deirdre frowned in response to the puzzled look on Carol's face. "What am I missing?"

"Deirdre, CCI is Cenotaph Charities Incorporated. It's based on Solaris." Carol opened her hands wide. "They pay all our bills, which means that for all intents and purposes, our boss is Kai Allard-Liao himself."

Tharkad
District of Donegal, Federated Commonwealth

Victor Davion clapped his hands as Curaitis finished his report of Peter's action on Lyons. "That's utterly fantastic news, and Lord knows I need it. I had Peter assigned to the Skye Militia because I figured it would minimize the amount of damage he could do on an assignment. I never expected him to handle himself so expertly." The prince's blue eyes half-closed with suspicion. "Are you certain the report is accurate?"

Curaitis did not reply immediately, but Victor had learned enough about the man to know the hesitation had nothing to do with trying to tailor his answer to curry favor. *He's just checking his facts and evaluating them.* Victor resisted the desire to smile, but he allowed himself some pride in having a man like Curaitis in his service.

"It is accurate, Highness. The words used may not have been verbatim, but it's close." Curaitis' expression darkened. "The report took a long time to reach Tharkad because the information about the Skye uprisings bumped it from priority transmission. Had the incident been specifically directed against Peter or had it resulted in any security breach, it would have gotten a higher priority. As things are going, though, Lyons is utterly cool."

Victor rose from his leather-upholstered chair and began to pace along the back wall of his office. He looked down, for a moment almost shocked out of his reverie by the matted path already worn in the carpet along the walnut bookcase. He realized that most of that wear had taken place while Skye and the border worlds where Ryan Steiner held sway had gradually been erupting into rebellion.

"It's not rebellion—*yet*," he muttered out loud. "Those who forget history are doomed to repeat it, but those who remember it sometimes turn to it for inspiration."

Curaitis nodded, just the slightest acknowledgment that he'd understood. "Duke Ryan Steiner is on his way to Solaris, so he won't be in a position to win influence by quelling the crisis as he did twenty years ago."

"I know, which is what convinces me he's the one behind this trouble." Victor stopped and turned to face the security man. "In thirty thirty-four the separatist movements in Skye went overboard. When Duke Aldo Lestrade died, his organization fell apart because he left no successor. The lesser leaders struggled among themselves, first one and then another putting on a show of power on his or her world, then others answering in kind, if not even more outrageously.

"Ryan, who had been handpicked by my grandmother's rival Alessandro Steiner, had hoped to inherit Lestrade's organization. Even though he had some of the keys to exerting control over it, Lestrade's people considered him a new player with nothing beyond a war record to commend him. But after he negotiated a settlement that kept my father's troops from destroying a rebel faction on Skye, his stock rose like a rocket among the separatists."

Curaitis nodded. "You're thinking that he would find the current situation analogous to the one in thirty-four."

"Correct." Victor slowly rubbed his hands together. "If Ryan wasn't in command of the situation, he wouldn't have gone to Solaris, but would be fighting to gain control of it. Ryan isn't stupid. He knows that to seem like a leader one need only determine which way the crowd is going and then run ahead of them. Perception becomes reality at that point."

He sighed aloud and, interlacing his fingers, capped his blond head with his hands. "By going to Solaris, Ryan makes himself visible. He has a soapbox and an alibi. He's hoping I'll make the same mistake my father did in calling out troops quickly. He'd love blood in the streets, but I can't afford it. At least, with the news you've brought, I don't have to worry about Peter going nuts on me."

"The protests on Lyons have been peaceful and the local constabulary has been able to handle them."

"Good. Intelligence has nothing directly linking Ryan to the riots, I assume?"

Curaitis nodded. "Ryan is decidedly cautious and the ELINT resources we had in his office on Porrima provided us only spotty coverage. The people he had sweeping his office were very good, and electronic intelligence-gathering devices are not very flexible. If Ryan had worked out an elaborate set of signals with subordinates—a sign language based on where he positioned the keyboard of his computer or the window shades in his office—our ELINT equipment would have missed them entirely."

"We have no one close to him?"

Curaitis looked over at the prince with the closest thing to a smile that Victor had ever seen on the man's face. "We came close, but Ryan hired Sven Newmark as his aide before we could put someone of our own in his path. The Secretariat now has a number of agents infiltrating the Rasalhague community to see if we can find a line on Newmark and to come up with a cover that would make the individual as attractive to Ryan as Newmark was."

"Commendable."

"Ryan's move to Solaris has provided us an opportunity." Curaitis clasped his hands behind his back. "Quentin Clark is the name of the man who has, so far, kept Ryan's office clean of our devices. He worked for us for a while and knows a few tricks. When Ryan prepared to ship out to Solaris, Clark liquidated a number of bank accounts. He has enough money to finance a high-rolling lifestyle on Solaris. In comparing the amount of money he withdrew with the amounts he's reported as income since first filing, we have a big discrepancy. When we mentioned that to him, Clark suddenly decided to sow ELINT devices instead of harvesting them in Ryan's offices on Solaris."

"Very good, very good, indeed." Victor smiled broadly. "I will settle for Ryan implicating himself in the growing Skye disturbances, but I'd like it even more if he would start bragging about having my mother assassinated."

"I doubt that will happen. I would not have thought him foolish enough to make that sort of mistake, but he has."

Victor frowned. "Mistake?"

Curaitis nodded once, curtly. "The mistake of placing himself on Solaris. There are many things that can happen on Solaris that could easily be ascribed to accident or bad luck."

"I see." The matter-of-fact tone in Curaitis' voice belied the gravity of his words. Victor thought about how they had found and captured his mother's assassin on Solaris, thanks to Fuh Teng soliciting for a contractor to have Kai's mother killed. The cover story had been that Fuh Teng had embezzled a great deal of money from Cenotaph and wanted Candace Liao killed so Kai would be forced to sit on the throne of the St. Ives Compact. The man who had killed Melissa agreed to take on another job of equal difficulty, and the Intelligence Secretariat had swept in and captured him.

Though Victor would never wish harm to Candace Allard-Liao, he found himself wishing Kai did sit on her throne. The year he and Kai had spent together at the New Avalon Military Academy and the time they had spent fighting the Clans had showed him how impressive Kai could be—not just in a Battlemech, but as a strategic and tactical planner.

Victor shook his head. "I was just thinking how different the whole situation would be if Kai weren't wasting his time on Solaris, but was here helping me deal with this crisis instead. The man never met a problem he couldn't defeat and I know he'd be as sharp at politics as he is in war. He would see opportunities to defeat Ryan where I see nothing but chaos."

"If Kai is that good, you're fortunate he's on Solaris."

"Because that's where Ryan's heading?" Victor cocked his head to one side as he reflected. "I suppose you're right. Ryan will doubtless do some meddling and Kai can deal with him there. Speaking of related items, has the approval for those Jade Falcons to go to Solaris been finalized yet?"

"ComStar has still not responded. The International Relations subcommittee of the Estates General is willing to report out of committee a recommendation for recognition of the Jade Falcons as a political entity. They're also willing to have a consulate established on Solaris, as we planned. But we might have problems if anyone in the Skye bloc learns that Jade Falcons will be passing through their space."

All I need is for Ryan to find out that I'm permitting Clanners to slip through Skye to a world beyond the line established by the ComStar treaty. "I'll have the Majority

Leader brief me on that situation. That old dog loves media opportunities."

It suddenly occurred to Victor that he shouldn't assume he understood Curaitis' remark concerning Kai. Making any assumption where Curaitis was concerned was a dangerous proposition. "You had something else in mind when you spoke about Kai."

"History is full of men who have been unseated by trusted advisors and comrades given too much responsibility in the power structure." Curaitis half-shut his eyes. "If Kai is the man you believe him to be, is having him close a good idea?"

Victor shook his head. "In that question you have underestimated me and totally misjudged Kai. He is not a political animal, but he could become one. He's changed a lot from when I first knew him. He has confidence in himself now. I gather, from things he has told me, that his time on Alyina had something to do with that. His performance on Solaris shows he's still testing, still pushing to see how good he can be."

Curaitis folded his arms across his chest. "What happens when he discovers Solaris is too small a scale on which to measure himself? Will he turn political and come after you?"

"Kai saved my life, twice. He did it on Twycross and again on Alyina." The blue flecks in Victor's gray eyes sparked with irritation. "How can I doubt the loyalty of a friend who saved my life?"

"Just like Galen Cox?"

"What is that supposed to mean?" Victor frowned. "Galen saved my life too, and has kept me from doing things that would have hurt the Federated Commonwealth. He's my closest friend."

"But he's not here."

"Right, because I sent him to escort my sister Katherine on her trip to Arc-Royal and then on to Solaris." Victor stared at Curaitis, searching the man's face for some clue to what he was thinking. "I trust Galen implicitly."

The security man's face deadened. "Galen Cox is outside your sphere of influence."

"But he's with my sister."

"Her name was on the *list*."

Victor stiffened as an icy claw closed around his heart.

The list! The investigation into the death of his mother had
produced the assassin, but it had failed to uncover the identity of the person who had hired him. A list of people who
had purchased tickets to the reception where Melissa had
died turned up only four names of those who'd had tickets
but had not attended the affair. Everyone else who was there
had either bought tickets themselves or been given them by
friends.

Ryan Steiner topped the list of no-shows, and Victor knew
he was the one behind his mother's murder. The current rebellion proved it. With Melissa out of the way, the glue that
bound the Federated Suns with the Lyran Commonwealth
was coming undone. The Lyran Commonwealth, having lost
a quarter of its holdings to the Clans, had suffered far more
than the Federated Suns portion of the alliance. Many Lyrans
resented that fact, and even more were afraid the Clans
would renew the war to finish the job. Ryan had used their
doubts and fears to increase his power and to position himself to assume the throne of an independent Lyran Commonwealth.

The second name on the list was that of the Precentor
Martial of ComStar, Anastasius Focht. Victor found it hard
to believe that Focht was involved in his mother's death,
though ComStar's virtual monopoly on interstellar communications could well have accounted for the frustrating difficulty of backtracking from the assassin to his patron. Still,
Melissa Steiner Davion had represented stability within the
Inner Sphere, and ComStar seemed devoted to preserving
both the stability and existence of the Inner Sphere in the
face of the threat posed by the Clans.

Katherine had been third on the list. Victor could never
have suspected her. He recalled what Curaitis had reported
Peter telling the group about the love Melissa had inspired in
all her children. Katherine, who had taken to calling herself
Katrina after their maternal grandmother, would have been
utterly beyond suspicion except for one tiny inconsistency—
she had not attended the reception despite being notorious
for her love of parties and people and attention.

"Do you think she had a hand in my mother's death?"

"I weigh alternatives and choose the most likely among
them." Curaitis shrugged his shoulders. "Your sister fell
asleep that afternoon. An agent checked on her and decided,

for whatever reason, not to awaken her. She has exhibited that sort of behavior before. Had you mother not died at the reception, your sister's absence would not have been noted."

"But she could just as easily have been faking sleep."

"The possibility weighs against her."

Victor nodded. His own name was fourth on the list, and speculation about his role in the assassination had often been used to boost the ratings on dying talk shows throughout the Federated Commonwealth. The fact that he had been the person to discover his father dying of a heart attack on New Avalon was coupled with his mother's violent death to create a strong case of circumstantial evidence to prove the son had slain them both.

"Katherine's name appearing on this list is insufficient reason for me to doubt Galen or his loyalty to me," Victor said. "I trust Galen and I want you to remember that."

"I do. My people only report on your sister, not him." The tone of Curaitis' voice almost suggested he found a paradox in that situation. "As you wish it to be."

"It is my prerogative to choose my own enemies."

"And my duty to see that *no* enemy can destroy you."

Victor glanced at his chronometer. "And you do a spectacular job of that."

"So far."

"Good point. Any chance a security alert can get me out of the meetings I have this afternoon? Surely these people who want prison reform must be dangerous. Furloughs, work-release, home arrest. That *has* to be a security problem, doesn't it?"

"No, sir."

Victor grumbled to himself. "Curaitis, when do Galen and Katherine arrive on Solaris?"

"They are in-system now. They arrive a day after Duke Ryan makes planetfall."

"Katherine will make a show of her arrival and eclipse Ryan, I have no doubt." Victor pulled on the formal jacket that went with his navy blue dress slacks. Half a dozen medals hung heavily on the left breast and a loop of gold braid encircled his left shoulder, dipping through his armpit, to be tied off at the epaulette. The Tenth Lyran guard crest rode on his right shoulder, with a tab above it that proclaimed him a member of the elite Revenant battalion.

He picked up a simple platinum circlet and let it hang from his hand like a magician's ring. It occurred to him, at that moment, that the damned thing was a magician's ring because it conferred on the wearer great majesty and power. *And responsibility, which men like Ryan Steiner never see until they've won their prize in a bloody war that tears apart a nation.* "Ryan Steiner would be willing to kill me to get this crown. I wonder if he would be willing to die for it?"

"He's putting himself in position to find out."

"Indeed." Victor flipped the coronet around, making it slap the inside of his forearm and back to hit the other side. "Curaitis, about the man in the leprosarium on Poulsbo, how is he?"

The security agent's voice remained emotionless. "He has healed from the leg fracture and has been rehabilitated. He is availing himself of computer simulation time. The system is isolated, so he is electronically quarantined as well. He has revealed no sources to us, and he appears to be as insulated from his patron as his patron is from us. He is arrogant and angry, but his simulations show he is quite good. He does not, however, like where he is being imprisoned."

"Homesickness, do you think?"

"Perhaps, Highness."

"We can't have that, Curaitis." Victor settled the coronet on his brow. "Bring his system up to date on Solaris and keep it that way. I'll want him ready just in case there *is* something to this idea of work-release after all."

12

Grace of God Leprosarium, Poulsbo
Periphery March, Federated Commonwealth
8 February 3056

The assassin realized that if he knew what day it was, he had a fighting chance of guessing on which world they had stashed him. The T-shaped cell where they were housing him had been whitewashed from floor to the ceiling five meters over his head. A pair of bright light bulbs burned incessantly overhead. Without windows he had no way of measuring the passage of the days, though even he acknowledged that some worlds within the Federated Commonwealth had so quick a rotation that tracking night and day would have been useless.

The cell's three arms each had its own purpose. He reckoned everything from the cell's single door, arbitrarily declaring that it was in the north wall. Opposite it, all the way against the south wall, sat his bed, sink, and toilet. He had no privacy screens and no way to shade his eyes from the eternal light. He knew there had to be dozens of listening devices and cameras secreted about the cell, so to frustrate his captors he made sure his daily routine was just that: routine and boring.

The cell's west arm held the most excitement for him. In it stood his treadmill. He used the device religiously, taking a certain amount of pride in the fact that he could walk without even the trace of a limp. The surgeons who had repaired the damage to his broken right leg had left a neat tracery of scars on his shin and thigh, but he was grateful that their work had returned to him use of the limb.

His computer sat beside the treadmill on a table. He noted with amusement that its manufacturer was the same as the one that had created the computer he'd used to kill Melissa Steiner-Davion. The difference was that this one lacked the modem which had made the crime possible. Instead it had been outfitted with a ten-disk CD ROM changer and a 150 gig Opdat drive that gave him access to more data than he'd ever found useful before. The oversize color monitor and detached keyboard made it possible for him to use the machine even while in the midst of his two-hour daily workout on the treadmill.

He walked over to the boxy computer and flipped it on. The monitor brightened, then went blank before flashing up the logo of the Federated Commonwealth Intelligence Secretariat. As the computer went through its booting ritual of checking all its onboard memory and loading programs, the assassin also went through his own checklist of reality, looking for any clue to how he might change it.

He knew that the Intelligence Secretariat knew that he was Melissa Steiner-Davion's killer. They had sufficient evidence in the form of fingerprints and hair and skin samples from the apartment he'd used on Tharkad to show he'd been present in the place where the bomb went off. They had the phone records to prove his computer had relayed the call from the spaceport to the cellular phone bombs he'd created to kill Melissa. If that were somehow insufficient, they also had transcripts of the various narco-interrogation sessions they'd conducted with him. While those might not stand up in any court, they left no doubt as to his guilt.

He labored under no illusions about the government and their stance on capital punishment. Though it was allowed under law, and even prescribed for assassination and treason, in reality it was seldom employed. The courts had repeatedly commuted sentences to life plus a hundred years. Even so, no court would have commuted his sentence, but there were plenty of ways a person guilty of his crimes could be induced or forced to "commit suicide" while in custody.

This all led him to the conclusion that the government wanted him alive. And that had to mean Victor Davion wanting him alive. Even while running from Tharkad to Solaris, the assassin had known Victor was taking a very personal and direct role in the investigation of his mother's death. Though many people mistakenly thought it was proof of Victor trying to cover his own tracks, the assassin put it down to a son's desire to see his beloved mother avenged.

That desire for vengeance could be the only reason he was still alive. He did not think himself vain in placing himself at the top of the hierarchy of assassins in the Inner Sphere. Yes, the Draconis Combine did have their *nekagami* and the Capellans their Thugee cultists, but he operated alone, without government or institutional sanction. In killing Melissa Steiner-Davion he had done what no one else had been able to do. He had no equal in his vocation and he knew it.

So does Victor Davion. The assassin's continued existence proved that, and the new disks he'd been given earlier confirmed it. The disks gave him information about Solaris—a world he already knew well—and, he chose to believe, even pointed out who he would be called upon to kill.

The most up-to-date information on the disks had been dated the seventh of February. Most of the "news" consisted of blow-by-blow descriptions of the latest fights on the Game World, though the assassin paid little attention to it. If Victor Davion wanted any particular fighter dead, all he needed do was have the local criminal cartels do the job for him. Fixing fights and punishing fighters were their stock in trade and well below the level for which Victor would be saving him.

Far more interesting was the information presented on the society page. The gossip columnist, an odious little man the assassin would have snuffed in exchange for a cup of coffee, previewed an upcoming party being hosted by Tormano Liao for his nephew Kai Allard-Liao. The guest list, which included a few local luminaries, boasted a truly interstellar cast of celebrities. In addition to the host and honoree, Katrina Steiner-Davion, Duke Ryan Steiner, and Omi Kurita would be in attendance. Katrina would be escorted by Galen Cox, a close friend of her brother, Victor.

Any or all of them could have been the person the assassin would be asked to kill. He was tempted to eliminate both Cox and Allard-Liao from the list because they played relatively minor roles in the politics of the Inner Sphere, but he resisted the temptation. He'd found nothing to suggest any trouble between the St. Ives Compact and the Federated Commonwealth, but he knew that governments often started, fought, and resolved conflicts well out of view of the public. Still, Kai Allard-Liao had consistently and regularly dedicated victories to Victor Davion, hinting at a close and cordial relationship there. Besides, killing Kai would gain Victor nothing—as nearly as the assassin could make out.

Galen Cox was an equally low-possibility target. If Galen were out of favor with Victor, the prince would never have assigned him the honor of escorting his sister on her current goodwill tour through the Commonwealth. If Galen had managed to dishonor himself while on that tour, he could have been recalled to Tharkad or summarily dismissed. Though it pleased the population to think of Katrina as *their* virgin princess, there were those who would love to learn of a romantic affair between her and the dashing hero who had saved her brother's life in the Clan War. The rumors of a falling-out between Victor and Galen, darkly hinted at in the society column, were yet one more reason *not* to have Galen killed.

The assassin, while on the run and even while living the identity of a florist on Tharkad, had heard the rumors linking Victor Davion with Omi Kurita. He thought it odd that the same people who speculated at great length about Katrina's romantic adventures found Victor's possible involvement with Omi distasteful and shocking. Were not Victor and Omi as star-crossed as Romeo and Juliet, the most famous lovers in history? Yet Victor's detractors considered even a hint of the prince's involvement with Omi the equivalent of high treason.

He doubted, therefore, that Omi would be his victim. Her death on a Commonwealth world would be a catastrophe of titanic proportions. Retaliation would be swift and certain, and likely would end the Steiner-Davion line. More important, though, Omi's death could serve no purpose for Victor. Even if the two were not lovers, her friendship with the prince made relations between the Commonwealth and the Combine more cordial, and that had a direct impact on how future wars against the Clans would be waged.

The remaining three people on the list are very viable targets. The assassin allowed himself a laugh over the oxymoron "viable targets," then began to sort out the reasons why he would be used against them. The process did not take long, but yielded very satisfactory results.

Tormano Liao seemed the least likely target. He did have political power and was quite capable of stirring up trouble between the Capellan Confederation and the Free Worlds League. Foolish action on his part could ignite a war between Federated Commonwealth forces and those two nations along their very long common border. But Victor would not want Tormano creating trouble for him while faced with the urgent necessity of building up to hold off the Clans on another border.

Besides, assassinating Tormano could bring more trouble than it was worth. Tormano and his Free Capella movement, no matter how small, presented a threat to Sun-Tzu Liao and the Capellan Confederation. If Tormano was eliminated, it would take some of the pressure off Sun-Tzu, giving him a chance to commit mayhem. Though the reports were weeks old, the *Zhanzeng de Guang* strikes in the Sarna March were just the sort of thing of which Sun-Tzu would be capable. Again, any increase in terrorist activity against the Federated Commonwealth would require Victor to send in Federated Commonwealth troops, and he could only do that by stripping them away from the Clan border. Exactly the thing he didn't want to do.

Victor's sister Katrina presented an interesting target. The assassin almost dismissed her outright, but something about how she looked in the pictures the computer displayed stopped him. She was pretty—bewitchingly so—yet she managed to look different in each one. Her chameleon-like ability to adapt her appearance to the various types of functions she was called upon to attend had helped endear her to the people. Adaptability was a survival trait without which leaders died, and she had it in abundance.

Her eyes. The assassin studied them in each image and noted that they did not change. In a short interview with her displayed on one disk, he saw an intelligence in her eyes that her easy answers and easier laugh belied. The only time he noticed it changing came when she stood with Galen Cox, her arm linked in his. The look softened, but did not dull, suggesting that she was able to enjoy her emotions without ever truly letting them override her brain.

Why would Victor want her dead? She had supported him in everything he had done since becoming the First Prince. She had run interference for him and helped repair his image with the popular media. She had done more to shore up his position than he had himself.

All this speculation brought the assassin back to a key point in his case for his own survival: vengeance. He didn't know if Victor suspected his sister of hiring someone to kill their mother, nor did the assassin know whether, in fact, she was the person who'd ordered and paid for Melissa's death. It was entirely possible that she was his secret patron, but then why wouldn't she have wanted Victor killed or otherwise neutralized at the same time she got Melissa out of the way? If Katrina had ambitions—and that look in her eyes told him she did—she had more patience and foresight than any other politician in the Inner Sphere.

The desire for revenge fit the last target perfectly. Duke Ryan Steiner had gained immeasurably from Melissa's death, and he had done enough other things to be at the top of Victor's hate list. Because Melissa's claim to the throne had been beyond dispute, Ryan had been little more than a whining puppy while she was alive. With her death, however, Ryan moved one step closer to the throne and could now make an excellent case for becoming regent, if not the outright ruler of a newly independent Lyran Commonwealth.

The separatist uprisings in Skye and along the Jade Falcon border pointed up the serious nature of Ryan's threat to the Federated Commonwealth *and,* in the assassin's eyes the shortsightedness of Ryan's ambition. If Skye and the border region pulled out of the Federated Commonwealth, Victor would be forced to commit troops to bring them back into the fold. He would have no choice because to lose that sector of space would be to lose important industrial capacity and a string of defensible worlds on the Clan border. Moreover, Victor was the sort of moralist who would believe it was his duty to protect the people of those worlds from the Clans, even if it meant military conquest and martial law to do so.

Ryan's Skye Federation, or whatever he would call it, obviously would not be able to stand. Because of the way the Isle of Skye worlds sat smack in the middle of the Inner Sphere, Victor could bring forces against them from both sides. The Draconis Combine, which might once have backed separatists in a Federated Commonwealth civil war, would no doubt prefer to maintain the status quo than have a weakened ally on the other side of the Clans. In addition, the Combine did not have the personnel or equipment to lend Ryan, because the only way Theodore could provide it was by stripping units off the long border with the Federated Commonwealth, leaving the Combine open to attack.

The Free Worlds League likewise could not support Ryan, nor, of course, could the Clans. Besides, the assassin seriously doubted that Ryan could survive politically if his people discovered that he had taken aid from either the Free Worlds League or the Clans. Ryan's only hope for success came if the Skye uprising were to trigger a popular uprising throughout the old Lyran Commonwealth, delivering it to him in one fell swoop. As the District of Donegal and Periphery March would back Victor, the miracle Ryan needed would not happen, dooming his effort to be nothing more than a boon to the funerary industries.

Ryan apparently assessed matters differently. With supreme confidence in his ability to control or manipulate events, he moved forward with his own agenda. If the Skye worlds were to pull out of the Federated Commonwealth and Victor had to tie up troops putting down the rebellion, the Capellan Confederation might step up operations in the Sarna March, the Jade Falcons might pull off more raids into the Commonwealth, and the Free Worlds League might even decide to try to recapture planets it had lost to Lyran predation centuries before.

Victor was not *required* to kill Ryan Steiner to eliminate the threat to the Federated Commonwealth. He certainly had other options. But the only final solution to the problem of Ryan was to assign his fate to an assassin. With the new disks and the potential of new information coming in every day to update him, the assassin knew he could do the job, and do it spectacularly.

That solved his first problem.

His second problem ran deeper and would take even more planning to solve. He harbored no illusions that Victor would thank the assassin for killing Ryan and then let him go on his way. He had, after all, killed the prince's mother, and he could appreciate the deep animosity Victor felt toward him for that. That animosity meant, of course, that after the assassin killed Ryan, Victor would have him killed.

The assassin's second problem was that he did not want to die.

He smiled as he sat down in front of the computer. Using the mouse he began to zip through Solaris City in a seemingly random fashion, turning left and right as new pictures flashed up on the screen. Victor was right to bring him up to date on Solaris because enough had changed even in the last three months that the assassin might otherwise never have been able to get to his target. The review and the study helped and the assassin was supremely confident because of it.

He would get his man.

And he would get away.

═══ 13 ═══

Kai gave the sleeves of his double-breasted, iridescent blue silk jacket a tug as he rode up in the elevator. Keith Smith seemed amused by his nervous fidgeting while Larry Acuff mirrored Kai, adjusting the sleeves of his own jacket. When Keith laughed lightly, Kristina Houpe slapped him on the shoulder. "You should wear a suit so well, Keith."

Keith blinked his eyes, feigning surprise. "I don't have to dress as well because I already have a date."

Kristina ignored him and reached out to straighten Kai's blue and gray striped tie. "There, that's perfect." She gently pressed his lapels flat, then returned to Keith's side. "The way these two look, you could be without a date by the end of the evening."

Larry smiled at Kai. "I told you she was smart as well as gorgeous."

Kai nodded solemnly in agreement. "And she obviously has compassion for the less fortunate." As Keith started to protest, he added, "As evidenced by her willingness to make sure my tie was straight—since I had no one here to do that for me."

Kristina laughed, then poked Keith in the ribs. "Losing ground here fast, Mister."

Keith looked at the other two men. "Just remember whose computer work makes sure those paychecks come out on time."

"Just remember who signs them," Kai shot back with a

laugh as the elevator came to a stop. "Have fun tonight. I won't be able to enjoy it much, so I expect you to have my fun for me."

Larry nodded quickly. "We'll keep our eyes peeled, in case you need rescuing."

"Thanks."

The elevator doors opened onto a vast room four times as wide as it was long. Eight huge, multi-armed chandeliers hung from the cathedral ceiling. The little flame-shaped electric bulbs set on each arm had multiple filaments that glowed in a random sequence to simulate real candlelight. The gold highlights sparkling from the chandeliers themselves found cousins in the glowing gold of the ornate wall paper.

The room's two longest walls had no windows to the outside because the hall was on the top floor of Tormano's palace. In their place stood massive floor-to-ceiling mirrors that reflected back and forth into their opposite number, making the hallway into a giant, Escheresque version of Versailles. At the far end, beneath the tall windows looking south over the city, a string quartet played soft chamber music that was just audible over the murmuring hum of the crowd.

The chandeliers and similarly styled wall fixtures provided a fair amount of light, yet to Kai it seemed somehow insufficient. Perhaps that was because he could recognize only one out of every five or six faces he saw, and could only put names to a quarter of those. He would have expected to see more people he considered friends present at a party ostensibly held in his honor.

Then again, if only your friends were here, we could have held the party in the elevator. Kai smiled in spite of himself, knowing that wasn't totally accurate. It was true that he didn't make close friends easily, but once he let people in, he enjoyed their company. Alone with his friends in the elevator, letting Kristina adjust his tie or engaging in quick banter felt natural and he liked it. In public he became more reserved. *And quite deserving of the nickname Steelsoul.*

He looked around to thank his uncle for the party, but Tormano was nowhere to be seen. Off to one side he saw Keith and Kristina making their way toward the bar, and thought he saw Larry deep in conversation with a woman who looked a lot like the cover model on the latest fashion holodisk. Then the milling crowd suddenly opened before him as if split by a wedge.

Recognizing the man who approached, Kai descended the three steps to the main floor to meet him on equal footing. Kai bowed, then extended his hand. "Greetings, Wu Deng Tang."

"It is my pleasure, Kai Allard-Liao." Wu stood as tall as Kai, but his brown eyes and sharper features marked him as being more fully Asian-blooded. Kai knew that Wu's family prided itself on the purity of its bloodline, though less from any sense of racial superiority than from a desire to preserve and protect a heritage dating from long before man's first steps away from Terra a millennium ago.

The crowd around them fell silent and waited breathlessly for something to happen. Wu took Kai's hand and shook it, then the two men bowed respectfully to each other. Kai saw a number of people look disappointed that they had not immediately gone for each other's throats, and he relished their frustration. Straightening up, he slapped Wu on the shoulder. "They want a show, but I have no desire to oblige them."

"Nor I." Wu picked at the shoulders of his gray jacket. "These are *not* my work clothes."

"I wouldn't wear these in a 'Mech cockpit even if someone wanted to pay me to endorse them." Kai saw something flash through Wu's eyes, but it vanished before he could identify it. "I'm glad to see you are well and looking fit."

"And you also." Wu's voice dropped to a whisper that could not be heard beyond them. "I would have you meet Caren Fung, but my fiancée could not join me this evening."

Kai's smile dropped away. "Nothing is wrong, I hope."

"Quite the contrary. She is fine, but the doctors have ordered her to rest. She is carrying our child, and after two miscarriages they have forbidden her any excitement." Wu's lips pressed together in a grim smile. "I've heard whispers that you have guaranteed her safety against those who would like to influence our fight. It is said the Red Cobras have already forestalled an incident."

Kai nodded. "There are those who do not understand that the fight between us is sport. Not a replay of the Fourth Succession War nor a prelude to another war. Being a sport, our duel should serve no other ends. Especially not political ones." Kai chose to refrain from adding that Keith had pulled a private detective's report about Wu's fiancée from Tormano's computer and had surmised what Tormano was intending to do to ensure a victory for his nephew. After a simple suggestion and a generous bribe to the Red Cobra Triad, no one would be able to get near her.

"When we meet in battle, it will be a contest of skill to decide who is the best between us, nothing more," he said.

"I agree."

Kai let himself smile. "Is this your first child?"

Wu nodded happily. "It is. I am told he will be a son. I plan to retire at least until he is two or three. I have enough savings to make that possible."

Kai raised an eyebrow. "Roger Tandrek might not like losing you. You've come up almost as quickly as I have."

"I know, but that will be his problem. I have no desire to die in the arena and leave my wife and child alone."

As Deirdre's father did to her. "I understand and agree with your thinking. If he starts to get tough about letting you go, come talk to me. I will buy out your contract and free you."

Wu was less than successful in hiding his surprise. "Why would you do that for me? We are enemies."

"Are we? I always thought of us as rivals, which is different."

"But my father commands a unit that might someday be used to attack the St. Ives Compact."

"At *that* time, and for the duration of that conflict, yes, we would be enemies; but not until then." Kai shrugged. "I understand your desire to be with your wife and child. If I can help you, I'm happy to do so."

Wu smiled. "Spoken like a man wise in the ways of fatherhood."

Kai shook his head quickly. "Not me, I have no children. Put it down to my visiting Arc-Royal and seeing Morgan Kell with his son Phelan."

"The Clan Khan?"

"Yes. Though father and son serve masters who are mortal enemies, they're very close. The bond is impressive. If I'm ever a father, I'd be happy with a tenth of what they have."

Sitting in his office, Tormano Liao smiled at the image of Kai on the screen of his holovid viewer. "And if my son had one tenth what you have, Kai, I too would be a very happy father indeed." The Mandrinn smiled and sat back in his chair. "Even the fact that you foiled my attempt to kidnap the Fung woman. *That* took initiative and bravery. You saw what needed to be done and you did it, just as I did in preparing to take her."

He looked up as the door opened and Nancy Bao Lee entered the room. For a moment he resented her uninvited entry, but part of him liked that she was so comfortable in his presence that she no longer thought that courtesy necessary. *And no woman so beautiful is ever an uninvited guest.*

Her black dress clung to her like shadow. The long sleeves had little triangular tabs covering the backs of her hands and were secured in place by a fabric loop encircling her middle and ring fingers. The mandarin collar and sweetheart neckline accented the fullness of her breasts, while the rest showed off her shapely legs. The floppy-topped black boots remained down around her ankles and the gold heel rims and toe caps matched the heavy, square-link gold chain around her neck.

She wore her black hair up and held in place with two golden sticks. Her makeup had been expertly applied and deepened the hollows of her cheeks to emphasize her high cheekbones. Mascara rimmed her eyes and, in combination with a deep mauve eyeshadow, heightened the almond shape of her eyes. A similar shade of lipstick made her lips more full, but without the cheap garishness that would have resulted if the application had been overdone. The purple-gray coloring on her fingernails topped off her graceful and cosmopolitan image.

"You are quite stunning, Nancy."

"Oh, really? Thank you, my lord."

Tormano killed the sound coming from the camera focused on Kai by hitting a button on his remote control. "You are early. I thought you were going to come for me in another fifteen minutes."

A blush rose on her cheeks, making her look yet more beautiful. "I was, I mean, that is what I had intended, in accordance with what you told me, my lord." She glanced down, refusing to meet his direct gaze. "I had my computer running a check on something while I changed and, well, it concerns your nephew and I thought you might want to know about it before this evening."

Tormano rose from behind his desk and crossed to the closet. He slipped a double-breasted black suit coat over his white shirt and adjusted the red necktie, snugging the knot against his Adam's apple. He glanced over at Nancy, watching her watch him dress, and smiled as he buttoned the jacket. "What did you learn?"

"What?" She blinked her brown eyes a couple of times.

"About Kai? What did you learn?"

"Oh. When I read the file you had on him, I saw a note about how he had taken special care or paid special attention to the people who had been prisoners of war on Alyina. My predecessor put that down to your nephew's reaction to Twycross and his accepting responsibility for people when he didn't need to. It was regarded as a flaw."

Tormano nodded as he opened the closet door and studied his image in the mirror on the inside. "Kai is known for having a soft heart and taking his responsibilities very seriously. It's for those reasons that I want him with us." It pleased Tormano to see in the mirror that Nancy listened intently to his every word and studied his every movement. "I recall reading about his POW work when the file was last updated."

Nancy smiled briefly. "I thought you would. I decided to run a check on the names of those people and see what he had done for them. Cenotaph's open report policy makes finding payments and the like very easy. I was able to track everyone who had been with him on Alyina and determine what he had done for them."

"And you learned that he's generous to a fault and obsessive about details. I bet he bought each one a house or a business wherever they wanted it."

"Yes, my lord, I mean, no. I wanted to see if there was someone special that we might be able to use to bring your nephew over to Free Capella. I think I found what I was looking for."

Tormano turned slowly. "I'm interrupting you, and obviously you have found something of significance. What is it?"

"I don't know how significant it is, my lord." Nancy's head came up and she clasped her hands at the small of her back, her breasts pushing up from her dress distracting Tormano for a moment. "Kai has helped everyone who was on Alyina with him except for one person. Her name is Dr. Deirdre Lear."

"The name means nothing to me." Tormano's eyes narrowed. "What do you know about her?"

"I've only started checking. She and David Lear obtained passage to Zurich last month. She is working at the Rencide Medical Center. Cenotaph Charities is funding that center, but all other aid has been more direct, so this is atypical. I've put out a request for further information, but it will be a while before I get anything back."

"David and Deirdre." Tormano curled his upper lip. "I think anyone who marries a person with the same initials ought to be taken out and shot. They're probably planning to name their children Dennis, Donald, and Doris."

"Yes, my lord." Nancy tried to suppress a smile, but it won through, brightening her face. "Shall I continue to follow up this lead?"

Tormano nodded. "Yes, by all means. Pay attention to when she and David were married. If Kai had an affair with her during the war, well, it's not much, but it might be useful."

"As you wish, my lord."

Tormano smiled and offered Nancy his arm. "Now, let us go and greet my guests. I will introduce you to my nephew, but don't say anything to him about this Lear woman. We'll save that surprise for later."

"Yes, my lord."

"Just make sure Kai enjoys himself." Tormano shot her a sidelong glance and a wink. "And with you beside him, I cannot imagine how he could possibly do otherwise."

14

Solaris City, Solaris VII
Tamarind March, Federated Commonwealth
12 February 3056

The turned heads and murmured whispers that accompanied his uncle's entrée into the room attracted Kai's attention immediately. He turned and looked up the steps toward where Tormano was coming through a door built into the wall between two of the mirrors. It was no surprise that his uncle had waited to make his entrance, for Tormano was known for his dramatic flare. What did surprise Kai was that he permitted the woman on his arm to upstage him.

She's gorgeous. Watching her take Tormano's arm, Kai was impressed with his uncle for the first time in his life. The knowledge that the man was still married did cut into the admiration, but Kai suddenly saw Tormano as so many others did: a powerful and wealthy man who did not show his sixty years. *I can but hope to age as well.*

Tormano led the woman straight over to the two MechWarriors. "Welcome, gentlemen, welcome. I am honored to be your host for this evening." Tormano bowed in turn to Wu Deng Tang and then his nephew. "Your presence pleases me more than you know."

Wu returned the bow. "Your invitation honors me and I thank you for it. Few would have expected a man in your position to wish my presence here."

Tormano brushed aside the caution in Wu's words. "Solaris is a world unto itself, with its own political and social currents. The outside world has so little to do with it."

He frowned slightly. "I had hoped Ms. Fung would come with you. Is she ill?"

Wu's face closed a bit. "She sends her regrets. Doctor's orders prevent her from being here, but she is well."

"Splendid." Tormano turned to the woman and smiled. "Nancy, please remind me to have flowers sent to Ms. Fung; if that would not be presumptuous of me, Mr. Wu. I know how this dreary world can make even the slightest illness seem grave."

"She would be most pleased with your gift, Mandrinn."

Tormano smiled at the use of his title, then looked down and shook his head. "Forgive me, I am being very rude. Kai Allard-Liao, this is my aide, Nancy Bao Lee. Nancy, this is my nephew, Kai Allard-Liao, and his challenger, Wu Deng Tang. Mr. Wu, may I present Nancy."

Wu bowed to Nancy, as did Kai. Straightening up, Kai took her hand in his, then raised her knuckles to his lips. "I am pleased to make your acquaintance, Ms. Lee."

Nancy blushed. "And I am happy to meet you, Mr. Allard-Liao."

Tormano shook his head. "I will have none of that formality, for I love you both and want you to be friends. Kai, Nancy here is quite a fan of yours."

"And of yours, Mr. Wu," she added politely.

Kai kept the smile on his face and murmured appropriate nothings as he withdrew inwardly. *My uncle playing match-maker? Why? Does he honestly think I need a companion, or is he trying to impress this woman with his access to me? Is she truly a fan, or is she a spy?*

Tormano deftly steered Wu Deng Tang away, leaving Kai and Nancy standing together. An awkward silence closed in on them, then both tried to speak at once. Their voices combined into gibberish, then they laughed. Kai gestured at her with his left hand. "You first."

Nancy shot a glance over at Tormano's retreating back, then let her voice sink into a husky whisper. "Please, Mr. Allard-Liao, don't think ill of your uncle for introducing us like this."

"An introduction to you is not something I will hold against him." Kai winked at her. "And do call me Kai. My surname is a mouthful at the best of times."

"Thank you, sir." She looked down, then her doe eyes

flicked back up. "I am a fan of yours, but not like, well, like . . . you know."

Kai raised an eyebrow. "Groupies?"

A quick nod. "Yes, exactly, not like that." She paused and took a deep breath, which sorely tested the elasticity of her dress. More composed, she began speaking again. "I'm making a mess of this, which is not what I wanted to do. You see, when I was writing out the check for your uncle's box at The Factory, I mentioned that I would love to see you fight some time. He asked if I wished to accompany him to your title defense and I'm sure he may have interpreted my enthusiastic response as that of a frothing fan. When he offered to introduce me, well, I mean, it is an honor . . ."

Kai gathered her right hand in his left and patted it gently. "Don't worry, I understand. My uncle wants me to have the best life possible and has trouble reconciling that with the fact that what I want may not be what he thinks I should have."

"He is a kind man. He knew I was not involved with anyone and he thought, well, that perhaps, we might . . . not that I would object to seeing you, of course." She smiled and blushed again.

"Of course?"

She gave his hand a squeeze. "In case it has escaped your attention, you are a very handsome and very eligible man. I rank you up here ahead of even Victor Davion."

"Ahead of Victor?" Kai frowned.

"All I mean to say is that Victor seems a little chilly to me." She smiled quickly. "And he's short."

Kai laughed aloud, then smiled. "Prince Victor is actually a very warm man and a good friend. But, you are correct, he stands well shy of the two-meter mark." He raised his right hand to her chin. "He would come up to here on you."

"Too small, warm or no." She caressed the back of his hand gently. "My preference runs to men of your height."

He met her eyes and read the interest in them. He waited for, hoped for, a jolt down in his guts that would tell him they had clicked and that she was the right one to win a place in his heart. It had happened before, once, and he wanted it to happen again.

He got nothing.

The inviting light in Nancy's eyes flickered and died. "I am embarrassing you."

Kai shook his head. "Not at all. You flatter me."

"But there is someone else?"

"No, not really." Kai pulled back emotionally. She had played coy and shy, yet she presented her hand to him in such a way that bringing it to his lips seemed natural. She had dressed seductively but denied being there to seduce him, then behaved in a way that could easily have led to seduction. Even so, she pulled back when he balked. *Was that another ploy, or is she back to her original, shy self?*

Kai gave her a wry grin. "My track record for relationships is less than stellar. For the next month or more I have to concentrate on my fight with Wu Den Tang, which won't give me much spare time for starting a relationship with a nice woman who would be deserving of all my attention."

Nancy brought her hands together and up toward her throat, her forearms hiding her breasts. She glanced down at the ground for a moment. Despite a commotion raised behind her at the elevator, Kai found himself focused on her hands. As she looked up he did too and their gazes met again.

"You're a wonderful man, Kai. Most would not have been so honest nor so considerate of my feelings. Those who name you Steelsoul are the biggest fools in the Inner Sphere."

Bigger fools than a man who lets a woman like you get away? "Shall we be friends then?"

Nancy smiled broadly and easily as she slipped her right hand through the crook in his left arm. "For the time being, I would be honored to be your friend."

"For the time being?"

She nodded. "Win your fight, then let us see how far we wish our friendship to go."

Zurich
Sarna March, Federated Commonwealth

Seated behind the emergency room desk, Deirdre Lear stifled a yawn. She'd been here for hours, getting sleepier and stiffer by the moment. She leaned back and stretched her arms overhead, trying to loosen up the kinks in her shoulders and to wake herself up a bit.

Still sitting back in her chair, she studied the report on the computer screen. It being a slow evening, she had offered to help Anne Thompson by typing in her own report on the little boy they'd seen earlier. She knew that to say "a five-year-old Zur male was running naked through his home when the family dog became excited and bit him on the scrotum" was the proper way to write up the report, but she balked at the idea of doing it that way. "There has to be another way to do this."

Anne glanced back at her, tearing her attention from the holovid viewer in the corner of the waiting room. "What's that, Doctor?"

"The report on little Donny Li."

"The boy who will have the interesting scars."

Deirdre smiled in spite of herself, then shook her head. "There you go, that's my problem. If I try to humanize this account, it becomes achingly funny. If I don't, and I treat it clinically, I can see colleagues reading the report in the boy's file and checking out my handiwork in putting him back together. It was bad enough that he got bit, but he'll relive that trauma whenever another physician looks at him."

"I see the problem." Anne waved her up and out of her seat. "You have to think like a doctor in a hurry. Diagnosis: Dog bite. Wounds: two punctures, one tear. Treatment: antibiotics and seven stitches—two per puncture, three for the tear. Prognosis: no scarring or disability." Punctuating her comments, Anne hit the Enter key and the emergency room report vanished from the screen.

Deirdre smiled and rolled her hands around to loosen them up. "Nice work."

"Thanks." Anne watched her for a second. "I had a boyfriend who used to do that. He was big into martial arts."

"So was I, once. I learned for self-defense."

Anne got up and drifted back over to the counter. "What did you study?"

"Aikido."

"Craig was into Kuk Sool Wan. We met when he removed an ugly growth from my arm."

Deirdre wandered over to the counter and stared out into the empty waiting room. The holovision set reflected in the window, but she could still see out into the dark of the Zurich night. "He was a surgeon?"

"Nope. The ugly growth was an ex-boyfriend who had trouble understanding the word 'no.' " Anne sighed heavily. "Craig was a nice guy. We had fun together, then he just up and took off one day."

"You don't know why?"

The brown-haired nurse frowned as she pulled a sweater from her chair and looped it over her shoulders. "Not really. He never told me, but I think it was because I'd entered my last semester of nursing school and was doing a lot of work with a hospice. Craig couldn't get used to me becoming so involved with terminal patients. I know terminal illnesses really get under some folks' skin, but I thought Craig could handle it."

She shrugged. "Anyway, my love life has been a history of disasters." Anne looked over at Deirdre. "So, what happened to Mr. Lear?"

"Ah, er, um, there, ah, was no Mr. Lear."

Anne blushed. "I'm sorry, I'm prying." She smacked herself in the forehead with the heel of her left hand. "I get that way on the graveyard shift. I'm sorry."

Deirdre frowned. "Seems I've got everyone saying that around here." She patted Anne on the shoulder. "Look, Lear is my family name—my stepfather adopted me when he married my mother. David's father and I, we met during the Clan War. It didn't work out. He was a good man, but he was younger than me and we each had our own career tracks going."

"I understand."

"You do?" Deirdre shook her head. "Maybe someday you can explain it to me."

The question on Anne Thompson's lips died as the doors to the emergency room burst open. *"Shangkou, shangkou!"* shouted one of the four Zur men rushing through the door. Between them, with two men on either side, they carried a thick, flexible mat woven from native fibers. On it they bore a man in the uniform of the local paramilitary constabulary.

Deirdre picked up the phone and punched down the intercom button while Anne ran around and pulled a gurney away from the wall. "Surgery team to the emergency room, stat!" Deirdre slammed the phone back down, then vaulted herself up and over the counter. She reached the constable's side just as the men heaved him up and onto the gurney.

The man was a mess. His blue shirt had three holes in it, each one like a black well in the middle of a growing crimson ocean. Deirdre pulled the shoulder strap of the black Sam Browne belt away from his right shoulder, then ripped his shirt open. Beneath it she saw a rapidly reddening kevlar vest. *Good, maybe the kevlar slowed the bullets down so they didn't fragment when they hit bone.* She mentally shut out the Zurs' chattering and listened closely for the sound of hissing air, but heard nothing.

"Anne, I need this man cross-typed and matched for whole blood. Start him with one unit and pump him full of penicillin." She looked over at the Zurs. "Do they know who he is? Do we have records on him. Is he allergic to penicillin?"

"He's Billy Hsing and was attending a meeting at their village. *Zhanzheng de Guang* ambushed him. Check the computer, he's a patient here."

Anne started pulling the gurney down the hallway toward the emergency surgical theater and another nurse ran down to help her. Deirdre pointed the men to the waiting room, and used one of the few Chinese expressions she'd learned thus far on Zurich. "*Juoxia*, yes, that's right, sit down, *jouxia!*"

As they complied, she punched up the name Billy Hsing on the computer. It showed three possibles and she picked the one whose age was listed as mid-forties. Then the screen showed the smiling picture of a man who looked very much like the body being wheeled into surgery. Deirdre hit the button to reveal his history of allergic reactions to drugs and discovered he had none.

"That's one little bit of a miracle, Mr. Hsing, that might let you live." His records showed him to be blood type O negative, which also worked in his favor. "Two for two."

She ran down to the surgery, tearing off her white coat and tossing it in a trash bin beside the door. She joined Rick Bradford at the sink and soaped up. "Forty-three-year-old Zur male, in good physical condition, has multiple gunshot wounds. The bullet penetrated the vest he was wearing, which suggests close range and or automatic rifle bullets. I think his right lung is collapsed."

Rick nodded as he lathered his arms up to the elbows, then lifted his head back while Anne Thompson tied a surgical mask around his face. "The lower-right quadrant wound is through and through, but I don't think it pierced the bowel."

"Third miracle in a row." Deirdre looked back over her shoulder. "He's O negative and penicillin allergy is negative."

Anne looped a surgical mask around Deirdre's face. "Looks like he has two bullets in him. One is resting against a rib behind his right lung. The other is right up against his spine. It missed the aorta by a millimeter and may be impinging on the spinal cord."

"The bullet near the spine worries me." Deirdre glanced at Rick. "Patch the lung first and reinflate it. Then we do the bowel and then, if we need to and he's up to it, we go for the second bullet, right?"

"Sounds good to me." Rick rinsed off his arms, then held his dripping hands up. "Gloves!"

Another nurse—it looked to Deirdre like it might be Cathy in the full surgical garb—stretched latex gloves over Rick's hands. As he stepped away from the sink and Deirdre started to rinse her hands, the doors to the surgery opened again. Rick turned toward the newcomer and started to shout at him. "You can't be in here!"

Flame lipped from the muzzle of the autorifle the man held and thunder filled the room. Rick ducked down away from the muzzle-flash, and behind him a glass jar full of cotton balls exploded. Anne screamed and backed to the wall, Rick still with one knee on the floor and the anesthesiologist raising his hands. Cathy stood trembling beside Deirdre, her hands rising toward the ceiling.

The gunman gestured toward the back of the room with his weapon. "Get away from him. Now! Do it!" He pointed the gun at the constable on the operating table. "This man is an enemy of the people. It is time for him to die."

Solaris City, Solaris VII
Tamarind March, Federated Commonwealth

Standing in the back of the elevator, Galen Cox smiled to himself and shook his head. The afterimages of the photographers' strobes still danced before his eyes. In traversing the gauntlet from the limousine to the door of Tormano Liao's palace, he had seen more flashes of light than he had in the battle against the Clans on Teniente. He had almost gotten used to everyone wanting to take Katrina Steiner's picture, but having the paparazzi call out his name and direct their cameras at him was a new and uncomfortable twist on the game.

He could well understand their desire to capture Katrina's image. Tall and slender, she wore her golden blonde hair long, yet styled in a dazzling variety of different ways. She had played a game with Galen, choosing outrageous hairstyles on some of their planetary visits just to watch a particular coif suddenly become a new rage among the people of that world.

Galen might have put that down to the cruel contempt of nobles for their subjects, but he had seen the serious, caring side to her. He'd been the one to mention the earthquake on Ginestra as they traveled to Arc-Royal, but it was Katrina who had bent heaven and earth to divert their route to the planet so they could help out. Wearing heavy boots, jeans, a work shirt, gloves, and a hard hat like all the other volunteers, she had worked as hard as he had to dig people out of the rubble. That included taking her turn in a construction exoskeleton.

Keeping his back pressed to the rear of the elevator, Galen watched her as she leaned over and spoke in hushed whispers to Omi Kurita. Tonight Katrina wore her hair in a long, thick braid that ran the length of her spine. Her backless evening gown was white with ice blue accents and sequins, long sleeves, and a short skirt. Galen recalled hearing the name of the designer who had created it back on Tharkad, but he'd long since forgotten it. He did notice that the blue-white diamond choker and matching earrings looked perfect on her.

Omi Kurita, escorted to the party by Thomas DeLon, was equally beautiful in her green silk skirt, blouse, and jacket. Galen smiled as he heard Victor's name pass between the women and he felt happy that his friend had the love of a woman such as Omi. Her grace, sensitivity, and intelligence made her a great prize. Galen thought it sad that Victor and Omi could never be together.

He realized, as the elevator began to slow and the two Davion bodyguards in the front shifted position, that Victor and Omi had about the same chances of being together as he and Katrina did. *Actually, that's not as bad as it might sound.* Omi and Victor were prevented because of the vast political and historical forces that had made their nations enemies for centuries. As much as they might love each other, their happiness would require an unheard-of alliance between the Combine and the Commonwealth. Because of hostilities that went back centuries, such an alliance would probably spark dozens of rebellions within the two nations.

The gulf between Katrina and him was not born of nationality differences, but it was just as wide. Katrina—he reminded himself that he would have to call her Katherine in conversations with Victor—was a noble, born far above his station in the universe. Galen's parents were ordinary citizens. His father had run a repair shop. The closest they'd ever come to the nobility ruling the Federated Commonwealth was when they licked a stamp or spent a coin.

When Victor had sent Galen out to escort his sister, Galen had entertained some fairy tale fantasies. He was a bit taller than Katrina and had almost the same coloring, which would make them a most handsome couple. He spent several hours imagining what old girlfriends and, better yet, their parents would think if he and Katrina were to wed. He would have paid money to see the kind of reactions that news would create.

Reality, in the form of cold self-assessment, hit him before he'd finished packing for his trip. He and Katrina were worlds apart. He and Victor were peers, but that was the equality of warriors who had shared the trial of combat. That bond did not extend to Katrina. Moreover, Galen knew Victor trusted him and he would never betray that trust.

That decision made things much easier and much harder. Because Galen knew he could never have Katrina, he had felt perfectly at ease around her and was often amused at the strained and nervous efforts other people made to impress her. He had quickly developed a sixth sense about when to rescue her from a socially awkward situation, and seeing the frustration of thwarted suitors made the game fun.

Because of his calm openness, Katrina began to reveal herself to him. He did not become a confidant so much as a friend. She and Galen spent many long hours talking about Victor, then their conversations came around to her and, eventually, to Galen himself. Though he was usually a fairly private person, he ended up giving her details about his life that he had long assumed he would tell no one save a wife or—Curaitis' unsmiling face flitted through his mind—a professional narco-interrogator.

About the time he realized he was telling Katrina his secrets, he realized how bad he had it for her. He immediately tried to disengage but simply could not. Because their positions and situation kept them apart physically, they had achieved a sort of intellectual intimacy that he had never known before with a woman. It was decidedly different than the bond he shared with Victor and intriguing enough that he wanted to explore it more and more.

The elevator stopped and the doors opened. The two mountain-like Davion security men exited the box and took up positions on either side of the door. The two smaller Combine security agents moved out next and became the point men for the quartet. Katrina and Omi exited next, followed by DeLon bringing up the rear.

As always, Katrina, your timing is impeccable!

The previous center of attention stood at the edge of the elevator landing. The scowl on his face disappeared quickly, but not before Galen saw it and smiled to let the man know he'd been caught. A venomous look flashed through the obsidian eyes, but Galen gave no sign that he either noticed or cared.

Katrina marched forward and gave the dark-eyed man a hug. "How good to see you, cousin! Congratulations on the purchase of your stable."

Ryan Steiner smiled politely, though the corners of his eyes wrinkled up in a distinctly pained manner. "I trust I can talk you into coming to my box to view some of the fights?"

"I would be delighted."

Ryan turned his back on the two men standing on the step below him and presented Katrina to a small, wiry Asian man. "Duchess Katrina Steiner, this is your host, Mandrinn Tormano Liao."

As with everyone else, Tormano's face lit up when Katrina smiled at him. "Your invitation was most kind, Mandrinn."

"And your acceptance has made this an occasion that shall live forever in the social annals of Solaris." He bowed to her, then kissed her hand when she extended it to him.

Ryan continued his introductions. "You know Mr. DeLon, of course. He has the honor of escorting her Highness, Omi Kurita."

Omi bowed respectfully to Tormano. "I wish the fortune of the ages on you and your house."

"Your presence, Omi-*san*, is proof that your wish has already come true." Tormano returned her bow in depth and duration. Coming back up he smiled and glanced expectantly at Ryan.

Ryan looked back at him, keeping his face blank. He waited just long enough for things to become weird, then let surprise show on his face. "Oh, I thought you two had already met, Mandrinn."

Galen took a step forward and offered the Free Capellan his hand. "Kommandant Galen Cox. Honor to be here."

"It is my honor to have you here."

"Indeed," Ryan laughed as he rested a heavy hand on Galen's shoulder. "What party would be complete without the presence of Victor Davion's lap dog?"

15

"**N**o one is going to die here tonight." Deirdre faced the gunman, her dripping hands hanging easily at her sides.

"Deirdre, he has a gun!" Rick Bradford yelled.

She ignored him and studied the gunman. *He's nothing more than a boy and a nervous one at that.* "Put the gun down. No one has to be hurt."

The boy took a step toward her, poking the smoking muzzle at her midsection. "I'll kill you, too!"

As he shoved the autorifle forward again, Deirdre moved slightly aside and took a step toward him with her left foot. She dropped her left hand onto the gunman's right wrist as she pivoted on the ball of her left foot and suddenly stood shoulder to shoulder with him. Her right hand closed on his as he tried to twist around to face her again. She locked his right wrist back and rotated it toward the outside, the muzzle of the autorifle describing an arc through the air as she did so. The movement froze the gunman's elbow and would have dislocated it, but off-balance and in pain, he went down onto his back with a thump.

Deirdre kept the pressure up with her right hand and yanked the autorifle free with her left. The gunman tried to spin on her to relieve the pressure, so she reversed the torque, forcing him onto his belly and locking the arm up behind him. She dropped onto his back with a knee in the spine and was rewarded with a satisfying grunt from the terrorist.

"Sedate him, now!" Deirdre looked up at Cathy. "I said

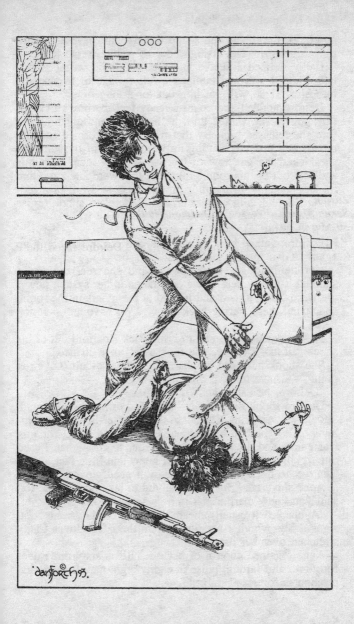

danforth 93.

now!" To the others she snapped, "We still have an operation to perform. Get Hsing under as well. Go. Do it."

Cathy stabbed a needle into a pulsing vein on the terrorist's trapped arm and pumped a full syringe of trophamine into him. "That will put him out for a long time."

Deirdre nodded and could already feel the boy's muscles slackening. She waited until he had gone entirely limp before she released him. By that time two uniformed security guards had arrived. Getting up from on top of the terrorist, she kicked the gun toward the two security men. "Get this and him out of this room. Take him to a ward and strap him in. Get someone to monitor him because he's full of a sedative. I'll look him over later and if there's a single bruise he shouldn't have, I'll have your heads. Got it?"

"Sure thing, Doctor."

Deirdre walked back to the sink and began scrubbing up again. "Give me his vital signs."

Her demand got no response and she realized she'd shouted it loudly, letting the adrenaline in her system power the words. She turned and looked at the others in the room, and found them staring back at her. "We have an operation here!"

Her milder tone seemed to bring Rick Bradford out of his shock. "Jesus, Deirdre, you took a hell of a chance."

She shook her head emphatically. "No I didn't. Let's get going, we have to save this man's life."

"Deirdre, he had a *gun!*"

Deirdre shook off her wet hands and turned back around. "Look, he was using a standard issue Stoner-Browning automatic rifle. The bolt had retracted and locked back. The gun was empty and the kid was too nervous to know that. I used one to kill a man on Alyina, so I knew that little fact, okay? Can we go back to surgery? Cathy, I need gloves."

Anne shivered. "But what you did to take him down. You said you knew martial arts but . . . you're good."

"A black belt usually means that, yes. What are his vital signs?" She wiggled her fingers into the latex gloves Cathy stretched over her hands.

Anne regained control of herself. "BP is sixty-three over forty-two and falling, pulse is eighty-eight and thready, respiration is forty and ragged."

Deirdre pulled on a surgical gown and approached the patient. "Okay, let's go in and fix him up."

Bradford looked at her from the other side of the operating table. "Are you sure you're able after what you've just done?"

Deirdre closed her eyes and looked toward the ceiling. *Give me strength!* "Look, everyone, I don't have time to think about what just happened. This guy is *dying* on us. I've performed surgery in the middle of firefights, so I'm okay. Let's get Mr. Hsing here healthy, then we can worry about the guy down the hall."

"Ready when you are, Doctor."

Deirdre smiled. "Good. Scalpel. Rick, be ready with the rib spreader—wipe it down with alcohol to get rid of the cordite traces. Anne, give me some suction right there. Here we go."

Solaris City
Solaris, Federated Commonwealth

Galen broadened the smile on his face. "It's true, Mandrinn, I *am* Victor's lap dog. He has, however, entrusted me to his sister for walkies. Don't worry, I'm housebroken."

One of the two men with Ryan sneered at Galen. "You just look broken to me."

Galen lifted his head and his smile died. "Even though I don't think you'll get this on the first pass, I'll only tell you once—from the duke I will tolerate abuse. From play warriors who stage fights on this toyland world, I won't."

Ryan smiled in a cautiously civilized manner. "I would watch my words, Kommandant, when you do not know to whom you are speaking." He reached back and guided the sharp-faced man up to the same level as the others. "May I present Victor Vandergriff, the number one fighter in the Skye Tiger stable. Victor, this is Duchess Katrina Steiner."

Vandergriff took Katrina's hand and raised it to his lips. "I am honored."

Galen pulled a handkerchief from his pocket and held it out to her. Katrina looked from it to her hand and back, then smiled and shook her head. "Always the gentleman, aren't you, Kommandant Cox?"

"I do my best." He put the handkerchief away and resolved to remain quiet. Her response to his offer had been tempered with amusement, but he read its true intent easily enough. He gave her a slight nod. *I won't create an incident.* He glanced at Vandergriff. *If I can help it.*

Ryan beckoned the other man forward as well. "And this is Glenn Edenhoffer, a rising star in my stable."

Katrina shook the man's hand. "My pleasure to meet you."

"I had never actually hoped to be presented to the embodiment of feudalism, but I find you charming."

Galen frowned. He had seen a holographic documentary about Edenhoffer that had suggested the man was eccentric. Galen could have told from the ill-fitting black clothes that Edenhoffer styled himself a bohemian, but he had no frame of reference to understand Edenhoffer's apparent desire to go through life as if it were one huge work of performance art. Were the man not known as being socially unschooled, his remark could have been taken as a grave insult to Katrina. Speaking so in front of Duke Ryan Steiner might even have been considered grounds for termination.

Ryan reinforced his smile. "Glenn is quite amusing in his own way. Refreshing."

The younger fighter raised his chin. "I am not so old that my cognitive network has ossified, blinding me to the greater realities of life."

Omi bowed her head in his direction. "In my nation it is believed that many years of contemplation can reveal the greater mysteries of the universe."

Vandergriff smiled politely. "Your nation is known for its grand tradition of melding mind, body, and spirit together to become one with the universe."

"And a totalitarianism that forces adherence to a mode of life that ended its usefulness before man left Terra," Edenhoffer shot in.

"I think, son, that your view of the universe is a tad limited by your lack of experience in it." Galen took a half-step forward and gently laid his right hand on Edenhoffer's left shoulder.

Edenhoffer's left hand came up in a windmill parry, knocking Galen's hand from his shoulder. "This from a servant of another repressive regime. I recognize your uniform. You're one of the people who helped ensure continuity for a government of dictatorial bureaucrats by rescuing Hohiro from the Clans. You deny the people of the Combine and the Inner Sphere the freedom offered by the upheaval the Clans have caused."

Galen's blue eyes flashed with anger. "You don't have a clue about the Clans and what they do or don't do to the people they conquer." He looked over at Duke Ryan. "Rein him in right now, or I will."

Vandergriff slipped from Ryan's side and inserted himself between Galen and Edenhoffer. "Remember your place, Kommandant, or you will have to be reminded of it."

Galen took a step back and laughed aloud. "By whom? You?" He laughed again and didn't mind the fact that he was attracting attention. "I've fought the Clans, boy, and I've defeated them. I've faced the best they had to offer, and I've walked away—in my *Crusader*. I've given better than I've gotten from the Clans, and I can guarantee you that they give better than you ever could."

Vandergriff shook his head and infused his voice with a patronizing tone that set Galen's teeth on edge. "You see, my lords and ladies, this is the sort of attitude we learn to endure here on Solaris. I do not doubt that Kommandant Cox is quite skillful in his use of a BattleMech, but he is not trained to the same high degree of expertise as we are. It would be akin to suggesting that a school child who had taken violin lessons was somehow the equal of a soloist with the Tharkad Philharmonic. This is an attitude we find common among the military men who come here."

Galen's eyes narrowed. "I am a member of an elite unit. I've fought more battles than you've studied in your career. You play at war here, I lived it."

Vandergriff dismissed him with a derisive chuckle. "You may have been in an elite corps, but that is only the best of one nation. Here on Solaris, we have the best of *all* nations. Were you to fight either one of us, you would lose."

Galen leaned in close to the other man. "Perhaps we ought to fight each other and find out if that's true."

Vandergriff raised his hands. "I would love to indulge you in your bellicose fantasy, Kommandant, but I am a professional fighter. For the protection of those who are not trained in fighting, we are not allowed to duel with anyone who does not have a licensing certificate—a certificate that takes months of training to obtain. I'm afraid you'll not be able to fight either one of us."

"I'll grant you're afraid, Mr. Vandergriff." Galen's hands knotted into fists. "You're both damned lucky you have laws to hide behind."

"Believe me, Kommandant," Vandergriff hissed, "it's you who is lucky, for it is now my fondest wish that you had a license so I could give you the lesson in humility you so achingly need."

"In that case, it will be my very great pleasure to grant your wish," Kai Allard-Liao said quietly. "I will give Kommandant Cox a license to fight."

Vandergriff hesitated, then frowned. "You cannot loan him your license to fight, my lord. It is not allowed."

Kai let Nancy precede him up the steps, then he followed and stood facing the entire group. "As Mr. Kindt, Duke Ryan's surrogate, so aptly pointed out at the last Compensation Committee meeting, I am not just a fighter. I own a stable. I can and hereby do grant Kommandant Cox an apprentice certificate. You can fight now."

Vandergriff kept his face neutral. "I beg to differ, my lord. An apprentice certificate is equivalent to a Class Two license. This would limit Kommandant Cox to a combat exoskeleton or a light 'Mech. I am a Class Six fighter and do not use small machines."

Kai shrugged easily. "Ah, but you know as well as I that regulations allow the apprentice certificate to be upgraded to the level of a senior fighter if the apprentice fights on the same side as the senior in a duel. As the conflict between you and Kommandant Cox was an outgrowth of his discussion with Mr. Edenhoffer, and I distinctly heard him offer to fight you both, I thought he and I could oppose the two of you."

Edenhoffer frowned. "You are in training to defend your title. I do not wish to wait a month for satisfaction."

"Nor should you. I have granted Mr. Vandergriff a wish, and now I do that for you as well." Kai's voice took on a razor's edge. "A week. Thomas, is Ishiyama available? Could we be fit into the schedule?"

DeLon smiled easily. "Without question, Kai."

"Good, thank you." Kai stared at Victor Vandergriff. "I assume you will accept this challenge. Mr. Kindt wanted to see me fighting you at this time, so now he will get his wish, won't he?"

Vandergriff straightened up, though his face had lost some of its color. "It will be my pleasure to meet you and Kommandant Cox in Ishiyama."

"You keep saying it will be your pleasure to do all of these things, Mr. Vandergriff." Galen threw a wink at Kai. "I hope you know how to handle disappointment."

Katrina slipped her hand through Galen's arm and smiled sweetly. "Well, now that you men have shown us how easy it is to make war, *I* shall show you how to enjoy peace." She nodded to Duke Ryan and his charges. "You no doubt have people to see and preparations to make, so we shall not detain you any longer. Dear cousin, I do hope to see more of you while we are on Solaris."

Duke Ryan bowed his head. "I shall make a point of it, Katrina." He withdrew, sketching a quick salute to Tormano Liao, his two fighters trailing after him.

Galen offered Kai his hand. "Thanks for the rescue. It's good to see you again."

"I confess to enjoying the look on Vandergriff's face." Kai turned to Nancy. "Please, allow me to present Nancy Bao Lee. Nancy, may I present you to Duchess Katrina Steiner-Davion, Lady Omi Kurita, and Kommandant Galen Cox." Nancy looked utterly flustered and fell into a tongue-tied silence as she bowed to each one.

Katrina smiled at her. "So, you are the woman who has captured Kai's heart? A year ago, when Morgan Kell retired, he was breaking hearts on Arc-Royal. Many women set their caps for him, but I can see how you won out."

"No, Highness, Kai and I are not . . ." Nancy blushed. "I mean, we are friends, I think."

Kai rescued her by looping her right hand though the crook of his left arm. "We are friends. My uncle introduced us this evening. Nancy works for him."

Tormano confirmed that statement. "She is my aide, and quite adept at her job." He looked up and around the room. "You will excuse me, but I have guests to attend to. I shall return."

"Thank you, Uncle." Kai watched his uncle walk away, then lowered his voice to a whisper. "This party is the social event of the year so far, especially with you and Lady Kurita here, Duchess." Kai maintained formality in his speech to minimize the social difference between Nancy and the rest of the group. As the heir to the St. Ives Compact, he was a peer of the other nobles and could treat them with the familiarity of equals. He knew Galen, Katrina, and Omi well enough to imagine they would take to Nancy with perfect ease, but it would take some time.

"If this is so, my lord, I suppose we should circulate." Katrina nodded to someone beyond their tight circle. "Given the goings-on in the Isle of Skye, some judicious stroking might be very helpful." She looked up when Galen reacted to her remark and gave his arm a squeeze. "I shall be the velvet glove, Galen, and you the iron fist. I approve of the way you handled yourself there. Such arrogance. I would have poked one of them in the nose."

"Then it shall be my honor to act as your surrogate."

Kai grinned as Katrina kissed Galen on the cheek. "A prize worth fighting for," he said.

The duchess winked at him. "Win and you shall have one, too, then. A loss will do Ryan some good." Katrina's voice grew icy as she spoke, then she shuddered. "Forgive me, but he possesses Steiner ambition, and I fear he will use it to sunder the Federated Commonwealth."

"Well, then, let us move about and meet people." Kai glanced down at the chronometer on the inside of his left wrist. "If we meet back at this spot at midnight, I'll take you to a place not far from here, but one that is worlds distant."

Omi smiled. "It sounds very special."

"It is, Lady Kurita, it is." Kai nodded confidently at them all. "I am certain Valhalla is unlike any place you have ever visited before, or are likely to again."

Duke Ryan Steiner watched the knot of royals break up and move into the crowd. Channeling his irritation away, he cleared his mind to run through all the implications of what had transpired. As he did so Edenhoffer prattled on about something of dubious import, but Ryan smiled in his direction and nodded at the right moments to keep the man going.

The challenge against Galen Cox would immediately attract attention, and the pro-Davion forces would probably promote it as a showdown between the forces of light and dark. Ryan knew his own backers would see it the same way, though they would reverse which side was white and which black. It could easily work to his advantage, *if* his side won. Victor could not afford a loss to his prestige, even in a morality play akin to what the fight would become, so it represented a very real chance to damage him in the eyes of Skye.

On the other hand, with the current champion of Solaris and a battle-tested veteran of the Clan Wars facing two younger and less experienced fighters, the chances of victory were the same as the chances of Melissa Steiner rising from the dead and reclaiming the throne. Ryan, despite the assurances of his fighters, harbored no illusions about their chances for victory. Why Kai Allard-Liao had chosen the Kurita arena for the fight, Ryan could not fathom, but he assumed it was for political reasons that would further embarrass Ryan and promote Victor Davion.

Ryan realized he would have to minimize the impact of the fight. Dismissing his two fighters would be a futile gesture and would cost his stable a great deal of revenue and fame. Unable to disassociate himself from the duel, he had to de-emphasize it, dilute it, so it could not hurt him. By the same token, *if* his fighters managed to achieve the impossible, Ryan could use it to good effect against Victor.

I need to divert attention from this whole fight. He smiled, which Edenhoffer took as a sign that he should continue his discourse on neo-retro cubism in the choreography of Class 3 arena battles. Ryan decided to have Hansau send out an order through the Free Skye underground network to step up the level of the protests on Skye worlds. To date they had been relatively peaceful, and Davion had played into his hands by repressing them rather vigorously.

With his next escalation, the Free Skye Militia would reappear and begin to commit terrorist acts against Davion targets in the Isle of Skye. Sun-Tzu's *Zhanzheng de guang* had proven Victor unable or unwilling to handle small-scale terrorist actions. In 3034 the actions of the Free Skye Militia had almost provoked a full-scale occupation by Hanse Davion. *How far will you go, Victor?* Because Ryan controlled Richard Steiner, the Field Marshal of Skye, any order to Federated Commonwealth troops to attack their own people would trigger a full-scale revolt in which Richard would denounce Victor while declaring for Ryan.

That will work, and work nicely. Ryan turned to his two fighters with an expression of extreme civility on his face. "You are fortunate, gentlemen, because I believe I have come up with a way to deal with the problem you have created."

"You won't have a problem to deal with, my lord." Edenhoffer smiled broadly and confidently. "We will win. I guarantee it."

"All I want *you* to guarantee is that you will not lose too badly!"

Vandergriff looked surprised at Ryan's harsh tone. "My lord, we are the best Solaris has to offer."

"You represent me now, so that is not good enough." Ryan's obsidian eyes flared. "Do me a favor—if you cannot win in the fight, have the good grace to die in it and thereby save me having to decide whether or not to have you killed for your failure."

Solaris City, Solaris VII
Tamarind March, Federated Commonwealth
31 March 3056

The procession of three hovercars glided through the grimy, rain-slick streets of Silesia like a pack of wolves trotting through game-rich forests. Though no one on the streets could have recognized the vehicles, people did seem to recognize their intent and purposefulness. The black aircars took the corners crisply and lunged forward through the streets, focusing on attaining their goal, not meandering aimlessly through the twisted warrens.

Kai Allard-Liao sat in the corner of the back seat more interested in the reactions of his fellow passengers than the world outside the windows. Nancy Bao Lee sat next to him, comfortably close, but uncomfortable because Omi was seated on her other side. Thomas DeLon sat across from Kai, with Katrina in the middle and Galen opposite Omi. The three visiting nobles studied the streets intently, gasping or frowning as the headlights froze in sharp chiaroscuro some improbably brutal or chilling street scene.

Katrina shook her head as she caught a glimpse of two people fighting over a scrap of cloth. "How can people live like that?"

"They live like that when they have no choice." Kai shifted around in his seat, wedging his spine into where the seat met the car's side wall. "In a free market system, there are always people who will not fit in and will be reduced to this level of poverty. If you don't want to see it, you create governmental structures and legislation that guarantee people housing, food, and employment, but that also gives you a police state."

The duchess frowned as Kai spoke. "Someone has to do something. They're living like animals."

"Some people do." Kai glanced over at DeLon. "I've been working here to fund a number of charitable enterprises and, by example, embarrass many of my fellow stable owners into doing the same. Ultimately, though, we can only provide opportunities for people. We cannot force them to take advantage of them."

Katrina nodded. "Forcing them would be akin to slavery."

"People can be educated and offered the chance to take responsibility for themselves." Omi's quiet voice barely sounded above the background hum of the hovercar's fans. "When they cannot accept responsibility for themselves, compassion dictates that we must do whatever possible to comfort them."

"Exactly." Kai's head came up as the hovercar slowed. The lead vehicle slued around in front of them to block Arnulf Street just to the west of a nondescript warehouse-like building. The car's doors opened as it settled to the ground and four Federated Commonwealth security men got out. Behind the middle car the vehicle carrying the Combine security forces likewise twisted around to block Arnulf Street to the east before its complement of security men also poured out.

The limo's doors opened and two security agents helped everyone dismount. Keith and Kristina, who had ridden in the lead vehicle, and Larry, who had directed the Combine car, joined the knot of nobles as they headed toward the smoky-glass doors of the building in front of which they had parked. Kai reached the door first and pulled it open. "Welcome to Thor's Shieldhall, the most infamous MechWarrior hideout on Solaris."

He could see from the pained expressions on the faces of both security crews that they were not thrilled at having their charges come to such a notorious place. But Kai would never have suggested it if he'd thought trouble might occur. Thor's Shieldhall had a worse reputation than it deserved, mainly because many society types chose it as a place to go slumming. A few negative incidents had become so magnified by multiple retellings that they had eventually come to the attention of the national security organizations of the various Great Houses of the Inner Sphere.

They walked through a short corridor and went up a set of steps to the left. Kai nodded to the doorman and gave him a one-hundred C-bill note. "Good evening, Roger. Access to Valhalla is highly restricted tonight, I understand."

The ComStar bill vanished beneath the long-fingered man's hands. "It is a shame that its capacity is limited, very limited."

"Thank you, my friend." Kai turned right and moved beyond the neon-illuminated bar. A Federated Commonwealth security man preceded him through a darkened section of the bar, ignoring the cherry glow of opium pipes, and held aside a thick curtain leading to a pair of ramps. The ramps doubled back to emerge at a landing roughly above where Roger maintained his post.

The ruby-red light of a laser identiscanner played over Kai as he stepped on the pressure plate beneath the carpet. Behind a bullet-proof pane of glass a security man nodded to him. "Welcome, Champion, to you and your guests."

A dark glass wall slid open, and Kai stepped aside to let two Combine security men enter first. They nodded and he followed them and his guests into Valhalla, smiling at their appreciative gasps and delighted laughter.

The Game World was possessed of two social realities. One pertained to the real world and was filled with the nobles and tycoons whose importance derived from who they were when not on Solaris. Money or inherited titles made them very powerful, and much of that power translated over to Solaris society. All were owed respect and received their due everywhere they went.

Everywhere except Valhalla.

In Valhalla, the second reality held sway. In it the true nobles of Solaris were the men and women who fought in the arenas scattered over the face of the planet. Only the elite of the elite were given access to Valhalla—as good as Larry Acuff was, he would have been refused entry had he not been in Kai's company. The warriors in Valhalla were culled from the top fifteen percent of those on Solaris, with Roger making all the judgments on access through some arcane formula that only he understood. Any MechWarrior in the Hall of the Dead could have bested ninety percent of the

MechWarriors in the armies of the Inner Sphere in single combat, which made them very much worthy of respect on Solaris or anywhere else.

Valhalla itself had an anachronistic feel that gave it a majesty and legitimacy that few other places on this synthetic and decaying world could claim. Long and wide, the whole hall had been built from genuine and rare woods. The planks had a rough, unfinished feel to them and the pillars holding up the tall roof still showed notches from the axes used to fell them. The hides from animals of two dozen different worlds decorated the walls, and handwoven curtains hid the alcoves along each wall.

A holographic bonfire in the center of the hall provided most of the illumination, with holographic torches set in wall sconces holding other shadows at bay. Huge, long tables and matching benches built by hand from thick planks ran down the center of the room, bre. king only at the bonfire. At the farthest end a dais and another table capped the room. On the far side of the dais were a number of highbacked chairs, including a thronelike one in the place of honor in the middle.

The shields tacked to the posts by each alcove were decorated with the crest of the fighter who owned it. The alcoves were assigned according to Roger's whims, with a fair number of those close to the door given to nobles who paid handsomely for the privilege of being allowed into Valhalla. Those closer to the dais were for warriors of great repute who had retired from the arena, or in certain cases, ones who Roger deemed most likely to survive to retirement.

Kai greeted and waved to many of the warriors as he made his way toward the dais. As Champion he could have taken his place on the throne, but instead he stopped at an alcove decorated with two shields. The top one showed a tombstone bearing the image of a black mechanical hand holding a flaring supernova. The disk in the heart of the nova had been transformed into a yin and yang symbol, the whole thing being easily recognizable to those assembled in Valhalla as the Cenotaph Stable logo.

The shield beneath it had a more comical symbol painted on its surface. A cartoonish ghost looked out with a shocked expression on its pale face. Glowing red cross hairs covered it, giving it good cause for its apparent alarm. Though slightly faded with age, the symbol conveyed a healthy contempt for the gladitorial system that spawned it.

Kai's guests filled the benches on either side of the table in the alcove. He took the seat at the head of the narrow table and nodded to the security man who pulled the curtain shut. Reaching down below the edge of the table at his end, Kai hit a button that brought a full array of antieavesdropping devices into play. "This is Valhalla."

Galen nodded appreciatively. "I saw the Cenotaph logo there, but what's with the ghost?"

DeLon smiled even before Kai began his explanation. "In thirty sixteen Gray Noton became champion here on Solaris and retained that title until he retired in thirty twenty-two. He designed that symbol to match the nickname he had been given: Legend-killer. He also gave his *Rifleman* the name Legend-killer. This was Noton's alcove and became my father's after Gray's murder in thirty twenty-seven. My father used Legend-killer to unseat the champion at that time, Philip Capet."

DeLon nodded in confirmation of Kai's story. "I saw one of Noton's last fights. He was very good and well deserving of the title and his nickname. No fighter before or since has held the Championship for that many years—though many think the current Champion may break that record."

"Two years and part of a third isn't even close to equaling the seven Noton had at the top." Kai shook his head. "Wu Deng Tang could end my reign, or Galen could decide we should go one-on-one after we finish off Vandergriff and Edenhoffer."

"I don't think so, Kai. I watched you polish off a Khan of Clan Wolf in that simulator battle on Arc-Royal last year."

"And Phelan killed me at the same time."

Galen shrugged. "Technicalities. The point is I'm happy to serve as your ally. I don't want to be your enemy."

Larry Acuff laughed lightly. "Not the first time you've heard that, is it, Kai?"

Kai would have preferred to let Larry's comment pass without need for an explanation, but being seated at the head of the table and nominal host of the party put him on the spot. "I suppose not."

Nancy, who was seated at Kai's right, laid a hand on his forearm. "It sounds like there's a story there."

"Quite a story," Larry added.

"Don't be modest." Nancy squeezed his arm. "We'd love to hear it."

Kai frowned and Larry looked stricken for a moment, but a quick smile erased the pain from Larry's eyes. Kai understood fully what incident had prompted Larry's comment and he *was* proud of it, but it had long been something he hadn't wished to talk about. Larry knew about it because he'd been on Alyina when it happened, but Kai hadn't shared details of his time on Alyina even with his family, let alone a group of people that included virtual strangers.

As he probed his feelings, they weren't as sharp and painful as he had expected. The whole of his experience on Alyina had been colored by his disastrous break-up with Deirdre Lear on the day before he left the planet. The only positive things in his time on the world had been centered around her, and their parting had mocked all of them. It had left him with a box full of memories tinged with terror, physical pain, and emotional torment which, for obvious reasons, he didn't enjoy rummaging through.

Working with people like Larry, getting to know them and helping provide them with opportunities, had helped him to separate some memories from his trouble with Deirdre. He could relate what Larry had witnessed without difficulty, but he wasn't certain he was at ease doing so to these people. The moment the idea occurred to him that he didn't want to let them in, he linked it to an unwillingness to be hurt again as he had been by Deirdre. Kai knew he had probably hurt her just as deeply, which did not deaden his pain, but opened the possibility of setting it aside so he could begin to trust others again.

It is ridiculous for me to assume that I cannot share this story with a man like Galen. I am willing to fight with him, yet not tell him of this incident, which is a minor anecdote at best. Kai smiled and sat back in his chair. "It is not modesty, Nancy, but something in my nature that keeps me a private person. However, you are all friends, so I will tell you about the matter to which Larry alludes. Of course, this preface makes it all sound far more important than it really was."

"You should have seen it from my perspective." Larry's grin broadened appreciably. "To him it was nothing, but to me it was everything."

Kai shifted uncomfortably in his chair. "This goes back to the time I spent on Alyina. I managed to avoid capture by the Clans, and when ComStar decided to take control of the world, I worked with some of the Clansmen to stop them."

Larry leaned forward, resting his elbows on the table. "Let me give you some perspective. I'd been captured and was in a firebase that had been converted into a prison camp. ComStar administered it. They treated us pretty rough and they had bounty hunters out looking for folks like Kai. After Kai escaped from them once, they wanted him bad. He brought a dead man into TZ—our camp was called Tango Zephyr—and claimed the reward for himself. That brought the Elementals down on him. He killed one in unarmed combat, which only made the other Elementals even more angry with him."

Kai raised an eyebrow. "I think that's all beside the point, Larry."

Galen shivered. "I've seen Elementals close up. They're huge, like monsters, and that's even before they put on their armor."

"Hey, the normal ones are nothing compared to Taman Malthus. He had a Bloodname and was out for Kai." Larry looked sheepishly over at Kai. "Sorry, boss, but it's the truth, and you know it."

Kai sighed. "Well, anyway, Malthus and I made a deal that included freeing all the POWs. He and I traveled to Tango Zephyr to liberate the camp. Malthus told the men there that he'd fought against me and had no desire to have me as a foe anymore. Instead he preferred I be his ally."

Katrina smiled at Larry Acuff. "I think you're right. The story needed the perspective." She arched an eyebrow at Kai. "My brother has told me none of this."

The Champion of Solaris frowned. "That's because he doesn't know any of it. He has too many things to take up his time. I don't like talking about the time on Alyina because I don't want to sound like a hero for what I did. It wasn't anything that Larry or any of the others wouldn't have done if given the chance. If I were a real hero I'd have found a way to get guys out of Tango Zephyr."

"You did, boss."

"I should have done it sooner." Kai held his hands up. "However, all of this is really beside the point. Malthus said he liked being my ally and I have the greatest respect for him. He was one hell of a commander, and winning a Bloodname among the Clans, well, that's quite an accomplishment."

DeLon nodded. "He sounds like quite a man."

"I think you'd like him, Thomas." Kai smiled. "You'll get a chance to meet him when ComStar and everyone agrees to let Malthus and his Star come here to visit. I expect them in time for the title defense."

"If the agreement comes through *and* the JumpShip schedule works out." Keith Smith looked a bit cross. "Some of the ships we reserved are moving around, but my chain is still intact."

"Yeah, *if* the connections work out. Thanks, Keith, for staying on top of that." Kai hit a second button underneath the lip of the table. "But now I think we've talked long enough without refreshment." A woman ducked through the curtain. "If it's available in the Inner Sphere, they have it here. Indulge yourselves. My guests will want for nothing."

Lyons
Isle of Skye, Federated Commonwealth

Peter Davion's eyes burned as he sat in the dark staring at his holovision monitor. In the foreground the holovision reporter whisked a wisp of dark hair from where the wind had whipped it across her face. She looked excited and exhausted, as befitted someone covering what was, to date, the biggest story of her career and possibly the piece that would get her noticed by a network on a larger world.

"The police have confirmed that the Free Skye Militia has claimed responsibility for this act of terrorism." Behind her three engine companies from the local fire department labored to pour water on the ruins of a burning building. "The spokesman said they had blown up the Prince Ian Davion Municipal Secondary School because the FSM believed it was—and I quote—'a Davion indoctrination center.' The Free Skye Militia, which was believed disbanded twenty-two years ago after the Skye Crisis was resolved through the intervention of Duke Ryan Steiner, is a group dedicated to, again quoting, 'fighting the cultural imperialism of the Federated Suns.' It has long opposed the formation of the Federated Commonwealth and it is unknown at this time if the FSM is the same organization from thirty thirty-four or merely an ideological offspring of that original group."

Peter ground his teeth in the dark. "It doesn't matter. They're terrorists and they're at the beck and call of Ryan Steiner. I know it."

The holovision reporter continued her commentary. "The bomb blast took place at three A.M., which was fortunate, because the school was empty at the time. Just twelve hours earlier, the school would have been packed with people attending Duke Peter Davion's presentation of the first Archon Melissa Steiner Memorial scholarship to one of the students. Experts believe that the bomb may have been intended to explode during the ceremony, which would have resulted in the death of Peter Davion in a crude parallel to his mother's assassination in a bomb blast nine months ago."

Peter felt a cold shiver run down his spine. Only twenty-one years old and he'd escaped death because a terrorist had been sloppy. In attending the New Avalon Military Academy and during 'Mech drill exercises with his fellow Militiamen, he'd faced imaginary death countless times. He often thought about how he would go out in some glorious combat, just as had his uncle Ian and innumerable relatives before on either side of the family. He had marveled at how Victor had escaped such a death. Peter resolved that when he died, it would be in the cockpit of a BattleMech.

That's how he envisioned it.

That was how he wanted it.

That isn't how it almost happened. The realization that he could be as much of a victim as his mother shook him. He had embraced the role of the warrior because of the romance and glory of it all. He had assumed that with his brother and sister ahead of him in line for the throne, his only chance to become a hero would be through his defense of the Federated Commonwealth.

He had never considered being martyred.

In a flash his introspection vanished as the smiling face of the young scholarship student entered his mind. She had been nervous, toying with red ringlets of hair as she listened to him read a list of her accomplishments to the five hundred people in the auditorium. She conquered her nerves when she thanked him and then gave a short speech on the meaning of citizenship and her dreams for the future. The crowd had applauded when she concluded her remarks, not just out of pride for her winning the scholarship, but in admiration of her bold wishes for the rest of her life.

She had impressed Peter, and it angered him to think of her vanishing in smoke and fire because of someone's twisted hatred of him and his family. The people of the Federated Commonwealth were his to defend, not to expose to danger through his very presence. That others would hurt someone like her just to get at him was insane, yet Peter didn't doubt the FSM would act again, and would not be so careless the next time.

If that's the way it has to be, I'm ready. He nodded to himself in the darkness and shut off the holovision monitor. "There will come a time when we go eyeball to eyeball," he murmured to the night, "and when that happens, I won't be the one to blink."

17

Tharkad
District of Donegal, Federated Commonwealth
1 April 3056

Give me the thunder of a thousand guns rather than the fanfare of one trumpet! Victor Davion didn't know if he remembered that quote from somewhere or if it was something he'd made up on the spot, but he did know it summed up his feelings perfectly. If it had been in his power to avoid having to make showy awards in the throne room of the Archon's Palace in the Triad on Tharkad, he would have exercised that power gladly. *And I can imagine that the man I honor today would just as soon avoid this circus as I would.*

A trumpet fanfare hissed, cracked, and popped through the public address system. Victor straightened the jacket of his dress uniform and tucked a last wisp of blond hair beneath his coronet, then held himself at attention. "His Highness, Victor Ian Steiner-Davion, Archon Prince of the Federated Commonwealth, Supreme Marshal of the Armed Forces of the Federated Commonwealth, Duke of Tharkad, Duke of New Avalon, Duke of Donegal, Landgrave von Bremen, Minister of the Crucis March, First Lord of the Star League." Another trumpet blast heralded the opening of the doors before him and Victor began his stiff-legged march down the red carpet toward the Triad thrones.

Many would have put his crisp step down to his desire for military precision, but in reality it came from a fit of temper. *I told the Grand Marshal to delete the First Lord of the Star League line from my introduction. I don't care if it's been part of the ceremony since the Star League collapsed three centuries ago, it's farcical and I will endure it no longer.*

As he stalked down the ribbon of blood-red carpet, the First Prince forced himself to slow down and rein his anger back in. The cathedral ceilings and massive stone pillars supporting their vaults harkened back to an age when strength was reckoned in stone and combat was fought between men wearing armor of steel. *In those days,* Victor thought, *I would have been fodder for another man's blade.*

Times had changed, but not so much that warfare had been eliminated. In the two millennia since Charlemagne had ruled on Terra, men had begun to settle to the stars. Just as their battlefields had become battle worlds, so had their weapons grown to accommodate their expanding conflicts. Instead of wearing a suit of armor, a warrior of the thirty-first century enclosed himself in a powerful and powered BattleMech.

On the dais toward which Victor Davion strode, two small thrones stood backed by a pair of BattleMechs. On the left stood a *Marauder,* a huge but squat 'Mech with two massive, blocky weapons pods on the ends of improbably slender arms. Its legs bent backward and the cylindrical body thrust forward, making the war machine both alien and terrifying in its appearance. The fact that it had been painted in the black and gold scheme of the First Kathil Uhlans moderated the terror, for the Uhlans were known to be fanatically loyal to the service of the Armed Forces of the Federated Commonwealth.

The other 'Mech, the one standing behind the throne representing the Lyran Commonwealth, looked wholly human, like a man at arms awaiting an order from his liege lord. The *Crusader* belonged to Galen Cox and had been placed in the throne room as a sign of his favor with Victor. Normally it would have sported the blue and gold of the Tenth Lyran Guards, but with Galen's permission it had been repainted with a red torso, black legs, and black trim in the manner of the Kell Hounds mercenary unit. Victor knew he should have had the 'Mech painted to match the color scheme of the Gray Death Legion, but the ceremony honoring them would only last one day, whereas the debt he owed the Kell Hounds required far more time to be repaid.

Victor reached the dais without looking at the people lin-

ing either side of the carpet. That had not prevented him
from nodding his head from time to time as he marched forward. It occurred to him idly that he tended to acknowledge
bright colors and the occasional young noblewoman forced
to the front of the line by an ambitious parent. Seldom, if
ever, had he allowed himself to be pressured into escorting
such a woman to a social function. In a quick review of the
few cases where he had been coerced into doing just that, it
dawned on him that he had enjoyed himself more talking
with the student holovideographer than he ever had with the
noblewomen.

*It could be, Victor, that you are too much a warrior to be
a good noble.*

He mounted the marble steps and bowed first to the Lyran
Throne and then to the one representing the Federated Suns.
Had Katherine and Peter been on Tharkad they would have
been seated in those thrones. He continued up two more
steps and stood in front of the tallest throne, the one capped
with the Sunburst and Fist of the Federated Commonwealth.

The Grand Marshal—Victor thought he was a distant
cousin or something—began to bring courtiers forward one
or two at a time. The old man announced the names, and
Victor smiled as if he recognized them all. Most of the pe-
titioners wanted small land grants or waivers on laws or
were being recognized for contributions in areas from agri-
culture to art and from cooking to the classification of scien-
tific trivia. They all seemed terribly nervous—except for the
hopelessly egotistical—and Victor was half-tempted to stop
the ceremonies to conduct a survey of those who, all things
being equal, would have preferred to have the award delivered to them by ComStar.

Victor had gotten so he could ignore the strobing of the
laser flash gun from his left. Each nod, each award, each
smile became immortalized in a holograph the recipients
would cherish or, in the case of political rivals, hide forever.
He did not really begrudge the people their rewards because
they had contributed to society even if it was a contribution
he could not understand or find a practical use for. What the
Prince most resented was the time away from handling the
political crisis that was threatening to bring down his realm.

*At least one of these rewards will kill two birds with a sin-
gle stone.* Victor kept the smile frozen on his face knowing

that the award to Colonel Grayson Death Carlyle would be a nice parry and cut back at Duke Ryan Steiner. Baron von Bulow, fiefholder of the planet Glengarry, had long been a Ryan loyalist and even though Glengarry was a tiny backwater, it was another potential hotbed of rebellion that would make the news and create an impression of widespread trouble in the Isle of Skye. It didn't matter if the demonstration pictured was the good baron's household staff doing what he told them to do under threat of firing, pictures made news and all the news coming out of the Isle of Skye had been bad lately.

The rebirth of the Free Skye Militia had worried Victor, especially when it looked as if their first act was the nearly successful attempt to assassinate his brother. Curaitis had assured him that Intelligence Secretariat teams had documented the absence of the bomb during Peter's visit to the school. The terrorists had slipped in later and only made it look as if the assassination had misfired because of a simple mistake. Even so, the presence of terrorists meant an escalation of the unrest in Skye, and that meant Ryan was upping the ante in the play for power.

Ryan had played his hand well. Intelligence had been flowing from Solaris, and Victor couldn't wait for Galen and Kai to pound Ryan's fighters into insensibility. Curaitis was pleased with the nature of the intelligence they were getting from Ryan's office, but he had pointed out that it might take a long time for them to figure out what the duke was doing. Ryan communicated with the subversives in Skye through a series of codes and unless Curaitis and his people could get a key to one of these preestablished codes, cracking them would be impossible. Even so, they were able to document portions of his network and they could be swept up at a time that would be most inconvenient for Ryan.

The antics of Richard Steiner—a cousin to Ryan and Victor both—had begun to annoy the First Prince. Richard was the AFFC Field Marshal in charge of the Skye March military district. As was proper and in keeping with his duties, Richard had been shifting troops around. The problem, however, was that the rotation had resulted in a number of Skye loyalist units being posted in Skye during a time Victor would have preferred to package the lot up and launch them into Clan space. *Richard will bear watching.*

Just before the start of the afternoon's festivities, Curaitis had dropped a bombshell that had Victor even more uneasy than the situation in Skye. *For Skye I have a solution I don't mind employing. For this ...* The health of Joshua Marik, the only son of Thomas Marik, the Captain-General of the Free Worlds League, had begun to deteriorate again. His leukemia, which had been held in check by treatments he was taking at the famed New Avalon Institute of Science, had recurred and was killing him. That sort of thing happened on countless worlds in the Inner Sphere on a chillingly regular basis, but the children who suffered those tragedies were not the heirs to the throne of a potentially hostile nation.

Curaitis thought it likely that Joshua would die and, because of that, he unveiled to Victor a project that his father had begun back when Joshua had first come to New Avalon. Joshua's health had been bartered in return for the Free Worlds League producing war materials for the Federated Commonwealth to use in fighting the Clans. Because those weapons and munitions were vital to stopping the Clans, Hanse Davion knew he could not let Joshua die.

And if the boy did die, he could not let anyone know. Hanse had initiated a program to create a physical double for Joshua. Such things had been done before by national leaders. Melissa Steiner-Davion had avoided death once by using a double. Victor could understand and condone it. *In fact, if I had a double, I'd not be here right now!*

What his father had planned, however, chilled him. Maximilian Liao, Kai's grandfather, had almost conquered the Federated Suns by putting a double on the throne in the place of Hanse Davion himself. For Hanse to turn around and plan a similar deception against Thomas Marik, well, it showed Victor how utterly desperate to stop the Clans his father had been. *And having benefitted from having those weapons in the war, I applaud his audacity.*

The trick of it was that now the Federated Commonwealth was no longer at war. Joshua's illness had allowed Thomas to keep Sun-Tzu at bay by giving him excuses to postpone Sun-Tzu's wedding to Isis Marik. That mean Sun-Tzu would not work actively against Thomas in case he would inherit through his wife what he could never take by force of arms. With Joshua dead, Thomas would have to accept Sun-Tzu,

which would give Sun-Tzu more power than could ever make Victor comfortable.

Please, God, make Joshua recover.

Victor's smile broadened as the Grand Marshal called forward the only person he wanted to see that afternoon. "Colonel Grayson Death Carlyle!"

The prince winced as the man mispronounced the mercenary leader's middle name. *It rhymes with* breath *you old goat—everyone knows that.* Carlyle seemed not to notice as he moved forward. The mercenary walked up to the dais with a quick, sure tread that marked him a military man of confidence and courage, and his bow set him well apart from the sycophantic courtiers who had dominated the afternoon's awards.

Victor descended the steps to stand before the man. "Ah, Colonel Carlyle. A pleasure to meet you at last."

"The pleasure is mine, your Highness."

Victor fingered the tight collar on his own uniform to let Carlyle know he abhorred the formality of the afternoon, then looked up for the benefit of all the others in the chamber. "You have served the Federated Commonwealth well over the years, Colonel. A distinguished record indeed. And even if that were not so impressive, the Gray Death Legion's discovery of the computer core on Helm would by itself entitle you to a place in the history books. The Federated Commonwealth is most grateful for the service of commanders such as you."

The Grand Marshal looked sternly at the both of them, then impatiently waved forward a liveried servant bearing an unwieldy broadsword. The prince accepted it from the man, then frowned as he looked at Carlyle. "Ceremony demands of you what I would not request. If you would kneel, please, and place your hands on the hilt of this sword."

The mercenary hesitated, then nodded solemnly. Though Victor sensed the man had no more love for the ceremony than he, Carlyle dropped to one knee in a very respectful manner. He placed his hands on the hilt, then he and Victor together set the blade's point against the lowest step of the dais.

"Let it be known on every world of the Federated Commonwealth, in the councils of the Clans, and among our enemies, that I, Prince Victor Steiner-Davion, do hereby recognize the many services of Grayson Death Carlyle to the House of Steiner and Davion. I hereby name you a Baron of the Federated Commonwealth. I bestow upon you and your heirs, in perpetuity, the fief and planethold of Glengarry in the Isle of Skye."

Victor saw the hint of a smile tug at the corners of Carlyle's mouth and he answered it with a partial smile of his own. "You have earned it, Carlyle," Victor whispered without moving his lips, "for your sake and mine I hope you are able to hold it."

Carlyle looked up with a fire in his eyes.

I have my answer. "Please, Baron von Glengarry, repeat after me. Before these witnesses here assembled I, Grayson Death Carlyle, Baron von Glengarry, do hereby take you, Victor Ian Steiner-Davion, Archon Prince of the Federated Commonwealth, to be my lord of life and limb, and I your man for my planethold of Glengarry."

Carlyle repeated back the oath of fealty, then further swore, at Victor's prompting, to defend the Federated Commonwealth from its enemies even unto his death. Neither Victor nor the mercenary underestimated the import of that oath because not only did Glengarry sit in the hornet's nest of Skye, but it was close enough to become a Combine target for attack if the truce between the Draconis Combine and the Federated Commonwealth should break down. Awarding the planet to Carlyle made it even more a target because of the Gray Death Legion's history of feud with the Combine.

"I, Victor Steiner-Davion, take you, Grayson Carlyle, Baron von Glengarry, to be vassal of heart and hand and mind, to support and sustain you, for as long as I bear this Sword of State." Victor handed the sword to the attendant, then grabbed Carlyle's hand and shook it. Without releasing the mercenary's hand, he bade him, "Rise, Baron Carlyle of Glengarry, and let citizens of the Federated Commonwealth look upon the rewards of selfless duty and devotion to their nation."

Zurich
Sarna March, Federated Commonwealth

"Rick, I don't want to do this." Deirdre looked over Rick Bradford's shoulder at the holovision crew and the reporter standing there with a wireless microphone. "Hsing isn't out of the woods yet. I can't take time to do a stupid interview."

Bradford looked uneasy. "Deirdre, I wouldn't ask you to do this, but it's a chance for some publicity. You know as well as I do that we can't help people who don't know we're here. And you also know that this story may get picked up by one of the syndicates and get broadcast throughout the Federated Commonwealth. That means we could get more donations. I don't want to press you on this, but it could really help us."

"I really, really don't want to do it." Deirdre wanted to stick to her refusal, but Rick's arguments made sense. "I answer a couple of questions. That's it. And *only* about the incident, right?"

Bradford nodded. "The reporter is Tod Chandler and I told him he could only question you about the incident." He waved Chandler forward and the cameraman trailed after him. "Mr. Chandler, this is Dr. Lear."

"Tod Chandler, Channel 47." The big man smiled in a friendly way, but Deirdre felt too much was going on behind his dark eyes to make her comfortable. "I know you don't want to be on camera much and I can respect that. Really. We just want some footage so we can build an angle on the story that will get it play outside of Zurich. It'll help you and help us."

"Just the incident, right?"

Chandler nodded. "Yep, just the incident. Let's get that angle, first, then we can go. I think we'll get spontaneity out of you."

Deirdre eyed him suspiciously, which put a smile on the cameraman's face. "Angle?"

"Yeah, a story hook."

"Taking down an armed terrorist in an emergency surgical theatre isn't an angle."

"Well, it is, Doc, but we want to maximize this." Chandler reached out and gently pinched her bicep between his thumb and forefinger. "You don't lift, do you?"

"Weights? No. I have a three-year-old and my work to keep me active."

Chandler's bushy black brows arrowed in at each other like fuzzy caterpillars racing toward his nose. "Okay, this kung-fu stuff, did you learn that from the Clans on Alyina?"

"It's *aikido* and, no, I did not learn it from the Clans." She folded her arms across her chest. "And Alyina isn't part of the incident."

"Angle, Doc, angle." Chandler smiled. "So this aikido kept you out of the hands of the Clans, right?"

Deirdre's head came up. "Mr. Chandler, before you 'angle' me one more time, let's try it this way. I am a doctor. I acted to save my patient. My patient was badly shot up and almost died because some kid was given a gun, fed some propaganda, and assigned a target. What happened here shouldn't have happened at all, and I'm just happy that no one was killed. *That's* the story I want told and *that's* the story you're going to tell."

Chandler laughed lightly. "I don't think you understand, Doctor . . ."

"I understand, Mr. Chandler, very well. You want this story to get you off this nowhere world. You have two choices: a story with me that runs along the lines I sketched out a moment ago, or a story without my participation and a promise of a lawsuit if you even hint at any of the other angles you were pointing to a bit ago." Deirdre shrugged her shoulders. "You need me a lot more than I need you, so you choose."

Chandler swallowed hard. "You are one tough woman."

"No, just one who is dedicated to her job and her patients." Deirdre let her arms hang at her sides and rolled her wrists around. "And that's your angle, Mr. Chandler. Shall we begin?"

Solaris City, Solaris VII
Tamarind March, Federated Commonwealth
7 April 3056

Though Kai made his bow as deep and respectful as befitted his uncle, he could not shake off the feeling that trouble loomed over the horizon. The invitation to join Tormano for lunch had come normally enough, brought round to the Cenotaph 'Mech stable by a messenger. Along with the invitation had been a separate envelope containing a thank you note from Nancy for the visit to Valhalla.

Kai had sent his acceptance back to Tormano by the same messenger, then showered and changed. He knew that his uncle would expect him to wear more traditional Capellan garb than was Kai's norm. He generally did just that when meeting with Tormano—just as he dressed to please his mother on visits to St. Ives. It was traditional and it was for family, so Kai paid these respects almost instinctively.

This time he did not. Instead he carefully chose green trousers and an ivory shirt made from good Capellan silk, both tailored in a style more appropriate for a business meeting on Tharkad or New Avalon. He also chose a black tie embroidered with the horse-head insignia of the St. Ives Compact. Already sensing what his uncle intended at lunch, Kai wanted to show he acknowledged his Capellan heritage, but that he had not abandoned his Federated Commonwealth blood.

The momentary flash of puzzlement on Tormano's face told Kai he had anticipated the man precisely. It was not a feat of telepathy or clairvoyance but a catalogue of clues that had led Kai to his conclusion. He was aware that his uncle was becoming increasingly desperate to find a powerful symbol for use in his fight against Sun-Tzu, and Kai was the likeliest one around. The abortive attempt at snatching Wu's fiancée, the sponsoring of the party, and even inviting Duke Ryan showed how desperate Tormano was.

"Thank you, uncle, for the invitation to lunch." Kai pulled out the chair at the opposite side of the round teak table and sat down. "And permit me to thank you again for hosting the reception the other night. I very much enjoyed myself and have also heard wonderful things from many others."

Tormano smiled easily. "It was my pleasure, Kai. You know you are my favorite and I would gainsay you nothing. Your successes bring glory upon us all."

Kai found Tormano's opening very polite, as befit the surroundings. The room was filled with treasures from the Capellan Confederation, many of them gifts from wealthy Capellans now living in the Sarna March. Kai had always liked the life-size bronze tiger sitting licking its paw in the corner, but even more valuable were the delicately woven and hand-embroidered silk robes hanging in frames on the walls. The walls also displayed a fantastic collection of rice-paper paintings of warriors of myth and legend, all by the same artist, and Kai noticed a new one among them today.

Tormano nodded toward the piece that had caught Kai's attention. "That one is from a private collection. There are four more in the series, three of which your mother owns. One more and the set will be complete."

"Good luck in your quest," Kai said, though he knew luck had little to do with Tormano's success. The new piece had formerly been housed in the Cultural Ministry on Sian. A year ago thieves had made off with it and several other pieces in a well-planned and executed robbery. Kai could easily imagine Tormano financing the operation, though his uncle tended to be more subtle than that. He had probably been an inspiration to the thieves, however, by making it no secret that he paid handsomely for treasures liberated from the current regime on Sian.

"And I wish you good luck in yours." Tormano pressed his hands together, fingertip to fingertip. "The challenge offered and accepted at my party has many people talking. You managed to embarrass Duke Ryan Steiner and will do so again when you and Cox destroy his fighters. Prince Victor will be pleased."

"I am happy if the prince has time to notice my fights. And if they please him, so much the better." Kai held himself back, warily, because his probe was coming in over a route Tormano had not explored before. "I am a simple gladiator and not worthy of the prince's notice."

"You are far from simple, my nephew, and you are a gladiator without equal." Tormano tapped his index fingers together. "You maintain a willful ignorance of your influence with the people. You have the power to make multiplanetary corporations bend to your whim. You are a symbol, an idol, to which countless people look up. You are a hero in a time that sorely needs heroes."

"I drive a machine that destroys other machines, as my father did before me."

Tormano smiled and Kai felt a trap closing around him. "Ah, but like your father you are more than you appear to be. He was a confidant and aide to Hanse Davion. Your father's deeds among the Capellans wrought the greatest change known in the Inner Sphere since the fall of the Star League."

"My uncle forgets the Clans."

"I do not. I remember them well." Tormano sat forward, leaning across the table. "I remember that you stopped them at Twycross. I know you frustrated them on Alyina. ComStar defeated the Clans at Tukayyid, but on Alyina you defeated ComStar. You alone can boast to winning out over the most powerful forces in the universe. You are most fittingly your father's heir."

Tormano's hands opened up innocently and spread apart slowly. "You are a combination of your mother and father. In you their destinies and legacies are intertwined. You are the eldest child of Maximilian Liao's eldest child. Your mother is heir to the Capellan throne, and your father did what he could to bring that throne into union with the Federated Commonwealth. Through you both things can be accomplished.

"There are people out there, Kai, who hunger to see a compassionate and sensible ruler at the head of their former nation. They look and weep at what Romano did to destroy the Capellan Confederation. They see Sun-Tzu planning to make the Capellan throne a groom-gift to the Free Worlds League. Even Maximilian Liao, mad as he was, would never have sunk to such base treachery. That is treason against the people Sun-Tzu has a sacred trust to rule."

Kai considered the words, becoming trapped by them until he looked at his uncle's warped reflection in the surface of the table. "There is nothing I can do about that, uncle."

"Yes, Kai, there is. You can do more than anyone else, and you can do it precisely because of who you are: the Champion of Solaris. Had you returned from the war and gone to live in obscurity on St. Ives, then, no, you would not be able to fulfill the dreams of billions."

"I think the dreams you ask me to fulfill belong to only one person: you."

Tormano's face closed up. "You do me a disservice, Kai."

Kai felt his anger rising, prompted by the oily, hurt tone in Tormano's voice. For once he decided to give it vent. "It is you who does the disservice here, uncle." Kai stood and looked down at his mother's brother. "Do you think I am blind to what you have done with your Free Capella movement? I am not, especially not here in your trophy room. For the past twenty-six years you have succeeded in feeding off the hopes of expatriots and refugees. For a quarter of a century you have been content to be a snarling dog on a short leash. Hanse Davion used you as a goad to drive Romano to madness. With the two of them now gone, and the years beginning to grind on you, you have decided the time is finally right to make your move.

"You want me to act as your surrogate, to lead people into battle for you. You want me to persuade them to contribute more money to your coffers so you can buy more weapons and someday take the rest of the Capellan Confederation. You want me to become a flag behind which everyone can rally. Well, I won't do it."

Tormano's face grew ashen. "You forget all the good things I have done for the people of the Sarna March!"

"No I don't, uncle, not at all." Kai shook his head. "You have founded schools and financed hospitals. Through your efforts millions of people who fled the Capellan Confederation have been reunited with family and friends in the Sarna

March. You have successfully managed to reintroduce extinct animals to their native worlds. Your efforts have not gone unnoticed or unappreciated. It is just that you do not give them the correct priority.

"When Victor cut back your budget, why do you think I had Cenotaph Charities begin funding the project you were forced to drop? Surely you did not think it was because I supported Free Capella? I funded the humanitarian projects you had begun because those were the first you cut loose. I have never given you money for guns or propaganda because I do not share your fervor for destroying the Capellan Confederation."

Tormano stood slowly, his head coming up and his eyes meeting Kai's stare without flinching. "You deny your own nature, Kai. You came here to Solaris to prove yourself the greatest MechWarrior alive because you know how much power that gives you."

"No, that's not true. Political power does *not* interest me." Kai thrust a hand toward the window opening onto the gray world of Solaris City. "I came here to honor my father, nothing more. I hate politics! I have no talent for it and a damned sight less tolerance for it!"

"I never thought I would call my nephew a hypocrite, but that is what you are." Tormano shook his head ruefully. "You are as political an animal as I am, yet you deny it."

"I am *not* political!"

"But you are, Kai. Yes, Cenotaph Charities does fund humanitarian causes and does not trumpet your name about. That is selfless. That is nonpolitical, and you cling to that idea as if it were the whole of your reality here." Tormano poked a finger against Kai's breastbone. "The fact is that you have manipulated the other stable owners as skillfully as an elder statesman. You have scourged them with your good works so they are forced to do the same. You set a trap, which gave them no choice. You do the same with the contracts you offer your fighters, forcing the other owners to make changes in their policies.

"You, nephew mine, have even dabbled in international politics by publicly embarrassing Duke Ryan."

"You're wrong."

"Am I? You've done it before—dedicating fights to Prince Victor, agreeing to have Omi Kurita in your box during your title defense. Now this, with Ryan, is one more data point on a chart that places you very highly in the precincts of political power. There is even a rumor that ComStar will permit a delegation of Clansmen to visit Solaris at *your* request. You have mastered ComStar and the Clans yet again."

"No." Kai's nostril's flared and his hands clenched as his uncle spoke. He denied the words out of reflex, but deep inside were bitter questions. *Have I been willfully blind to my own motives? It's true that I have manipulated the other owners, forcing them to do things my way because I gave them no other choice. But is that politics? No!*

"I am a fighter, nothing more!" Kai hoped his denial didn't sound as hollow to Tormano as it did to him.

Tormano laughed aloud. "Delude yourself, if that makes you happy. I have not spoken falsely. You suckled at your mother's breast, drinking in politics with her milk. You learned deception from your father, watching him twist up Hanse Davion's enemies, and politics pervaded your childhood home as sunlight pervades a desert. Join me. Become my heir and one day you will free Capella from the madness that dominates it. Politics is you, it defines you and empowers you. You cannot escape it, so use it."

"No!" Kai slammed his right fist into the palm of his left hand. "I learned many things from my mother and father, but the greatest lesson was that killing must never come easily, and killing is what you are asking me to do."

"This from a fighter on Solaris?" Tormano barked harshly. "You must think me insane!"

"No, just obsessed." Kai felt himself back in control of his anger and he directed it at Tormano. "Look at my record, uncle, I have a string of victories, a handful of defeats and only one kill. That kill came when my opponent punched out in The Factory and hit a wall. Time and again I have refused to deliver the coup de grace to a downed foe. I do not want to be responsible for the death of another human being. I've already done enough of that as a soldier, and if I can help it, it will never happen again."

"Death is death. On Solaris or in freeing the Confederation, it's all the same."

"You're wrong, uncle, very wrong," Kai said calmly, despite the shock he felt at his uncle's callousness. "Here on Solaris death is a matter of choice. The lawyers have a legal term for the reason why another stable or a fighter's family cannot sue me if I kill someone in a fight: it's called assumption of risk. What would be murder in the streets is acceptable in an arena because everyone who steps into that arena has agreed to accept the consequences of his actions.

"The same is *not* true in the outside world. In conquering what is left of the Capellan Confederation, we would cause the death of billions of people. Whole planets might be destroyed. Why? To salve the ego of a man who believes he know best how a people should be ruled? Perhaps you can accept such responsibility, but I cannot."

"You must, Kai. It is your duty."

"No, it is my duty to prevent that from happening." Kai's voice dropped to a sepulchral whisper. "I am not a political animal. I'm a *warrior*. You have reminded me of my duty, so now I will execute it."

Kai rose and took a step toward the door. "I will continue to fund your humanitarian efforts, Uncle, and will even undertake to continue your pension if Victor decides the Federated Commonwealth can no longer afford it. This I promise you, both as your nephew and as a fellow Mech-Warrior. It is a deal, bargained well and done, as the Clans would say.

"Continue your snarling. Give Sun-Tzu bad dreams. Oppose the *Zhanzheng de guang* with your network of spies. Give value to the lives of those who share your dreams. Do what you wish short of starting a war and I will not gainsay your efforts."

Tormano's eyes became dark slits. "And if I defy you?"

"I am the Champion of Solaris because I destroy my enemies." Kai bowed his head curtly at Tormano. "Have you a wish to become my enemy?"

Tharkad
District of Donegal, Federated Commonwealth

"You're certain it's the Tenth Skye Rangers?" Victor stared at the holographic display of the Isle of Skye hovering above the black lozenge shape of the briefing table.

Alex Mallory, Secretary of Intelligence, nodded solemnly. "The Tenth is away from its base, and the story is that the unit is off on an exercise. The Field Marshal's office is disclaiming any knowledge of an operation, but ComStar communications logs leaked to us through the liaison officer from the Precentor Martial's office show that Duke Richard has had communications with the JumpShips that showed up with the Rangers in the Glengarry system on the first of April."

"I had expected Ryan to move against Glengarry, but not this quickly."

Mallory sat stiffly back in his chair, looking very much his age, reminding Victor that the man who had also advised his father for a quarter of a century had once endured torture on Sian in service to Hanse Davion. "I can't be certain that either Ryan or Richard Steiner have authorized his activity. It looks as if Baron von Bulow might have launched the attack on his own initiative, trying to regain ownership of Glengarry. Richard Steiner is aiding and abetting the action by doing nothing, but most of the units now stationed in Skye would likely support the action, not oppose it."

"I had just awarded Glengarry permanently to the Gray Death Legion on the day those DropShips appeared in the Glengarry system. The Rangers must have jumped into the system on the day I made the award."

Curaitis, seated midway between the other two men, nodded. "The Baron was given advance notice of the investiture."

"How much advance?"

"Twenty-four hours."

Victor smiled. "Good. That means this action is hasty. With Glengarry being such a backwater world, the Rangers will have problems keeping up their supplies. The Gray Death Legion won't give up the world without a fight."

"Only half the Legion is on the planet, my lord."

"I know, Curaitis, but the rest will be on their way back there soon enough."

Alex shook his head. "That might not be enough for the Gray Death to win the fight, but we can't support them any more than that, either. We have no loyal troops in Skye and to send some in will seem like Davion aggression. And that will only play further into Ryan's hands."

"Good point, yes, but there are some things we can do." Victor leaned forward and began ticking items off on his fingers. "First, we're going to reprioritize the recharge stations so they service merchant ships first, *my* military transports second, and Richard's ships last—dead last. I also want to open up our strategic stores of grains, other foods, and fuels on the hottest planets. Flood those worlds with low-priced food and fuel. Tell everyone the Federated Suns is enjoying bumper crops and the people are sending this bounty along to help their Lyran cousins. Declare the anniversary of my mother's death a holiday with pay for everyone."

Alex Mallory looked shocked. "Highness, this largess will be very expensive."

"More so than losing Skye?"

"No, but corporations will want to be indemnified against losses from the cheap food and fuel."

"Fine, we'll do that. I need this massive distribution because I'm going to nationalize the local militias. I want them under my direct control. I know, I know, I can't trust all of them, which is why we'll be keeping some very busy playing Santa Claus to their worlds. We'll give them bonus pay, too. The rest of the units will keep the peace and keep an eye on Richard's units. If we can localize the conflict and keep it on Glengarry, we have a chance to shut down this rebellion before too many people die."

Alex nodded appreciatively. "It's just the sort of plan your father would have put together. Are you going to speak with Carlyle?"

"How can I? I'd have to make promises I couldn't keep. What I want you to do is hire two regiments of the Northwind Highlanders in Carlyle's name as Baron of Glengarry. If he tries to defend the world with just his own men, that might not be enough. We can't risk losing Skye, but we can't intervene directly with our own Federated Commonwealth troops. However, reinforcements hired by the rightful Baron of Glengarry to protect his fiefdom should help Carlyle do the job *and* keep my name out of it."

"I understand, my lord." Alex set his face with an uncompromising expression. "Is there anything else?"

"Two things. First, see what pressure we can put on ComStar to get those damned Elementals to Solaris for Kai's fight. We'll have to route them well outside the Skye March because all hell will break loose if Ryan learns they passed through his territory to get to Solaris."

"Agreed on Ryan. I'll get on it. And the other thing?"

Victor smiled broadly. "Talk to Kai's people and get an agreement for broadcast rights to the fight that pits him and Galen against Ryan's fighters. Let's let everyone in the Isle of Skye get a good look at Ryan's embarrassment."

Curaitis' eyes narrowed. "What if Kai and Galen lose?"

"The chances of their losing are about as good as Ryan's chances of making the Isle of Skye secede from the Federated Commonwealth." Then Victor's voice dropped, becoming so soft the other two men might not have made out the words. "But if it's a game of chance, may luck be on our side."

Solaris City, Solaris VII
Tamarind March, Federated Commonwealth

The scowl on Tormano Liao's face failed in its attempt to become a smile despite Nancy Lee's jovial expression. He still seethed with frustration over his disastrous meeting with Kai. "Yes, Nancy, what is it?"

She handed him a holodisk, which he inserted in the viewer on one corner of his desk. She flicked the device on, then graced Tormano with a smile. "I've found Deirdre Lear."

Lear? Tormano nodded as recognition of the name surfaced in his mind. "She was on Zurich, correct?"

"Yes. She works in a medical clinic there."

"And her husband? Dudley or D something or other."

Nancy shook her head. "David." She punched a button on the viewer and a picture filled the screen. "He's not her husband, he's her son."

Tormano's heart leaped as he saw the frozen image of mother holding child. "How old is he?"

"Three years. Born on Odell, in the Sarna March."

Tormano sank back in his chair. "Very good work."

"Thank you, my lord, but it was due more to luck than anything else." Nancy tapped the screen with a long fingernail. "This is from a news story out of Zurich. Dr. Lear disarmed a *Zhanzheng de guang* terrorist, then operated on the man shot by the terrorist, saving his life."

"Sounds like an extraordinary woman." Tormano's thoughts began to race at breakneck speed. Dozens and dozens of scenarios unfolded, then withered and died just as quickly in his mind. Yet at the center of it all, two things remained constant. One was the frustration he felt at Kai's spurning of his offer.

The other came from the conversation between Kai and Wu Deng Tang on which Tormano had eavesdropped electronically. *My nephew said he had no children.* A quick glance at the image on his viewer confirmed what Tormano had known intuitively at first sight. *The child has Kai's eyes and his chin.*

He smiled almost gleefully at his aide. "Yes, quite an extraordinary woman. I would like to meet her, reward her for her bravery. Have her brought to Solaris as a guest on my estate on Equatus."

"As you wish, my lord."

"And, Nancy, no word of this to Kai. I want to surprise him."

The woman smiled. "If that is his son, he will be very happy."

"Indeed, he will." Tormano stared at the image. *But only if he does as I wish.*

$$ \equiv 19 \equiv $$

Solaris City, Solaris VII
Tamarind March, Federated Commonwealth
8 April 3056

Duke Ryan Steiner sat back in his office and laughed aloud as David Hanau finished an anxious explanation of what Prince Victor had done within the Isle of Skye. "Brilliant, Victor, brilliant. Well played."

Hanau looked confused. "My lord, his efforts have essentially frozen the rebellion and left only one Skye unit in mutiny. He has blunted your efforts. Il Pompiere is ready to act, to intervene, but the federalization of the planetary militias means we could have citizens of Skye fighting citizens of Skye."

Ryan held out his hands and pressed them gently downward as if he could physically lower Hanau's alarm. "Il Pompiere is to do nothing at this time." They had chosen an Italian code name for Richard Steiner because of the duke's desire to honor an old Skye family's quirky insistence on using that tongue in polite company. Ryan had chosen the name "Fireman" because of Richard's ability to handle a crisis.

"But if Il Pompiere does nothing, Glengarry could fall into the wrong hands."

Ryan shrugged. "Il Fuco has overstepped his ambition. If he succeeds in wresting his planethold from Carlyle, he will need supplies to consolidate his victory. And that means he will come begging to us. If his attack on Glengarry fails, we denounce him as a dangerous and deviant force, and thereby win praise for being reasonable. If we support him now, we invite a wider conflict, which I do not want at the moment. The time is not yet right."

"I see," Hanau said, but his face still showed confusion. "I thought you'd be worried and would want to do something."

"Oh, I do. The level of protests going on in Skye is sufficient for my purposes. Victor's quick fix of supplying goodies for the populace plays into our hands because at some point he will no longer be able to afford this beneficence. When that moment comes and he is forced to cut the people off, the outcry will be loud and long."

"So we wait?"

"Some of us, yes." Ryan Steiner turned to Sven Newmark. "You will execute an Oyster Three Window immediately; severity can be subject lethal, though I would prefer it not be so."

The ex-Rasalhagian nodded. "That would put it close to the date of the fight here. Is that what you wish?"

"Most satisfactory." Ryan smiled as he saw Hanau's bald puzzlement. "Believe me, you don't want to know."

Hanau held his hands up. "Greater good for the greater number."

"Exactly." Ryan clapped his hands together. "Il Pompiere does nothing, Il Fuco twists in the wind, and we let Victor Davion pay for his audacity. It's a good day's work."

Sven Newmark left the meeting to prepare the message that would initiate the Oyster Three Window. The code name had been created from three parts, two of which became obvious if one shared the same frame of reference as Ryan, Sven, and the Free Skye Militia cell coordinator who would receive it. Window as a command suffix meant that Ryan wanted visual confirmation of the results of the operation and, in this case, they were to be disseminated to the news media. Had the suffix been Keyhole, the evidence would have gone only to Ryan, whereas the absence of a suffix would have instructed that no visual record was needed. Finally, Coffin would have meant to keep any and all connection with the operation secret. A host of other suffix words could have affixed blame on a variety of other parties, but in this operation the blame would be self-evident.

The word "three" indicated that Peter Davion was the target of the operation. Each of Hanse and Melissa's children were designated by a number corresponding to their birth order, though Ryan also used "the corporal" as a derisive name for Victor who was as small as Napoleon. The message would be directed to Lyons, which was Peter's current location, and the operation would be carried out by the local Free Skye Militia cadre.

Oyster had a simple meaning in the scheme of things. An oyster operation was one that seemed to be routine, even boring on the outside, but contained a surprise within. Ryan had outlined a number of general ideas for Oyster operations involving Peter, all of them centering on his well-known temper and low tolerance for any threats or slights to his family. Though he had shown remarkable self-control in the bar incident, reports indicated that the school bomb had shaken him a bit.

The designation of "subject lethal" for the operation meant that Peter Davion's death was a permissible outcome. In many ways Ryan considered Peter no more than an unsupported piece on a chessboard. He was useful to the opposition only in that he could be placed in jeopardy, forced to retreat, or be taken, any of which would hurt Victor. Most people in a similar situation could be "turned," but it would never be possible to persuade Peter to support Ryan. Given that Peter was a Davion, turning him would also blunt the anti-Davion focus of the rebellion.

The whole of the message Sven Newmark wished to send was Oyster Three Window Subject Lethal, incomprehensible in itself, which was just as it should be for a secret message. It was also true that such enigmatic messages might attract attention for exactly the reason that they might contain important secrets. Duke Ryan did not discount the possibility that Victor Davion's Intelligence Secretariat had ways to penetrate his security, but that didn't stop him from trying to make obtaining information the most difficult of tasks—and understanding it all but impossible.

One of the more interesting aspects of Sven Newmark's employment with Duke Ryan Steiner was his study of countless catalog disks from worlds throughout the Inner Sphere. He sought out small publishing houses, university presses, and private firms that issued limited-run information disks or special editions of classic or contemporary cutting-edge fiction. The more obscure and esoteric the work, the more Sven wanted it.

Working through a series of cutout companies, he engineered the purchase of a hundred copies of each bookdisk in question. The Federated Commonwealth produced enough of them that his purchases amounted to a dozen volumes each month. These disks were subsequently shipped to large-volume bookdisk retailers along with a description to be entered into their computer system catalogs. Sven wrote these descriptions personally, laboring to make the books sound as impenetrable as steel and as exciting as watching fingernails grow.

Each description had a keyword, derived from a previously sent message, for which each cell leader would search the catalog on a monthly basis. When a description contained that phrase, the cell leader would immediately place an order for the bookdisk in question. Two months later the books became "live" and formed the basis for the whole code system Ryan used to communicate with his people.

Sven fired up his computer and typed in the message to be encoded. The computer sorted through the vocabulary lists for the dozen books in use that month. Only three contained all the words, and from among them he selected a mystery anthology titled *Pearls of Murder*, edited by the Bonsai Writers' Club. Within an instant the computer reported back the results of the encryption: 16-2-36 223-1-45 143-0-3 45-5-32 88-6-2.

The numbers referred to page, paragraph, and number of the appropriate word. Sven knew that if he loaded the bookdisk and looked at the sixth paragraph on page eighty-eight, he would find its second word to be "lethal." Without the correct book to facilitate decoding, the message would be gibberish.

Sven copied the numbers down on a sheet of paper, then

shut off the secure computer in his office and turned on the computer with the outside link. It was little more than a dedicated terminal, though a few of its chips had been burned with highly specialized programs. When the system came up, Sven initiated a connection into the local news service and picked his way through the menus to locate the off-planet news service.

Once he had access, he punched in a password that got him beyond the public-access area and deep into the service itself. Hitting a function key, he triggered a rom program that took him further down into it. The screen went blank, then a single blinking square of light appeared.

Resting his sheet of paper at the top of the keyboard, Sven laboriously typed each of the number sequences into the computer. The remote system accepted the input, but gave him no clue as to its disposition. When he finished the transcription, he hit the Escape key twice, then return once, then severed the connection by killing the power on his machine.

Turning away from it, he laid the slip of paper in an ashtray and set it on fire. He watched it to make sure it burned completely, then he pulverized the ashes with one finger until they were nothing more than a smudge. Satisfied that the paper could never be reconstituted, he poured the ashes into a waste receptacle. Now he could leave his office for the day, confident the message would go out and Peter would have his surprise.

The remote computer system took the numbers Sven had provided and broke them down into digital codes. This information was loaded into an unused, sideband track on an outgoing tape of a 'Mech match fought in one of the D league arenas on Solaris. The whole information packet was squirted over to ComStar, repackaged, and then transmitted via hyperpulse generator from Solaris to be distributed throughout the Inner Sphere.

Three days later the fight in question was broadcast by a low-power holovision station on Lyons. The local cell leader was sleeping at the time, but her computer monitored the broadcast and picked up the coded information. When she awoke she was instructed to insert the mystery disk into her computer. After she did so, her machine carefully reconstructed the message Newmark had sent.

She read it from the screen. "A piñata for Peter, with pictures." She smiled slightly. "That I can do. And with great pleasure."

20

Solaris City, Solaris VII
Tamarind March, Federated Commonwealth
9 April 3056

Kai Allard-Liao sat patiently in the combatants' waiting room far below Ishiyama as Katrina Steiner-Davion gave Galen Cox a kiss. "That's for luck," she said loud enough to be overheard, "and so you won't do anything foolish out there."

Kai felt the last remark directed at him and he gave her a covert nod. She had spoken with him several times without Galen's knowledge, expressing concern for Galen's safety and winning Kai's promise to protect him from harm. A lucky headshot by Ryan's men or a piloting error could still get Galen killed, but Kai was confident he would be able to keep that promise.

"Duchess, Lady Omi Kurita and Mr. DeLon are waiting for you in the DeLon Stable box." Kai smiled at her easily. "Your security detail knows the way. We will be with you shortly."

Katrina looked at Galen. "Promise?"

"Your wish is my duty, Duchess."

Katrina gave him another quick kiss, then turned away. Kai couldn't see her face as she left the waiting room, but tears in her eyes wouldn't have surprised him. *Does she fear losing Galen as she has already lost the other people closest to her?*

Galen shook his head as he fished his apprentice license from the breast pocket of his jumpsuit and clipped it to his lapel. "What was that all about?" he asked.

"Kommandant, you are too bright to have missed the fact that the Duchess Katrina is enamored of you."

The distant thunder of war machines battling over them vibrated through the room. Galen shrugged helplessly. "Wanting what you can't have isn't a pleasant way to go through life."

"As Victor and Omi have discovered." Kai clapped his friend on the shoulder as they walked back into the South Side dressing room. "I think you understand that the situation could become rather delicate, but I wouldn't be concerned about Victor's reaction. He loves you both."

"But is this a violation of the trust he has in me?"

"I'm not Victor, so I can't really say, but if I'd entrusted one of my sisters to you, I'd be neither surprised nor displeased at a romance developing." Kai steered Galen over to the well-lit dressing room where two big Red Cobra tongsmen stood guard. "In fact Victor might be very pleased that after tonight a career opens up to you that could provide both plenty of money and lots of positive exposure."

Fuh Teng waited for Kai and Galen in the dressing room along with two others he introduced as grandnephews. Laid out in readiness were a pair of body suits, which were black except for the gold stripes that ran from the underside of the wrist up to the armpit, then down the torso to the outside of the thigh. At the knee the stripe crossed over to the interior of the shin and ended at the ankle of each leg. The head piece had been chopped off above the forehead level, with a gold band running around the brow. Everything else was black, with an opening for the face.

Galen looked around the room, then shook his head. "We get our cooling vests and neurohelmets in the cockpit?"

"No, these do the job." Kai picked up his cowl and turned it inside out. "These silver patches are the neuroreceptors normally found on the inside of a neurohelmet. The cowl even has a throat mike and earphones built in. The interior fabric is a goretex weave that wicks sweat away from the body. The whole suit has coolant lines in it, but because it covers the entire body, the coolant lines are slimmer and decidedly less bulky than in normal cooling vests. The suit has medsensors inside too. Just connect that plug on your right hip into your command couch and you're in business."

Galen frowned. "No neurohelmet?"

"The helmet is a holdover from when a pilot needed it for protection in warfare outside the cockpit. We'll be wearing impact helmets, but we've eliminated the bulk and weight of the conventional neurohelmet." Kai shrugged. "Ditto the bulk of the cooling vest. We can afford to run with lighter equipment because we're much closer to help here than in a war and because things are generally much more under control."

When Galen looked suitably impressed, Kai couldn't help a sheepish grin. "To tell the truth, though, the major reason for the switch is that this is show business and the performers look better in these snazzy outfits."

"And here I thought the light gear was just for the simulators we've been using all week." Galen unzipped his jumpsuit and sat down on the edge of a table. One of Fuh Teng's grandnephews immediately whisked off his shoes and helped him change. Kai likewise perched on the table while the other grandnephew helped him.

No one spoke as they worked, and Kai used the relative silence to focus his mind in preparation for the battle. The one thing he preferred in fighting on Solaris over combat in the field against an enemy was that he needn't worry about anyone else under his command. Yes, he had promised to keep Galen safe, but Galen wasn't likely to need any help taking care of himself. The simulator runs they had done to acquaint him with Ishiyama's cavernous layout had forged the pair into a team operating almost instinctively. Larry Acuff and other fighters from Cenotaph had taken the roles of Vandergriff and Edenhoffer in the simulations, but no matter how good they were, Galen and Kai were victorious every time.

Kai's choice of Ishiyama as the venue of the fight had been something of a snap decision, but it was still a good one. Vandergriff fought in a four-legged, eighty-ton *Goliath*. The 'Mech had good armor and speed as far as machines of that class went, but the *Goliath* was designed for optimum performance in open battles where long-range combat predominated. Its Gauss rifle and machine guns would function well enough in the close quarters of Ishiyama, but its long-range missiles would be relatively useless.

Edenhoffer's eighty-five-ton *Stalker* suffered similar limitations. Ishiyama's close ranges and narrow tunnels negated the advantages of the 'Mech's twin LRM canisters. The extended-range large laser would still work in Ishiyama, as would the short-range missile racks and the four medium lasers, but Edenhoffer might not be up to his usual brilliance. His record in Ishiyama was far worse than his overall record, and he had lost a number of times to underweight and under-powered enemies in the precincts of Stone Mountain.

Galen tugged the head piece into place, then rubbed at his now-hidden ears. "So, our strategy is to keep our holographic display on infrared scan, hit hard and fast, and risk running hot to pour fire in on the other guys."

"Right. You have to go with IR in Ishiyama because all the stone is artificial and full of girders and rebar. Fighters who like running in magnetic resonance mode have nicknamed the place 'Iron Mountain' and one guide book even offers that as the translation for the word Ishiyama." Kai adjusted the forearm of his suit to a more comfortable position. "If you get hit before you see the other guy, fire back, break quick, and then start pounding again when he begins to broil."

"You're the boss. I just hope my *Crusader* is a help."

"The kills will be yours." Kai understood Galen's concern about the *Crusader*. It was a missile-boat BattleMech that normally used its high maneuverability to flank foes and generally end up where the enemy didn't want it to be. Its flamer, machine gun, two medium lasers, and twin SRM launchers gave it a better array of close-in weapons than the *Goliath*. But it only massed sixty-five tons, making it the most vulnerable of the 'Mechs in the contest.

Galen shrugged. "I'm not much for having my food pre-chewed for me, but I'll gobble up anything you send my way."

"Bon appetit!" Kai jumped down to the floor as his dresser zipped up the rear of his suit. The grandnephews opened the double doors at the back of the dressing room and bowed as the two MechWarriors passed into the 'Mech bay. Opposite the dressing room stood a huge archway that led into the vast network of tunnels that allowed Battle-Mechs to move from training areas and repair facilities to the various arenas where they would fight, without the need for surface transport. The tunnels had been built because the constant movement of 'Mechs on the surface of Solaris would have destroyed much of the city, not to mention that BattleMechs obviously required a much bigger right of way than the average human.

The Ishiyama 'Mech bay itself resembled any of a thousand similar places scattered throughout the Inner Sphere, except for one thing. *The Kuritans keep this place spotless!* It was so clean Kai imagined he could eat off the floor without getting a speck of coolant fluid in his food, though he wasn't planning to test the theory. The myriad carts and tools needed by techs preparing 'Mechs for battle had been whisked away and hidden, so as not to disturb the thoughts of the warriors heading into combat.

Their two 'Mechs, each painted in a black and gold pattern similar to that of their cooling suits, stood side by side on an elevator platform. Galen smiled when he saw his *Crusader*. "I don't know what amazes me more: that you had a *Crusader* I could use, or that you got your hands on one of those *Penetrators* to pilot."

Kai shrugged. "Kallon Industries has been after me for a sponsorship, so they think my using a *Penetrator* in a fight here will help spur sales. They also make the *Crusader*, so it wasn't too hard coming to a mutually satisfying agreement."

He extended his hand to Galen. "Look, these guys are good, but all they've ever done is play at war. We've been there. Let's show them what made the Clans run."

Galen pumped Kai's hand firmly. "Hard-lock and firing, Kai."

They parted, each to climb into the cockpit of his machine. As Kai worked his way up the gantry he allowed himself a little laugh. The Kallon Industries representative had not been as ready to give Kai one of the new *Penetrators* as he had led Galen to believe. It had taken Kai pointing out that the St. Ives Compact would doubtless give extra weight to any positive report he made concerning the machine when next they needed to purchase new BattleMechs. With that consideration in the picture, Kallon had suddenly become more generous with equipment and technical support.

Politics got you this ride, so you can use it for political gain. Kai frowned as he climbed in through the open face plate on the squat, stocky BattleMech. He realized that ever since his conversation with Tormano he'd been thinking more and more about politics, and he didn't like it. He found himself going back to reexamine decisions made in the past to see whether politics might have unconsciously influenced him.

His decision to help Galen out of an awkward spot at the party was one of those choices that made him wonder. Kai knew that Ryan had been working against Victor for a long time and probably had put Vandergriff and Edenhoffer up to provoking a fight with Galen to embarrass Victor. Holding open the jaws of Ryan's trap so Galen could escape had been an act of friendship toward both Galen and Victor, not some political ploy on Kai's part. *The truth is I acted without thinking, yet people like Tormano take that as a sign of political shrewdness and cunning.*

Kai frowned. Victor must also have seen it that way, or why else would he have ordered the fight broadcast throughout the Isle of Skye as soon as it was over. Having the fight in Ishiyama also meant the battle vid would likely be circulated in the Combine. As Galen had been among those who rescued Hohiro from the Clans, the broadcast was almost guaranteed a favorable reception. Letting the people of the Combine see a friend of the next Coordinator fight in Solaris would certainly help Omi in her quest to legitimize the ronin in society. Finally, it wouldn't hurt to remind the people of Skye that the Combine still lurked too close for comfort, which ought to dampen the desire of some people to escape the Federated Commonwealth's protective umbrella.

"No, I did not make these decisions, consciously or otherwise, for political gain." His sharp denial echoed within the close confines of the 'Mech's head. "At least, I didn't intend any gain from them."

Enough! Kai cleared his mind for the task ahead. He pushed a big switch upward and locked it into place as the thrumming of the Vlar 300 fusion engine started from within the 'Mech's chest. The face plate slowly swung down into place, sealing the cockpit, then Kai heard a hiss and his ears popped as the cabin pressurized itself.

He settled into the command couch and pulled the impact helmet on over his cowl. He buckled it beneath his chin, then plugged the lead from the command couch into the socket on his suit. Immediately the coolant in the suit began to chill him, a sensation he savored because he knew it would not last very long. He snapped the safety restraining straps into place, then tightened them down.

"Computer on."

The computer's artificial voice purred through his earphones with a throaty seductiveness that surprised him until he remembered old men like his uncle often made purchasing decisions for the military. "This is Penetrator 3XF32, honored to be given to Solaris Champion, Kai Allard-Liao for his ..."

"Computer, initiate cross-check."

"Voiceprint pattern match obtained. Proceed with cross-check phrasing."

Because BattleMechs were incredibly powerful machines, capable of razing a city merely by walking through it, each one was equipped with a series of security measures to prevent unauthorized use. The first was a voiceprint check of all authorized pilots in the machine's memory. Though it was possible to counterfeit that match, getting past the second security check was all but impossible for anyone not authorized to use the 'Mech. Each pilot, when first checked out on the 'Mech, programmed it with a phrase that had to be repeated exactly during the startup sequence or the machine would shut down automatically.

"Killing a man is not easy, and never should be," Kai said softly.

"Authorization confirmed."

The cockpit immediately filled with light as half a dozen monitors and button arrays came to life. Kai watched as the computer cycled through a full range of diagnostics. One screen drew a picture of his blocky, chicken-legged 'Mech and pronounced all limbs fully mobile and powered. Another screen showed a list of his weapons as they came online, each of them checking out normally.

The *Penetrator* had been built for combat against the Clans. The extended-range large laser in each arm gave the 'Mech the long distance firepower needed to keep shooting while the 'Mech closed with its foe. The six medium pulse lasers, three located in each breast, made the *Penetrator* a nasty medium-to-close range machine. The center torso-mounted antimissile system provided some protection against missile-boats, making it able to survive the process of getting close, and the jump jets gave the 'Mech the kind of mobility that had made the *Crusader* so feared on the battlefield.

Kai made a quick change in the *Penetrator*'s standard combat program. The joysticks on each arm of the command couch had a thumb-button and three trigger switches. Kai remapped the weapons, putting all the pulse lasers on his index-finger triggers. Whenever he hit that trigger, all three pulse lasers on that side of the 'Mech would fire. In a real battle a warrior might want the ability to trigger each laser individually, but in Ishiyama Kai wanted a lot of firepower delivered all at once. He left the large lasers slaved to the joystick thumb-buttons.

Kai keyed his throat mike. "Taph one is green."

"Taph two is green," Galen answered. "Ready here."

Kai smiled. "Great. Let's talk a lot up there. Locating the enemy is the first step in beating him."

Lyons
Isle of Skye, Federated Commonwealth

"Say again, Angel Two." Glancing at the *JagerMech*'s auxiliary monitor Peter Davion saw that Carson's *Locust* had already crested the hill and entered the Bellerive Valley, which accounted for her message breaking up. He'd already seen the flash of light from beyond the hill, so he'd come up prepared to take hostile fire. "Angels Three and Four, deploy wide and back. Dicky, you're my back door."

At sixty-five tons, Peter's *JagerMech* outmassed all the other 'Mechs in his lance. The *Locust* and Angel Three's *Commando* together didn't weigh as much as his machine, but the mix of light and heavier 'Mechs made perfect sense in a militia light attack lance. The *Locust* and *Commando* could move fast and gather intelligence, while the *JagerMech* and Dicky's *Trebuchet* could provide long-range cover and fire to help extract the other two from difficult situations.

Reaching the crest of the hill, Peter flipped his holographic display over to Starlight. The computers compressed the full three hundred-sixty degree circle around him into a one hundred-sixty degree arc that hung in front of him. A gold targeting cross hairs floated delicately through the scene, which the computer painted in blacks and greens. The designator tag for the *Locust* below him identified it as friendly.

Down in the valley Peter saw exactly what he'd expected to see. The sleepy little hamlet of Bellerive clung to the wooded hills on either side of the river that cascaded down from the mountains to the north. As with many other settlements on Lyons, this one had been established by a religious community whose people wanted nothing to do with modern technology. Peter could respect that despite his particular group's denunciation of his brother as the anti-Christ. The citizens of Bellerive, whatever their view of Victor, had taken to prayer instead of violence to oppose him.

"And now those Free Skye Militia rat-bastards have brought the most evil of technology here to you," he growled softly. His lance had seen sent out to chase down a Free Skye terrorist cadre that had overpowered the peaceful locals and taken refuge in their town.

"Angel One, I have fire from the church steeple in the center of town."

"Roger, Angel Two." Peter punched up the magnification on his holographic display and centered it on the steeple of the whitewashed wooden church. There he saw what looked like a number of portable SRM launchers arrayed to protect the town. As he watched, another short-range missile launched from the steeple and headed out toward Carson's *Locust*.

The anti-missile cannon in the birdlike *Locust*'s stubby left wing spat flame into the night. One of the SRMs exploded in mid-air as the *Locust*'s shells shredded it, but the other remained on target. It slammed into the *Locust*'s left leg, shattering ferro-fibrous armor. The small 'Mech staggered for a second, but remained upright.

"Two, report."

"Lost some armor, Skipper. No problem." Deb Carson sounded her usual confident self. "What do you want to do?"

"I'm on it, Two." Peter dropped the cross hairs on the tower. His *JagerMech*'s right arm rotated up into firing position. Peter opted to use one of the autocannons instead of a laser because the energy beam might well touch off the fuel in the missiles left in the launchers. The resulting explosion could turn the wooden town into an inferno, the last thing he wanted to do. Unless he had no luck to spare at all, the autocannon's shells should take the steeple down without detonating the missiles.

He nudged the cross hairs lower so they would undercut the launchers by five meters, then double-checked the area backstopping his shot. He quickly flicked his scanners over to infrared, but nothing registered behind his shot. "Standby, Angels, the steeple goes down now."

Something halfway between a scream and a mechanical whine sounded as Peter triggered his autocannon, the resulting hail of metal slicing through the steeple like a giant buzzsaw. The upper half of the steeple hung in the air for a second, then slowly fell to the ground, disintegrating as it hit.

Peter felt one instant of elation before disaster struck. He saw the steeple crash into the ground and a launcher bounce free. As the launcher rotated slowly through the air, time moved slowly enough for Peter to start remembering the procedures for recovering dangerous munitions from a civilian area. *Don't explode!*

It didn't.

The building behind it did.

The decapitated church's windows glowed with a golden light before suddenly exploding outward. Curling flame talons shot from the windows, then closed around and crushed the entire structure. A roiling fireball burst up through the roof, bringing the light of noon to midnight Bellerive. The ball of fire seemed to hang there, an ill omen.

It did not remain alone for long. Another half-dozen buildings in the town also began to explode. Like an epidemic sweeping through the village, houses spontaneously combusted, spraying fiery debris in ragged circles around themselves. Infected by their flames, yet more buildings went up, and within twenty seconds of Peter's hitting the trigger, Bellerive had been consumed by fire.

"My God, oh my God." Peter stared down at the burning town. "What have I done?"

Zurich
Sarna March, Federated Commonwealth

"Yes, I'm Dr. Lear." Deirdre bowed reflexively in response to the man rising from the chair in front of Rick Bradford's desk. "Is there something I can do for you, Mr ...?"

"Chiang, I am Feng Chiang. At your service, Doctor." The slight man smiled politely and bowed with a precision that Deirdre knew marked great respect.

"Rick? Is this another media thing?"

Bradford shook his head. "No, Deirdre. Mr. Chiang has come all the way from Solaris to talk to you. News of what you did has reached there."

Kai? She swallowed her fear and held her head up. "Why are you here, Mr. Chiang?"

"My master wishes me to convey his greetings and a request that you join him as a guest at his estate. You and your son, that is." Chiang apologetically ducked his head. "He wishes to reward you for your heroics on behalf of the hospital."

"You can tell Kai Allard-Liao for me that all we needed to say to each other was said on Alyina years ago." She spun on her heel and started toward the door.

Chiang's voice stopped her. "No, Doctor, Kai Allard-Liao is not my master. He did not send me." The little man sucked at his teeth as if in pain. "I am sent to bring you to Mandrinn Tormano Liao."

Kai's uncle. Deirdre hesitated. "Please convey my thanks to the Mandrinn, but as you can see I have much work to do here."

"He appreciates that, Doctor, and hopes you will accede to his request when you learn that his reward to you is a magnetic resonance imaging suite for the hospital here. He understands the hospital's need for it, and hopes you will humor an aging man's desire to converse with a real-life hero."

Her eyes narrowed. "He can speak with his nephew if he wants to talk to a hero."

"Alas, he does not. He and his nephew have recently become estranged."

Deirdre looked past Chiang at Rick Bradford. *He's staring*

off into space, already adding the MRI equipment to our emergency wing. "When do we leave?"

"This evening, Doctor. The Mandrinn has set up a command circuit from here to Solaris so your arrival will not be delayed." The man smiled happily. "I brought two doctors with me to fill in during your absence."

"How long will I be away?"

"Barely two weeks to reach Solaris and participate in the ceremony, then we will get you back to Zurich as fast as possible." Chiang bowed his head respectfully. "I am certain, Dr. Lear, that you will find all the arrangements most satisfactory."

═══ **21** ═══

Galen Cox resettled his hands on the joysticks of his new *Crusader*. He felt utterly comfortable in the machine, and actually liked the feel of the cooling suit and the lighter helmet. In fact, only one thing disturbed him: the scent of the cockpit. It was the first time he'd ever had a 'Mech that smelled brand new.

That won't last very long, he thought, seeing the massive doors opening in front of him and feeling a nervous sweat start to slick his skin. His initial glimpse of Ishiyama's dark caverns took him back to Trellwan and the first combat against the Clans. He and Prince Victor had engaged in a running gun battle with warriors of Clan Jade Falcon through a series of linked caves. They had not known then who or what they were fighting, and to this day Galen believed only luck had let them escape.

He stepped the *Crusader* from the elevator and saw Kai's *Penetrator* on his left. Galen keyed up his radio. "Deuce here. Do you know where we are?"

"Affirmative. We're about a half-klick from the Grand Gallery. Take that first tunnel to the right."

"Roger, Ace." Galen realized he knew the Grand Gallery better from having watched holovids of fights held in Ishiyama than from all the training he had done with Kai. A huge crevasse ran through the center of Stone Mountain, neatly splitting the lower reaches in half. A narrow ledge on the north side linked it to a number of tunnel mouths. Those openings led back into a maze of tunnels and ramps that provided access to the various levels on that side.

On the south side was a long ledge with pillars that looked like they'd been formed from stalactites and stalagmites growing together. These gave the south passage the appearance of a monster's gap-toothed grin. Galen could easily imagine the open tunnel having some correspondence to an ancient Japanese myth or Combine legend.

The *Crusader* entered the tunnel heading north and slightly up slope toward the Grand Gallery. Kai had predicted that the Kurita operators of Ishiyama would place the two teams relatively close to each other. In contrast to Federated Commonwealth audiences, the people of the Combine liked quick and violent firefights. Since their market dwelt on the heroic nature of battle and the perfection of technique, the hunting and chasing sequences that built suspense in other markets left Combine audiences merely bored.

In their preparatory simulations Galen and Kai had practiced fast and deadly battling. As the *Crusader* came to the level spot from which the Grand Gallery shot off to the east, Galen held up one arm of his 'Mech and gave Kai the standard FedCom signal to slow his advance. "What little I can see of the caverns on the other side is clear. No heat registering."

"Roger, Deuce. I'm up to cover you." The *Penetrator* sidled deep into the landing, then eased over near the opening of the southern passage. "Enfilade or frontal, do you figure?"

Galen shook his head as he punched a command into his computer. He already had the holographic display on infrared, which rendered everything the scanners picked up in colors corresponding to a rough breakdown of heat level, with purple being coolest and white the hottest. The new program he brought on line broke the scan down into finer gradations, but scant little changed on the display.

"I've got no trace temperature changes to suggest they're over here. Enfilade." Galen returned the computer to the original program. "Ready when you are."

"I'll cover the middle hole. Go."

In accordance with a strategy they had worked out during their simulations, Galen started the ten-meter-tall *Crusader* sprinting down the southern passage. The sensors in the cowl allowed the machine to use Galen's own sense of balance to regulate the gyroscopic stabilizers that kept the 'Mech upright. Though not as agile or reflexively quick as a man, the *Crusader* moved with a spritely élan that would have surprised everyone except perhaps its pilot and the engineers who had designed it.

As he broke from cover and dashed down the ledge, Galen caught movement on the opposite side of the Grand Gallery. It was Edenhoffer's *Stalker* coming through the opening of the centermost tunnel over there. The covers over the square LRM launchers mounted in the 'Mech's boxy shoulders snapped down, and fire ignited in the missile racks.

A full score missiles shot out at the speeding *Crusader*, but fewer than half locked on to their target. Galen felt the *Crusader*'s head buck as the antimissile system kicked in. The gun mounted in the 'Mech's forehead spit flame as it labored to blast missiles out of the air. It succeeded in picking off one of the incoming LRMs, and two more slammed into a pillar before the last seven hit their target.

The missiles hammered the *Crusader*'s left arm. As the explosions sent armor plates whirling away, the auxiliary monitor reported that the limb's protection factor had dropped by twenty-five percent. Two other missiles tagged the 'Mech's right leg, chipping away about ten percent of its armor, but Galen wasn't much concerned over the damage. Resisting the temptation to shoot back, he kept the speeding 'Mech upright despite the shock from missile detonation.

Two searing white lines linked the iconographic representation of Kai's *Penetrator* with Edenhoffer's *Stalker*. The first large laser slashed a furrow through the armor of the ride side of the 'Mech's torso. The second traced a diagonal cut through the riotously colorful armor on the *Stalker*'s right leg. Galen knew the damage to Edenhoffer's machine exceeded what his had taken, but given Edenhoffer's advantage from the start, it didn't even come close to making them even.

On the far side, just about even with where Kai fired out at Edenhoffer, Galen caught a glimpse of Vandergriff's elephantine *Goliath*. The tiger-striped, four-legged 'Mech moved ponderously from the tunnel it had been using for cover. As it half-turned to sight back along the line of the

crevasse, its turret swiveled around to sight somewhere forward of Galen's path.

*Going for the long precision shot and waiting until it's at
my weak back armor!* Galen shook his head. *Predictable.
When the Clans got predictable, we beat them by being unpredictable. Like now.*

Leaning to his right slightly, Galen brought the *Crusader*'s arms up and, as he slackened his speed, pushed off hard
from the passage's wall. His 'Mech's right foot pressed
down on the ground, sparks shooting up from beneath the
heel. Galen twisted his own body around, leaning heavily to
the left as he did so to make the *Crusader*'s torso mimic the
motion. The pilot then stabbed his feet down on the jump jet
pedals, igniting the jets on the *Crusader*'s back and launching the 'Mech out from between stony teeth into the
crevasse.

A quick feathering of the jump jets made the sixty-five-
ton BattleMech dip down into the crevasse itself. That immediately provided him cover by putting him beneath the
line of sight from the ledge on the north side. The *Stalker*,
which had shifted around to target Kai, vanished from Galen's holographic display. A forward-jutting section of the
crevasse eclipsed the *Goliath*, eliminating any threats to the
Crusader for the moment.

Above him he caught the quick flashes of laser light and
the sustaining fire of a missile launching that marked another exchange between the *Stalker* and Kai's *Penetrator*.
"Ace, what's the score?"

"Deuce, I knocked down all his incoming missiles and
took laser damage to my left arm. I hit him in the chest and
right arm. I'm operational and he's fixating on me."

"His mistake." Galen hit the jump jets for a sustained
burst of thrust. A wave of heat passed up into the cockpit,
but the cooling suit shunted it away quickly enough. Galen
centered the cross hairs for his weapons controls in the middle of his tactical display, then let the jump jets bring the
'Mech up to superimpose them on the *Stalker*.

The *Crusader* came up to land on the narrow ledge to the
east of the *Stalker*'s lair. Galen kept the cross hairs on his
cylindrical body as he bent the *Crusader*'s knees to cushion
the landing, then he cut loose with both his LRM racks and

the medium lasers built into his 'Mech's arms. *Let's get rid of even more of that ugly paint job.*

One of the lasers missed low, but the other flensed armor from the top of the *Stalker's* right shoulder. The missiles leaped from the forearm-mounted launchers and arced in at the *Stalker* like comets falling in toward the sun. Explosions ringed the 'Mech and bathed it in fire. Armor shards flew out of the firestorm, leaving armor over the 'Mech's left leg, flank, and chest in tatters.

Two red spears of laser light stabbed into the *Stalker* from Kai's position on the far side of the Grand Gallery. More armor dropped in molten gobs from the right side of the BattleMech. The *Stalker* returned fire on Kai, but one swarm of missiles swerved off down into the crevasse to explode far below. The large laser melted a big hole on the right side of the *Penetrator's* chest and then four missiles from a second launching exploded on the center chest.

Despite its counterstrike, the *Stalker* had been hammered badly. Galen could see no signs of an armor breach, but the 'Mech had definitely taken a physical pounding. The missile and beam assaults were powerful enough to momentarily kick the gyros out of phase with each other, and Edenhoffer could not keep the 'Mech on its feet even though his life might depend upon it. To his credit, he seemed to know he was going down, and managed to have his 'Mech fall backward and into the cave that had been giving it shelter.

Its departure from the battlefield allowed Galen to see all the way along the narrow ledge to the *Goliath* lumbering toward him. The muzzle on the turret gun flashed a brilliant electric blue as the Gauss rifle vomited out a silvery projectile. The long-range missile pods blossomed with fire on either side of the 'Mech, and Galen found himself at ground zero for their attack.

The Gauss rifle's ball slammed into the *Crusader's* right shoulder and rocked the 'Mech back with the sheer force of the impact. Ferro-ceramic armor crashed to the ground like so much broken glass and the auxiliary monitor reported he had lost seventy-five percent of the protection on that arm. *One more hit and its gone!*

The missiles corkscrewing in on him met a hail of antimissile fire head on. Over a third of them died there, with the remainder peppering the right side of the *Crusader's* chest and left leg. Compared to the damage done by the Gauss rifle, what they did was negligible and decidedly survivable. Aside from his vulnerable right arm, the *Crusader* could weather anything the *Goliath* could throw at it and keep coming.

Even as he had braced for the assault, Galen had been lining up his own shots and then returned fire, hoping he would give at least as good as he got. Both lasers hit. One stabbed into the middle of the *Goliath*'s chest while the other undershot the torso and hit the right rear leg. The missiles swarmed all over the boxy 'Mech, shredding armor on both the hind right leg and chest, then grinding it away on the turret and right foreleg.

Over on the south side of the crevasse, the *Penetrator* launched itself into the air. The large lasers in each arm cut loose at the slothful *Goliath*, but only one hit. It opened a wound in the heretofore pristine armor on the orange and black-striped 'Mech's right flank. The *Goliath* faltered for a second, but Vandergriff kept it right and moving in toward the *Crusader*.

Galen did not shy from the confrontation, despite the gross weight difference between the two 'Mechs. Once again he cut loose with missiles and beams as Vandergriff walked his 'Mech straight into Galen's fire. The LRMs gouged huge chunks of armor from both of the *Goliath*'s forelegs and shaved some off the hind left leg. The twin medium lasers lanced into the armor on the 'Mech's chest and right foreleg, but neither they nor the missiles even slowed it down.

The *Goliath*'s answer to Galen's attack staggered the *Crusader*. The Gauss rifle's silvery sphere ripped into the *Crusader*'s left arm, shattering the rest of its armor. The falling armor left the arm naked, exposing the bunched myomer fibers, which looked as if someone had stripped the flesh from a man's arm. The LRMs Vandergriff launched at the *Crusader* failed to hit the unprotected limb. Those that got through the antimissile system's counterfire exploded against the *Crusader*'s chest and left leg, crushing armor plates.

The *Penetrator* lighted on the ledge with the delicacy of a mosquito descending on unprotected flesh. The 'Mech's legs absorbed the shock of landing, then, as the 'Mech came back up to normal height, the trio of pulse lasers in its left breast sprayed ruby darts at the *Goliath*'s hindquarters. Fully a third of them shot wide, but the rest ripped away steaming gobs of armor from the *Goliath*'s back.

The *Goliath*'s turret swiveled around to cover its rear arc, and that contributed greatly to the confusion that seized the battlefield as the *Stalker* reentered it. In retrospect, it seemed to Galen that it was as foolish for Edenhoffer to trap himself in a cavern too narrow to permit him to turn around and retreat as it was for the *Goliath* to similarly position itself on the narrow ledge. The two stable mates, both egotistical and driven, fought as individuals and not a team, which hurt them seriously.

The *Stalker* emerged from the mouth of the cavern just in time to interpose itself between the *Crusader* and one of the two LRM barrages Vandergriff had launched at Galen. The *Goliath*'s LRMs blasted into the *Stalker*'s chest and right leg, tearing armor from each. All but one of the missiles that remained on target went down to Galen's antimissile defense. That one nibbled at the armor on the *Crusader*'s chest, but failed to do any real damage.

The same move that brought the *Stalker* in between him and the *Goliath* spitted the cylindrical 'Mech on Galen's cross hairs. He hit the thumb buttons on his joysticks, launching two flights of missiles at the *Stalker*, then tightened up on his triggers and slashed at it with his medium lasers. The beams ripped up from the *Stalker*'s left leg to left shoulder, whittling away the armor on both limbs.

The missile flights had no antimissile system to overcome, so they flew in at the *Stalker* unmolested. They detonated against the 'Mech's cockpit, then arced over to impact on the right side of the *Stalker*'s body. The resulting explosions stripped the last of the armor from the right flank and ate away at the internal structures holding the 'Mech together.

Hardly dead, but gravely wounded! Galen watched as the *Stalker*'s two port-side medium lasers angled toward him and sent scarlet beams of coherent light at him. They sliced armor plating from his right breast and right leg, yet failed to open a hole through to his 'Mech's interior. *I get at least one more exchange.*

Beyond the *Stalker*, Vandergriff triggered his Gauss rifle. Its silver ball nailed the *Penetrator*'s right leg, but the smaller 'Mech hardly seemed to notice even though more

than half the armor on that limb fell away. The impact
slewed the *Penetrator* around, but Kai swung his 'Mech's
torso back around and opened up on both Skye Tiger
'Mechs.

The right-side pulse lasers sent stuttering lines of laser
fire into the *Goliath*'s back. The datafeed coming from Kai's
'Mech showed up on a secondary monitor and revealed a
gaping hole in the *Goliath*'s back, as well as internal damage. The computer painted more damage on the quadruped
'Mech's right flank.

Two of the three lasers directed at the *Stalker* hit their target. One clawed armor off the center of the 'Mech's chest,
while the other one stitched a nice line of flaming holes in
its right leg. Somehow, Edenhoffer kept his 'Mech upright
despite the damage done by both Cenotaph fighters.

The gaudy *Stalker* pivoted on its left leg and started along
the ledge toward the *Crusader*. Edenhoffer's move firmly
screened the *Goliath* from Galen's fire and vice versa. It also
left Galen in a position to go one-on-one with a 'Mech that
both outweighed his and out-gunned him at close range. *I
have no choice.*

Galen stabbed his feet down on the jump jet pedals. The
jets in the rear of his 'Mech's torso ignited, hurling the humanoid war machine up and in toward the *Stalker*.
Edenhoffer snapped off shots with his LRMs and large laser,
but everything passed well below the flying 'Mech.

Jammed deep into his command couch by inertia, Galen
abandoned any thought of returning Edenhoffer's fire. Instead he concentrated on what he expected to be a very hot
landing zone. *I don't know if this will qualify as the sort of
foolish thing Katrina warned me not to do, but unless Kai
does something quick, it* could *be suicidal.*

Below him the *Goliath* again fired into its rear arc with
the Gauss rifle. The argent projectile drilled into the right
side of the *Penetrator*'s chest, scattering armor like fragments of shattered crystal. The *Penetrator* faltered for a second, then came on trailing bits and pieces of broken armor
plating. Stalking forward, the *Penetrator*'s pulse lasers
blazed away at the larger BattleMech.

The energy needles stabbed through deep into the *Goliath*'s heart. Galen saw the large 'Mech shudder, then stagger
to the left. Its left shoulder hit the north side of the crevasse

wall, then the 'Mech rebounded to the right and its legs collapsed beneath it, giving Galen all the classical indications
of total gyroscope failure. The 'Mech crashed down on the
ledge, bouncing once, then teetered on the edge before the
stony ledge lip crumbled beneath it.

Galen landed with his back to the wall as the *Goliath* disappeared from view. Off to his left, Edenhoffer's *Stalker*
reared up and started a quick pivot to the right to come
around and face the 'Mechs in his rear. His effort, born of
desperation, was the only thing a non-jumping 'Mech could
do in that situation, yet it exposed his damaged right flank
to both Galen and Kai.

Galen gladly sent a flight of LRMs at him and followed
it up with the medium laser built into his 'Mech's left arm.
Had he decided to turn and face the *Stalker* he could have
brought all his weapons to bear, but that would have put him
in Kai's line of fire, and he had no desire to do that. *Here
you go, Edenhoffer, art this!*

Galen's missiles all landed dead on target. Five dove
through the hole others had previously opened in the right
flank, and detonated within the *Stalker*'s breast. A secondary
explosion and black smoke marked the death of a short-
range missile launching rack and the destruction of the
'Mech's large laser. The other missiles powdered armor on
the right arm and leg. The single laser boiled armor from the
left leg by undershooting the rising torso.

Kai could only use the right-side weaponry on his *Penetrator* without chancing a hit on Galen's *Crusader*. Galen
smiled as he saw the *Penetrator* thrust his right arm forward
and the large laser beam shoot out. The coruscating light
spear vaporized the last of the armor over the *Stalker*'s boxy
right shoulder and melted away internal support structures.
One of the smaller pulse lasers pumped its energy into the
same hole, letting a hail of half-melted bits of metal fall
through the opening.

Only one of the other two pulse lasers hit, but it burrowed
in through the 'Mech's ruined right flank. The wound blossomed white on the IR scan, telling Galen the fusion engine's shielding had taken damage. *He'll run hot for as long
as he runs.* The MechWarrior shook his head. *That won't be
long.*

The tremendous pressure generated by Edenhoffer's maneuver stressed beyond all tolerance the few remaining structural supports in his *Stalker*'s right side. Screaming like an animal in pain, the metal gave way as the 'Mech tried to complete its turn and plant its right leg on the ledge. The impact drove the *Stalker*'s hip straight up through its shoulder, then ripped it free. The left foot lost all traction on the ledge and slipped out into the air above the crevasse. The *Stalker*'s body hit the ground hard enough for Galen to feel the tremors in his cockpit, then slowly began to slide toward the abyss.

It would have gone over, too, but the 'Mech's right leg flopped over and on top of the barrel-shaped torso. The added weight pinned the broken 'Mech in place. The *Stalker* lay there, motionless, smoke billowing out of the gaping hole in its right side, like an animal too exhausted and too wounded to even think of escape.

Galen kept his cross hairs on the downed 'Mech as he keyed his microphone. "What do you think, Ace?"

"I think we won, Deuce." Galen heard Kai laugh heartily. "And I don't think anyone else is going to bother you for the rest of your time here."

22

Even though he feared it made him look like a besotted fool, Galen couldn't help but have a huge grin on his face. Sitting in Kai's alcove in Valhalla, with Katrina seated beside him, he felt like the king of the world as they watched a holovid replay of Ishiyama workers prying an irate Victor Vandergriff from his battered *Goliath*. *I'm alive, we won, and the Duchess seems to be happy with both of those facts.*

"I don't think I've ever really seen myself in combat before, well, not like that, anyway." Galen poured more Timbiqui Dark into his mug, letting the beer form a thick head. "I've seen shots of me in battle ROMs, but never like this."

Kai nodded and slowly rotated his wine glass by manipulating the stem. "Not many battlefields have the number of camera angles as these arenas. Ishiyama is very good, and their directors are great at cutting to the next angle at precisely the right time. The fight actually starts about ten minutes before any 'live' images are available. It allows the directors and editors to put together a cohesive package without having the combatants stop for advertisement time-outs."

"I hope the fight we put on was a good one."

Katrina smiled at both of them. "It was, very good. I don't like these fights, especially when good friends are involved, but others in the DeLon box seemed very pleased." She wrinkled her nose up in a sign of distaste. "Well, not Ryan, of course, but that's his problem. But I was thrilled, too." Her voice trailed off into a husky purr that made Galen blush.

Kai nodded and sipped his wine. "Fuh Teng said it went very well, Galen. You've gotten a lot of praise for that daring jump over Edenhoffer's *Stalker*. Not many pilots would have had the guts to do that."

"Guts?" Galen shook his head. "It was that or die. Not much of a choice."

"Really?" Kai arched an eyebrow at him. "Most pilots I know would have balked at jumping onto a seven-meter-wide ledge in front of a speeding *Goliath*."

"But . . ." Galen closed his mouth and thought for a second. "Well, when you put it like that, I guess the LZ was a bit narrow and a tad warm, but I expected you'd finish Vandergriff off, as you did."

Kai looked over at Katrina. "Do me a favor and take him away from here. I don't need the competition for the Championship. Anyone who would describe that landing zone as 'a bit narrow and a tad warm' is a contender."

"We'll leave after you successfully defend your title," Katrina said, winking at Galen. "If you lose he'll want to avenge you."

Kai laughed sincerely. "He could do it now. That Apprentice ticket became a Class Six license with his win. I'd be happy to have him in my stable, but I doubt I could pay him enough to stay here."

Galen was about to thank Kai for the compliment when a hand shoved the alcove's curtain roughly aside. The violence of the action prompted the thought that Vandergriff or Edenhoffer had come to continue with fists what they failed to do in their 'Mechs. That idea died as a man in the red robes of a ComStar demi-Precentor filled the opening.

Kai looked up at the man. "Can I help you, Precentor?"

The ComStar agent shook his head then looked directly at Katrina. "Duchess Katrina Steiner-Davion?"

"Y-yes," she replied, the tremor in her voice no doubt prompted by the stern expression on the man's face.

"I have a holodisk for you, one you will likely wish to view in private." He pulled the disk from inside his robe. "It is confidential and concerns your brother."

Tharkad
District of Donegal, Federated Commonwealth

The sensation of déja vu hit Victor like a hammer as the ComStar official entered his office. He expected it to be a holodisk of the fight on Solaris, but even Galen and Kai going down to defeat couldn't have brought such a serious expression to the woman's face. The last time he had anticipated the message of a ComStar official, it was when someone brought him news of his mother's death. That was one night he had no desire to relive again. *Something must be very wrong.*

Victor's guess was confirmed when he realized the Precentor wore the robes accorded an off-duty member of the ComGuards. They looked similar enough to the garb worn by normal ComStar couriers that no one would have noticed the difference as she passed by. She wore her black hair longer than most MechWarriors, and her petite figure wouldn't normally have marked her as a warrior, but Victor's own small size had taught him to look beyond initial impressions.

"Precentor III Andra McGwire, Highness." She stood at attention in front of his desk and snapped a salute. "The Precentor Martial sends his regards."

Victor returned the salute and waved her to a chair, giving himself time to think. *The Precentor Martial and I have never met, but my mother always spoke highly of him, as if there were some bond between them.* "Please convey my best wishes back to him."

"As you wish, sir." She remained standing. "You are expecting the holodisk from the Kai Allard-Liao/Galen Cox fight, were you not?"

"Yes I was." Victor brought his chin up. "I wouldn't have expected a member of the ComGuards to bring it to me, however. Is there a problem with it?"

"With the battle, no. I shall not spoil it for you . . ."

"Go ahead. I'll watch it when I have time."

"Your friends demolished the opposition." Her expression eased ever so slightly. "Duke Ryan Steiner's fighters were humiliated and both the opposition 'Mechs were heavily damaged. The fight cost Ryan dearly in both prestige and money."

"Very good." Victor wanted to leap from his chair and laugh aloud, but the expression on McGwire's face kept him firmly rooted to the spot. "There is more."

"I am afraid so, Highness." She removed a holodisk from inside of her robe. "This contains the fight and more."

"More?"

"Late last night your brother Peter was mobilized to pursue members of the Free Skye Militia. They had been reported taking refuge in a little hamlet called Bellerive."

Victor frowned. "A religious community, I know it."

"When your brother arrived, his lance immediately encountered hostile SRM fire coming from the steeple of the church in the middle of town." She motioned toward the holovision monitoring system in the corner of the room. "If I may."

"Please."

She walked over and slid the disk into the viewer. Victor used the remote control on his desk to power the device up. As McGwire backed away from the screen, Victor frowned. "That looks like a broadcast from Solaris VII. Is that the start of Galen's fight?"

"It is, Highness." She glanced over at him. "If you please, hit the mute button, then the menu button, then ninety-nine."

Victor did as he was told, but before he could tell her the menu had no option ninety-nine, the screen changed. It showed a nighttime scene of a small village in a wooded river valley. On the far side he saw a 'Mech silhouette itself on the crestline—a move that earned a frown from Victor because it placed the 'Mech in immediate danger from below—and raise one of its arms. *JagerMech skylining itself. Just like Peter.*

The *JagerMech* fired one salvo from the larger of its two autocannons, and the church steeple crumpled and fell. As it hit the ground, the whole village exploded in a sea of golden flame.

"My God, what happened?" Victor hit the pause button, freezing Bellerive's pyre as flames reached for the stars. "An autocannon couldn't have triggered that."

"The Precentor Martial agrees with the assessment, which is why I have showed this to you." McGwire's voice dropped in volume, yet rose in intensity. "What I will tell you now will be denied if it is ever brought up in private, and openly denounced as Davion deception if mentioned publicly. You will see that to do either would be foolish and useless, so I trust whatever sanctions my superiors would wish to impose upon you will be left undiscovered."

Victor sat back in his chair and folded his arms across his chest. "I understand."

"Good. It is readily apparent to anyone who understands BattleMechs that a single shot from a *JagerMech* could not have caused that conflagration. Obviously, the hamlet of Bellerive was rigged to explode and was probably detonated remotely. It may have been done by the camera crew who recorded this holovid of the incident. We do not know."

The woman from ComStar clasped her hands behind her back. "ComStar has had investigators on site and a preliminary report indicates that everyone in Bellerive was killed. We put the death toll at approximately 550 people. We cannot say if there were more or less there, and any remains will have been incinerated beyond recognition or classification."

"As would any traces of explosives, detonation devices, or other things that might implicate the Free Skye Militia in this," Victor cut in. "And, because Bellerive was known to be hostile to me, the logical conclusion is that I had my brother employ some secret weapon to wipe out the whole settlement." He slammed his fist onto his desktop. "And there's no way to prove it's not true, which means this holovid will send Skye into full-scale rebellion!"

"It would, Highness, if it were distributed."

Victor's eyes narrowed. "What are you saying?"

"Whoever produced this video decided to hoist you on your own petard, Highness." McGwire gave him a sly smile that he at once loved and mistrusted. "They digitized the holographic record of Bellerive's destruction into a computer system that attempted to marry it to the Allard-Liao/Cox fight. You have seen how that works here—only those who know how to program their viewers to pick up the sidecar information can get it, but they can copy it onto a regular holodisk and make it available to anyone else who wants it.

"However, they attempted to send it through ComStar linked to the aforementioned fight. We picked it up when an acolyte noticed that the fight package had come in at one transmission length, but would be going out at something roughly 20 percent greater than that. He located the sidecar information and, because it was of a military nature, presented it to the Precentor Martial. Anastasius Focht correctly pointed out that because the sidecar was attached to a program you were paying to have distributed, it was up to you to decide whether you wished the original or the adulterated version to be distributed."

Victor sat back, steepling his fingers. "You bring the information to me not as a report of ComStar's discovery of a spy network, but merely as evidence of tampering with a message of mine. You allow me to quash it without involving yourself in politics. Very good, Precentor.'

"Do I take it that you do not wish the adulterated version to go out?"

Inspiration struck and Victor smiled. "I have a better idea, actually." He opened the central drawer of his desk and pulled out the holodisk copy of the interview the student had sent him. "I think we should substitute this for the footage of Bellerive. I'm sure those who expected something special will enjoy it."

"The Fox bred true."

In at least one of his children. Victor frowned. "But, tell me, how is it that I learn of this from ComStar before I hear of it from my brother?"

"Your brother sent out two messages. One went up through the chain of command . . ."

"And was stopped no doubt by that idiot Richard."

"His office did receive it, yes." McGwire nodded carefully. "The other message was of a personal nature and went to your sister, Duchess Katrina."

"Her name is Katherine." Victor frowned. "Is there much of this sidecar stuff going on in your message traffic?"

"It is not unknown, nor illegal unless covertly joined to a message for which someone else pays." The Precentor shrugged. "I understand an audit has been undertaken of such things, but it is well outside my area of concern."

"And you have no way of stopping the distribution of physical copies of this holovid." *Preventing broadcast of it will slow the distribution, but won't stop it.* "It can't be stopped, can it?"

"No, Highness, that would be almost impossible." She shook her head. "The images you have seen here will get out, but at a much slower rate of speed, to be sure. Were it possible to stop direct copy duplication and distribution, the entertainment industry would not be constantly lobbying you to strengthen the laws against piracy."

"Yes, that's it!" Victor stood and clapped his hands. "I can have my people dummy up titles and information that will make that footage look like an advertisement for a holovideo drama. I could even fund the development of such a project—the people at Virtual World Entertainment would do it quickly and well. Ryan's people would end up being branded frauds because it could be claimed they just stripped the overlays from the images to fake the footage. The only way they could claim it was real would be to admit having destroyed the village."

McGwire nodded appreciatively. "It appears to be a workable plan, Highness. I will leave you to it."

"Thank you, Precentor." Victor came around from behind his desk and shook her hand. "Please, tell the Precentor Martial I am in his debt."

Solaris City, Solaris VII
Tamarind March, Federated Commonwealth

Though he would have preferred to be nowhere near the front of the room, Galen Cox took his place behind and to the right of the podium to which Katrina moved. The bright lights put in place by the media nearly blinded him, but he wouldn't let himself look down or away. He knew the people in the audience, and those who would later watch holovids of the event, would be observing him to see if he squirmed or shied away as Katrina delivered her message.

Katrina placed note cards on the podium and adjusted the microphone before her. Galen knew she had memorized the whole speech, but he had helped her prepare the cards in the wee hours of the morning. He was confident she would not falter, but Katrina was obviously leaving nothing to chance.

"I would like to thank you members of the media for coming here on such short notice. I have a statement to make. I will take no questions afterward." She cocked her head slightly forward in a gesture that Galen recognized as meaning she would brook no resistance to her intended plan.

"It struck me last night," she began slowly, "that I have been in shock since the death of my mother. You all recall it—a nation wept when a terrorist's bomb ripped the Archon apart. You have seen holovideo of it, I am certain, and know how horrifying it was to see her life snuffed out.

"I have labored in this state of shock to support my brother, Victor, as he attempts to take over for our mother. He is Hanse Davion's rightful heir, loyal son to our mother, and as much a son of the Lyran state as any other man born and schooled on Tharkad. I had thought that those who opposed him did so out of some misguided impression that his ambition had contributed to my mother's death. As I said then and reiterate now, Victor is blameless in that crime. I would stake my life on that fact, and I have done so by agreeing to place *our* nation in his hands."

Her left hand delicately brushed a wisp of golden hair from her eyes. "I would have remained in shock except for several things that have conspired to wake me from it. The time I have spent traveling with Kommandant Galen Cox has opened my eyes to everyday life within the Federated Commonwealth. Until I had traveled with him to help out in the aftermath of the earthquake on Ginestra or had attended the memorial services for the Kell Hounds on Arc-Royal I had not realized how insulated from reality my life really is.

"Second and equally important was the Free Skye Militia's attempt to murder my brother Peter. You all know of my brother. The most warlike thing he has done in his time in the militia is to protect helpless animals against cruel poachers.

"Peter is as unpretentious a man as exists in the Inner Sphere, yet hateful people target him for destruction because of his genetic heritage. They strike at him as if his death were the solution to a problem that cannot be solved in any other way. They are quite simply and clearly wrong. Misguided, misled, and woefully *wrong*."

Katrina half-turned and smiled back at Galen before continuing. "Last night I watched Galen and Kai Allard-Liao fight against two warriors from Duke Ryan Steiner's Skye Tigers stable. Though the battle was a contest of skill between highly trained and experienced warriors, others have tried to make it so much more. I heard men exclaim that if

Victor won his other battles as well as he won this one there would be no Skye Rebellion left to speak of.

"*Victor* did not fight last night. Galen and Kai were *not* his surrogates. The other two fighters did not substitute for Duke Ryan. They fought over a point of honor that had nothing to do with politics, yet their battle was reduced to a coup for my brother or defeat for Duke Ryan. This is nonsense and, yet, this was the third thing that brought me out of my shock."

She took a deep breath and used the silence to draw her audience more deeply in. Even though Galen knew what was coming next, he found himself leaning forward in anticipation.

"I have neglected my duties—no, my responsibilities—as far as the people of the Federated Commonwealth are concerned. For this I apologize. Yes, my mother's tragic murder was quite a burden to bear, but I should have shouldered it more stoutly and should have borne it with more strength. I owe you more than I have given, which means now that I will labor tirelessly to repay you.

"I hereby call upon Duke Ryan to use his vast influence within the Isle of Skye to bring an end to the riots and bloodshed terrorizing the worlds of Skye. No one should have to fear having a child slain by a madman's bomb nor their business burned in riots. Duke Ryan should remember that we are a civilized people and can settle our differences in other ways."

Galen saw her eyes tighten in profile. "I likewise call upon my brother Victor to help ease the tensions in the area. We all know there is fighting on Glengarry, but he must protect against that conflict spreading. I wish him to return control of the militias to the local governments and I charge them with the duty of maintaining the civil order. Blood in the streets stains everyone and murder in the name of liberty is thinly disguised tyranny.

"Both Victor and Duke Ryan are proud, intelligent, and headstrong men. In knowing one so well I know the other. I open my hands to both and offer to mediate their differences. I will guarantee that no reasonable grievance will go without redress, and I vow no crime will go unpunished. I offer myself as the buffer between ambition and the people it would oppress."

Katrina's head came up. "This is what I was born to do, and it is the job I demand to be allowed to complete. Each citizen who dies takes a piece of my heart with him. I will allow no one to destroy me or my people."

= 23 =

Even with the years he had devoted to self-discipline, Duke Ryan Steiner had to struggle mightily to keep his temper in check. He stared one last time at Victor's smiling face on the holovision viewer, then mashed a finger down on the remote button that killed the power. *Oh, that I could eliminate him so easily.*

Ryan looked at Hanau and snarled. "What happened? That wasn't supposed to be an interview with Victor!"

Hanau looked stricken. "I don't know. I set up your distribution network and worked out how we can sidecar messages, but I didn't actually arrange for the transmission. What was being sent?"

Newmark remained cool as ice. "We had graphic images of Davion aggression that we wanted to bind to the Cox fight."

"Graphics? How much? What was it?"

Ryan frowned angrily. "Holovid material."

"What length?"

Newmark shrugged. "Not more than ten minutes."

Hanau slumped back into his chair. "No wonder they found it."

Ryan took an odd comfort in the relief in Hanau's voice. *At least something here makes sense to someone.* "Explain."

The portly man leaned forward in his chair, his stomach stressing the buttons on his tunic. "The system I created was designed to pass coded messages. Those messages are always very short and, in computer storage terms, very small. They are smaller than most rounding errors. At the very worst they would add only a kilobyte of data to any message to which they are attached. Most often they go out unnoticed because most communications programs round up to the nearest kilobyte for billing purposes. As far as they're concerned, our messages are rounding errors."

"Graphics and holovideo data is really thick. It takes up a lot of computer space. The Cox fight weighed in at something like ten gigabytes. That includes ads and translations and the like. But that's only an approximation, you understand."

Ryan nodded. "Understood. Go on."

"Even if this holovid you tacked on were only five minutes or so, that would add about two gigabytes. You bumped the size of the packet ComStar was sending by twenty percent, which is a big enough anomaly for them to notice. They took a look and immediately asked Victor if he wanted the other signal to go out with the fight, since he was paying for the fight's transmission. He obviously substituted this message, both to confuse our people and to let us know this form of information transfer has been compromised."

Ryan's breath hissed in between clenched teeth. "This does not please me at all. The Cox fight proved to be a disaster for my fighters and made me look like a fool. Then this sidecar message is something warm and fuzzy from Victor himself."

David Hanau smiled cautiously. "I don't think any of our people will believe anything he says in this interview."

"Of course they won't, you fool. It's pap and anyone with enough brain cells to make a working synapse can see it." Ryan's nostrils flared as he sat back in his thickly padded leather chair. "The fight has done the most damage. Galen Cox comes off as a hero. He had the lightest 'Mech of all and used the most daring tactics. My people had him. They could have destroyed his 'Mech. They had his arms naked, but then they let him escape.

"Next, Katrina makes her little statement. My God, she all but accused me of being the mastermind behind the Free Skye Militia and of murdering her mother. The bitch needs to be reminded that if she wants to move into the forefront she too becomes a prime target."

Newmark's tone urged caution. "You cannot have her killed."

"Of that I am well aware. Regicide has ever made people uneasy." The duke rested his chin between the thumb and forefinger of his left hand. "Still she must be reminded that anyone who jumps into the political waters risks being attacked by sharks. She can only stay safe if she remains on the beach."

"Pity your fighters didn't kill Galen Cox in Ishiyama." Hanau shrugged. "He wouldn't be much of a symbol dead, but his death would likely have traumatized Katrina enough that she'd have retreated to lick her wounds."

Sven Newmark nodded halfheartedly. "You're probably right. She seems quite fond of him."

Well, now, there's an idea. Ryan's obsidian eyes became dark slits. "We have circulated the rumor that Galen Cox is estranged from Victor, have we not?"

Hanau nodded. "The idea has an appeal among those who think Victor killed his mother and tried to have Kai Allard-Liao killed on Alyina."

"Good. We have to modify that rumor. Point to Katrina's statement and Cox's support as proof of the distance between Galen and Victor. We should also note that Galen has Katrina under his influence and has, as she said in her statement, opened her eyes to reality. We need to drive a wedge between Victor and Galen—in appearance if not reality."

Hanau nodded. "That will be easy enough to accomplish. We'll build on what we already have. Skye is ripe for it, but it will also play in other parts of the Lyran Commonwealth. Maybe even in the Federated Suns, too, though our influence there is much less."

"How long will it take for the campaign to move past the initial stage?"

"Two weeks. By then it should have newsbyte opinion pieces and have become a topic of discussion on various talk shows. It will have begun to germinate."

"Good, very good." Ryan smiled as the plan crystallized in his mind. "In a week Kai Allard-Liao will defend his title. He will likely win and after all the hype leading up to his defending duel, there'll be a bit of a news vacuum. I think we should fill it."

Hanau smiled. "With copies of the stuff from Bellerive?"

"Yes, the Bellerive bonfire will do nicely for starters, but we'll need more."

"More?"

Ryan glanced over at Newmark. "Melissa Steiner-Davion liked flowers, as I recall."

Newmark nodded slowly. "She did indeed."

"Perhaps we can see if Cox does as well, Herr Newmark." Ryan's smile broadened as he saw a look of horror spread across David Hanau's face. "Cox will be leaving Solaris after the title fight, and we should present him a nice bouquet to send him on his way!"

Tharkad
District of Donegal, Federated Commonwealth
13 April 3056

Victor saw instantly that the rapid trip from Lyons to Tharkad had taken a lot out of Peter. Regret at not meeting his brother at the spaceport assaulted Victor but he suppressed it as remorselessly as he would have liked to put down the Free Skye Movement. *Perhaps his being fatigued will make this easier.* "Welcome home, Peter."

"Welcome is the least you can offer me, brother." The fire burning in Peter's eyes told Victor he had a fight on his hands. "Thanks very much for pulling my whole lance off Lyons. I'd never have run on my own accord, so you pull me out and make me look like a coward!"

Victor waited for Curaitis to shut the doors to his office before speaking. "Better you be thought a coward then end up a dead fool."

The controlled, quiet reply stopped Peter Davion dead in his tracks. "Choosing the greater of two evils for me, Victor? I am in your debt, but then, what happens to me is beyond my control anyway, isn't it?"

"If you think that is so, *little brother*, then why fight it?"

"Because I have responsibilities, Victor." Peter's eyes flashed, and Victor felt his own ire rising in response. "I care about my people. The members of my lance worked hard and are as good a scout lance as any in the Inner Sphere. I demand you take care of them."

"You *demand*?" Victor came around from behind his desk and steered Peter into one of the two wingbacked chairs near the holovision viewer. "I understand your concerns, Peter, but their lives are in jeopardy, as is the whole of the Isle of Skye. I have made arrangements to have them join the Kell Hounds. Morgan will take them on, no questions asked, and you know we can trust his loyalty and discretion."

"He should be damned proud to have them, too!" Peter nodded distractedly, then his head came up. "You're playing cute with me, Victor. Why should Morgan be discreet? What are you going to do?"

Victor straightened up. "Your lance is being court-martialed. The charges are reckless disregard for life, reckless endangerment."

Peter shot to his feet. "You can't do that. They had nothing to do with the village exploding. You know that, dammit, and you're marking them for the rest of their lives."

"The records will be sealed—they've already been sealed."

"With no trial?"

"What kind of trial would you want, Peter?" Victor fought to keep his anger in check. "A show trial? Would that suit you? Would you like it known throughout the Federated Commonwealth that you caused the death of some 550 people who were known to oppose me? Even if you wouldn't, I'm absolutely certain Ryan Steiner *would*—and of that I have proof. What were you thinking, Peter?"

"You would have done what I did."

"No, I wouldn't." Victor shook his head adamantly. "I would have weighed the alternatives. I would have viewed the situation against the political context."

Peter sneered down at his brother. "That wasn't part of my operational orders."

Victor tapped his brother's forehead. "That should *always* be part of your operational orders, Peter. You're a Davion, dammit!"

"I'm a *Steiner*-Davion, Victor." Peter growled, his hands balling into fists. "If you didn't want me in that situation, you shouldn't have put me there."

"That's a mistake I won't make again." Victor turned away from Peter and noticed Curaitis had been poised to take Peter down had he turned violent. "Suffice it to say your people will be taken care of. The Steiner-Davions always take care of their own."

Peter clasped his hands behind his back. "And how will you take care of me? Am I to become a mercenary, too?"

Victor shook his head slowly. "No. Once burned, twice shy. Your days in a 'Mech are over."

"What?! Over? Why? I was set up!" Peter slammed a fist into the arm of his chair hard enough to crack the wood beneath the leather. "Victor, you can't do this to me. I'm good, I'm damned good, I'm goddamn great, and you know it. I'm your brother, for God's sake."

"Which is exactly why I must do it." Victor held his voice to a calm, even tone in the vain hope his words might get through to his brother. "You and I know you were set up by the Free Skye Militia. They picked the target. They planted the explosives. They provided the tips that put your unit into the setup position. That you were the one who took the initiative to take out the steeple, well, that could have been anticipated. You're so convinced of your own importance that you'd never have allowed anyone else to do it."

"I would have given them a new church."

"Oh, *that* would have required a sell-job beyond even the most skilled Lyran merchant." Victor shook his head to stave off a shudder. "You just don't have a clue as to how deep was the pit you fell into."

"Enlighten me."

"Will you listen?" Victor allowed that to sink in for a heartbeat, then continued. "What you have not been told is that the Free Skye Militia had a holovideographer in the hills opposite your position and they made a holographic record of the whole thing."

Peter's face drained of color. "I thought our battle ROMs were the only record. I didn't pass them on to Richard, you know."

"Thank God you started thinking that night, albeit far too late to help the residents of Bellerive. Your battle ROMs provide an accurate record of the incident because they clearly show a time lag between your action and the explosions. The holovideo the Free Skye people produced is inconclusive in that matter. The FSM tried to distribute copies of their holo out into the Isle of Skye, but ComStar gave us a chance to restrict the distribution." Victor sighed wearily. "The Precentor Martial himself did that—obviously he doesn't want to see Skye secede from the Federated Commonwealth."

"So things are at status quo ante, but I'm destroyed by it anyway."

"I'm sure the prayers of the people of Bellerive are with you, brother."

Victor's sarcasm visibly stung Peter. "Victor, you can't dispossess me, not for this, not for something I didn't do."

Peter looked so forlorn that Victor almost regretted the decision. "Peter, I have no choice. If I do not, you remain a target for another tragedy like this one."

"For God's sake, Victor, I'm not going to fall for something like this again."

"Blinded by your ego, I'm surprised you've survived this long without doing something equally as stupid." Anger slowly trickled into Victor's voice. "Peter, you are a political liability. You don't seem to understand that. If ComStar hadn't stripped the holovid of your action from material we were sending out, right now I'd be forced to try you *and* your lance for crimes against humanity in a public trial. Moreover, I'd have to convict."

"You would reward the criminals for framing innocent people."

"You're Davion—Steiner-Davion—but in the Isle of Skye being Davion means you're already guilty."

"In my experience, *Victor* Davion is the only man presumed guilty there."

"And in *my* experience, Peter, you are seen as a way to embarrass *me*!"

"There it is, there's the core of it." Peter stabbed a finger in his brother's direction. "You're afraid of me. You're afraid that the people care more for me than they do you! You're afraid I'm more popular. Admit it!"

"That's ridiculous, Peter!" Victor shot up out of his chair and began to pace. "You are really insignificant in the grand scheme of things. An annoyance, yes, but not a threat. I must deal with Ryan Steiner right now, and though you only serve as a distraction, I can ill afford to have one in the way right now."

"You're lying!"

"You might wish that, but it's not so. Frankly, Peter, had Kai and Galen not destroyed Ryan's fighters on Solaris so easily, and if Katherine hadn't made her recent statement, Ryan would be in a very strong position. As it is his scheme has backfired and Katherine has him scrambling to deny ties with the Free Skye Militia. Because the Gray Death Legion is still holding its own on Glengarry, the rebellion is stalled. Had circumstances not shunted the Bellerive issue to the side, you would be looking at actual prison time for your actions there."

Peter sat on the edge of his chair, his anger no longer fully able to counter the fatigue etching lines on his young face. "Politics, Victor, is a business not fit for warriors. I *am* a warrior. You cannot dispossess me to satisfy some political gambit."

"That's the problem, Peter, you see yourself as a warrior, but you fail to realize that *everything* is politics."

Peter's eyes glazed over. "You're wrong."

"Am I, Peter? You see yourself as a warrior. I see you as a pawn. While you were in the Lyons Militia you were a very valuable pawn. The Militia meant nothing and, to be quite frank, aside from your lance, I was and *am* not now much more confident of the unit's loyalty. Your presence and the good works you did with the conservation forces there helped me immeasurably. I saw that. Ryan saw it too, which is why he had to force me to take you out of the game."

"I can't believe you would dance to a tune called by Ryan Steiner."

Victor ignored the scorn in Peter's voice. "Better that than having to leave the dance."

"You're dancing when you should be fighting."

"If that's what you think, I pray God you're never forced to sit on the throne."

"Then let's hope you open your eyes to reality soon. Remember, Victor, if you die, I am one step closer to the throne."

Victor shook his head sharply. "If *I* die, the Federated Commonwealth goes down with me."

Peter's jaw dropped open, then snapped shut. "Even I would never have imagined you were *that* arrogant, Victor."

"It's not arrogance, Peter." Victor's gray eyes narrowed. "I *am* the state, Peter. I am everyone in it. I have to feel it all, be aware of it all, so I can deal with it all. I have had to sublimate the warrior in me in order to best serve the people of the Federated Commonwealth."

"And do a disservice to me."

"Now who dabbles in arrogance?" Victor fixed his brother with a hard-eyed stare. "You may see it as a disservice, but the service I require of you is in the name of the Federated Commonwealth. That may discomfit you, but you *will* perform it."

Peter raised his chin. "If it makes sense to me, I will do it."

"You will do it without question, Peter." Victor shot a covert glance at Curaitis. "You will be briefed on what you need to know, nothing more."

"What I *need to know*?" Peter blinked incredulously. "Do you think I cannot be trusted?"

"What I think is immaterial. The Intelligence Secretariat makes those decisions."

"So the Intelligence Secretariat absolves you of responsibility?"

"Not at all."

Fire flared in Peter's eyes. "Then accept some of it, dammit! Don't keep me in the dark. How many secrets to you know, Victor?" His eyes narrowed. "Who killed our mother?"

"I don't know."

"Don't lie to me, Victor. You know something." Peter turned and looked at Curaitis. "Do you know? Tell me. I *command* it."

"Say nothing, Curaitis." Victor came around to interpose his own body between Peter and the agent. "I tell you I do not know who ordered our mother killed. If I did know, if I had *proof*, I would avenge her instantly. This I swear, Peter, on her grave and the graves of every Archon who ever sat on the throne here on Tharkad."

"That's the first truthful thing you've said today, Victor. I'm glad to know you're still capable of honesty." Peter settled back in his chair, his eyes still smoldering. "I will not be dispossessed. If I don't have a 'Mech, if I cannot perform my duties as a warrior, I might as well be dead."

"That is one solution, but I find it unacceptable."

"At this time," Peter added.

Victor took a deep breath, then sat down across from his

brother. "Look, my first assignment was to the Twelfth Donegal Guards. It wasn't where I wanted to be, but that is where our father felt I would be most useful."

"My assignment to the Lyons Skye Militia, by your very own words, was just such a post for me." Peter frowned heavily. "I deserve more. I deserve better."

"The truth or falsehood of that aside, you are not going to get a command."

"Why not? Our father placed you with the Tenth Lyran Guards and you went on to reap military glory in the war against the Clans. Why can't you place me *there*? They don't have a Steiner-Davion in their ranks and you know you'll use them when it comes time to crush the rebellion. I can lead them." Peter's voice became edged with ice. "Our father would have done that if he were still alive."

"He tried to do just that in thirty thirty-four and he made a grave mistake."

"Oh, so now *you* can decide when our father was wrong?" Peter snarled. "What is going on with you, Victor? How can you arrogate yourself so much?"

"Try another tune, Peter, and some new lyrics. This is old." Victor stabbed a finger at his brother. "I do know what I'm doing. Our father nearly lost the Isle of Skye two decades ago and, because of his action, I must now deal with the same problem all over again. I intend to end this so my children, *our* children, won't also be saddled with the same problem."

"Doubtless that is what our father intended." Peter shook his head. "How dare you presume to second-guess him?"

"I can and I will because I *learned* from our father! I learned from his mistakes." Victor pounded his right fist into his left palm. "This is a delicate game."

"And I am but a piece in it?"

"*That* fact has already been established. You'll go where I send you. You'll do what I tell you, and that will be that."

Peter forced himself down further into the padding of the chair, then folded his arms slowly. "Where, then, Highness, will your humble servant be sent? Are you going to put me in the Saint Marinus House on Zaniah so I can spend the rest of my time in prayer and meditation?"

"Considered and rejected, at this time, but I might revise my opinion. Staying there worked for Morgan Kell. Perhaps it would work for you." Victor waited until he saw the fear of exile rise in his brother's eyes, then slowly shook his head. "No, Peter, you are too good at dealing with people for me to waste you there, *and* you still attract interest because of who and what you are. Now that I've had to cut funding for Tormano Liao's Free Capella movement, Sun-Tzu Liao's *Zhanzheng de guang* is getting more adventurous and Tormano is screaming all sorts of things as a result. I am assigning you to be Tormano's liaison and military advisor. I want you to be very visible, very solicitous, and as helpful as you can be. And in all that, I want you to keep Tormano from doing *anything*."

"Tormano is a dog that growls on command and I am to be his hush-puppy."

"Hardly. You are the kennel master who will prevent him from biting anyone while inspiring him to growl more loudly." Victor nodded curtly. *And the kennel master will have a keeper all his very own. Kai will be able to settle Peter down, I hope.* "You already have a rapport with him because of your conservation work, so that is your new assignment."

"It makes Saint Marinus House look inviting."

"Perhaps. Do you really want to make the comparison?"

"No." Peter's head came up. "So, you're sending me to Solaris. Will I be allowed a 'Mech?"

Victor hesitated. "For ceremony? Yes. And I will speak to Kai so you may train with his fighters and keep current against a time when I need you in a military capacity."

"Can I fight, as Galen did?"

"No. Fighting on Solaris is a narrow alley to glory. Picking a fight with one of Ryan's fighters and attempting to duplicate Galen's feat could only go against us. If you lose . . ."

"I would not."

Victor shrugged. "That doesn't matter. Peter, stop thinking like a warrior. Political battle requires more than a 'Mech and a target-lock."

Peter slowly rose from his chair. "Is this a life sentence?"

"That will depend on factors far beyond your control." Victor wanted to tell Peter he was sorry to have to give him this assignment, but that would only show a weakness he couldn't afford. "I've had your things transferred over to another DropShip. You are leaving immediately."

That took Peter completely by surprise. "Do I have time to visit our mother's grave?"

Victor hesitated, then nodded. "Yes, yes, of course, but then you're off. You must get to Solaris as quickly as possible."

"Why?"

"Kai is defending his title, and I want you there with Tormano." Victor smiled. "I need you highly visible, and that is the best exposure we could hope for."

"You have me, Victor. I will do what is required of me." Defiance glittered in Peter's eyes for a second, then faded. "But I won't forget what you have done to me here."

Peter stalked sullenly from the room and Curaitis closed the door behind him. "Highness, your brother may prove to be difficult."

"Agreed. I will send a message to Kai to ask him to watch over Peter." Victor returned to his desk and dropped into the chair. Tapping the screen of his computer, he looked up at Curaitis. "I gather from this report that the only thing keeping Joshua Marik alive is life support."

The Intelligence agent nodded. "Even that will fail. The cancer is out of control."

Victor nodded mechanically. "We have no choice but to institute Gemini. We start by telling Marik that Joshua has had a stroke?"

"It covers alterations in speech, memory, and personality."

"Do it, and let Joshua die naturally."

"Understood."

Victor sat back in his chair. "I know you'll advise against this next thing, but I want it done. Send the assassin to Solaris. Put him in a safe house."

Curaitis' head came up, but his face betrayed no emotion. "Is it not premature to kill Ryan Steiner?"

"You and I know he did it. We don't have the smoking gun yet, but I want the assassin in position for the moment we get it. Ryan will make a mistake. I'm certain of it." Victor curled both hands into fists and rammed them together. "And when he does, I'll see him dead."

Solaris City, Solaris VII
Tamarind March, Federated Commonwealth

The listening device the Intelligence Secretariat had placed in Duke Ryan Steiner's office was of a variety that was very hard to detect. It consisted of three parts and had been assembled in such a way that uncovering it would require synchronicity and luck in equal proportions. It could only provide audio, but that had been deemed sufficient because all of Ryan's visiphone traffic was tapped and two of his household servants were in the Intelligence Secretariat's employ.

The device's pickup microphone was a metal cylinder no bigger than a pencil, and had been inserted into one of the wall studs. It picked up the vibrations of conversation and transmitted them along two wires to a fully shielded recording device. It was set low on the wall, near an electrical outlet, so that any normal magnetic fields would cover any trace activity from the device. It could store twenty-four hours of audio. By carefully tracking Ryan's time in the office, the agents knew when the device was full, and could schedule a purge to recover the information.

The output device had been built into a window casing. Its job was to pump the audio data out in a high-speed pulse that would make the big front window vibrate. Ultraviolet lasers directed at the window would read the vibrations and a computer would collect the data for later transcription. A sonic pulse shot against the window would start, stop, and pause the output device in order to halt information collection if someone entered the office.

The audio information underwent encryption and a sixty-to-one compression, which meant that it took a minute to collect an hour's worth of coded data. As that data was sent out, the device purged its memory and was ready to collect more. This was the trickiest part of the device because information lost could never be recovered again. It was deemed a necessary evil, however, because the purging meant that even if someone discovered the device, Ryan would have no idea how much data had been recovered.

While the output was vulnerable to vibrations from street noises, sampling the sound during the collection process gave the Intelligence Secretariat the data they needed to eliminate those sounds from the final records. Once the background noise had been filtered out, the sound was decrypted and decompressed, then filtered again to separate all the voices. Each voice was checked against voiceprints of Ryan's known associates so the IS could track who was given what duties or entrusted with what missions. From that information they built up a chart of Ryan's organization.

When agents came to harvest the last twenty-four hours of data, they had no way of knowing it contained Ryan's order to Newmark to set up Galen Cox's assassination. Though that would not have been the smoking gun Victor so dearly wanted to prove Ryan's complicity in his mother's death, the man's willingness to have someone murdered would have helped confirm that he was capable of assassination.

The agents had set themselves up in the usual position and were using an ultrasonic whistle to start the feedback from the unit. As the sound resonated against the glass of the window, the sensitive microphone in the wall picked it up. It relayed the sound to the recording device, which instantly recognized it. Then it began to send material out along a fiber optic cable, which ended at the feedback device located at the window casement. What played out first was a check-sequence that let the agents know if the lasers were reading things correctly. They were, so a second whistle started the machine pumping out the data it had gathered.

The check sequence had told the agents the device was full, so they nervously prepared for a half-hour spent in their listening posts. A broadcast device could have pumped the information out far more quickly, but it would also have been easier to detect. By using ultrasonics and ultraviolet lasers, their collection method was all but invisible. And, at 3:00 A.M., the chances of anyone entering the office were nil.

The agents kept an eye on the neighborhood and were pleased that it looked completely normal. The rain-slicked streets had oily puddles spreading out from clogged gutters. People shuffled in and out of shadows, generally keeping to themselves. Most crossed the street so as not to trod on the unblemished sidewalk in front of Duke Ryan's newly renovated brownstone for fear that this very powerful man might take notice of them and adversely alter their miserable lives.

All stayed away from the brownstone except for one man.

The agents smiled as they first heard his voice. They had taken to calling him the Screamer, and believed him to be utterly mad. Like clockwork the Screamer would walk down the street in front of Duke Ryan's home. The man, obviously a schizophrenic with paranoid tendencies, tended to rant and rave at himself, alternating between two voices. His arguments were incomprehensible and remarkable only in that both sides seemed to be losing.

The agents remembered him because one of the tech boys had asked who were the two men arguing in the street. That had made all the field agents burst out with laughter, indelibly burning the Screamer's dirty, hunched silhouette into their minds. The incident was one of the few times when the tech boys had made a mistake within earshot of the field agents and the field agents were determined not to let them forget it. As a result they secretly rejoiced when the Screamer made his sojourn during their collection runs.

Their unofficial mascot would betray them on this night. Locked in a battle with his inner demons, the Screamer picked up a stone from the street and flung it with all his might at the lair of the individual he knew to be the anti-Christ. He did not know Duke Ryan Steiner lived there, but had he, the Screamer would gladly have awarded him the title of anti-Christ. All he did realize was that the building seemed out of place in the neighborhood and, in a moment of lucidity, he realized that breaking a window would bring it down into the gutter with the rest of the buildings on the street.

The rock shattered the window being used for collection. The agents doing the run remained shocked for a second or two, then one of them had the presence of mind to blow the whistle that stopped the output. The sound pickup in the room did register the whistle and stop the recording, but the whole incident had trimmed a full ten minutes from the data in the device.

The loss of ten seconds of compressed data was not deemed important. And it would be another week and a half before anyone could have even guessed what the ten-minute gap had contained, and then another day would pass after that before anyone would link the gap to Galen Cox's assassination. By then, however, the information that could have

stopped the plot before it began was as effective as closing
a barn door after the horses had all fled.

Sven Newmark's caution provided a second chance to
save Galen's life. Newmark assumed that Davion intelligence had spies within the Steiner household and taps on the
communications links. To contact the broker needed to target
Galen for assassination, he left the house where glaziers
were replacing all the windows with bulletproof glass and
walked to a nearby transit station. He checked numerous
times to see if he was being followed. Detecting no surveillance, he proceeded to a bank of visiphones and placed a
call.

Newmark placed his hand over the visiphone lens to prevent the person answering the phone from seeing who he
was. "Good morning, I am looking for the florist."

The Asian man in the window nodded his head. "He is
out. May I take a message?"

"We require a bouquet delivered to il Capo after the title
defense." Newmark kept his voice level, never betraying the
fact he was ordering a man's death. His reference to il Capo
came from the nickname Ryan had decided to use for Galen
Cox. Cox's rank, Kommandant, could have been rendered as
il Comandante in Italian, but il Capo served just as well and
Ryan liked the way it made Cox sound like a criminal.
Sergei Chou, whose people had already been engaged to
provide covert surveillance of Katrina and Galen, understood the reference and had used it in various reports on
their activities.

"Understood. Five thousand C-bills."

"Done. Charge the Moonbeam account," Newmark instructed him. Moonbeam was one of a dozen different
shadow corporations Ryan maintained for making payoffs.
Chou would have his computer people break into the account and loot it, which would permit Ryan to deny complicity in the crime if the account were ever traced back to
him.

Newmark broke the connection and returned to the house.
A recording of his conversation, made by the Solaris City
Constabulary through its taps on Chou's lines, were down-
loaded into the Constabulary computers. The machines made
a transcript of the conversation, then read it over for key
words. The florist reference went right by it, but it picked up

on the term "il Capo" precisely for the petty criminal over-tones that Ryan Steiner liked so much.

The machine shunted the recording and report to the Organized Crime division of the Constabulary. The voices on it were immediately checked against known organized crime figures. The computers identified Chou instantly, but came up blank on Newmark. The computers queued the recording to be checked against Known Criminal, Media, Celebrity and, finally, Political voiceprints. The first three checks, each of which took a full day, came up blank because Sven Newmark had never made a public statement that had been recorded on Solaris.

The last check, Political, would correctly identify his voice, but it would take an additional four days to be completed because the technicians were so preoccupied with trying to figure out how to reconstruct the data sent out at the instant the Screamer's stone hit the window of Duke Ryan Steiner's office.

Solaris City, Solaris VII
Tamarind March, Federated Commonwealth
16 April 3056

Peter Steiner-Davion had difficulty deciding what amazed him more: having traveled from Tharkad to Solaris in three days or Victor's highhandedness. He had towered over Victor even when they were children, and it had always irked Victor that people took him for the younger brother because of it. Peter thought Victor should long since have grown out of his jealousy, but he realized that Victor's insecurities must run deep to the bone.

Peter never had and never would avoid a fight that must be fought. He could take care of himself, and because of his sheer size, had never been forced to learn to be as sneaky as Victor. As far as Peter was concerned, they could settle their differences in an honorable way, on the field of battle. Victor, however, would know that he couldn't win, so his only choice was to humiliate his younger brother.

Peter felt betrayed by Victor, yet vowed he would not be broken by his bother's actions. *Assigning me a role as Tormano's handler is a slap in the face, but it was also a big mistake for Victor. He missed it, and I shall profit from it.* The mistake, as Peter saw it, was to have given his younger brother a public platform on which to perform, a platform that was too far away for Victor to easily exert any control.

Peter laid out the conflict and attacked it in his mind like a long campaign. His first step would be to identify and isolate himself from Victor's agents on Solaris. Security men he could do nothing about, but they would follow his orders regardless. They were not a problem. It was people like Kai Allard-Liao and Galen Cox who would be.

Second, he had to perform all his duties with Tormano perfectly, giving Victor no cause for reproach. By exerting a subtle influence over Tormano, Peter knew he could push the man to do things Peter wanted done. Then, in his role as Tormano's keeper, he could claim glory or punish failure as he saw fit. People would see him in a leadership role, which is what he wanted when he next confronted Victor.

"Peter!"

A smile involuntarily spread across Peter's face as his sister Katrina ran toward him in the spaceport's VIP lounge. He dropped his shoulder bag and swept her up in a hug that lifted her off her feet. She gave out a most undignified yelp, which dissolved quickly into laughter that he shared with her. "Hello, Kath . . . Katrina. I'll get used to it yet."

He set her back down on her feet and she danced back a step or two. "You look wonderful, Peter. I'm so happy you're here."

Peter's smile began to disintegrate at the corners of his mouth. "Your presence takes the sting out of my exile."

Katrina looked at him with surprise in her eyes. "Only the sting? I must be losing my touch. Aren't you glad to see me?"

"Yes, of course I am. As always . . ." Peter frowned as he tried to decide how much he would tell her, then realized he could never keep secrets from Katherine—Katrina. "I'm not pleased about losing my command."

"Of course not." Katrina turned and pulled a man in a uniform forward. "Peter, you and Kommandant Cox have met, haven't you?"

Peter shook the man's hand, then noticed how easily his sister took Cox's arm. "Yes, good to see you again, Kommandant. I congratulate you on your victory in the arena. I saw a replay on my way in."

"Not the sort of example an officer of the AFFC should be setting, I'm afraid." Cox smiled self-consciously.

Katrina gave Galen a peck on the cheek. "Be a dear and get Peter's bag there." She released Galen's arm and took Peter's hand in hers. "Do come with me, Peter, because it's truly wonderful that you're here. This is definitely a step up from the Skye Militia."

"It is?" Peter frowned. *You're not a MechWarrior, Katrina. You can't know how it feels to be dispossessed of that which you were born to have.* "I would prefer any position that permitted me to pilot a 'Mech."

Katrina laughed throatily. "I'm certain you would. Kommandant Cox thought that when first ordered to escort me. But his mind has changed, has it not, Galen?"

Cox shouldered the bag. "Of course, Duchess." He winked at Peter. "I still manage to get into a 'Mech from time to time, though."

"And he's not above bringing chaos to a social gathering to do it, either." Katrina rolled her eyes, then squeezed Peter's hand. "Though you may not be in a 'Mech, your work as Tormano's Liaison Officer is important. It elevates you from militia officer to a player on the Inner Sphere stage.'

"Anyone could have been assigned to do it." Peter frowned deeply. "I could record a holovid tape and have a loop set up for my visiphone to do the job. 'Yes, Mandrinn, that sounds very interesting. I will take it under advisement and report back to you, but for now, do nothing.'" Peter purposely shielded his intentions from Galen, but he knew Katrina saw through his deception.

Katrina smiled knowingly. "What, and deprive Tormano of the wise counsel he so desperately needs? Listening and making decisions will be good training for you."

"The only training I need is in a simulator."

"Oh, has someone invented an Archon simulator while we've been away from Tharkad?" Katrina shivered and Peter threw an arm around her shoulders in a reflexive hug. "Victor is not without enemies and they might destroy him. In that case . . ."

Peter looked down at her. "In that case, you would become the Archon Princess."

"I could govern, Peter, but I cannot *lead*." The emphasis she placed on the words did not escape him. "It may be that the responsibilities of the Federated Commonwealth are so great that we require two rulers—just as it was when our mother and father were still alive."

And if Victor had his way, Omi Kurita would govern beside him. Peter nodded to Katrina. "Now you give me the same sort of wise advice you expect me to give Tormano."

"It is in your nature to defend and destroy, and it is in mine to heal and help."

"I hope, if the time comes, we will know all we need to do our jobs." Peter caught her frown and bowed his head. "Victor is keeping secrets from us."

Katrina stopped and turned to face him in the corridor leading away from the docking bay lobby. She did it carefully, concealing her surprise, but he felt her shudder as she pulled away from him. "What kind of secrets?"

He looked past her toward Galen. "Family secrets."

Galen hesitated for a moment, then nodded. "I feel the urge to buy a pack of mints." He headed off toward a concourse gift shop. "Anyone else need anything?"

"No, thanks." Katrina smiled after him, then looked up at Peter. "What secrets?"

"He knows who killed our mother."

"What!" Katrina's hand came up to cover her mouth. *"Who?"*

"I don't know. He wouldn't tell me." Peter shrugged helplessly, suddenly angry with himself for having built things up so much without being able to deliver for her. "He said he didn't have proof, so he couldn't act, but he said he would when he did."

"I see . . ." Katrina woodenly slipped her arm back through Peter's and guided him over to where Galen stood studying a memorial plaque mounted on the spaceport wall. As they approached, Katrina's movements again became fluid and a smile returned to her face. "Interesting reading?"

Galen nodded. "It struck me that I used to watch the fights from Solaris when I was a kid, but never expected to be here—especially not fighting here. It's incredible how things never turn out the way you expect."

"If they did, that would be really *incredible*." Peter aped his sister's smile, slowly growing used to the plastic feeling it gave his face.

"You're right. All set to go?"

Katrina linked her other hand through Galen's. "There, I have the two most handsome men on Solaris as my escorts. I couldn't be happier."

"Let's hope it's contagious," Peter grumbled lightly.

"It will be, you'll see. Now, Peter, you've got just enough time to go to The Armored Fist and unpack, then we go to dinner and afterward to watch some fights at Ishiyama in the box of Thomas DeLon." Katrina pulled at him when he slowed down to protest. "And don't argue, Peter. It won't do any good. You're a Steiner and this is an order."

Peter laughed, then shot Galen a sidelong glance. "She hasn't changed at all." He roughly sketched a salute at his sister and smiled graciously. "I hear and obey, Archon Katrina. I am a slave to your whims."

The assassin knew from the holovision feeds he watched from Solaris City that Peter Steiner-Davion had arrived at the spaceport barely four hours before he did. That information impinged on him only because it added another possible target to his list. He dismissed Peter as a target almost immediately, however, because Victor could get rid of his brother without having to hire an assassin. All the prince had to do was send Peter on a covert mission to Glengarry, where he could make sure the Free Skye people captured and killed him.

The DropShip *Columbus* landed with no difficulties and taxied to a military hangar. A legion of Intelligence Secretariat agents ringed the place, and a group of five escorted him to a waiting limo. The assassin caught a whiff of Solaris City's moist air and smiled. *Home again, home again. I will be away from my captors soon enough.*

The IS agents hustled him to a darkened limousine and drove through the city in an aimless pattern the assassin thought was intended to limit his ability to guess at where they would finally deposit him. Even though he could see nothing through the black windows, the assassin could have told them not to bother with the little game because he knew they would house him in the Black Hills. Silesia would be too close to his target, and the Davionist sympathies of the people of the Black Hills would make it much easier to limit information about him.

The limo drove into an underground parking area, then the agents pulled the assassin from the vehicle and took him up into the safe house. They placed him in a spartan room with minimal furnishings and a built-in mirror that he readily assumed was two-way. The assassin smiled at his own reflection, then sat down on the edge of the cot.

A tall man with hard, icy eyes came in and dismissed the

other agents with a mere nod of his head. He waited until they had left the room, then he sat on the edge of the table with his back to the mirror. "You are here in case you are needed."

"I am always needed, sooner or later."

"I expect that is so. You will want equipment. We will supply it when your mission is determined."

The assassin smiled. "I believe I know what my mission is. I know Solaris, and I know what I will need."

"Do you?"

The assassin nodded. "It will save us time. There is a man here named Sergei Chou. He is a Capellan and you know of him because I gave you his name during my interrogation. He has access to some things I left behind here. I need a rifle."

"We will get it." The big man watched him with raptor eyes. "You will need other things."

"Your analysis of my computer's files will have highlighted one called 'SLAP.' I have to give the specifications to Chou."

The IS agent shook his head. "We will get what you need."

The assassin shrugged. "Chou knows me. He will deal with me. He'll smell you out and will run." He forced a nonchalant yawn. "Ask your prince. He will approve my request to meet with the man."

"You presume a great deal."

The assassin smiled. "I know he needs me. He will not gainsay me any request."

"Were I you, I would not be so confident."

"No?"

"No." The ice-eyed man paused before he opened the door. "You murdered his mother. That is something he has not forgotten. Nor is it something he is likely to forgive."

Standing in the living room of the penthouse suite in The Sun and Sword Hotel, Galen Cox looked out toward the northeast. The city's neon lights stole the night's tenebrosity, but gave it a sinister edge. In many ways the cityscape made him think of a fading dowager trying to cover her age with cosmetics and dim lights.

He half-smiled, knowing his morbid thoughts about

Solaris City only came in contrast to his mood. The evening had gone fairly well. He and Peter had taken steps toward tolerating each other, though Peter obviously thought Galen was little more than a spy in his brother's service. The fact that Katrina trusted Galen completely had won Peter's respect, and as the evening wore on, the young man began to relax.

Katrina seemed to have used Peter's reaction to him as some sort of a litmus test. Galen and Katrina had been growing closer with each passing day, their evenings since the fight filled with emotion and heart-to-heart conversations. Galen reveled in Katrina's openness, yet his knowledge that they could never be together held him back. He felt confused, but wonderfully so, and not a little bit afraid of what would happen that evening. He felt—he knew—things would come to a head and either proceed further than was likely to be prudent, or fall apart completely. Neither of those outcomes were ideas he could abide.

"Pfennig for your thoughts, Galen." Katrina stole up gently behind him and rested her chin on his shoulder, then wrapped her arms around him. "It looks so decadent and corrupt."

"Save yourself the pfennig because you've got my thoughts for free." He disengaged himself from her arms, regretting the separation immediately. "Duchess, we need to talk."

"We do that quite a bit already, Galen." She smiled playfully, then glanced down almost shyly. When her eyes came back up he sensed a change in her. "Yes, we probably should."

Taking his right hand in both of hers, she led him over to the couch that had been the site of their nocturnal conversations. "I want to thank you for everything over this last week, Galen," she said, patting the seat beside her. "I couldn't have survived it without you. If not for you, I would have exploded or broken down."

He shook his head. "That's not true. You are much stronger than that, Katrina. Had I not been here, you would have coped."

"Maybe so, Galen, but you made it easier for me." She reached up and caressed his face. "I feel so close to you,

I . . ." Katrina leaned forward and kissed him full on the mouth.

Galen returned her passion in kind, then regained control of himself. He took firm hold of her shoulders and gently eased her back away from him. "Wait, Duchess, wait."

"No, Galen, no. There is no rank between us." She plucked his right hand from her left shoulder and kissed his palm. "I want to hear you call me Katrina. I want to feel your caress on my face, my throat." She pressed his hand to her cheek and slowly let it slide down as her blue eyes closed.

"Katrina, Duchess, stop." Anguished frustration twisted through his words. "Please, don't make this any more difficult for me than it already is." Galen brought his hand back up to her cheek. "Please, don't do this."

"Do what, Galen? What I feel for you I've never felt for any other man." She pulled away from him and slumped on the arm of the couch. "You don't know what it is to live your life in a fishbowl. Ever since I was fourteen years old I've been matched up with every eligible bachelor from age eighteen to eighty. Politicians consider me chattal best suited to sealing alliances. Petty nobles see me as a way to make their grandchildren special. The scandal vids see me as a way to spike sales."

Her gaze flicked up at him. "When we started on this tour I expected to see the scandal vids link us. They did, but it was different this time. They weren't nasty. And everywhere we went, on every world, people seemed pleased to see you and me together. They say we make a beautiful couple, a fairy-tale couple."

Galen held his hands up. "I know. I've heard them too, but I know better than to believe them. You are incredibly beautiful and desirable. I would give anything for us to be together."

"But you push me away." She leaned forward and pressed a finger to his lips. "Let me finish, Galen. I noticed you at my father's funeral, then again when Morgan Kell retired. You struck me as a man of dignity and Victor's trust in you impressed me. Victor and I do not always see eye to eye, but he is a shrewd judge of men. You stand up to him and force him to recognize things he doesn't want to acknowledge. That takes a strength of character few men possess."

Katrina looked down. "That is a trait I would have in the man who becomes my husband."

Husband? "No, Duchess, it would never work."

"Why not?"

"I'm twelve years your senior."

"So? My father was *twenty-seven* years older than my mother."

"He was also Hanse Davion and no one could have stopped him from winning your mother."

"And I am his daughter. Do you think I will compromise any sooner than he would?" Katrina threw her head back and laughed aloud. "I'm not a little girl, Galen. I'm twenty-four and I do have a brain. You would be an excellent choice for my husband. You are a war hero who is loyal to my brother. You are from the Isle of Skye. You have won fame here on Solaris and you helped rescue Hohiro Kurita from the Clans. You even know and have fought in concert with a Khan of Clan Wolf. You are a prize, Galen, and I know more about you than just the surface material."

Katrina playfully poked him in the chest. "I have seen your heart. I know you are a thoughtful, compassionate man. You can be supportive without trying to solve my problems for me. You are considerate and kind. You work tirelessly in service to others, be it my brother or earthquake victims. You are brave and strong. You would make any woman proud to call you husband."

"This is going too fast." Galen shook his head, not even permitting himself to consider the possibilities. "I am no one, Duchess. I am not a noble."

"Perhaps not in blood, Galen, but in here you are." Again she tapped a finger against his chest. "If you want a title, I can arrange that. Victor just made Grayson Carlyle a baron. He can do that or even better for you. Would you like to be Duke of Solaris? It can be arranged. I would do that for you, Galen, if it would make you happy."

Galen felt his resistance crumbling. "And I would accept it, if bestowing a title on me would make you happy."

Katrina shook her head. "It would only make me happy if it were something you truly wanted."

"I want whatever makes *you* happy, Duchess."

"And if I tell you having you in my bed tonight would make me happy?"

Galen closed his eyes and made a decision. "I would have to tell you that it would force me to betray the trust your brother has placed in me, and that would make me very unhappy. Don't play games with me, Katrina."

"Just hearing you say my name makes me happy, Galen." She smiled radiantly. "And I will not force you to choose between Victor and me, if you will promise me something."

Galen swallowed hard. "And that is?"

"When next you see Victor, you will ask him for my hand in matrimony."

═══ 26 ═══

Solaris City, Solaris VII
Tamarind March, Federated Commonwealth
19 April 3056

It took Kai a couple of seconds to shift his attention from the 'Mech duel he was about to fight to the two men entering his dressing room. A smile followed the flash of recognition in his eyes, then he stepped forward and offered Galen his hand. "I didn't expect to see you here."

Galen shrugged. "You've been cloistered away out in Joppo all week getting ready for the match, so I figured this was my only chance to wish you good luck before the fight." He pumped Kai's arms, then half turned toward the other man with him. "Duke Peter Steiner-Davion, may I present Kai Allard-Liao?"

Kai nodded and shook Peter's hand. "We overlapped at the New Avalon Military Academy. The duke wasn't in my company, but I remember him well. I've not seen you since your mother's funeral."

"Good to see you again, Kai." Peter nodded rather formally. "I, too, wish you good luck tonight."

Peter's words were proper, but his tone was a strange mixture of apathy and mild hostility, and he held his body very stiffly. *I'm obviously missing something,* Kai thought.

"Thank you," he said aloud. "You will be in my box for the fight, yes? And then, tomorrow night, you will be my guest at the Sesame Inn for dinner?"

Peter glanced at Galen briefly, then nodded. "If I must, I mean, I would be honored. Forgive me, please, I am still getting acclimated."

"I understand." Kai glanced at the holovision monitor built into the dressing room wall. It showed a closeup of his box, with Katrina and Omi standing side by side in conversation. A digital counter in the corner of the screen reeled off the time until his fight. "Only half an hour left, gentlemen. So now I must go to work again. Please, consider my box another home. Fuh Teng will see to it that you have whatever you need."

"Well, again, good luck." Galen waved as he turned back toward the door. Peter looked as if he was about to take offense at the dismissal, then turned brusquely and followed Galen from the room. Kai bowed to their retreating backs, then straightened his spine so Tsen Teng could zip up the back of his cooling suit. "Tsen, go up to my box and make sure your grand uncle takes care of Peter. Have him pamper the man and, if he deems it appropriate, make sure to moderate his alcohol intake."

"*Wo dong,* Kai." The young man bowed and exited the room, leaving his master alone.

Kai preferred solitude before a fight, and Peter's presence had disturbed him. Even during his training for the match, Kai had worked as much on his mental preparedness as the physical. Because of the pressures generated by Tormano's antics concerning the fight, Kai had even absented himself to the little town of Joppo, where he had friends at a villa who were able to put him in the properly martial frame of mind. Their efforts had worked remarkably well, though Peter's actions threatened to distract him.

Peter had seemed grossly out of sorts. He and Kai had not mixed much at the New Avalon Military Academy. It was easy to attribute that to the division of classes, but Kai knew it was more than that. In those days Kai had been so unsure of himself that being around Peter and his egocentric view of the world had been downright painful to him.

Despite the strengthening of Kai's self-confidence that the war had wrought, he still felt uneasy with Peter. The duke seemed resentful of his duties on Solaris, as though he still hadn't decided whether to endure them or not. If he was dissatisfied, felt he had no purpose, no goal, Kai knew that Peter Davion was a man who could make for trouble.

Maybe Kai could help by getting the young man involved with Cenotaph in some way. Then he frowned, knowing he must clear these thoughts from his mind. They were distractions from the task at hand.

"Tonight I face Wu Deng Tang," he said to no one in particular, shaking off the strange mood. "He is worthy of my respect and my concentration, and he shall have them entirely."

Tormano Liao smiled politely as Nancy Bao Lee brought Ryan Steiner a snifter filled with a clear mixture of peppermint schnapps and grain alcohol known as a PPC. "I trust, Duke Ryan, that you will find this to your liking."

Ryan accepted the drink, but set it down on the arm of his chair without tasting it. "Yes, Mandrinn. I'm sure it will be perfect. I thank you for the invitation to join you in your box to watch this fight."

Tormano followed Ryan's gaze to the holovision screen set up in the corner of the room. It showed Peter Davion and Galen Cox joining Katrina Steiner and Omi Kurita in Kai's box. "Yes, I'll wager neither of us would have been welcome guests up there."

Ryan shrugged. "I've never seen the virtue in being a gracious loser."

"I have never seen the virtue in being a *loser*." Tormano smiled cautiously. "I do, however, see the virtue in not stealing from another or meddling in his affairs."

"Yes, quite," said Ryan. "Personally, I consider defeat merely a temporary obstacle on the road to total victory." He finally took a sip of his PPC and managed to choke down a swallow of it without too much trouble. "My compliments to your aide."

"Graciously accepted, Duke Ryan." Tormano smiled at Nancy, who returned the smile. "If you will permit me, I have a matter to discuss with you."

"Please proceed."

Tormano again looked at the holovision screen as the camera zoomed in for a close-up of Peter. "As you know, Prince Victor has given his brother Peter the assignment of liaison between the Federated Commonwealth government and my Free Capella movement."

"So I have heard." Ryan looked supremely indifferent to Victor's action. "Does this concern me?"

"I believe, my lord, that you have a certain proprietary interest in Peter. It is because of your actions that he has come here to Solaris."

Ryan leaned forward, more amused than anything else, it seemed to Tormano. "That is, *if* you believe the gossips who take Davion coin to spout Davion lies."

"I have always felt actions speak more loudly than words, Duke Ryan. Peter was an obstacle in the Isle of Skye. He is removed." Tormano also sat forward and lowered his voice to a conspiratorial whisper. "What I wish to ask of you is this: are you through with Peter? May I have him?"

Ryan took another drink of PPC, then cupped the snifter in both hands as he swallowed. "Will your plans for him discomfit Victor?"

"I imagine so, yes."

"Then, by all means, he is yours." Ryan looked straight at Tormano, his dark eyes full of fire. "Will you get him killed?"

"That is entirely likely."

"Then do me one favor. Make sure there is no question about who caused his death."

"That, my dear Duke, is not a problem." Tormano sank back into his chair and steepled his fingers. "When I am done with Peter Davion, no one in the Inner Sphere will doubt who took his life."

The assassin smiled as Sergei Chou entered the back room of the Mongolian barbecue restaurant on the border between the Black Hills and Cathay. "*Buona sera,* Sergei. It has been a long time."

"It has indeed, my friend, a very long time." The Capellan sat down across from the assassin, his face betraying nothing. The assassin wondered for a moment if Sergei had missed the signal, but the other man's next words banished that worry. "*Come sta?*"

"I am well." The assassin pulled an optical data disk from his pocket and slid it across the table. "On this you will find the plans for some special ammunition I will need. I also require the custom rifle your people made for me."

"*Bene.*" Chou looked around at the small room. "How many rounds?"

"Fifty. Use half to run some ballistics checks on them for

me. Bring me the data, the brass, and the unused shells when next we speak. *É importante.*"

"*Capisco.*" Chou shook the man's hand and walked out of the room. As he did, the assassin observed that a couple who had been siting near the door also got up and followed him out, by which he identified two more of the team they had watching him. That made for eight, and he knew they must have at least four times that many keeping track of him.

One shell for Ryan, and twenty-four more to use as I make my escape. He smiled for an instant, then killed the smile as the ice-eyed man entered the room. "Chou will not fail me."

"Good." The security agent jerked his head toward the doorway. "You've done your shopping. It's time to go."

The assassin nodded, forcing resignation into the motion. *It won't fool this one, but his other people will believe I'm beaten. That will make them sloppy, less attentive. One slip and I am away.*

27

Strapped into the cockpit of Yen-lo-wang, Kai Allard-Liao allowed himself a smile. All the weapons systems reported themselves operational, all armor appeared whole and strong, and the 'Mech's limbs were all working fine. Cathy Kessler—an artist of unparalleled skill—had overseen the painting of the *Centurion,* returning it to the bold red and white color scheme his father had used when piloting this same 'Mech in The Factory.

The image of Yen-lo-wang stalking Peter Armstrong's *Griffin* through the tangled warren of metallic debris and crumbling ferrocrete appeared in Kai's mind's eye as vividly as if he had ridden in the cockpit alongside his father twenty-nine years before. *How odd that my father was masquerading as a loathsome Capellan, and Armstrong was out to kill him for being a Liaoist. That would have been my uncle's way today. If it were up to him, he'd have me out to kill Wu Deng Tang merely because of his nationality.*

Kai would never forget the time his father had talked to him about killing Peter Armstrong. It was a deed that had haunted Justin Allard all his life, a deed he could never stop regretting. Thinking about it made Kai angry at Tormano for wanting him to destroy Wu Deng Tang like some kind of overture to a war over rule of the Capellan Confederation that would only result in massive death and destruction. *This is not a fight of nation against nation, but of man against man. My father would not have killed Peter Armstrong if he*

could have avoided it, and I will find a way to keep from having to kill Wu Deng Tang.

He knew the odds-makers were having a field day with this match-up. Wu had twenty tons on Kai because his *Cataphract* weighed in at seventy tons. Both machines had comparable armor, though Wu's 'Mech had a slight advantage in the chest and on the arms. The pulse lasers of the two 'Mechs canceled each other out, but Kai's Gauss rifle was more powerful than Wu's extended-range PPC. Wu's LB-10-X autocannon more than made up the difference, however.

Kai's main advantage was that the *Centurion*'s weapon balance was better than the *Cataphract*'s. By approaching from the left, he could bring all his weapons to bear while Wu would have trouble bringing the autocannon mounted on the 'Mechs right side into play. The Factory's relatively close quarters eliminated the PPC's advantage at long ranges, but Wu was known for his ability as an in-fighter. Kai had planned his strategy with that in mind.

He took one last look around the cockpit and decided everything was ready. He hit a switch on the console. "Fight Control, Yen-lo-wang is good to go."

Galen looked up as Keith Smith pointed with his beer stein out through the picture window toward the huge display area that the luxury boxes surrounded. "They're bringing the laser holosimulator online."

Because The Factory had once been a working industrial complex, the only way to watch fights held here was through closed-circuit holovision transmissions. The holosimulator built a map of the whole complex, then slowly zeroed in on the starting points for the two 'Mechs involved in the match. The display itself expanded or shrank to whatever scale best showed the relative positions of the BattleMechs. It could even zoom up to one-for-one scale if the pilots actually closed and started physically beating on one another.

Keith directed Galen's attention to the glowing gold *Centurion* model in the upper area of the tallest building. "That's Kai. They gave him a good position. If Wu comes up after him, Kai will have the high ground."

"What if Wu waits for him to come down?" Peter Davion

asked as he joined the other two men at the window. "Wu could ambush Kai."

"Possible, but not likely. Kai's not easy to ambush."

Galen laughed. "As the Jade Falcons discovered on Alyina."

Keith Smith nodded, but a frown creased his forehead. "Got word today that it looks like ComStar will finally sign off on having Kai's Elemental buddies visit Solaris."

"But they miss the fight?"

"Right, which defeats the whole purpose of the visit." Keith drank some beer. "I had a circuit set up that could have gotten them here in time had ComStar okayed it yesterday. The problem was that the circuit would have passed through Skye—and one of the conditions for the visit is that they would *not* enter Skye space, for obvious reasons. I still haven't been able to arrange the new circuit for them yet."

"Tough break." Galen squinted as the 'Mechs began moving. "Looks like they've both decided to go hunting."

Kai instantly recognized his placement in The Factory. Largely because of gravity, the upper levels tended to be freer of debris, but because of the incredible amount of damage down in the lower reaches, the structural integrity of the upper floors was doubtful in many places. The phenomena of a 'Mech falling through a weakened floor was not unknown and generally not healthy for that unfortunate BattleMech.

Picking his way through a tangle of half-melted girders, Kai worked Yen-lo-wang toward the ramp in the northeast corner of the building. When The Factory had been a real industrial facility, there had been ramps strong enough to bear 'Mech traffic in the four corners of the facility. When the place was refitted to become an arena, the ramps had been rebuilt so Fight Control could open or seal any or all of them. Because Wu and Kai were known to be game fighters, the controllers had opened the ramps at opposite ends of the two floors. Had they been more timid fighters, they'd have been placed on the same level, with no ramps made available for escape.

The sound and vibration baffles between the floors would trap all indicators of the *Centurion's* movement, but Kai knew the baffles wouldn't stop thermal bleed through the ferrocrete. The climatic controls that had been installed during The Factory's last renovation weren't being used to modify the temperature, which would help disguise thermal bleed. The level of light in the arena meant vislight scans would function well enough. Better yet, they would provide spectators with the best look at the battle as it unfolded.

If they started me up here, then they probably started him down below. That means we'll meet in the middle. They'll use the delay of us cutting to the chase to show some ads. Which means they figure this fight will be quick and dirty. Kai smiled to himself. *Quick I can handle, but only if I keep moving. If we stand and slug, I'm dead.*

He started the *Centurion* heading down the ramp to the lower levels. *Ready or not, Wu Deng Tang, here I come.*

The softness of Omi's half-whispered question surprised Peter Davion. "Excuse me, Lady Omi, what was it you asked?" He smiled at her as he stepped back from Galen's side.

"I was wondering, Peter-*sama,* if you could explain to me why Kai would so willingly move his 'Mech in toward a confrontation with a larger, more powerful BattleMech?" Omi returned his smile, then looked down shyly. "This must be a strategy which I, not being a MechWarrior, fail to understand."

Peter shook his head and watched Omi as he considered what she had asked and *how* she had asked it. Her question had been phrased to praise his ability as a MechWarrior and to draw him out. She put herself in a subordinate position so he could help her understand something that puzzled her, and in so doing begin to build a bond between them. That she was in love with his brother might almost have made him think her stupid, but he'd already seen enough to know that couldn't be true. *She is a crafty witch who would be happy to have me underestimate her.*

"I do not know for certain, Lady Omi, but I can hazard a guess." Peter pointed to Kai's 'Mech as it moved swiftly across the level below where it had started, then moved down the ramp to the next lowest level. "The *Centurion* is a fast 'Mech, almost fifty percent faster than the *Cataphract.* That means Kai can get to a lower level faster than Wu can come up. He'll be able to meet him somewhere unexpected, and that gives Kai a gross advantage."

"That is a tactic worthy of a warrior." Omi smiled politely, then bowed her head to Peter. "You are quite insightful."

"And you are very kind." Peter graced her with his plastic smile. "I now understand why my brother thinks of no one but you, Lady Omi." *And as any physical liaison with you would likely cost my brother the throne, I can truly wish you both the happiness you desire.*

Kai would have been impressed with Peter's analysis of his strategy, with the addition of only one minor refinement. As his *Centurion* descended the first ramp, Kai covered the next level with the Gauss rifle mounted in his 'Mech's right arm. That sparked an idea that sent him racing to the ramp leading to the next level down. Once again his Gauss rifle commanded the new level, bringing a smile to Kai's face.

Coming down I expose my right side. Going up, Wu will have to expose his left flank. He pushed Yen-lo-wang on through the third level and came to the fourth. Here he slowed his speed, his approach becoming more cautious. Supports ran in tandem down the middle of the rectangular factory floor. Walls that had once separated sections of the floor were now reduced to rubble, and chunks of ferrocrete from previous reconstructions of upper levels littered the floor.

The metal from girder scraps and rebar roots hanging out of ferrocrete boulders made using magres scans impossible. Kai almost switched over to infrared to pick up heat from Wu's approach below, but he decided against it, instead pushing on toward the ramp leading up from the lower level. He brought Yen-lo-wang up onto two ferrocrete boulders fifty meters from the opening, then hunkered down and waited.

The ferrocrete will absorb some of the thermal energy I'm putting out, so I'm safe from detection for a bit here. Now for how long . . . ? Not very.

Wu Deng Tang was neither a stupid nor a suicidal fighter, which was why he was mounting the up-ramp at full speed. Had he been coming up more slowly or had he stopped to peek up over the edge of the floor, it would have left his

'Mech's head vulnerable. As it was, the difficulty of negoti-
ating the steep slope meant he had to hunch his 'Mech's
torso forward for balance, preventing him from being able to
bring the weapons on the right side of the machine's body
into play.

Kai dropped the gold cross hairs onto the *Cataphract*'s
outline. As the computer flashed a golden dot in the heart of
the cross, he hit the thumb buttons in quick succession and
squeezed the trigger on his joysticks. Both pulse lasers sent
out their ruby energy flechettes to boil away armor on the
Cataphract's left arm. The silvery Gauss rifle projectile sped
from the muzzle at the *Centurion*'s right wrist and arced in
to hammer the right chest area of Wu's 'Mech. Armor plates
crumbled under the onslaught, and Kai knew the exchange
had done significant damage to the *Cataphract*.

In response Wu did what would have been all but impossible for anyone save a superior 'Mech pilot. He lurched his
'Mech up and forward, racing for cover on the upper level
instead of retreating to the lower one. Most fighters would
have chosen the latter, taking the position of waiting below
for Kai to come down to them. Fight Control would have
opened another ramp to give Kai another way down and to
preserve the advantage his bold strategy had given him.

As Wu moved forward, he swung his 'Mech's left arm
wide and triggered a burst with the pulse laser mounted beneath its forearm. The energy darts found their mark on Yen-
lo-wang's broad chest. Part of the beautiful Kessler paint job
combusted when molten armor poured down over it. The
auxiliary monitor in Kai's cockpit showed that he'd lost
thirty-three percent of the armor over his 'Mech's midline,
and that brought the two opponents back even closer than
Kai would have hoped.

Wu's shooting impressed him. *If that was just a snapped
shot, he's damned lucky—and even more dangerous than I
thought. Still, I'm nearly through on the right side of his
chest.* Kai leaped his 'Mech back off the ferrocrete boulders
and hunkered down behind them. *Could be one shot and out,
for either of us. Gotta be careful.*

DropShip Qianlian, *Inbound to Solaris VII*
Tamarind March, Federated Commonwealth

Deirdre stroked David's hair as he lay with his head in her lap. Pulling the blanket up over him, she dearly wished the man in the seat opposite would keep his voice down. He had been polite enough to plug his headphones into the portable holovid viewer, but whatever feed he was getting from Solaris apparently had his blood up.

She could see the reflected light from the LCD display on his face, and when the reflections looked less like explosions and other excitement, she reached out with a slippered foot to touch his leg. "Can you keep it down?"

The man looked from her foot to her face and back down, then he frowned. "What?" he asked much too loudly, then blushed and removed the headphones. "Excuse me, what?"

"Can you try to control your voice?" She gave him as kind as smile as she could. "My boy is very tired. I don't want him to wake up."

"Sure," the man said, giving her a friendly smile. "But I bet he'd like to be watching this, too. Hell of a fight so far."

Deirdre shook her head. "I don't allow him to watch fights."

"This isn't just a fight, ma'am, this is art. Kai Allard-Liao is defending his title. This is *history*." The man shook his head. "He's piloting his father's 'Mech in The Factory."

She closed her eyes, feeling tears suddenly well. "Please, sir, can you see if they're showing the fight in the saloon here. My son . . . I lost his father to the Clans and war."

The man nodded sympathetically, accepting her lie. "I'm sorry. Sure, I'll go. This screen is too little to see much anyway."

"Thank you." She gave him a brave smile that covered her regret at having lied. It was only after the door to the compartment closed that it occurred to her that *her* Kai *had* been lost to the Clans and war. *And to my stupidity.*

Deirdre turned to face the viewport, and stared at the planet toward which they sped. Pressing her hand to the clear plastic, she suddenly found herself doing something she'd never have dreamed of before. With all her heart, she offered a silent prayer for Kai's safety.

Solaris City, Solaris VII
Tamarind March, Federated Commonwealth

Speed is my advantage. Kai brought the *Centurion* to its broad flat feet and came around the ferrocrete boulders he had been using as cover. He darted directly for the narrow archway through which the *Cataphract* had vanished. Reaching out with his 'Mech's left hand, he posted off the archway and cut back to the left. Moving laterally down a narrow pathway through the debris, he let his cross hairs drift to the right.

Come on, you've got to be there.

Kai had expected Wu to step out through the archway. He knew the *Cataphract* had been hiding behind it because Wu would have fired on Kai's left flank from cover had he moved further west through the debris on the far side of the level. Kai had intended to draw Wu out with his feint toward the opening, but the other MechWarrior wasn't going to play the game by Kai's rules.

Had Wu done what Kai had expected, he'd have kept his damaged right flank behind the arch, giving Kai another chance to blow off the damaged arm. Instead of staying half-in and half-out of the archway, Wu pivoted his 'Mech on its left leg and mirrored Yen-lo-wang's lateral drift. When he appeared on Kai's tactical display, he was a bit more to the center than Kai had expected, but correction of aim was no problem.

Both men fired their weapons at the same time, but this time Wu's aim wasn't so flawless. Both pulse lasers tracked low, evaporating hunks of ferrocrete instead of armor, but the PPC was right on target. The jagged beam exploded the armor plates off Yen-lo-wang's right arm, tracing a blackened scar from elbow to shoulder. The autocannon in the right side of the 'Mech's chest whined loudly as it spat out a hail of projectiles. Most of the hits ground away at the already-damaged armor on the *Centurion*'s center torso, while some chipped the armor on the 'Mech's left breast.

Kai leaned forward and to the left to fight the twisting motion imparted to his 'Mech. Yen-lo-wang withstood the assault without much trouble while Kai kept the *Cataphract* covered with his cross hairs as his weapons hit back into it. Both pulse lasers eroded the armor over the *Cataphract*'s midline, flirting with but failing to carry over to the nearly naked right flank. The Gauss rifle ball smashed into the 'Mech's left arm just above the elbow, blasting the last of the limb's armor into ferro-ceramic flinders, then crushing two heat sinks in a spray of yellow-green coolant fluid.

Kai knew he had Wu. *One more exchange at this range and he's done. He's got only one chance.* The moment the thought occurred to him Kai knew that his foe wouldn't hesitate to do what he must. The one shot he had could win the fight for Wu. He was damned good, as the trap at the ramp had showed, and the tactic he would use was worthy of a champion on Solaris.

Another time, Wu, against another foe. Kai stopped his 'Mech's leftward movement and darted straight forward. He leaped the *Centurion* over a low pile of rubble and dropped into a crouch, the 'Mech's massive legs cushioning its landing. Kai's skill as a pilot made the war machine move cat-light and cat-quick despite its enormous size. Damned few other pilots could have matched the move, and even fewer would have anticipated it.

Which is why I *am champion here.* Kai twisted his 'Mech's torso to the left and dropped his cross hairs onto the *Cataphract.*

Wu's 'Mech had also moved forward and had thrust its right arm through one of the archways supporting the roof. Had Kai remained traveling to the left for another exchange, the move would have caught him naked out in the open against a foe in heavy cover. Because he had instead crossed over to Wu's side of the floor, he caught the *Cataphract* with its most awesome weapon out of position.

One of Kai's pulse laser's stitched laser needles along the roof support shielding part of the *Cataphract,* causing no damage. The other one hit on target, melting away the last of the armor on the right side of the 'Mech's body. The energy darts, hardly spent by the armor they devoured, skewered the LB-10-X autocannon and reduced the breech mechanism to molten sludge.

The Gauss rifle's silver sphere pounded into the *Cataphract*'s left knee, snapping the leg out straight. It blasted away more than seventy percent of the armor and knocked the limb askew. The 'Mech's left arm flailed through the air in a vain attempt to rebalance the machine. Amid a cloud of armor shards, the *Cataphract* went down on its back.

Were Wu any other fighter on Solaris, Kai would have opened a radio channel and demanded his surrender. He knew that Wu, being sensible and honorable, would likely have accepted even though his 'Mech was still operable. The loss of the autocannon and the breeches of armor on the left arm and right torso left little doubt as to the outcome of the fight, but Wu could have kept going.

Kai advanced carefully and targeted the *Cataphract*'s legs, the pulse lasers stripping armor from the 'Mech's right leg. The Gauss rifle's silvery ball whipped through the armor-fog created by the lasers and slammed into the *Cataphract*'s left thigh. The little armor left on that leg joined the pile of debris below it, then the ball burrowed in through the thick myomer muscles and hit the ferro-titanium femur. The ball shattered the bone, then ricocheted off deeper into The Factory.

Kai keyed his radio. "You have fought well, Wu Deng Tang. We shall stop now, if you do not mind."

"Thank you, Kai Allard-Liao. I would be willing to continue, but there would be no purpose in it. I have a son I want to see born."

Kai laughed. "And I want your son to have a father. It is over. I may be the victor, but in no way should you feel the vanquished."

28

Mandrinn's Estate, Solaris VII
Tamarind March, Federated Commonwealth
20 April 3056

Tormano Liao smiled broadly as Deirdre Lear and her young son were ushered into the informal dining room of his estate on Equus. "How very nice it is to meet you finally, Doctor." He bowed to her, then shifted slightly to bow to David. "And you, young man."

David executed a smart bow. "*Zao,* Mandrinn Liao."

Truly surprised, Tormano clapped his hands. "Bravo, David, your Chinese is excellent."

His mother blushed appropriately. "He's been learning a little on Zurich."

"That's good," Tormano said. "I believe the sharing of languages is the first step toward the reunification of mankind." He waved the two of them toward the table, which had been set with common crockery and flatware to deemphasize the opulence of his estate. The table itself sat in a glass-walled porch which, as the day neared noon, just happened to be bathed in sunlight.

"I apologize for not meeting you at the spaceport last night," Tormano said smoothly, layering a pained expression over his face. "My nephew was engaged in another of his battles and my attendance was required. I would have tried to escape it, but Duke Ryan Steiner was my guest, and well, in these times of political tensions, to abandon him would not have been wise."

Deirdre picked David up and settled him on a chair facing the expanse of rolling lawn and heavy forest surrounding the estate. "I guess we're both prisoners of politics, my lord."

Tormano frowned momentarily, then forced a smile. "Doctor, believe me when I say I realize you would have preferred to remain on Zurich treating your patients. Your dedication to your work is not in question, and the two doctors I sent to fill in during your absence should be an indication of how highly I value your services to my people."

Deirdre took a seat opposite him. "*Your* people? Forgive me, but Zurich is part of the Federated Commonwealth."

Tormano smiled and raised his hands. "Ah, yes, a point well taken. I have tried to repress the paternal feelings I have for those worlds once part of the Capellan Confederation. Still, I feel a greater rapport with their people than Prince Victor or any of the other Steiner-Davions apparently do. I had once hoped Kai would share my interest, but . . ."

Deirdre raised an eyebrow. "But Kai funds the medical center where I work."

"Pressured into it, yes, he does." Tormano stopped as a frown flashed over Deirdre's face. *She does not like Kai, but she refuses to believe the worst of him. I must be careful here.* "He knows that I cannot continue many of my funding efforts ever since Victor Davion slashed his financial support of free Capella. Appointing Duke Peter as my liaison officer should help fund-raising as will, I hope, the presentation I wish to make to you."

Servants brought Deirdre and David fruit cups, and after a moment Tormano casually raised a hand. "I had not planned to eat right now, but that looks very inviting. If you don't mind, Doctor, I will join you."

Deirdre looked appropriately apologetic. "By all means, of course."

David plucked a grape from his bowl and put it in his mouth, then his eyes grew wide as he pointed across the table toward the window. "Birdies and deers."

The Mandrinn smiled as a male peacock spread its tail while a herd of small spotted deer meandered into view. "We have many exotic animals here. One of the programs I fund recovers and helps reestablish endangered species on war-ravaged worlds. I allow myself the luxury of having some of them here."

Deirdre reached over and dabbed the corner of David's mouth with her napkin. "You mentioned a presentation?"

"Ah, yes, I did. The presentation of a check in the amount needed for the MRI unit at your medical center. The ceremony will be somewhat formal and it will be recorded so that I can show it and some of the new pieces done on you to philanthropically minded individuals within the expatriot Capellan community. It is all private and small-scale—I know you are a person who prefers to avoid the spotlight. I would gather that is especially so here, on Solaris."

Deirdre's eyes hooded cautiously, though she kept her voice light. "Why should Solaris be special?"

The Mandrinn planted his elbows on the table, pressed his hands together fingertip to fingertip, then leaned forward and watched her from around his hands. "It is no secret, Doctor, that you knew my nephew on Alyina. At no time during your trip here or since your arrival have you asked after him. I conclude from this that you are indifferent or perhaps hostile to him, and that any publicity that might draw his attention to your presence on Solaris would be distasteful to you. Am I incorrect?"

"No, no you're not." She looked down and used her spoon to surgically dissect a piece of melon.

"Good, then we are allies in working for the benefit of people less fortunate then ourselves." Tormano pulled back as a servant brought him a fruit cup. "You will get what you want, and I will get what I want, and no one will suffer in the process."

David filled the silence with a whined question. "Mommy, can I play with the deers?"

"David, the deer are not toys."

"If I may, Doctor, the deer are quite tame and used to visitors." Tormano looked at the boy, then smiled at Deirdre. "He is such a bright, inquisitive child."

"Thank you, my lord." Deirdre ran her fingers through David's dark hair. "He is the true joy of my life."

"Yes, of that I have no doubt." Tormano chuckled as he popped a cherry into his mouth. "Intelligent, curious, and adventuresome. An interesting child." Placing his hands on the table, Tormano straightened up as though struck by an unexpected thought. "A most interesting child. In fact, my dear, David very much reminds me of my nephew Kai when he was about the same age."

Solaris City, Solaris VII
Tamarind March, Federated Commonwealth

Katrina's presence in the lobby of the Sun and Sword Hotel surprised Galen. He saw the security men around her and, standing in one corner of the lobby's marble checkerboard floor, a knot of giggling girls in Land Scout uniforms. He was definitely running late. "Forgive my tardiness, Highness."

Katrina greeted him with a smile, resplendent in her smart blue skirt and jacket. "Don't worry, Kommandant. I wasn't waiting impatiently for you." She threw him a covert wink, then added, "Mr. Chelsey's niece is a member of that scout troop over there and he's asked permission for them to make a presentation to me. I agreed and decided to do it here."

So the hotel manager can have the publicity, and the girls can be center stage in their home town. Galen smiled. "I understand." He looked down at his casual clothes. "It won't take me long to change. I stayed a bit longer than I should have. Kai was out of town again, but made arrangements for me to practice in the *Penetrator* Kallon has loaned him. I lost track of time."

"No matter, the presentation is waiting for the district scout leader." Katrina laughed lightly, but the sound died prematurely as a short, stocky man threaded his way through the security gauntlet to her. The man looked nervous, but when the security crew passed him through, Galen assumed he must be no threat to Katrina. Even so, he moved to his left to bring the newcomer into intercept range in case the IS men were mistaken.

The man bowed to Katrina. "Highness, forgive me, but I bring you a message from your cousin." He drew an envelope of ivory paper from the outer pocket of his mackintosh and held it out to her. "With his compliments, Highness."

Galen frowned. *Cousin? There are only two families that Katrina acknowledges as cousins: the Kells and Ryan Steiner's line. Could that be a message from Khan Phelan?* The instant the idea occurred to him, Galen rejected it. Catching the faint scent of flowers as Katrina opened the note, he wondered for another wild instant if this man had bluffed his way past the bodyguard phalanx to give her a love note. But Katrina's eyes were already flashing anger as she read the note and then immediately tore it in half. Galen saw not only that he'd been wrong but got a big clue to the identity of the sender.

Katrina focused her gaze on the messenger. "You are?"

"David Hanau, Highness, the duke's assistant."

"Then, Mr. Hanau, you can carry my reply to your master." Katrina tossed the torn message and envelope into a nearby trash receptacle. "Tell the good duke that I would sooner dine with dogs than accept his invitation to dinner. Do you have that?"

Hanau looked as if he would melt beneath her stare. "H-Highness?"

Galen took Hanau by the shoulders and spun him around to face the door. "Allow me to translate: Her Highness declines the invitation because she has no tolerance for treasonous agitators who have the blood of innocents on their hands." A light shove sent Hanau beyond the perimeter the security men had established, and one of them escorted him to the door.

When Galen turned back to Katrina, he saw that she'd been rattled by the encounter. "What's wrong?"

She shook her head. "Nothing. And thank you for the help." She reached out and caressed his cheek. "Hurry, Galen. I am so impatient to have you by my side."

"As you command, Highness." Galen winked at her, then headed toward the elevators. *One more day on this world, then it's back to Tharkad.* He smiled as the elevator doors opened before him. *And then we will never have to be apart again.*

Kai Allard-Liao had arrived at the Sesame Inn intentionally early so he could be on hand to greet his guests. Walking through the restaurant he recognized a number of individuals from 'Mech battles on Solaris and, curiously enough, from his mother's court. Beyond the table where a Solaris fighter named Dick Thunder sat with a bevy of Asian groupies, he saw three men in the uniforms of the mercenary unit known as Khorsakov's Cossacks. Two looked enough alike to be father and son, while the third man's scarred profile was as unmistakable as it was unforgettable.

What would they *be doing here?* The Cossacks were famous for their almost fanatical hatred of Romano Liao, a hatred so intense that even Romano's death could not end it. The mercenaries had merely transferred their enmity to Sun-Tzu, Romano's son and heir. The Cossacks were from Tikonov, a world heavily populated with people tracing their ancestry to Russia on old Terra. Kai did not know the source of Nikolai Khorsakov's hate for his Aunt Romano, but he did recall having seen the man at court on St. Ives. He also remembered well how adamantly Khorsakov had vowed to oppose any Capellan aggression against the St. Ives Compact when Kai's mother hired the Cossacks for garrison duty.

What struck Kai as odd about seeing the elder Khorsakov in uniform was that he'd recently read a news piece about the old man's retirement. Only an operation against Sun-Tzu could have brought Nikolai out of retirement, and his presence on Solaris meant Tormano Liao was playing with fire. Kai had thought his warning to Tormano was loud and clear, but perhaps his uncle's viewing the fight in the company of Duke Ryan Steiner had inspired him to make mischief.

I will deal with my uncle tomorrow. Tonight is a celebration.

Kai caught up with George Yang as the handsome Asian left a table filled with others in uniform—members of the Legion of the Rising Sun, if Kai remembered the insignia correctly—and bowed in greeting. "You seem to have a full house this evening, George."

"Word of mouth has been very good to our establishment. Many of your fellow stable masters have recommended us to their friends." George shook Kai's hand. "The mention in the newsfax today that you were hosting a party here had the visiphone busy from the moment we opened this morning. Many people are here to be seen, I believe."

"Your cuisine will bring them back." Kai followed Yang into the Dragon's Realm, where he saw that everything was perfect. The table was set with places for the dozen guests he had invited. Above each plate, between the wine glass and water glass, was a blue velvet box. Kai pulled a similar one from his pocket and handed it to George.

"I had fourteen of these coins struck in platinum. Twelve are on the table, one has been sent to my mother, and the last is yours in gratitude for all you've done to make this celebration possible." Kai watched as the man opened the box, then smiled. Similar coins minted in gold, silver, and bronze had also been released to the collector's market. Because the coins were limited runs, collectors were buying them up for much more than the metal itself was worth, and the profits were being funneled into Cenotaph Charities.

"You are most kind, my lord." George lifted the coin from the box, holding it carefully by the rim of the protective plastic case as he turned it over. One side showed Kai's profile and was inscribed with the date of the fight against Wu Deng Tang. The other side showed Wu's *Cataphract*. Kai would have preferred having the image of Yen-lo-wang to his profile on the coin, but because it was legal tender within the St. Ives Compact, Grand Duchess Candace Liao had ordered that her son's portrait be engraved upon it.

George bowed and withdrew as the first two of Kai's guests arrived. Wu Deng Tang bowed to Kai, then led a pretty, petite, and very obviously pregnant woman forward. "My lord, may I present my fiancée, Caren Fung. Dearest, this is Kai Allard-Liao."

Kai bowed to the woman, then took her right hand and kissed it gently. "I am very pleased to make your acquaintance, Caren. When Tang told me you would be joining us, I was very pleased to hear it. Cenotaph has a helicopter waiting on the roof in case your condition requires a quick trip to the hospital."

"That is very kind of you, but I regret that you should have gone to such expense."

Kai shook his head. "No expense: that's how I got here tonight."

Caren looked up at Wu, then smiled at Kai. "My lord, I came to thank you for what you did for Tang in the fight. I was not allowed to watch it, of course, but he has told me of the great honor and respect you showed him. You could have hurt him, but you did not. Thank you."

Kai shook his head. "An honorable and skillful rival always deserved to be treated with the respect. Besides, how could I harm him with your child so soon on its way?"

He turned and opened his arms to the table and vista be-

yond it. "Please, you are my honored guests." Smiling, he
pointed toward Solaris City by night. "I promise you a tran-
quil evening with no surprises and no undue excitement."

Much later, the sheer irony of those words would echo
again and again through Kai's mind. The next instant, as Kai
looked from Caren toward the dark view of the city, took the
top floor off The Sun and The Sword Hotel in a fiery explosion.

═══ 29 ═══

Mandrinn Tormano Liao smiled as Nancy Lee guided Peter Steiner-Davion into the room. Still in a state of shock, Peter seemed not to notice Nancy's smile, and his eyes barely flicked up when Tormano offered him his hand. *Excellent, he can barely think. So much the better for what I need.*

"Please, Duke Peter, forgive me for insisting that our first meeting take place so soon after the tragic death of Kommandant Cox. I wish it could have been otherwise."

Peter's lifeless handshake satisfied social convention and gave Tormano a quick indication of the depth of Peter's apparent depression. "There is no problem, Mandrinn Liao. I should keep busy."

"Please sit. Nancy, I would like some tea. Highness?"

Peter frowned in thought, then nodded. "Tea would be fine."

Tormano watched calmly until Nancy had left the room, then he turned to Peter. "Forgive me, my lord, but I sense much discomfort in you. If I may be so bold, might it be that you wonder why your brother has left you here, on Solaris, in a dangerous situation, while your sister has been whisked away back to Tharkad?"

The younger man's gray eyes showed their first spark of life. "Are you a mind reader, Mandrinn?"

"No, no, not at all. Were I such, you and I would have no need for this meeting." Tormano leaned forward in his chair, resting his elbows on his knees, with his hands clasped together. His voice quieted to a confessional tone. "It is just that I used to wonder the same thing when my father abandoned me on a world in the path of your father's juggernaut almost thirty years ago. The question ate away at me, sapping my strength and weakening my spirit. It left me wondering why my own sire, my flesh and blood, wished to consign me to death. It is a dreadful thought."

"It is, Mandrinn, it is that." Peter stared down at his hands.

"What gnaws at a man is the question of motive," Tormano went on, a grim smile of satisfaction twisting up the corners of his lips. "And once I had the key, everything fell into place and I felt, for the first time, that my eyes were truly open."

Peter looked up, his gaze searching Tormano's face for the answer. "What did you decide? Why did he do it?"

"Jealousy."

"You *are* a mind reader, and you must have read my brother's." Peter leaned back in his chair and forced a laugh. "What makes you think this?"

"Is it not obvious?" Tormano arched an eyebrow at Peter. *Clever boy, you want me to praise you. Are you that vain and also that vulnerable because of it?* "You are doubtless too modest to mark all the reasons your brother would envy you. On the most basic level, of course, you look more Hanse Davion's heir than Victor ever did. He has the classic Steiner coloration—pale and washed out. On Katrina it is quite fetching, but it only makes Victor look weak. You, on the other hand, have your father's ruddy coloring and his red hair. Your imposing stature and deep voice also give you an air of command that few men, noble or otherwise, possess. You remind me of the days when your father was a young man and no one even dared to contemplate waging war against the Federated Suns."

Tormano fell silent as Nancy arrived with the tea and poured for each of them. He noted with satisfaction that Peter watched her every move and gave her a smile when she noticed his attention. *Wounded pride always makes molding inexperience so much easier. Distractions help as well.* Nancy let her hand brush across Peter's shoulder as she withdrew, as if she had read Tormano's mind and conspired with him.

Tormano opened his arms wide. "Of course, physical appearance is mostly beyond our control, which the wisest among us realize and accept. I would have thought your brother wise enough not to worry about those things he cannot change."

"Victor is not half as wise as he needs to be, nor a quarter as wise as he thinks he is."

"You know him far better than I, Highness. But anyone can see that it is not merely your appearance that makes you a leader. Your successful efforts at conservation and the incident in the tavern on Lyons . . . Yes, yes, I heard all about that and, quite frankly, it was one of the things that gave me heart when I learned your brother was sending you here. You dared take a stand in a situation that was hostile to you, and you won your enemies over. That is a rare ability.

"Victor, on the other hand, seems to *react* to situations rather than act to head them off." Tormano frowned and shrugged his shoulders. "You are different, a leader, one who inspires. Your presence on Lyons kept its people from declaring openly for Ryan Steiner. Your surviving the assassination attempt mocked the Free Skye Militia's efforts to destroy you. It made you very strong and people began to look up to you. And then your brother *reacted* to that situation."

"Hence my exile to Solaris, where assassins can get close enough to place a bomb in my sister's suite." Peter's eyes reflected a trace of fear. "If he wanted me dead, he should have just shot me."

"It might have occurred to him, but he has uses for you. He cannot afford to have you as a rival and so he sends you here to keep you from achieving the same kind of military success that catapulted him into the spotlight. Everyone know that if Victor had not fought so well against the Clans, your parents would have passed him over as heir."

Peter smiled graciously. "It must gall you that my brother's victories were won through the unsung efforts of your nephew."

"Victor's neglect of the Sarna March troubles me even more than that, Highness." Tormano shook his head. "He mocks us both, to his detriment and possible danger."

Peter sipped his tea, then watched Tormano through narrowed eyes. "What danger?"

"It is good we come to this, because it is what I wished to speak with you about. I have received word that a Capellan Confederation unit is staging on Shiloh for an attack on the Federated Commonwealth. The unit is the newly formed Harloc Raiders commanded by Wu Kang Kuo. I can show you the report." Tormano raised his hand and beckoned Nancy into the room. "Nancy, will you please get a copy of the Harloc Raiders report for the duke here?"

Peter smiled faintly at her, then turned to Tormano. "Have you told my brother about this?"

"Believe me when I tell you how hard I have tried to communicate to him the danger here. He thinks me a stupid old man who is crying wolf just because he cut my appropriations. It is not true, the threat is real, and anyone who has watched Sun-Tzu's *Zhanzheng de guang*'s predations in the Sarna March can see what I am saying." Tormano stopped himself and drank some tea. "Forgive me, Highness, but the gravity of the situation and your brother's cold indifference have me agitated."

"I can understand that, Mandrinn Liao."

"Being a warrior, you can also understand this. I have engaged a mercenary unit, Khorsakov's Cossacks—you know of them, of course, and how they have supported my efforts against the illegitimate regime on Sian—to undertake a recon-in-force of Shiloh. I hope they will come back with physical evidence of the Harloc Raiders' presence because the photos and holographs my agents have obtained—at such great risk to their own lives—have been decried as inconclusive by your brother. He will not believe me."

Tormano held his hands up in a gesture of hopelessness. "I beseech you, my lord, to take the information the Cossacks bring back to your brother. Convince him of this threat. The evidence we recover should be sufficient to make the case, and if you deliver it . . . well, there will be no way he can deny my report."

Peter smiled warily. "I can guarantee he will have no choice but to accept it."

Tormano blinked his eyes innocently. "How?"

"I will command the Cossacks. I will see what they see, and I will report it from personal experience."

Tormano shook his head adamantly. "No, I cannot allow that. You would be in grave danger."

"More danger than here on Solaris?" Peter gestured to the window behind Tormano. "I could be in a sniper's gunsight right now. A bomb could destroy my hotel tonight. I am under a death warrant here and the most galling thing about it is that I am a MechWarrior. You were a MechWarrior, Mandrinn. You know what it is to be able to crush your foes. If I am to die, I would prefer that it be in the cockpit of a 'Mech, not a pool of blood in the street. You will let me go."

"Please, Highness, do not insist. If something should happen to you, I . . ."

Peter's face hardened as his eyes flashed with triumph. "Think of it this way, Mandrinn Liao—I am your liaison officer. You have told me of your plans to send an armed incursion into another sovereign nation, a deed that could bring us to war. If you refuse to let me go with them, to oversee the mission, I will shut it down. It will go nowhere." Peter sat tall in his chair. "You have a decision to make, but you really have only one choice."

Tormano opened his mouth, then shut it and let his shoulders slump forward. "No wonder your brother fears you as a rival. You are as hard as he is. As hard as was your father."

"I am even harder than that, Mandrinn, as you will see on this mission."

The older man nodded wearily in defeat. "I wish you godspeed, Highness. I will not rest easy until you return, and when you do I will rejoice. This victory over our enemies will guarantee that your brother can never shove you aside again."

"My thoughts exactly, Mandrinn." Peter stood, rejuvenated by the meeting. "You will have details on the expedition communicated to me. I will be preparing my kit. I assume we leave soon?"

Tormano nodded. "Their DropShip is already headed out of the system. I can have a shuttle at your disposal in four hours."

"Very well." Peter smiled cautiously. "If the Harloc Raiders are on Shiloh, we will find them, destroy them, and deliver their ashes to my brother as proof of their elimination."

Peter marched from the room, taking the report from Nancy as she showed him out. Tormano remained seated until she returned to say that Peter had left the building.

"Thank you, Nancy. Now I must ask you to do two things

for me. First, please send a message to Nikolai Khorsakov and tell him that Case Prokofiev is in effect." In deference to Khorsakov's sensibilities, Tormano had chosen to name the operation after the composer who had created "Peter and the Wolf." It gave Tormano a certain grim satisfaction that Khorsakov would think the title meant that he had real value to the Mandrinn.

"Easily done. And second?"

Tormano's eyes narrowed. "We still have a file of known agents working for the Maskirovka and Sun-Tzu?"

"Active and unfortunately expanding."

"Pity, yes. Pick one, a reliable one, and let him know that a mercenary unit will hit Shiloh ten days from now. Let Sun-Tzu know that it's the Cossacks, but do *not* let it slip that Peter is with them."

Nancy stared hard at him. "But that will get the Cossacks killed. And Peter, too."

"Indeed, it very likely will." Tormano shrugged. "And then Prince Victor will have to avenge his brother and let me destroy Sun-Tzu, won't he?"

Tharkad, District of Donegal
Federated Commonwealth

Victor hesitated at the threshold of his sister's suite. *I have never seen her so devastated. She must blame herself.* He knocked lightly on the door casing, then entered the dimly lit room. The drawn shades kept out the light reflected by new-fallen snow, and the illumination coming in through the doorway barely served to dispel the shadows. "Katherine, we must talk."

The quilt-shrouded lump in the overstuffed chair did not answer. The lighter shade of gray that marked her hair moved slightly, giving him evidence that she heard but no way of telling if she understood. All she gave out was the occasional congested sniff followed by the addition of another crumpled tissue to the pile surrounding the chair.

"We have some information about the bomb. It was radio-controlled. Whoever set it off, did so deliberately." Victor remained in control, letting no emotion bleed into his voice. "It was not a bomb like the one that killed our mother. And we have reason to believe you were not the target, Katherine. Galen was."

Her voice came as a harsh croak. "What do you know?" An intake of breath punctuated each word, as if saying anything taxed her unto death.

"The Solaris City Constabulary made an intercept of a message to a 'broker' on Solaris asking for a hit on someone called il Capo. As that is underworld slang, the tip went to the organized crime people, but they could make nothing of it. The Intelligence Secretariat now believes that call was placed by a man who wanted Galen dead. We checked other records, because we have that man under surveillance but we believe a technical problem destroyed the evidence we need to show that his boss gave the order."

"Who?"

"The man was Sven Newmark. He is in the employ of Duke Ryan Steiner. We believe the order came from Ryan."

The lumpy figure in the chair became smaller. "Ryan? Ryan killed Galen?"

"He didn't have his finger on the button, no, but he gave the orders." Victor folded his arms across his chest. "There is something else you should know."

"Galen is gone."

"He is, Katherine, but no one could have prevented it. We know who did it, but only because of hindsight." Victor watched her for a reaction, then shook his head. "The man who arranged for Galen's assassination was the same man who hired the assassin to kill our mother."

"What are you saying?"

"I have all the evidence I need to convince me that our mother was assassinated on the orders of Ryan Steiner."

Katherine's shadowed head rose slowly. "He must die, Victor."

"Katherine?"

"You must kill Ryan. He has committed treason. You cannot try him in court and keep the Federated Commonwealth intact."

Victor shook his head. "The evidence would not stand up in court. I know he did it. I have no doubt that he did it. But I cannot prove it."

"He killed Galen. He killed our mother." Tears filling her

eyes picked up enough light to make them glitter. "He wants to destroy us, Victor. Kill him."

Victor slowly nodded his head. "I concur. That is what I will do."

"How soon?"

The prince shook his head. "As soon as can be arranged."

"How?"

"You don't want to know."

"Make it soon, Victor, very soon." Katherine's head sank again and he saw her shoulders wracked with sobs. "Only then will our dead rest in peace."

"They will, Katherine." Victor withdrew from the room and left her suite. He met Curaitis in the hallway outside. "Tell the people on Solaris it's time to act."

The agent nodded. "Did she tell you anything useful?"

"She wants Ryan dead." Victor shook his head. "So do I. Your people can do it?"

"By the end of the week."

Victor looked up at the man walking beside him. "Shouldn't I feel something in ordering a man's death?"

"The lack of feeling is not a problem, Highness." Curaitis did not look at Victor, but stared unseeing down the hallway. "It's when you start enjoying it that you've got trouble."

Solaris City, Solaris VII
Tamarind March, Federated Commonwealth

Kai Allard-Liao smiled in spite of the distracted look on Peter Steiner-Davion's face. "Sorry to surprise you, Peter. I tried to call before coming over, but I couldn't get through."

"I'm not answering right now." Peter hung in the doorway of his room blocking the view of the interior. "Is there something you want?"

What's going on here? Kai kept his smile in place. "I wanted to apologize for not getting in touch with you before this. The night of my title fight there wasn't time, then, well, after the explosion I had to get Caren Fung to the hospital because she went prematurely into labor. I should have been here sooner."

Peter's expression eased just a bit. "Apology accepted, but I can't talk long. I have some things to do."

"Things to do with my uncle?"

"Are you spying on me?" Peter's face flooded with color as his hands tightened on the door jamb. "I knew Victor would put you up to that."

"Hold on, Peter." Kai looked both ways down the hotel corridor and noted the concern of the security people posted nearby. "Don't you think we should go into your room to discuss this?"

"Don't evade my question! What have you told my brother about me?"

Kai paused for a moment to rein in the anger and suspicion that he knew were more rightly directed at Tormano. "I am not spying on you. The only reason I know that you visited my uncle is because I *do* have people watching him. I have no idea of the nature of your meeting. But from some things I've recently learned, I'd have to classify my uncle as an unsavory individual. I would prefer to insulate you from him."

"There's nothing wrong with your uncle."

"He meddles in affairs of state that are beyond him."

"Better than to be like you, hiding here, acting as a spy for my brother." Peter stabbed a finger into Kai's chest. "He told you to come here, didn't he? Don't deny that you've talked to him about me."

A million different ways to phrase his reply as a shield for Victor came to Kai, but he rejected all of them in favor of the truth. "Your brother did send me a holodisk with a message saying he hoped we'd become friends. It arrived while I was in training. I have failed him in that I did not attend to his request immediately. I have come so I do not fail you as well."

"So you showed up because I talked to your uncle. You don't think I can take care of myself, do you?"

Kai held up his hands and took a step back. "I know you are a very capable individual."

"But you came here today, now, because you think Tormano has found a way to force me to do something I don't want to do, right?"

Kai couldn't reconcile the question with the confident grin on Peter's face, but he answered in spite of the paradox. "I was concerned, yes."

"And if I had not met with him, you might not have come today, right?"

Kai winced. "Probably not."

"I thought not." Peter folded his arms across his chest. "Listen up, Kai. I don't need you to watch over me. I'm a big boy. I know Victor wants me to fail, and he wants you to witness it. Well, no sale. I'm not going to fail at anything. I wouldn't give either one of you the satisfaction."

This is not going at all the way I expected or intended. Right then and there Kai decided to back off and try again later. *If I meet with the same problem, or he meets with Tormano again, my uncle and I will have a showdown. Should I have the Red Cobras watch Peter the way they watch Tormano or . . . ? No, if Peter or his security men spotted them, there could be trouble.*

"Peter, forgive me. I've come at an awkward time for both of us." He thought for a second. "I'll tell you what, why don't you come down to my training facility and log some 'Mech time. How about tomorrow morning? Shall I come by for you at ten?"

Peter nodded. "Sure, ten is fine."

"Until tomorrow, then."

"Until we meet again."

Solaris City, Solaris VII
Tamarind March, Federated Commonwealth
24 April 3056

Kai saw a smile blossom on the hotel manager's face when she recognized him. "May I help you, my lord?"

Kai nodded. "If you would be so kind as to ring Duke Peter's room for me. I'm here to pick him up."

The dark-haired woman hesitated. "There must be some mistake."

Kai glanced at his chronometer. "Well, I was supposed to meet him at ten, so I guess I'm a bit early."

"No, not that." She hit some keys on a computer console. "Duke Peter checked out last evening. He is no longer a guest here."

"Gone?" Kai blushed. His mind raced back over their conversation of yesterday, and suddenly Peter's final remark hit him as both incongruous and ominous. "Has the room been cleaned? I have to get in there now!"

"No, not yet, but I don't know if I can . . ."

"You have to." Kai pointed to the ComStar satellite office just off the Armored Fist's lobby. "I can have a priority message sent to Tharkad and have their answer back immediately if you want."

The manager thought for a second, then shook her head. She punched some numbers into the computer, then slipped a blank magnetic key into a slot. Lights flashed and the machine beeped before spitting out the key. Then she came around from behind the desk and ran with Kai to the elevators. "What will you be looking for?"

"I don't know." Kai fought to keep his anger down. "Anything that will help me stop Peter before he gets himself in real trouble."

DropShip Zarevo, Transient Pirate Point -1.33763
Solaris VII, Federated Commonwealth

Peter felt the familiar tremors run through the DropShip as it linked up with the JumpShip *Remagen*. "Your crew is to be commended," he told his companion. "That link was quite smooth."

Nikolai Khorsakov nodded proudly. "Discipline and training are the two things that keep MechWarriors alive."

"That is so." Peter glanced at his chronometer. "How soon until we jump out?"

Khorsakov's face darkened. "We could jump now, but that wouldn't put us any closer than six days from the planet at one gravity acceleration. We can get closer, but because of the gravitational dynamics of the Shiloh system, pirate points open and close with annoying irregularity. A two-day wait here and we could jump in almost on top of Shiloh."

"I think we should go now." Peter realized that by now Kai Allard-Liao would have discovered his deception and might have gone straight to Victor to try to stop him. *Not that I would obey any order from my brother, of course.* "After all, a six-day run into the system makes sense for a merchantman. It also allows us to collect background data from the world. We might actually get the evidence we need through holovision broadcasts."

Khorsakov nodded, but Peter could read the frustration in his eyes.

"Of course, Nikolai, this doesn't mean we won't attack the Raiders." Peter smiled boldly. "It just means we'll know where they are, and that will make our job much, much easier."

Solaris City, Solaris VII
Tamarind March, Federated Commonwealth

"What the hell have you done with Peter Davion?" Kai stormed into his uncle's office, barely noticing Nancy Lee at her desk in the outer chamber. "I warned you."

Tormano looked up from a stack of holographs, patiently

and slowly, as if he hadn't a care in the world. "Ah, good morning to you, nephew. What is it, then?"

Kai resisted the impulse to leap over the desk. "Where is Peter Davion?"

"Why ask me? He merely liaises with me. I am not his keeper."

"Enough of your games, Tormano." Kai forced his fists to open. "I know that you had Khorsakov's Cossacks brought to Solaris and I know you spoke with their leaders. That means you're up to something. I also know you met with Peter, and *that* means you're up to something. Peter has vanished from Solaris and so have Nikolai Khorsakov and his people. If you got Peter mixed up with those mercenaries, you've got trouble."

As he spoke, Kai saw the light shift in his uncle's eyes, and he started putting two and two together. *I wouldn't put it past Tormano to have hired the mercs to hit a Capellan-loyalist base in the Sarna March, or even an actual Confederation world. If he has Peter liaising with that unit, it covers his ass.* He felt his stomach begin to suck in on itself. "Where have you sent them, Uncle?"

"Nikolai was here because he is an old friend and has recently retired. Peter and I had tea yesterday. Beyond that, I know nothing."

"You lying bastard." Kai wanted to put his fist through the bland smile Tormano was giving him. "If you think stonewalling me will do any good, think again. I'll find out where they are and I'll stop them. You can believe it."

"What I believe, Kai, is that you will do nothing of the kind." Tormano picked up one of the holographs on his desk, and casually flipped it toward Kai. "You have too much to lose."

Kai snapped the holograph out of the air and looked at it. *Deirdre?* It showed her and a little boy petting some deer. Kai looked back at his uncle, but the million questions he wanted to ask all jammed in his throat and not a sound came out.

Tormano stood, his smile taking on a cruel edge. "That is Dr. Deirdre Lear and her *son* David. He's already more than three years old, Kai. And you last saw her just shy of four years ago. Allow me the pleasure of presenting to you your son."

The words hit Kai like a hammer blow. *My son!* He studied the picture and tried to deny what Tormano had said, but he could not. The boy looked so much like him that no one could doubt they were close kin. He wanted to deny the evidence before his eyes, but he could not.

Tormano's voice cut through the emotional turmoil raging through Kai's mind and heart. "For the next ten days, Kai, you are going to do absolutely nothing. Just as you have people watching me, so I have people watching you. I will know your every move. If one of your DropShips leaves Solaris, I will know. Do not disappoint me and I will unite you with your son. Defy me and the holograph you now hold will be the last view you'll ever have of your son's face. You are dismissed."

Kai felt a hand tugging on his elbow. Seeing it was Nancy Lee, he followed her without conscious thought, letting her lead him out of the room. As they passed through the long hall and then down the curving staircase to street level, Kai gradually came back to his senses, and it was the awareness of Nancy Lee crying that brought him out of it.

Kai conquered the sympathetic impulse to join her. "Nancy?"

"It's my fault. I didn't know."

"What is?"

"Doctor Lear. Your uncle knew nothing about her until I found an anomaly in some records. You'd helped all the other folks from Alyina, except her." She swiped at tears with her hands. "I thought he wanted to bring you two together, especially when I heard she had a son. He's a beautiful child, but I should have guessed."

Kai grabbed her by the shoulders. "Nancy, do you know where she is? Do you know where they are?"

"No, oh God, I wish I did. I'd tell you, I would." She reached out and hugged Kai and began to sob again. "I want to help, I do, but I don't know—"

"Nancy, Nancy, get a hold of yourself." Kai held her out at arm's length. "Look, this isn't your fault. Tormano is a twisted, bitter man. I should have done something about him sooner. This is *my* fault. I do need your help."

"Anything."

"Keep your eyes and ears open. If he lets anything slip about Deirdre, let me know. Please."

"I will. Promise."

Kai gave her a kiss on the forehead. "Thanks."

"What are you going to do?"

"Anything I can, Nancy, and a hell of a lot of praying."

"Bon giorno, Sergei." The assassin greeted the broker as he entered the back room of the Red Hart Tavern and Grill, *"Come sta?"*

"Molto bene. I have what you wanted." Chou deposited a briefcase on the table, then added a small package wrapped in brown paper and tied with a string. "The rest of the reports are in the briefcase. I think you will be most pleased with the results. Everything was done to your specifications."

"As always, your work makes mine much easier. *Xiexie."*

"Bu xie." Chou bowed to the assassin and backed his way out of the room.

The assassin made no move to touch any of the things the broker had delivered. He knew, from the few words they had exchanged, that Chou had gotten all the information he had secreted in the computer files. That meant his escape plan would go into effect immediately. The sooner the security people walked him out of the room and set him on his target, the sooner he would be free.

Mandrinn's Estate, Solaris VII
Tamarind March, Federated Commonwealth

Deirdre did not like the portents offered by the smug expression on the Chief of Security's face. "I said I wanted to know when we would be leaving Solaris, Captain. The Mandrinn has made his presentation and you told me yesterday that the magnetic resonance imaging equipment is bought and ready to transport. When do we head back to Zurich?"

The man did not bother to try to conceal the lie in his reply. "Forgive the Mandrinn's caution, Doctor, but there are rumors that a *Zhanzheng de guang* assassination team is present on Solaris. It is believed they have targeted the Mandrinn and may actually be watching this estate." He patted the pistol on his right hip. "That's why my people are armed and have orders to shoot to kill. The danger should be past in two weeks or so, but until then we cannot afford to move you from here in case they should try to ambush you."

Deirdre shook her head. "I appreciate your caution, Captain. Is there nothing that you can do to get us out of here sooner?"

"Nothing, I'm afraid. The Mandrinn has told the staff to do everything to make you feel completely at home on the estate. We are at your service."

"But you won't get us on a DropShip and headed for Zurich?"

"No."

"Very well." *Let's see just how much of a prisoner I am.* "Please summon the local ComStar Precentor so I can send my family a message not to worry."

The captain smiled. "That has already been done, Dr. Lear. The Mandrinn wished to save you the expense."

"I see. Well, then, I would like to use a visiphone to call to Kai Allard-Liao."

The man blinked in surprise, then shook his head. "I'm afraid no outside contact is possible. Our communications may not be secure, and Kai has been implicated in the terrorist organization."

That is just flat not possible. Kai and Sun-Tzu would no sooner work together ... Pieces began to drop into place for Deirdre Lear. "I see."

"Please, if there is anything else I can do for you." Light mocking tones underscored the words as he turned to leave the suite.

Deirdre sat down on the edge of the couch. *David and I are hostages, we're prisoners. Tormano is using us against Kai.* She felt a sharp pang of regret as old emotions awakened in her. *I knew Kai's nature would be the death of our relationship, and now it could kill my son.*

She looked over at David playing with wooden building blocks. *Our son. Kai ... why are you doing this to us?*

Her mind flashed back to the six months she had spent with him, running from the Jade Falcons. Never would the old Kai have done anything to harm her. He'd even bargained with a Clansman, risking almost certain death, to win her freedom on Alyina. How had he gone from being a quiet warrior who accepted responsibility for all his actions to a money-grubbing play-warrior? The change must certainly have something to do with her rejection of him. *If I hadn't been so harsh, David's life wouldn't be in jeopardy now.*

She tried to reconcile her old and new views of Kai, but they fought in her mind until only the old Kai, the one she had known on Alyina, remained. Her thinking had gotten so twisted. How could she have begun to think of him in any other way?

I've been ignoring the evidence I didn't want to see. Cenotaph Charities, Inc., that's vintage Kai. And his uncle is the one who brought me here, obviously to use me against him. Tormano is the one pushing for a military conquest of the Capellan Confederation, and didn't he say he'd had a falling out with Kai? Kai must have opposed him and his plans. Oh god, Kai hasn't changed. He's still the man I knew, the man I loved. And now we're a knife being pressed to his throat.

"What's wrong, Mommy?" David reached up and brushed some of her tears away.

Deirdre snatched the boy up into her lap and hugged him tightly. "Oh, baby, I've been wrong about someone very special, and now he's in trouble because of it."

"Can we help?"

"I hope so, David." Deirdre's face hardened into an angry mask. *Kai and I eluded ComStar and Clan hunting parties for six months on Alyina. There's no way a handful of Capellan ex-patriots are going to keep me here against my will.* She kissed her son, then held him close. "We have to do some planning, but then we'll help a lot."

Solaris City, Solaris VII
Tamarind March, Federated Commonwealth

It pleased the assassin that the security men brought him and his equipment directly back to the safe house. They gave it to him without checking it first, a mistake the ice-eyed man would never have made. The assassin didn't know where the ice man had gone, but it was a good thing he had. *That* man wouldn't be sitting back watching the monitors connected to the cameras that tracked the assassin constantly. *He'd be here, probably sensing me getting ready to bolt.*

The assassin opened the case with the rifle first. The weapon had been broken down and carefully placed in the foam rubber pockets of the interior. Everything looked just as it had when he'd first stored the rifle. The scent of fresh gun-oil told him that Sergei Chou had cleaned the weapon after the ammunition had been run through it.

Pulling on a pair of white cotton gloves from within the case, the assassin looked up at the two security men in the room with him. "This is a Loftgren Supreme Model One-fifty. I modified it, did a trigger job on it and trimmed the interior of the stock so it balanced perfectly. It's a twelve point seven millimeter rifle and with the scope in place I can hit a target at two kilometers. Because I'm going to be shooting at a man who lives in a section of Silesia undergoing gentrification, I'll need that distance. I also need you to engage Room eight-oh-seven at the Armored Fist Hotel for me."

The surprised look on the men's faces told the assassin that they did not even know the name of his target. He knew he had gone too far, but without the ice-eyed man to direct them, someone had to take the lead. Determining his target had been simple: Katrina had departed the world and Victor was showing support for Tormano by appointing his brother Peter as his liaison officer. That left Ryan Steiner from his list of possibles. Ryan's complicity in the explosion that killed Galen Cox was nearly transparent. And so Ryan it would be.

The assassin pulled the report on ballistics from the case and set it on the table. He then pulled the clip from the case and shut it. One by one he thumbed the bullets from the clip and set them on the table. The first had a thick black stripe on the case and the second had a green stripe. A bullet with gold and pink stripes came next, followed by a brown and black striped shell and one with silver, red, and scarlet stripes. The last had blue and white stripes on it.

The assassin wanted to smile, for the bullets told him everything he wanted to know, but he kept up his act for the security men. He turned to the ballistics report. "The bullets I ordered for this job are boat-tailed, sabot-loaded, armor-piercing bullets. The target will be in an office, behind a window that your information claims is made of bullet-proof glass. Many people actually believe glass can stop a bullet, but that is not true."

He picked up the black bullet. "A bullet this heavy, accelerated in the rifle, will contain enough kinetic energy to deal with the glass problem and still be able to take our target out."

The assassin pointed to the graph on the first page of the report. "See here, the black bullets have a mid-range trajectory of plus one point twenty-four centimeters at a range of two hundred fifty meters. That's as close to flat as one could hope, but the accuracy tails off at five hundred meters. Which is not good." Page by page he continued through the report, impressing the men with facts and figures that they obviously did not understand. All that was important to him was to check that the charts had been bound into the report in the same order as the bullets had been placed in the clip.

"Because the gunsmith made up four of each configuration, I have four of whichever bullet I want." The assassin looked up and smiled. "I think the silver-red-scarlet bullet is the one I want to use, don't you?"

He held it up and one of the men went to take it from him, but the assassin pulled it back. "No, no, gentlemen, you don't have gloves on. I doubt your prince would like Intelligence Secretariat agent fingerprints on the shells that killed Ryan Steiner. Very bad idea."

The one man blushed while the other one laughed, and that brought a smile to the assassin's face. It occurred to him that this was the first time he had ever allowed victims to see him preparing to cause their deaths. "Yes, the tri-color it will be."

A third man entered the room. "Get your gear together. We have the room you want."

The assassin looked up expectantly. "It's on?"

"Yes," the new man said with a nod. "Tonight Duke Ryan Steiner dies."

=== 31 ===

Kai nodded as Keith Smith severed the visiphone connection with Kristina. "Sorry to ask you to break a date, Keith, but this is very important." He looked over at Larry Acuff and Fuh Teng to acknowledge their presence as well. "Right now you're the only people I can trust with this, and I'm going to need your help. After I lay it out, floor's open and we bring in anyone else we need, provided we can keep a lid on this stuff."

All three men looked sufficiently intrigued and cautioned that Kai knew he had their undivided attention. "Peter Davion has left Solaris in the company of Khorsakov's Cossacks. That unit was infamous for being virulently anti-Romano and they have no love for Sun-Tzu either. They've jumped out of this system on a mission somewhere. I understand it will take approximately ten days for results to be reported back to Solaris."

Larry frowned. "Ten days is a long time. A JumpShip can go quite a distance in that time, and with a good pirate point, troops could be on a planet almost as soon as they arrive."

Keith reached out and turned Kai's computer console around, then pulled the keyboard into his lap. "Keeping track of JumpShips for those damned Jade Falcons has got me a database full of stuff. Do you know the ship the Cossacks are using?"

Kai shook his head. "Sorry."

"Not that much of a problem, really." Keith hit a few keys

and a screen full of information scrolled into place. "Peter was here yesterday, which means we need a JumpShip on station within the last twelve hours. Only three here: the *Remagen,* the *Darlington,* and the DMCS *Shojo,* which is here to get Lady Omi and carry her home. The only one that wouldn't be limited to a one-jump range or the need to recharge in another system is the *Shojo,* which has lithium-fusion batteries."

Fuh Teng frowned. "It would not seem to me that mere arrival in a system would produce sufficient results for a report."

"I agree. I think we also have to look at hostile worlds." Kai looked at his computer expert. "What have we got for hostile worlds within thirty light years of Solaris?"

"Well, now, that depends on how you define hostile."

"What do you mean?"

Keith typed a command into the computer. "New Kyoto, Rahne, Algorab, Zaniah, and Fianna are all within range."

"But those are Federated Commonwealth worlds, Keith." Larry shook his head. "They wouldn't be heading out to a FedCom, would they?"

"A couple of those worlds do lean toward Skye in terms of politics." Keith shrugged. "Peter's got no love for Ryan Steiner."

"True, but the Cossacks have no beef with Steiner. Besides, my uncle had a hand in this."

"You should have said so." The information on the computer screen changed, bringing a frown to Keith's face. He hit another command, but the screen remained unchanged. "Not that I doubt the machine, but there isn't a single Capellan Confederation world within striking distance."

Kai's eyes narrowed. "Could my uncle have set up a command circuit?"

"I honestly doubt it, Kai. I've been tracking JumpShip traffic and I have the computer set up to recognize patterns that could improvise a circuit." Keith adjusted his glasses. "I knew you wanted to get the Jade Falcons here without having to pay JumpShip masters to wait around for ComStar and everyone else to approve the trip. So I've been looking for patterns of ships. We had one seven weeks ago that looked real good, but it fell apart before we could use it. We're close again now, but the title match is over so it doesn't matter. Anyway, I don't show anything like a command circuit going toward the Capellan Confederation."

"Can't rule it out entirely, but let's assume it has a low probability." Kai leaned forward on his desk, pressing his palms flat against the sheet of glass covering the mahogany top. "If it's not Capellan, what is it? Free Worlds League?"

"No offense, Kai, but your uncle could easily have planned something just about that crazy." Larry's face darkened. "I'd have thought Duke Peter would be too smart to go along with it, but reading Chinese is easier than reading him."

"Eight worlds in range in the Free Worlds League. Want a list?"

Kai was about to answer when the intercom buzzed. He hit a button on the control console. "Yes?"

"Gatehouse, sir. Perkins here."

"Yes, Mr. Perkins?"

"Sir, Mr. Wu Deng Tang is here. He wants to see you."

Kai shook his head. "I'm very busy right now, Mr. Perkins. Please tell Mr. Wu I will call him when I'm able."

"Yes, sir, but he says its urgent. He says he has to return the favor you did him before your fight. Return it in kind, he says."

Before the fight? I had people watch over his wife so she wouldn't be hurt. Kai felt a cold chill work its way down his spine. "Please, Mr. Perkins, send Mr. Wu up."

"On our way, sir."

Fuh Teng got up and headed toward the office door. "What do you think it is, Kai?"

Kai's head came up slowly. "I don't know." *Dare I guess he knows something about Deirdre and David?* Kai slipped his hand into the pocket of his jacket. The holograph felt cool to his touch.

Fuh Teng opened the door and Wu walked in. He looked tired, and perspiration dotted his brow. He looked around at the other men in the room, then at Kai. "I've had a message from my father."

"He was pleased to hear of the birth of your son?"

"Yes, he was, but that's not what brought me here." Wu paused to catch his breath, then began to speak slowly. "First, he asked to be remembered to you and said he hoped you served Prince Victor as well as your father had served Hanse Davion."

"I've never met your father and for a Capellan officer to mention my father . . ."

"If it's not a curse, it could get him killed, I know." Wu shook his head. "He said that our fight and the honor you showed me would have to suffice for honor in the Wu family this year. He had hoped otherwise because he has been told enemies are inbound and his Harloc Raiders are ready for them. However he has been ordered to pull his people into the fortifications they have created there, and is to leave the defense of the planet to the local forces."

Kai's jaw shot open, then snapped shut again. "Did your father say who the enemies were? Did he mention Khorsakov's Cassocks?"

It was Wu's turn to appear stunned. "How did you know?"

"Where is your father stationed?"

"Shiloh. He's training there with the Third Sirian Lancers in a joint operation."

"Shiloh's on my list."

Kai sat down hard and sank back into his chair. "This is even more monstrous than I would have imagined. The Cossacks make for Shiloh with Peter Davion at their head and your father kills them because he's been tipped off that they're coming."

Wu blanched. "Peter Davion is with them?"

Kai nodded. "His death would force Victor to attack the Capellan Confederation because it would be one of their units on a League world that killed Peter. And that's just what my uncle wants. And if the Cossacks did get back out, along with Peter, suddenly the Federated Commonwealth has proof that Sun-Tzu is staging Capellan troops on League worlds within striking distance of Federated Commonwealth holdings."

Larry Acuff shivered. "Why order the raiders to pull back?"

"So they won't kill Peter." Kai looked up at Wu. "You said your father is conducting training operations with the Third Sirian Lancers? Has he talked about them?"

"He said they're game troops, but as green as spring leaves. The Cossacks will destroy them."

"Which means that Peter Davion is leading a strike against a Free Worlds League planet." Kai's breath hissed in between his teeth. 'That, in turn, will cause Thomas Marik to declare war on the Federated Commonwealth, which is something Sun-Tzu would love to see."

"But Thomas can't do anything against the Federated Commonwealth because his son Joshua is with the doctors on New Avalon. He's a hostage." Keith combed his fingers back through his light brown hair. "A man can't take an action that might get his child killed."

"I could not," Wu said in a whisper.

"Sometimes a man has to." As the other men in the room looked at Kai, a lump caught in his throat like a fishbone. He pulled out the holograph and slid it across the table. Keith caught it before it could fall to the carpeted floor, then held it for Wu and Larry to see.

Larry pointed at the woman in the picture. "That's Dr. Lear, right? She was on Alyina."

Kai nodded. "That's my son with her. Tormano has them both. He said I'd never see them again if I do anything to oppose him."

Fuh Teng hung his head. "But to do nothing means a war erupts."

"I know." Kai felt helpless, but he forced the feeling away and sat forward in his chair. "We have to stop this idiocy before millions of people are killed. If doing that means . . . it just has to be done."

"Do as my father suggests, Kai." Wu pointed to the visiphone on the side table. "Send a message to Victor through ComStar. Have him recall his brother."

"Can't, for two reasons. The first is that Victor can't send troops into the Free Worlds League without triggering the war we're trying to avert. In fact, if Victor knew about the Harloc Raiders being on Shiloh, he might just send his own forces there to destroy them. The second reason we can't have Victor recall Peter is because Peter would go in just to spite his brother. My Uncle Tormano has Peter absolutely full of himself. That's why we're going to have to stop him."

"What do we do?" Keith set the picture of Deirdre and David back on the desk. "Tell us and it's done."

Kai thought for a second, then looked at his companions one by one before speaking. "This plan is probably full of holes, but I think it could work. Fuh Teng, you'll use the visiphone to call up every fighter Cenotaph has under contract. We'll need them ready to move because we're going to send a force after Peter. But this has to be kept quiet. Give them no details, just tell them I need their help."

He looked over at Wu Deng Tang. "Look, you don't need any part of this, but if you want to help you could get people here in Cathay to start spreading rumors. All kinds—about my being very, very depressed and in seclusion or my being manic and out celebrating insanely. The wilder the better. Tormano is going to be watching me and I want his information network flooded with so many reports and rumors that he won't be able to sort the wheat from the chaff."

"I owe you my son's life. I'll do what I can to safeguard yours."

"Thank you." Kai turned to Larry. "Larry, you'll have to get us the supplies the folks Fuh Teng brings in will need. Include you and me in that mix."

"You going to be driving Yen-lo-wang?"

"Can't. Tormano or one of his people would notice it missing." Kai cracked a wry smile. "Kallon Industries won't mind me doing an extended field test with that *Penetrator*. Order stuff in odd lots, duplicate purchase orders, buy from small distributors. It will have to be here in one day, so stay local."

"You got it, boss."

"Good." Kai looked down for a moment, trying to impose order on the chaos in his mind. "Tormano will be watching the *Zhangshi* and the other ships we use. I'll arrange for alternate transport, then I'll help Fuh Teng bring people in."

Keith set the computer keyboard on top of the monitor. "That leaves me. You want me to use my incredible computer skills to find your son for you?"

"Yeah, Keith, I do, but that's your second priority." Kai glanced down at the holograph, then looked up again. "You're going to have to provide cover for this whole operation through the computers. There can be no records of our purchases after they're delivered. People who will be gone must appear to have all the normal computer traffic coming in and going from their homes. We need bills and bar tabs and clothing orders and anything else you can think of dumped into the computer pool so Tormano's people will think they're still tracking us.

"My uncle is a man who prides himself on being both intelligent and subtle. He will listen to an eyewitness sighting, but he will *believe* in a credit card bill for a meal or a pilfered telecom statement that says I was here making calls. His people will be watching all those things anyway, so we have to satisfy him."

Keith nodded slowly. "You know, this is going to be a full time job until you're gone, because I'll be making up new things and erasing old things. Won't be until after you leave that I can start looking for your son."

Kai's guts twisted around at those words. "Yes, and I know that puts him at risk. My uncle's given me no other choice, really, because if Tormano can use the boy successfully against me here and now, he'll keep him. This time Tormano demands my inactivity. What do I do next time when he demands I act?"

"I'd make sure there isn't a next time." Keith picked up the holograph. "Uncle or no, he threatens my kid, I'd stamp paid on his account."

"I agree, but I can't do that until I know David's safe." Kai stood up. "And we can't make sure he's safe until we've stopped this war."

Duke Ryan Steiner smiled as Sven Newmark made his report. "You're certain, Sven?"

"Yes, my lord. We can find no trace of Peter Davion on Solaris. That fact, coupled with Mandrinn Liao's report, would seem to indicate that Peter is no longer a problem." The Rasalhague expatriot offered Ryan his hand. "Congratulations, sir, I think we may have turned the corner."

Ryan rose from behind his desk and pumped Sven's arm heartily. "You may be correct, Mr. Newmark." The duke allowed himself a low chuckle as he gathered his hands at the small of his back and walked to the window. Looking out toward Cathay and the Black Hills, he saw uneven, fire-blackened crenelations crowning The Sun and The Sword tower. "Two birds killed with one stone there, and now Peter has been thrown to the wolves. Victor is quickly losing his supporters."

"There is no doubt, my lord, that the legitimacy of his

claim to the title is in question." Newmark sat down in a chair near Ryan's desk.

Ryan nodded, then smiled as he looked down into the street. "This squalid scene below me is indicative of how unsuited the Davions are to rule over the Lyran Commonwealth. Davions believe in symbols. You have a street full of decay and what do you do to improve it? You festoon it with these colored banners on the lamp posts. Not only does it do nothing to solve the problem, but silver, red, and scarlet is hardly an eye-catching combination of colors.

"Steiners, on the other hand, have ever understood the problem of poverty and its solution. As I did in coming here and investing in rehabilitating this building. My presence in the quarter will encourage others to come in with improvements. We bring money to a community, and it creates jobs. Money makes more money, but the Lyran Commonwealth has suffered because of three decades of the Davions vampirizing our capital assets."

Ryan half-turned, presenting his profile to both Newmark and the window. "The Lyran Commonwealth will not be a banquet at which the Clans and Davions can sup. I will see to it. This I vow, on pain of death!"

Half a kilometer away, at an elevation approximately twenty meters above the point where Duke Ryan Steiner stood in his window, a gloved finger tightened on the trigger of the Loftgren 150. That tripped the sear, pulling it from the notch in the striker that held it back. Freed of resistance, the spring bunched behind the striker in the bolt assembly and pushed it forward. The striker, in turn, drove the firing pin forward and into the bottom of the cartridge in the breech.

The firing pin smashed into the cartridge right where the primer had been placed. Inside the primer a small anvil moved forward, compressing the primer explosive. As it had been designed to do, the chemical exploded, introducing fire into the propellant in the base of the cartridge. Less than .05 seconds had passed since the trigger had been squeezed.

The cartridge had been filled with 9.72 grams of high explosive propellant. It ignited very quickly and pressure built in the cartridge from the expansion of the burning propellant. As the pressure increased, the cartridge itself began to warp and the fire sought escape. The easiest route it could

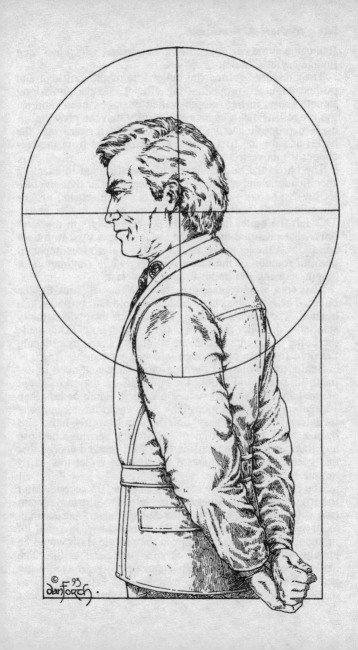

find came at the narrow end of the cartridge, which had been plugged with a bullet.

The pressure squirted the bullet free of the cartridge and pushed unburned propellant out after it into the gun's long throat. There, in the smooth-walled chamber, even more of the propellant had a chance to combust and the pressure increased proportionately. The bullet hurled forward into the barrel and for the first time since being freed from the cartridge, it met resistance.

The barrel the bullet entered had been milled to exacting specifications and was .254 millimeters smaller than the bullet itself. The six flat lands inside the barrel planed off the offending .254 millimeters of excess metal on the bullet. This left the bullet its original 1.27 centimeters in diameter only where it fitted against the six grooves scored in a tight spiral down the length of the barrel. These grooves imparted one full rotation of the bullet for every 17.78 centimeters of length, causing the bullet to spin very fast.

That spin would guarantee stable flight ballistics for the bullet. The bullet had been cast in a mold that provided it a boattail. The bullet's tail end tapered back so it was actually smaller in diameter than it was at its widest point. This made the bullet much more efficient at longer ranges by reducing the drag from the air through which it passed.

Behind the bullet the burning propellant continued to expand. Its fire would follow the bullet all the way up and out of the barrel. It would produce a muzzle flame of less than 15 centimeters. Much more than that would have been easy to detect in the dull gray Solaris sky. It would have also been a mark of an inefficient load in the cartridge because any flame that showed outside the barrel marked energy that had been unused in the act of sending the bullet toward its target.

The bullet left the rifle's muzzle a scant .075 seconds after the trigger had been squeezed. Its velocity as it moved into free flight came in at just under 868.68 meters per second. With the target only five hundred meters away, it would hit in under a second. The light from the muzzle flash would be enough to register in Duke Ryan's peripheral vision. The .61043-second flight time from muzzle to target would not permit him to even begin to evaluate that data.

As the bullet flew it lost velocity and started to lose in its fight with gravity. The rifle had been sighted in to take this into account. When the sight showed the target centered in the crosshairs, the muzzle actually aimed at a point 15.24 centimeters higher than that. At closer ranges that would have meant the rifle would shoot high, but because it had been sighted for a half a kilometer, it married aimpoint to bullet flight trajectory.

Bullet-proof glass is actually a misnomer. Glass, while it can be thickened, strengthened, and hardened, is like any other armor. It is subject to the laws of physics, which do not allow for the paradoxical existence of both an immovable object—the glass—and an irresistible force—the bullet. Bulletproof glass will stop or deflect many projectiles—at least the most common ones, which are the types the vast majority of assassins and terrorists and lone nuts might possess. Even so, a heavier than normal caliber will shatter it.

So will specialized ammunition.

When the sabot-loaded, armor-piercing round hit the glass, it transferred an incredible amount of kinetic energy to the glass itself. The glass, which is in reality a very slow-moving liquid, began to bulge inward. As the energy stressed its crystalline lattice, the glass began to give way. Microfractures began to spread through the glass at the point of impact, forming a cone that expanded in toward the room.

The microfractures might have been seen as a failure of the glass, but, in effect, they were just the glass doing its job. Creating the fractures bled off energy. While the glass gave way in a very small area, it managed to resist the rapidly spent bullet. The rest of the structure held and the 34.02 grams of lead flattened itself against the glass without penetrating it.

The tungsten sabot around which the bullet had been formed did not surrender as easily as its softly malleable lead sheath. The metal needle shed its metallic coat and punched through the microfractured portion of the glass. Barely 3.175 millimeters in diameter, it crossed the thirty-six centimeters between the window and Duke Ryan's head in .0007 seconds and, because of the uneven fracturing of the glass, had become slightly unstable in flight.

The needle's point hit Ryan just above his left ear. It penetrated the hair and flesh as if they were not there, then struck bone. As the bullet itself had done to the glass, the needle transferred much of its energy to the bone structure of Ryan's skull. The dome began to compress and would fracture because of the stresses. Unfortunately for Ryan, that fact would only be discovered upon autopsy.

The needle had twisted in flight, fishtailing slightly toward the back of his skull. This really made no material difference in results of the damage, but it did cause the entry wound to have a peculiar shape. This would confuse ballistics experts and forensic scientists and would create a microeconomy of authors and investigators who would continue to argue for decades about the number of shooters there had actually been. Though they would never uncover anything of substance in the matter, their speculations would hound and harry Sven Newmark to the point where the man would commit suicide.

At the point of impact, the skull's interior surface exploded. It filled the cranial cavity with bone fragments that ripped through Ryan's brain. The organic shrapnel destroyed cells and severed both synapses and blood vessels. The damage from bone splinters alone would have been enough to paralyze Ryan Steiner, akin to the effects of a massive stroke, and kill him were medical intervention not available.

The sabot pierced the brain and had turned enough that it moved sideways through the collection of neurons. The actual number of cells it destroyed was insignificant compared to the overall make-up of the brain. It quickly outstripped the bone shards in their flights and approached the far side of Ryan's skull.

What did the most damage, ultimately, was the shockwave traveling behind the needle. It homogenized a cone-shaped segment of Ryan's brain, fatally disrupting all his bodily functions. It stopped all reasoning and destroyed sensory portions of his brain. It also tore apart the brain's circulatory system, rendering the body incapable of bringing to the brain the things it would need to repair itself.

The needle had spent all but a fraction of its energy when it hit the far side of the skull. It impacted almost broadside and blew out through Ryan's right ear. As it came out, so did a jet of blood and organic material that actually snapped Ryan's head back toward the window through which the shot had come. His body fell to the left and his head struck the window. He left enough of a smear on the window to fuel the speculation that, in fact, he had been shot from the right and below head level.

According to experts, that put the murder weapon in the hands of Sven Newmark. They decided he had been an agent placed in Duke Ryan's service by the Rasalhague underground. People pointed to the dissatisfaction among some of the Rasalhague community over Ryan's involvement in the attempted kidnapping of Prince Ragnar on Arc-Royal the year before. It was the flimsiest of motives, which made it that much stronger to conspiracy theorists. The fact that Arc-Royal belonged to Morgan Kell, and Morgan was a cousin to Victor Davion, all seemed to make sense in a twisted sort of way.

In the end, none of that would matter. In under two seconds from the time the assassin's finger stroked the trigger of his gun, Ryan Steiner, his plots, and all the secrets he knew lay dead in an expanding pool of blood on the floor of his office.

32

The assassin backed away from the window and shucked his arm from the sling he had used to help steady the rifle. With a trace of regret he tossed the whole weapon onto the bed, then knelt at the foot of it and snaked a hand under the coverlet and between the mattress and box spring. There he felt a leather strap and pulled it free. With it came a shoulder holster and needle pistol with two reload blocks.

He had been told to wait for his control officers to return to the room after he had shot Ryan, which was a mistake. Despite the very slim chance of someone spotting and later identifying an Intelligence Secretariat agent on the scene, one of them *should have* stayed in the room with him. The assassin knew the ice-eyed man would never have left him alone, which also meant he'd be dead by now and the secret of who shot Ryan Steiner along with him.

The door to the connecting room opened, and the two agents who came through it did not have their guns drawn. They had apparently expected him to believe the fiction they'd told him on the way over, but the assassin knew better than to think Prince Victor would ever let him get away. He pointed the needle pistol at the two agents, then pulled the trigger repeatedly.

The needle pistol carved its projectiles from a block of ballistic plastic and propelled them through an explosion of propellant gas in the chamber. The first cloud of needles took the face off the lead agent. The second shot hit him in

the shoulder, with enough getting past to hit the woman behind him in the forehead. The assassin's finger hit the trigger
a third time, blowing a hole in her chest. He shot a fourth
time, guaranteeing the death of the first agent, then rose and
jumped over both bodies.

He sped into their room, then opened the door to the hallway. A quick look showed no agents in the hall, so he ran
down to room 827 and knocked once on the door. It opened
to admit him, a smiling punk waving him in. The assassin
crossed the threshold, waiting until the punk had shut the
door and gone to sit on the bed before turning on him. He
shoved the needle pistol up under the punk's chin, then
pulled the trigger, killing him instantly.

The body fell back on the bed. The assassin pressed the
needle pistol into the punk's hand, leaving his fingerprints
on the weapon. In keeping with the instructions and coded
terms on the disk he had given Sergei Chou, the dead boy
had been the person to sight in the sniper rifle, fill the clip,
and pack everything away. Trace evidence on the body and
clothes would prove the kid had fired the weapon. The Constabulary would also find a suicide note implicating the
young man in Ryan's murder when they searched the apartment. The assassin did not care what motive Chou's forgers
had invented, all that mattered was that the kid be a fall guy
that no one would question.

From the room's closet he pulled a long black rain slicker.
He donned it, keenly aware of the weight of the knife in the
right sleeve and the feel of the sawed-off shotgun dangling
beside his right leg. He slipped his hand in through the right
pocket and felt straight through to the weapon's pistol grip.
In the left side pocket he found shells, though he was certain
he wouldn't need them.

In the bathroom he found a plastic bag with a fake goatee
and mustache, which he pressed into place. He knew the disguise would never hold up to close inspection, but they
changed the shape of his face enough to conceal his identity
under initial scrutiny. Also in the bag he found what looked
like an ordinary eye patch, though its weave actually permitted him to see out through it and enough space existed at the
corner of his eye for his peripheral vision to function. He
settled the patch over his left eye, the one which he closed
when shooting anyway, then greased his hair back and used

the hotel's courtesy comb to change the part to a centerline stripe that made him look like a person in from a hick town like Joppo.

He flushed the plastic bag down the toilet and put the comb in his pocket. He left behind some stray hairs he had combed just so Victor would have something to remember him by.

Peering through the peephole in the door, the assassin saw that the hall was empty. He left the room with the door ajar slightly, then walked to the stairs at the end of the corridor and went up a flight. On the ninth floor he went to the elevators and pushed the Down tab. When the elevator arrived with a discreet hiss, he selected the lobby and waited patiently as the box descended.

He had just reached the lobby and turned into the corridor leading into the north wing when he began to hear police sirens keening in the background. He waited to hear if the sirens were getting closer or going away toward Ryan's office, but it was impossible to tell. He pushed that concern into the part of his mind that catalogued and dealt with trivia, then continued down the corridor. In another twenty paces he would be at the auxiliary north lobby and free.

The assassin was surprised that he'd been able to make it even this far. If he had anything to thank it was the malaise affecting most of the Lyran Commonwealth. The ice-eyed man had Tharkad written all over him. The locals would have strongly resented the man's arriving to take over coordination of activities concerning the assassin. But the assassin had not seen the ice-eyed man since Galen Cox's assassination, so he must have left Solaris with Katrina. Freed from the ice man's scrutiny, his subordinates must have suddenly relaxed.

The lobby was empty, so the assassin continued out through the door and on up Dusseldorf Street. The street was festooned with orange and white banners on both sides, while the lamp posts of Demien Street, back on the south side of the hotel, were strung with black banners. Yet further south were green banners, gold and pink banners, silver red and scarlet banners, and blue and white banners—all corresponding to the stripes on his bullets.

The assassin let no smile reach his lips as he sauntered along Dusseldorf Street for the requisite five blocks. The code was simple, having been set up with Chou long ago. The assassin speaking in Italian would indicate he was under surveillance and he needed an escape arranged. Surveillance on him meant Chou would also be watched, so the latter would have to coordinate things through subordinates. That was no problem, however. The plan had been put together in such a way that matters could be handled piecemeal without revealing the whole plot.

Chou had selected the punk who would be the scapegoat for the assassination. A substantial bribe to a member of the housekeeping staff had placed the pistol in room 807—the people involved would later be killed. Chou's people had created the banners and had put them up to decorate the better part of Silesia. That had been the best part of the plan and doubtless had the Intelligence Secretariat people chasing around well south of the assassin trying to figure out the code in the banners.

The Intelligence Secretariat agents would remember the sequence in which the bullets had been ordered in the clip. They would assume the assassin would go down Demien Street, in the direction of the black banners, then turn where the banners became green and again when the gold and pink banners appeared. It would not so much lead them away from him as all over the place, especially when banners went in two directions at once. It would confuse them, leaving him in control and better able to make his escape.

The assassin cut east on Ashing Street, then crossed in mid-block to head north on Bruno. He went up the left side of the street, scanning the façades that would give him the last piece of the puzzle. He was concerned that he had still not been able to figure it out, but he trusted Chou enough to know the man would not have left him hanging. *It is here, it has to be. You will find it.*

The code in the bullets was not related to the colors, however, but to the words for them. Where the Intelligence Secretariat people saw the color black, the assassin had keyed on the Italian word for that color: *nero*. The initial told him to head north. Green came next, which in Italian was *verde*. The initial *v* did not correspond to the direction, but became a roman numeral and told him to head north five blocks. Gold and pink combined through *oro* and *rosa* to form "or," or the first two initials of the Italian word for east, *orientale*.

Chou had gotten fancy with the fourth bullet. Brown was *bruno* in Italian, which designated the street he should take. Black sent him north again. Silver/red/scarlet produced *argento rosso scarlatto*, which he interpreted to be *angolo retto sinestro* or right-angle left. In the code they had established that meant he would be entering an establishment on the left side of the street.

The last bullet, the blue/white one, had him stumped. In Italian that became *azzurro bianco*, which had no clear meaning. He had puzzled over the meaning of blue/white or the initials *a* and *b* and had come up with a number of different possibilities. *AB* would denote a blood bank and blue/white could cover anything from an aquarium or seafood store to a holovid theatre showing a feature on Terra.

Then he saw it and recognized it more by how it looked than the meaning of the sign over the door. The little tavern had no front on the street, just a doorway and stairs leading up. The sign over the door showed a Steiner fist holding a short axe and the chipped and peeling wording beneath it read, The White Hatchet.

The assassin nodded once. *Accetta bianco*, white hatchet. It bothered the assassin a bit that Sergei had slipped and used a color as its equivalent in the coding, but his hunger to be inside the sanctuary let him dismiss the concern. He mounted the stairs and came up to a large common room filled with smoke and a lot of wooden furniture. Most of the chairs were missing bits and pieces, and many more were held together by a combination of rusty screws and lumps of wood-glue. At first glance it seemed the same was true of the place's stinking patrons.

The bartender looked at him the second he entered, then reached under the bar. His hand came up with a key dangling from a length of leather, which prevented the assassin from cutting the man in half with a shotgun blast. "In the back, to the right."

The assassin took the key and found the room. It lay just beyond the bathrooms and had a sign reading Manager hanging from one screw on it. He opened the door and slipped inside, then closed and locked it. The door was too flimsy to make him feel secure, but he didn't expect to spend much time there. Had there been a chair in the room, even one as flimsy as those in the common room outside, he would have wedged it under the door knob.

The accommodations were primitive, but that was to be expected. An old four-poster bed dominated the room, allowing for maybe half a meter or so between it and the wardrobe on the side. The sink in the wall shared with the bathroom on the other side had rust stains on the porcelain and a flyblown mirror above. A chest of drawers alongside the bed sagged a bit and balanced on two bricks in lieu of one of its legs.

The assassin knew the key to his escape lay in changing his appearance. He pulled open the top drawer of the chest and pulled out a toilet kit. He opened it and removed a battery-operated clipper. He placed it by the sink, then shrugged off his coat and the shirt under it. He tossed both of them on the bed, leaving the shotgun lying on top and within easy reach.

Flipping the clipper on, he cut a stripe down the center of his head. His dark hair hit his shoulders, some of it also drifting to the floor. It came off quickly enough, only leaving a faint trace of stubble in its place. The assassin would use the razor in the kit to complete the job of shaving his head, but first he had to get the longer hair off.

Though the buzz of the clippers was deafening, the assassin did not feel in jeopardy. Sergei Chou's blunder at the end of the code would have been a disaster had the target not been Duke Ryan Steiner. Because of Victor's paranoia about Ryan, no agent who had grown up in the Isle of Skye would have been part of the assassination plot. A high percentage of people in Skye understood Italian, but it remained remarkably low in the rest of the Federated Commonwealth. And so did the chances of his detection.

Shorn, his head felt cold. He ignored the sensation and completed the job by covering his pate with shaving lather, then taking a razor to it. He dried his head with his shirt, then stripped out of the rest of his clothes. Digging into the second drawer of the dresser, he pulled out and wound a saffron-colored cotton sheet around his body. Over that he pulled a brown cloak, quickly completing his transformation into a Buddhist monk.

After lacing up a pair of well-worn sandals and donning a beat-up pair of glasses, the assassin looked at himself in the mirror. He did not look his best, which was desirable. He added a slouch and locked his right hand into a claw as if it were crippled. Moving stiffly, he pulled the door open and slowly shuffled out into the bar.

He passed unnoticed among the patrons, then became virtually invisible once outside among the crowd of townsfolk and tourists. Moving on, he felt more confident about his escape with each step away from the Armored Fist. Indeed, he yearned to be free of Solaris as quickly as possible.

A hand landed heavily on his shoulder. "Wait."

He turned, remaining in character, but ready to strike with his gnarled hand. "Yes?"

A smiling young woman pressed a coin into his hand. "I won a wager, and you should share my good fortune." She smiled and winked, then disappeared into the crowd.

The assassin looked down at the gold coin. Melissa Steiner Davion's face smiled up at him from one side and when he flipped it over he saw Victor's image. *I have worked against your house once, Victor, and in its favor another time. We are even.*

As he moved on, the assassin reflected for a bit on whether he would work for or against Victor in the future. He reviewed many possible scenarios as he headed for the spaceport, but rejected all save one. *Whether for or against, the decision will not be made in my heart or my mind.* He hefted the coin and smiled. *My loyalty goes to the highest bidder, and if you're smart, Prince Victor Davion, that person will be you.*

danforth © 93.

Solaris City, Solaris VII
Tamarind March, Federated Commonwealth
25 April 3056

So intent was Kai Allard-Liao on watching the BattleMechs march themselves into the ovoid hull of the DropShip *Taizai* that he remained unaware of her presence until she touched him on the shoulder. He jumped and she uttered a gasp, then he bowed. "*Konnichi-wa*, Kurita Omi-*sama*." Kai straightened from his bow slowly, both out of respect and to give his mind a chance to refocus. "Your loan of this DropShip is most generous."

Omi smiled carefully. "I enlisted Victor and his people to save my brother from the Clans. It is the least I can do to help you and your people to save his brother from treachery."

"It is a pity that this is a secret we must both keep from him." Kai winced. "I regret deeply having to ask that you keep this hidden from Victor. He deserves your trust more than I."

"Victor must save his concern for threats that have yet to be averted. Revealing to him how his brother was duped will serve neither one of them." The Kurita woman remained composed despite the march of garishly colored BattleMechs through the hangar and into the ship. All had moved to the spaceport via the tunnels underneath the city, marking the unique status of Solaris City, where a mass migration of BattleMechs could take place without causing any commotion or alarm. "I see many 'Mechs here that do not show the black and gold of Cenotaph Stable."

"Only a dozen of my people are going." Kai shook his head. "We tried to keep it quiet, but word got out and a number of fighters showed up offering to go. They had no idea what the mission was, but it was enough that they'd heard I was putting a call. Keith says he's got the security breach under control by now, though."

"You sound surprised by the response."

"I suppose I am. It's true that I've helped a number of fighters with little things, but I never thought . . ."

Omi smiled and patted him on the shoulder. "You are a man many would emulate."

"Am I?" Kai breathed in slowly. "Will Deirdre understand if the worst occurs?"

"Perhaps, but you cannot dwell on the worst. You have your mission to perform. You are doing it to save the lives of countless people. You must succeed. The rest is in the hands of the gods."

"I know, though I hate trusting in fate. I did what fate seemed to dictate once and that's exactly the reason I've only seen my son in a holograph." Kai turned toward Keith Smith as the man came walking over with a comp pad in his hands. "Anything good to report?"

"Lots, as long as you're not Tormano Liao." Keith glanced at the comp pad's LCD display. "I've covered all the orders Larry made and have arranged for the bills to be paid so no one will squawk about that. I've got you involved in your normal routine of training and have a couple of reminders going from you to ComStar to ask about the Jade Falcons. You're also inquiring about the costs of sending them a copy of the fight holodisk. I have routines worked out for everyone else, including those last two guys, Simpson and Taylor. Oh, and I even have Cathy Kessler engaged to repaint Yen-lo-wang."

"Nice touch, that. Tormano will track the 'Mech and assume I'm not far from it."

"That's what I assume. By the way, flight clearance has come in for the *Taizai* to carry Lady Omi back to the Combine." Keith looked up from his comp pad. "I'll take her back to your house and get her squared away before I really start working."

"Thanks, Keith." Kai said, then turned to Omi. "Omi, thank you for the loan of this ship and for agreeing to hide out in my home until our return. If this goes bad, remember, we coerced you into letting us use the ship."

"It will not go bad."

Larry Acuff came running over to the group. "We're all loaded up, Kai. I've got one company, Chris Taylor has another, and you're leading the third. We're all good to go."

"Then we shall." Kai bowed to Omi, then offered Keith his hand. "Thanks for everything you've done, my friend."

"I'll find your boy, Kai."

"I know you will." Kai pulled a card from the pocket of the vest he wore over his cooling suit. "If you get the information before we've reported back from Shiloh, shoot the whole packet to this number. It's a computer on the other end and they'll know what to do when they see it."

Keith accepted the card. "Four-four-nine prefix—that's Joppo, isn't it?"

"Trust me as much as I trust you."

"It's your son, Kai. I'll do as you ask." Keith pocketed the card. "Shoot straight and dodge the incoming shots."

Kai drew strength from Keith's confident smile. "Will do. We'll report when we have results."

Glenn Edenhoffer, thinking himself an artist, wallowed in the realm of emotion to the detriment of his relationships with others and his whole life in general. He used emotions as inspiration, but his humiliation after the fight with Allard-Liao and Cox had cut deeply into his self-confidence. Cox's death in the explosion at The Sun and The Sword had removed any chance of self-redemption, only deepening Edenhoffer's depression.

The mood darkened Edenhoffer's world and so skewed his view of everything that he had begun to see the fight in new terms. Cox's death elevated him above the fray and allowed Edenhoffer to focus his ire and anguish upon Kai Allard-Liao. Kai's victory over Wu Deng Tang looked to Edenhoffer like yet another display of noble disdain and contempt for the more common folk.

Given his biases, Edenhoffer should have welcomed the death of Duke Ryan Steiner at the hands of an assassin. He would have considered it an example of just the kind of action necessary if humanity was to awaken from its lethargy and reclaim its heritage of greatness. Of course, Edenhoffer would never admit that he had no concrete ideas to back the rhetoric he spouted—as an artist dwelling in the realm of emotion it was only necessary to inflame. The rest, he presumed, would come naturally.

In his current state of mind the duke's death became a sacrilege, a heinous act with only one purpose. That purpose, as Edenhoffer saw it, was to place the ownership of the Skye Tigers in the hands of Ryan's widow, Morasha Kelswa. As that lady had never taken the slightest interest in the stable, she immediately offered it for sale and had provided no guidance on how the stable was to be managed. Which meant Edenhoffer could not arrange a fight with Kai Allard-Liao to redeem his honor.

He decided that Kai had ordered Ryan's murder specifically to deny him a rematch. This put Kai at the top of Glenn Edenhoffer's list of enemies—a distinction because it usually took someone a considerable amount of time to work their way up that very long list. Kai's placement at the top meant that Edenhoffer began to focus on the man and everything about him and his activities in hopes of finding a way to thwart him as Glenn had been thwarted.

Because of his obsession, Edenhoffer correlated two facts. The first was that Tormano Liao had people interested in knowing where Kai was at any given moment. He had also gotten wind of a number of MechWarriors being called out on a mission, though it had been difficult sorting through the lies and rumor. That message indicated that MechWarriors who felt they owed Kai a favor should bring their 'Mechs through the tunnels to the spaceport because Kai had something going.

Glenn garnered all the details he could and determined that Kai was planning to leave Solaris. He decided this was information that Tormano Liao might find useful. Walking to the wall of his apartment, where he had pasted the invitation to Tormano's reception into the collage he had started before the fight, he located the number for Tormano's office. He punched it into the visiphone, raking his hair into place with his fingers as the call was answered on the other end.

Tormano looked up from the pile of notes concerning Kai that had been accumulating on his desk. He frowned, his hands crushing slips of paper into balls. "Did that call bring another rumor?"

Nancy Lee shook her head. "It was Glenn Edenhoffer. He was one of the two fighters who lost to Kai and Galen Cox."

Tormano smiled and leaned back, leaving crumpled paper on the desk. "And did Mr. Edenhoffer have anything useful to offer?"

"I'm not sure," she said, but Tormano could tell from the way her nose wrinkled up that she sincerely doubted it. "He suggested that with Duke Ryan's death, you might want to buy the Skye Tigers. I thanked him and told him you would speak with him late next week."

"What an idiot that man is." Tormano shook his head, then looked up at Nancy. "Thank you, my dear, for handling him so adroitly."

"It is my pleasure to serve you, my lord."

"Indeed. I don't know what I would do without you."

34

DropShip Zarevo, Inbound Shiloh
Free Worlds League
27 April 3056

As far as Peter was concerned, the background chatter from the three Shiloh holovision networks mixed incongruously with the intensity of the discussion in the *Zarevo*'s ready room. There was no disguising the disappointment in the voices of the troopers as they reported negative information about the Harloc Raiders. *Normally, folks would be happy to know the enemy is bottled up in their base, but we all wanted to hit hard and destroy them in a sharp, decisive battle.* He glanced down at the holographically displayed order of battle for the Harloc Raiders and wondered where they were hiding. *It's as if they knew we were coming.*

The Cossacks had originally planned to land their DropShips on the plains of Chatham and deploy both regiments south, toward the Raiders' last known area of operation. Initial data from Shiloh had looked normal and placed the Raiders near their intended landing zone. Then, suddenly, all information about the Raiders stopped flowing.

As nearly as they could tell from the data they monitored on Shiloh, the only forces that would oppose them on planet were the Third Sirian Lancers. Nikolai Khorsakov had dismissed them because the virtually green Lancers had no chance against a highly trained, elite mercenary unit like the Cossacks. "I would never suggest they'd simply fold up like a house of cards in a tornado, Highness, but I really have no respect for them."

Peter, though he found the assessment as foolish as it was

frank, tended to agree with the aging mercenary leader. Even their intended prey, the Harloc Raiders, were not much of a threat. The unit was too new to have been blooded in battle, so the only way it could present much challenge was if Sun-Tzu had stripped the elite fighters from all his other units and sent them here. Peter thought that possibility very unlikely.

For Peter, Wu Kang Kuo became the key to the puzzle. Khorsakov denigrated Wu's past experience, but Peter thought the Capellan officer smart enough to be planning a trap. Obviously, Wu would dispute their landing, for any commander knew that landing was a 'Mech unit's most vulnerable moment. For Peter it became a question of *when* not *if* Wu would engage them, but he couldn't seem to convince the Cossacks of that.

Peter rested a hand on Nikolai's shoulder. "Colonel Khorsakov, I believe we will flush our quarry when we land, not a moment sooner. As I recall, we had indications that their main base is sixty kilometers south by southwest of our LZ." The eagerness to do battle freed a low chuckle from Peter's throat. "Shall we land closer and invite them out?"

The mercenary smiled graciously. "We have two days yet to map our landing. I shall prepare the contingency plans."

"Good." Peter yawned and stretched. "Too much traveling, too much anticipation. I think I'll try to get some sleep. Wake me if anything happens."

"As you wish, Highness. Pleasant dreams."

Peter smiled broadly and gave the other man a sharp salute. "All of our coming battle . . . pleasant dreams indeed!"

Solaris City, Solaris VII
Tamarind March, Federated Commonwealth

It cannot be this hard. They have to be on some world or another! What am I missing? Keith looked at the holograph, then back at his computer. *The key is here, I know it.*

He took off his glasses and rubbed his eyes. He had begun the process of trying to figure out on which world Tormano had stashed Deirdre and David with the rather simple tack of examining the holograph, then cataloguing its unique features. Because of the clouds in the sky he had no constellations as a point of reference. Had such data been available he could have pinpointed the world by having his machine pull down all available astronomical data bases and do a point by point comparison until he got a match.

In the holograph he tagged two things immediately: flora and fauna. The deer were the easiest to track, mainly because of their rarity. The data that came up on them showed that they had come to the brink of extinction during the Fourth Succession War a quarter-century before. Because of a breeding program funded by Tormano Liao, the Prudolm dwarf deer had been reintroduced in viable numbers on their native worlds of Tsitsang, Hunan, and Kansu.

"Only good thing you've *ever* done, Tormano," Keith commented drily.

The flora proved much easier to track down. He identified the grove of trees in the background as iron elm, and the computer produced a list as long as Keith's arm of worlds where they could be found. Unfortunately it included Tsitsang, Hunan, and Kansu, which meant he could not further narrow down the choices of worlds. *I'm looking for a needle and this haystack is getting bigger, not smaller!*

In narrowing his search to the three worlds that were home to the deer, he ran into a problem that threatened to destroy everything already accomplished. The Prudolm dwarf deer preferred a dry climate and usually roved in vast herds across plains. As the iron elm grew only in temperate zones, the chance of the two things being found together was very slim.

The obvious solution to the paradox was that the deer were present in a private reserve, but that could be on *any* of the 137 worlds where the iron elm grew naturally. Then again, if the holograph had been made in a zoological or botanical garden, Deirdre and David could have been anywhere.

Not accepting defeat, Keith had gone through and pinpointed everything else in the picture. He knew the likely point of origin for all the clothing worn by Deirdre and her son. He'd even made a passable shot at identifying the manufacturer and interstellar distributors of her eyeshadow. He was particularly proud of having traced back to Odell, in the Crucis March of the Federated Commonwealth, the brand of mirrored sunglasses Deirdre had tucked into the neckline of her blouse.

If they were prescription, I bet I could even figure out the correction. He looked at the holograph, then called up the digitized version of it. Using a mouse he drew a square around Deirdre's chest. He started typing in the commands to blow it up, then stopped and redrew the square so it only contained the glasses. Satisfied that he'd have nothing to explain to Kristina, he increased the magnification by a factor of ten.

For the first time in two days he smiled. *Yes, this could be it.* In the magnified lens he saw a reflection. He added two more levels to the magnification, then punched up a correction of the data. The computer evaluated the image pixel by pixel and decided, by comparing each with those surrounding it, what its most likely color and composition should be. Once it had begun to transform the picture from a collection of blocks to something more recognizably human, Keith ran another filter that corrected for and lightened shadows, which stopped the figure's nose from spreading over its face like an inkblot.

Using the mouse he drew a new box that isolated the top lens. He pulled up the data on the sunglasses and had the machine do a flat projection of the image to eliminate distortion from the curve of the lens. That took the figure from being tall and slender to shorter and more solidly built. Again he corrected for pixel distortion, then again blew up the image by a factor of ten.

Keith ran another correction just to be certain, but he knew who he was looking at. The picture resolved itself and Keith found himself unconsciously snarling at the man who faced him. "You son of a bitch, Tormano. I've got you now. The question is, *where* in the FedCom have I got you?"

Keith's eyes stopped burning and new vitality flowed through him. He saved the picture he had created, then used his computer to plug straight into the Solaris information network. First stop was the local newsfax database. He punched up a search program that analyzed the last two months of data to find any mention of Tormano Liao. Every article, every picture, every caption that did was logged into a text file and sorted by time and date—first of those attributed to the article and second by date of publication of the item.

He let the computer perform that task in the background

while he zeroed in on what he hoped would produce his target. Operating from the premise that Tormano Liao had not left Solaris in the past two months, he was certain Deirdre Lear had to be on Solaris itself. Just to be certain that memory of Tormano's comings and goings served, he was running the other check. The iron elm was native to Solaris, so it would not be much of a clue, but the Prudolm dwarf deer might just prove to be invaluable as a locator.

Keith steered directly through the system to the Solaris VII Holovideo Production Commission database. The S7HPC did everything it could to promote the shooting and production of holovid dramas on the world. As part of the service it offered to production companies, it maintained a massive database of locations throughout the world. Cenotaph had even given permission for one of its satellite training facilities to be used in an episode of a Constabulary Drama and had been paid handsomely for the privilege.

"C'mon, Tormano, you need money. Have you got a place with nifty little deer where you want folks to come make holovids?" He started a search program using every key he could think of from the holograph. As the computer began the task, he sat back and wracked his brain for any other ideas that might help pinpoint their location, but the machine kicked out an answer even before he'd gotten his feet up on the desk.

"Tormano's estate on Equatus! How could I have missed it?" Keith closed his eyes tight and raised his face toward the ceiling. The computer beeped at him and he opened his eyes to find the remote system wanting to know if he wished to download the survey packet of the Estate site. His expression of pain turning to one of joy, Keith replied in the affirmative and watched the light on his drive flicker as he pulled in the data.

The other check turned up a full schedule with two gaps. The first report was of a weekend rip by Tormano to his estate on the other continent and the more recent gap was for the day after Kai's title defense. "Yes!"

The packet of S7HPC data provided full visual scans of the estate, and Keith easily located an image that contained the area where Deirdre and David stood. He cropped the image and brought it up so it and the holograph were on the same scale. Using the date of the S7HPC image as a starting point,

Keith had the computer check astronomical databases and create a projection for when or if the shadows in the holograph were correct for 20 April 3056. It came back and informed him that, according to the shadows, the holograph had been made at one-thirty in the afternoon, local Equatus time.

Keith built the S7HPC data and a file with his information into a packet and used a compression routine to shrink it all down. Using the number Kai had given him he created a connection with the remote system. With the touch of two keys he started the download.

"I didn't even know they *had* computers out in Joppo." Keith shivered for a second, wondering if Kai truly did know what he was doing. "No, dammit, I trust you, Kai. I'm not going to be the one to botch up your plan."

The download finished in less than ten minutes. Keith waited a second, then typed: TRANSMISSION ENDED, REQUEST RECEIPT CONFIRMATION.

It took a minute as the reply appeared letter by letter. TRANSMISSION RECEIVED. MISSION UNDERSTOOD, SITE DATA APPRECIATED. Random letters and numbers then flooded the screen as the remote system terminated the communication.

Keith stared at the screen for a moment, then smiled. "Well, I've done all I can." He reached over to shut his system down, then hesitated. "No, I've done all I was *asked* to do. I can do much more."

Settling his fingers on the keyboard he smiled and wormed his way into the Solaris data stream again. *Whatever the Joppo crew is going to do, it can't hurt if the estate doesn't know they're coming.* He typed in a command that took him over to the area of the computers through which the telecommunications of the world flowed. From there he very methodically began the isolation of the Mandrinn's estate and the destruction of its security system.

Mandrinn's Estate, Solaris VII
Tamarind March, Federated Commonwealth

In the two days since Deirdre Lear had begun planning the escape she had learned some important things. The first was that escape *was* possible. She had studied the grounds and security arrangements with eyesight and perceptions honed on Alyina. Several times she found herself wondering what Kai would make of a given situation, but she stopped short of trusting what *she* thought *he* might think. *I have to trust myself in this.*

The security staff was attentive and did roam the grounds with assault rifles slung over their shoulders, but they were not wholly alert. The night before she had been able to roam the manor house without being challenged until she neared the kitchen. And the resistance she met there only happened because she surprised a guard helping himself to a late night snack. From the deference the man showed her, Deirdre concluded that even if the guard knew she was a prisoner, he remained awed by her previous status as a guest.

An escape plan formed itself quickly and she knew it would work. A quick strike from the house to the deer compound would enable her to open the heated corral where the deer were penned at night. She could release them and scatter them over the grounds, giving the guards a multitude of targets to hunt. More important, if the guards used infrared scanners to try to track her, the compound itself would be a big heat source helping to blind them to her presence. They might know she had been there to release the deer, but trying to differentiate her heat signature from that of the deer would not be a simple matter.

From there she could head out and go over the wall. Outside the compound she would have to go to ground and hope she could elude pursuit or, if forced to do it, defeat them.

That led her to the second realization. David weighed just over seventeen kilograms, which meant she could not carry him. Nor could she fully explain everything to a three-year-old ahead of time because he might innocently blurt it out. Finally, because of his size he could not run as fast or as long as their escape attempt demanded.

Her logical side screamed at her to leave him behind, but her emotions wouldn't let her abandon him even briefly. She did not want to believe Tormano Liao would have the boy hurt, but he was quite capable of spiriting David away and using him against Kai and her. She realized her choices lay between the smart things to do and that which she *had* to do.

Deirdre thought back to her time on Alyina. At one point, she had been trapped by an Elemental and Kai could have run, could have escaped, but he did not. Detriment she might have been, but he came for her and defeated the Elemental in single combat.

If David's father would not abandon me, how can I abandon his son? That decision made, she set aside all her concerns about it. She dressed David in the darkest clothes she could find and similarly attired herself. She caught a nap in the afternoon, then waited until nearly midnight on the clock to begin her operation. She let David sleep through the first part, hoping to shield him from the violence that would be necessary.

Leaving the lights in the room dim, she walked to the door of her suite and tore it open. The guard—a man who usually spent the evening sitting in a chair propped back on two legs against the wall—was on his feet with his right hand holding an earphone tight into his ear. "Quickly, I've seen a scorpion in here. It's under the couch. You have to kill it."

The guard looked none too pleased with the report. "I'm sorry, my lady, but I have my orders."

"You must! It could kill my son!" Deirdre put as much hysterical power into her voice as she could. "You have the gun, you can't be afraid."

The man listened intently to his radio, then smiled and chuckled lightly as he walked into the suite. "In or out, it won't matter." Hitching his rifle over his shoulder by the sling, he looked around the living area at the three different couches, the scratched his head. He turned to face her, the obvious question on his face, but words never made it past his lips.

Deirdre drove her knee deep into his groin. Grabbing double handfuls of his hair, she brought his face down to meet her knee's second strike. Without releasing his hair, she twisted her hands and yanked down, accelerating him toward the ground. His head hit with a satisfying smack and his body went limp.

She pressed her fingers to his carotid artery and found the pulse slightly elevated but strong. She stripped off his gun and web belt. The guard was big enough that the only way she could wear the belt was to sling it over her left shoulder like a bandolier. Using curtain cord she had pulled from the shades in the bedroom, she bound the man and gagged him with a ball made from a rolled-up pair of David's socks.

Slinging the gun over her right shoulder, she turned and saw David standing in the doorway to the bedroom. "David?"

The boy rubbed sleep from his eyes. "Did you do that, Mommy?"

She nodded.

"Cool."

Deirdre reached out for David's hand and the little boy came to her. "You have to be quiet. Come on." She led him out the door and down the short corridor to a pair of doors that led out onto the grounds. Crouched beside it, she looked out into the darkness and saw no one. She opened the door and slipped through to the outside. She pulled David after her.

"David, we have to run to that bush over there. Can you do that? Quietly?"

The boy nodded solemnly.

"Go."

He sprinted off, running with a bouncy, wild-legged gait that marked a youthful lack of coordination. Despite his awkward strides, he reached the bush quickly. She followed him closely, then pointed out a stand of iron elms. They made it and crouched in the shadow of the trees to catch their breaths.

"Are we doing good, Mommy?"

She kissed him on the forehead. "We are, David. I love you."

"I love you too, Mommy." He kissed her on the lips with a big smacking sound that she loved despite the way noises carried at night.

"David, see the funny-looking tree there?"

"Uh-huh."

"Go."

As he ran, Deirdre watched the whole area for movement, but saw no one. She pulled the rifle from her shoulder and curled the sling around her left forearm. Checking the selector lever she flipped it from safe to the setting for a three-shot burst, then she worked the charging lever and eased a bullet into the chamber. Keeping low, she moved as quietly as she could and reached David's side.

The stand of trees in which they had taken cover widened ahead. In shape the whole forest swath resembled a lollipop, with the slender handle being the section closest to the house. They had made it halfway up to the bulbous head, with another two hundred meters to the top round part. From there they could reach the compound with a short sprint across some open territory.

They pushed on in short bursts of movement. Deirdre quietly praised her son at each stopping point and urged him again to be quiet. She couldn't tell if he thought it was all a game or not, but she suspected that some of her nervousness was getting through to him. He smiled brightly when she hugged and kissed him, but the smiles quickly faded into the expression he wore when he concentrated on something. His eyes searched the area around them and, having watched her advances, he began to move from shadow to shadow as he went forward.

Suddenly the floodlights mounted around the manor house blazed to life and a siren's keening sliced through the night. The lights illuminated the vast lawns, but made the forest into a zebra-pattern of brightly lit patches and black shadows. Deirdre froze where she huddled in the shadows and glanced over at David hunkered down behind a fallen tree trunk. *If I can't see him, neither can they.*

Men shouted from behind her, running out from the house. She shifted around so she could cover them, but under the siren's undulating shriek she heard something else. Turning back toward David, she saw two black quadruped shadows galloping across the lawn. Sharp barks were accompanied by the flash of even sharper fangs as the dogs zeroed in on her son.

Without thinking, Deirdre broke and raced toward him, stopping only as the dogs closed on her boy. Leaning heavily against a tree, she steadied herself. The rifle came to her shoulder and she tracked as the dogs cut from right to left across her field of vision. She pulled her left hand back until the sling tightened painfully on her arm, then she hit the trigger.

The gun's muzzle flash momentarily blinded her and the report started her ears ringing. The first burst hit the lead dog in the chest and flank as it leaped up over a fallen branch. The animal squealed as it tumbled through the air, then yelped as it slammed into a tree and fell to the ground.

Where's the second one? She didn't so much see it as she

saw movement. Swinging left she triggered one burst, wrestled the gun's barrel down and triggered a second. She heard an agonized bark, then she dove forward and pulled David down with her as the world exploded.

The men coming up from the house, and the two handlers who had released the dogs, opened fire on the woods. Deirdre jammed her face into the moldy leaves on the forest floor as bullets crisscrossed just over her head. Wood exploded, branches fell, and the ground shuddered as bullets traced lines of fire through the leaves. She felt David trembling and crying, but she couldn't hear him and dared not pull him to her for comfort. Her right hand kept him pressed against the ground like a mouse beneath the paw of a cruel cat.

As suddenly as it had begun, the gunfire ended. Deirdre heard words shouted, then heard the order repeated in English. "Throw down your gun!"

Deirdre rolled on her right side, pressing her back against David and disentangling the weapon from her arm. She tossed it aside, then screamed, "It's down, it's down. We give up." She fervently wished she was actually wearing something white that she could use to signal her surrender.

She heard the heavy tramp of men running through the woods. Rolling back on to her face and then the other side, she pulled David to her. "We have to be brave, baby, very brave."

He nodded, but his lower lip trembled. She could see tears welling up in his eyes.

"It's okay to cry, David." She stroked his hair, then cautiously came up in a sitting position. She shifted David to her lap and held him close as Tormano's guards advanced with their weapons out and ready to be used. Striding boldly through the center of them, his hands empty, was the captain.

He stepped over the fallen log, the other men following in his wake as if the captain's courage would shield them. He kicked Deirdre's gun further away, then nodded a salute to her. "I congratulate you, Doctor, on almost making your escape. You, of course, made only one mistake."

"And what was that?" Deirdre's eyes narrowed. "Or don't you want to tell me for fear I might avoid it next time."

The man smiled in a fashion Deirdre found almost reptilian. "When you introduced the virus into the computer that controls our perimeter security system, you assumed you had neutralized our ability to track you. Technology, as wonderful as it is, can fail." The man tapped the earpiece in his ear. "That is why we have radios and keep dogs for use. A quick radio check showed us that you had dealt with Li, so we came after you."

Deirdre's mind reeled. *Computer virus? What the hell is he talking about?* "The Mandrinn is holding us prisoner. I know Prince Victor Davion. Tormano will have much to answer for."

The captain reached down and pulled David away from her. She started to contest him for the possession of her son, but a half-dozen rifles immediately pointed in her direction, most of them still smoking from the muzzles. "If you hurt him ... Holding him won't keep me here, you know."

"I know that very well, Doctor." The captain shrugged almost apologetically. "You see, the Mandrinn has been keeping you alive as a courtesy. Ultimately your son is the only person who is important here because he gives the Mandrinn leverage over his nephew Kai. You, Doctor, are merely a nuisance."

He looked up at one of the guards. "She was on the grounds without authorization and did not stop when you called to her to do so. Fearing she was a terrorist, you shot her."

"Mommy! Mommy!" David squirmed in the man's arms and the captain cuffed him sharply over the ear.

"Good bye, Doctor Lear. Don't worry about David." The man laughed aloud, drowning out David's crying. "The Mandrinn will take care of your son and make him into a model heir for the Celestial Throne of the Capellan Confederation."

DropShip Zarevo, *Inbound Shiloh*
Free Worlds League

A booming thump brought Peter awake. He thought at first that they were under attack, but that couldn't be it because Khorsakov would have awakened him, long before any fighters had gotten close. As his mind became clear enough for him to reason that far, other echoes in the ship confirmed what the noise had been.

A shuttle has docked with us. Peter glanced at the viewport in his cabin and saw a distant orb trailing flame. *Overlord Class DropShip. Reinforcements?* Peter frowned because he did not think Tormano could have afforded more mercenaries, yet the reception of a shuttle from that ship clearly indicated that the forces were friendly. *Or at least not hostile.*

He dressed quickly, pulling on a jumpsuit and combing a hand quickly through his red hair, then headed out the companionway. He saw no one, which was not surprising, for most of the warriors were catching whatever sleep they could in preparation for the battle. Still, the fact that Khorsakov or his son had not come for him made Peter uneasy.

When he reached the ready room he saw two men with their backs to him wearing black and gold uniforms. A pale Colonel Khorsakov looked up as Peter entered the room. The man began to mouth an apology, but Peter never gave him a chance. "I'm disappointed in you, Colonel, and will deal with you later."

He grabbed the interloper nearest him and spun him around. "Who the hell are you? Where are you from? Why are you here?"

The man slipped his shoulder free of Peter's grasp in one smooth motion. "You know who I am, Peter Davion, and you know I'm from Solaris. It's time for you to turn around and leave before you destroy the Inner Sphere."

35

DropShip Zarevo, *Inbound Shiloh*
Free Worlds League
27 April 3056

DropShip Zarevo, *Inbound Shiloh*
Free Worlds League
27 April 3056

Peter's face went from shock to naked fury. "So, my brother thinks you can stop me?" Peter began to laugh and shake his head. *"You?"*

A chill puckered Kai's flesh at the strained, abnormal sound of the laughter. "Your brother didn't send me, Peter. He doesn't know anything about this."

"You acted *without* his approval?" The scorn in Peter's voice lashed Kai. "Be careful, Kai, you could find yourself the object of my brother's lethal jealousy, as was Cox and as am I."

"Peter, get hold of yourself. There's more going on here than you imagine. Have you asked yourself how I knew you would be here?" Kai did his best to force compassion into his voice. "Have you?"

Peter folded his arms, a superior sneer on his face. "You're dying to tell me, so go ahead."

"My uncle duped you."

"Ha! I forced him to let me join up with this mission. He refused, but I insisted."

"Just as he assumed you would." Kai felt his stomach clench. "He wanted you here, he *needed* you here. Without you here, his whole plan would fall through. Can't you see that?"

"What I see before me is a man who hasn't the same courage as his uncle to do what's necessary to guarantee the safety of the Federated Commonwealth. You play at games on Solaris when you should be here with me, leading men on this mission."

"I *am* here, and I *am* leading men on a very important mission. I've got a full battalion of warriors on the *Taizai* waiting to see what you're going to do." Kai fought to rein in his frustration. "Use your head, Peter. You still don't see it, do you? How did I happen to be here? Why have the Raiders gone to ground? It's obvious! Your mission is blown. The forces on Shiloh knew you were coming, and they're under orders not to fight you."

"They're afraid!" Peter walked around to Kai's left until the commanders of the Cossacks backed him. "We're going to prove the Harloc Raiders are here by bringing back pieces of their 'Mechs."

"If you try to do that, Peter, you'll go down in history as the man who started the war that destroyed the Inner Sphere. Sun-Tzu has issued orders to the Raiders to avoid an engagement. They're leaving the defense of the world to the Third Sirian Lancers. If you go after the Raiders, the Lancers will go after you."

Colonel Khorsakov shook his head remorselessly. "Then we will destroy the Lancers."

"Oh, very good." Kai channeled his anger into sarcasm, hoping he could make someone think clearly. "If you fight with the Lancers, the Free Worlds League will declare war against the Federated Commonwealth, which was *exactly* what Sun-Tzu had in mind when he gave the Raiders their orders."

"You're speculating about the Raiders' orders."

"No I'm not. The man who commands the Raiders supplied me the information that told me where I'd find you."

Peter's laugh had a sinister ring. "Consorting with the enemy, are you, Kai?"

"That's unworthy of you, Peter. Wu Kang Kuo felt he owed me a debt because I prevented my uncle from hurting his unborn grandson and because I honored his son in our duel. He repaid me, even though doing so could put his career *and* his life in jeopardy." Kai shook his head. "Damn you, Peter, use your brain, How do you think Wu knew you were coming here with the Cossacks? I'll tell you—my uncle leaked the information to the Maskirovka so you would be trapped and killed. And if *that* happened, Victor would have to declare war on Sun-Tzu and support Tormano's private war."

Kai stepped forward. "You're being used Peter. You're a pawn and you're being played by masters at politics. Tormano uses you, pitting you against your brother, so he can pit your brother against Sun-Tzu. Sun-Tzu deflects you toward Thomas Marik so he can use Thomas against Victor."

"And you, Kai Allard-Liao, how are you using me?"

"I'm not, Peter, I'm trying to save your life."

"You're trying to stop me from uncovering a threat to the Federated Commonwealth." Peter's tone grew more strident as his temper surged out of control. "You're trying to preserve my brother's power, when we both know his rule will destroy the Federated Commonwealth!"

"Listen to yourself, Peter, you've lost it. Give the order, turn this ship around. Recharge and jump back out to Solaris!"

"Never! You're the one who's lost it. You've abrogated your responsibilities to your family by playing on Solaris. I'm willing to accept my duties and execute them faithfully for the good of the Federated Commonwealth!" Peter poked Kai in the chest with a finger. "You've been on the run since Alyina, Kai, and perhaps even before that. Everyone has seen your actions and labeled them modesty, but I call them *cowardice*. This isn't Solaris, Kai, this isn't a game and we're not in 'Mechs. There's only one way you can stop me."

Kai shook his head. "I don't want to fight you, Peter."

"Then the stories about you fighting against Elementals are untrue, eh, Kai Allard-Liao?" Peter raised his fists in a challenge. "I am the future of the Federated Commonwealth. Stop me if you dare."

Mandrinn's Estate, Solaris VII
Tamarind March, Federated Commonwealth

Though she knew it could mean her death, Deirdre Lear acted the moment the captain turned away from her. Still seated on her left hip, she pushed off the ground with her hands and scooted forward. She swept her right foot forward, catching the captain behind his left knee. As he began to fall, the sound of gunfire erupted all around her, but barely impinged on her consciousness as she moved to save her son.

Rolling up onto her left knee, Deirdre ignored the bullets flying and the flashes of light and explosions. She focused on the captain, and when he landed on his broad back, her upraised right hand struck. She brought it down, fingers flattened, and smashed the fleshy edge of it into his throat.

The martial artist in her knew the blow would crush his windpipe like a soggy cardboard tube.

The doctor knew the man would suffocate.

The mother who had watched him strike her child did not care.

David extricated himself from the man's arms and ran to her. Deirdre hugged and kissed him, waiting for the bullet that would claim her life. She didn't want to die, but if it had to be now, she exulted in these last moments with David.

"Doctor Lear." The voice, all metallic and distant, made her realize she was no longer hearing gunfire. She opened her eyes and saw the men who had captured her all scattered across the ground. The shadows hid most of them, but she could have sworn she saw parts disassociated with the bodies to which they had once belonged.

Clutching David's face to her chest so he couldn't see the carnage, she rose and turned. What she saw sent ice running through her veins, and made her breath catch in her throat. Her knees buckled, but she steeled herself and refused to go down.

Approaching her through the shadows she saw a dozen oversized humanoid figures. The bright light stained the right halves of their bodies with darkness, but it fully brought out the jade green plumage and burning amber eye painted on the helmets of the exoskeleton armor. The lead figure extended his left arm to her in a gesture of friendship whose tenderness contrasted the three-fingered claw of a hand and the smoking machine gun slung under the forearm.

It's impossible. How can they be here? Deirdre started to tremble. *I must be dead and this must be my personal hell!*

The claw beckoned her forward. "I do not know if you remember me, Doctor, but we have met before. I am Taman Malthus and these are my men. Kai Allard-Liao asked us to escort you home."

she slowly backed her forward. "The only way to stop you is to *dare*, Peter. . . . but you leave me no choice."

36

DropShip Zarevo, *Inbound Shiloh*
Free Worlds League
27 April 3056

"**D**are, Peter, dare?" Kai shouted at Peter. The fury in his own voice surprised him and he fought to control the emotions raging through his body. "I have no choice *but* to stop you."

"Words, Allard, words." Peter smiled cruelly. "Actions speak louder than words."

For a second Peter dropped his fists and Kai knew he could take the man down with a roundhouse kick to the side of his head. Muscles tensed, nerves fired, but Kai withheld the kick. *It's not enough for him to be defeated. He has to understand why he cannot be allowed to win.* "Then look to your actions and tell me what they say."

"They say I am Hanse Davion's true heir. They acknowledge the destiny of a Steiner-Davion to once again forge a Star League and unite all the Houses under one ruler." Peter's bright eyes burned with a fanatical light. "Victor will destroy it all, he will let the Federated Commonwealth fall apart, nibbled away by threats like the Harloc Raiders, and his confederates will aid and abet him in this treason."

Peter closed and hooked a right at Kai's head. Kai ducked low and to the left, slipping the blow. By reflex his right hand shot up straight between Peter's hands. Though Kai pulled the blow at the last second, the heel of his hand still mashed Peter's lips against his teeth.

"I'm sorry, Peter." Kai bounced back out of Peter's reach, and Larry Acuff pulled a chair out from Kai's line of retreat.

Peter looked stunned. He probed his split lip with a finger that came away bloody. "More treason. Has Victor sent you here to kill me?"

"No, dammit, Victor does not know I'm here!"

"Lies!" Pain filled Peter's voice and everything came together for Kai as Peter rushed at him, fists flying. The flurry of punches pummeled Kai, coming too fast and too chaotically to be blocked effectively. Flailing away, Peter's forearms hit as often as his balled fists, but the sheer manic fury of the assault battered Kai and forced him to retreat.

Peter must have sensed he was overwhelming Kai because the rhythm of his flurry broke as he focused on winning and took conscious control of his body. This gave Kai just the opening he needed. As the punches slowed, he ducked his right shoulder and hammered Peter with one sharp blow that caught him just beneath the breastbone. Air left Peter's lungs in one explosive *oof!*, then Peter collapsed to the deck, his face turning red.

Kai shivered, partly from anger, but more from fear. He reached down and grabbed the belt on Peter's jumpsuit and pulled up, forcing the downed man to arch his back and pull air into his lungs. That stopped Peter's immediate distress, but having the wind knocked out of him also took the fight out of him.

"Listen to me, Peter, I understand what you're thinking. I know the pressures you feel. You have the Free Skye Militia out for your blood, just as I've been hunted by the Capellan Confederation and the Clans. You are heir to great responsibilities and traditions, as am I. We want to do many things, accomplish many great goals, but we are hamstrung. Your brother sent you to Solaris and my uncle"—Kai swallowed against a lump rising in his throat—"holds my son hostage or else I wouldn't be here trying to stop you from starting a war."

Something in Peter's eyes cleared and his body relaxed. Horror flashed across his face, then he closed his eyes and slowly shook his head.

Kai released Peter's belt, then slowly straightened up. "Colonel Khorsakov, my family has ever appreciated your dedication and loyalty to the true Liao bloodline." Kai chose his words carefully. He wanted to salve the old mercenary's ego, yet could see no reason to spare the man any of the anger still boiling around inside him. "Your service has been invaluable, and no other unit could have come this far or come as close to fulfilling its mission here."

"You are most kind, my lord."

"Indeed, and perhaps you would wish me to remain so *kind* in the future." Kai paused for a moment, letting the sting of that remark settle in before he continued. "It is time for you to leave, Colonel. Send the *Zarevo* back to the *Remagen* and return to Solaris."

"You must understand, my lord, that I am not in your employ."

The look of insolent defiance on the old man's face made Kai want to drop him with a punch, but he opted for a less physical means of cutting him down. "My Uncle Tormano engaged you under false pretenses. He is insolent, but to avoid the embarrassment of a scandal I will indemnify you and fulfill the monetary requirements of your contract." Kai folded his arms slowly. "That is, I will do so if you leave now."

"But we have a mission to fulfill."

"Colonel, there is no mission, you have no sponsor and no sanction for this action. You can choose between a glass that is full or one that is empty, and you don't know how empty it is. One word from me and the Federated Commonwealth will never engage your services again. The same goes for the St. Ives Compact. And were I to speak with Lady Omi Kurita, who is a guest in my home at this time, well, the Cossacks would be low on the list if the Combine should ever decide to use mercenaries again. You would never work for Sun-Tzu and, unless you missed it, you have invaded the Free Worlds League." Kai shook his head ruefully. "I suppose you could find employment in the Periphery."

"My lord!"

"Consider yourself lucky, Colonel, because you have avoided triggering a war that would have anointed you with the blood of millions. Save your hatred for my cousin's soldiers. You will quench your thirst for their blood another day. Am I understood?"

"Yes, my lord." The reply came tight and full of wounded pride, but Kai expected that and was suddenly pleased to have so easily manipulated Nikolai Khorsakov. "About Duke Peter, my lord."

"He is coming with me to the *Taizai*. You can return his kit to him on Solaris. Farewell, Colonel. Enjoy your retirement." Kai grabbed one of Peter's shoulders as Larry Acuff came around to help him. "I've got him, Larry. Go to the shuttle and tell Wilson to do his preflight. We're going home."

"Roger, boss."

Alone, in the companionway, Kai let Peter rest against a bulkhead and get his legs back under him. "I couldn't let you start a war, Peter."

"But your son, I never knew you had a son—and to risk him." Peter's chin sank to his chest as words failed him.

Kai took firm hold of Peter's jaw and lifted the man's head back up. "Acting against your own best interests, acting in the way you *must* instead of the way you *want to,* that is what leaders like your brother must do. Setting aside ambition and personal satisfaction for the benefit of what is right and good, not expedient, isn't easy. It must be done, though, or else others will use you to advance *their* goals."

"As I was." Horror and anguish bled through Peter's voice. "You're right, I was a pawn. Pawns get used and swept from the board."

Peter tried to pull away from Kai, but the smaller man refused to let him go. "Don't give up, Peter, don't surrender to despair. Pawns that win through battles, that survive to the final rank on the board become very powerful. You want everything *now,* and that comes from youth and inexperience. You have time, and impatience is merely energy you should direct into pursuits that will make you a better man in the future."

Kai let him go and started walking him toward the shuttle bay. "Your hopes and dreams have made you define yourself against your brother. Peter Steiner-Davion has to be his own person, not the anti-Victor. You also don't have to be Hanse Davion reborn. You can be you."

"This insight from the man who traced his father's footsteps and attained the same honors his father did?" The weak riposte came tinged with humor, so Kai ignored the barbs in it. "Have you found out who Kai Allard-Liao is?"

"Self-discovery is a journey, Peter, not a goal. The minute you think you've discovered who you are, you're wrong because that discovery changes you. All you can do is follow the path that lets you be true to yourself."

Peter nodded, then frowned. "Wise words from a man whose sole ambition is to be Champion on Solaris. Your coming here, your stopping me, this points to other abilities and greater destinies. Are you certain that path is letting you be true to yourself? You're right, I can't be my brother's antithesis, nor the reincarnation of my father. How about you?"

Kai felt a chill cutting at his spine. "That's a question I've never even dared ask myself. In Cenotaph I honor him, but only by emulating a very small part of his life."

"Meaning?"

"I don't know what it means," Kai laughed, his tension evaporating, "but I think I see little glimmers of an answer in studying the question. If you are willing, Peter Davion, perhaps we can continue this conversation on the *Taizai* and set our feet on the right paths by the time we return to Solaris."

Solaris City, Solaris VII
Tamarind March, Federated Commonwealth
29 April 3056

Tormano made no attempt to conceal his surprise when Kai entered his office. "I had expected you sooner, nephew. The *Taizai* landed four hours ago."

"There were many things to take care of upon landing, uncle." Kai's face became a mask Tormano could not read, and this disturbed him. *His father used to wear that same expression.* "There are going to be changes, Tormano."

"Indeed? Will they include replacing the staff your thugs killed at my estate?" He waited to see what sort of effect that would have, but Kai gave no sign of having heard him. "I must admit I erred in keeping Dr. Lear and her son there after I gave you the holograph. I will do better next time."

"No, Uncle, there will be no next time." Kai moved deeper into the room, surveying it as if seeing it for the first time. "And, yes, you will have more staff at your estate. Fuh Teng has grandnephews and cousins who will oversee the security arrangements. They will take pains to assure that you are quite happy there."

Tormano blinked in surprise. "You are exiling me to my estate on Equatus? Ho, this is a bold Kai Allard-Liao I have before me. What makes you think I will give all this up?"

Kai's face took on a hint of a smile. "You will, for you would not want to face the shame of being evicted. You see, I own the estate now."

"You what?"

"You heard me. Even before the *Taizai* landed I had Keith

Smith put together a complete analysis of your financial situation." Kai clasped his hands behind his back. "When your finances ran short because of Prince Victor's cutbacks, you used your estate and your home in Solaris City to secure a number of short-term loans against your hopes that the next Estates General will approve a bill for new funding. I bought the paper from the bank."

"Those loans can't be called for another three months. I can arrange funding to pay them off in that time."

"Wrong, uncle. The loans cannot be called until the Estates General has refused funding. I sent a message to and have received a reply from Victor Davion. You will get no funding. All this is mine."

Tormano felt his heart pounding in his chest. "You can't . . . You can't have told Victor Davion about his brother because that means you'd have had to tell him about the Harloc Raiders being on Shiloh. So that means you're withholding information from him. I can send him a message that will win his gratitude."

Kai slowly shook his head. "He won't believe you. In my message I told him that you and I had spoken. I had determined that the stress of leading Free Capella was too much for you. I dropped some hints to let him assume that you've had a breakdown like your father and are now a shell of a man, a doddering imbecile likely to fall prey to all manner of delusions."

"I don't believe this, none of it." Tormano's mouth remained open as alternating waves of horror and awe washed over him. That his nephew could depose him so simply in the course of four hours horrified him, yet it also excited him. In doing so Kai had exhibited all the skills that Tormano himself had hoped to instill in him. Kai had usurped what Tormano would have offered willingly. "This is incredible."

"No, it is quite credible." Kai's gray eyes glittered like ice chips in the room's dim light. "You have made it readily apparent to me that you are too dangerous to be left to your own devices. Your bitterness has made you reckless. You almost started a war that would have caused untold destruction on hundreds of worlds. Never again will you have that opportunity."

"There is only one way you can guarantee that, Kai." Tormano opened a drawer in his desk and pulled out a pistol.

"You won't kill me, Uncle."

"You're quite right, I won't." Tormano laid the gun down and turned it so the butt pointed in Kai's direction. "You now lead Free Capella. You have become what I wanted you to become. Doing this, deposing me, cutting me off, this was all very good. You display the abilities you will need to destroy Sun-Tzu. But if you expect your victory to be complete, your mastery absolute, you must be ruthless. Pick up the gun and kill me."

"No."

"No? If you do not, Kai, you will not be rid of me." Tormano jerked a thumb toward the window looking out over Cathay. "I have loyalists, Kai, I have allies about whom you know nothing. You will never keep me on that estate. I will get away, I will get funding, I will get support and I will be outside your control."

"I will not kill you."

Tormano laughed in his face. "You must, Kai. It is the final act. You have to learn how to deal with rivals. Victor knows! If you think he didn't have Ryan Steiner exterminated, you're a fool. If you think he didn't send Peter here to die, you are an even greater fool. I will die happy if I know you are ruthless enough to kill me. That means, when the time comes, you'll not spare your rat-faced little cousin Sun-Tzu. You will do what must be done."

"I've already done that. I've arranged for you a gilded cage. I will not kill you."

"Blake's blood, Kai! I held your child hostage! I threatened him with death!" Tormano nudged the gun toward his nephew. "Do it, kill me. Prove yourself."

"To whom? You?" Kai shook his head implacably. "No, Uncle, I don't need to prove myself to you, not here, not now. You'll have many days—many years—at your estate to decide if I am sufficient to inherit your mantle. You see, I don't have to become you or Victor to do things the right way. I am Kai Allard-Liao and that, I think, is more than enough."

Peter Steiner–Davion felt slightly uncomfortable sitting back on his heels, but he endured the pain in his knees as Omi Kurita poured him a small cup of tea. Showered and shaved, wearing a black and gold jumpsuit on loan from Cenotaph Stables, he felt truly human for the first time since leaving the *Zarevo*. His discussions with Kai on the return trip had helped him focus on the turmoil boiling deep inside, but they had not fully resolved the problems.

Upon his return to Solaris four hours before, Peter had sent a note to Omi requesting a chance to speak with her in Kai's home. Larry Acuff arrived to say that Omi had agreed to the meeting, then he drove Peter to Kai's house. The servant answering the door had ushered him into a side room where Omi was waiting with tea.

She offered him the cup and he accepted it with a half-bow. The steaming liquid made the porcelain hot enough to cause discomfort, but he did not set it down. *Penance comes in many forms.* He waited for her to pour another cup, then he drank with her. Following her lead, he set the cup on the low table between them.

"Thank you for meeting with me, Lady Omi."

"It is my pleasure, Duke Peter. I am very happy to welcome you back to the Federated Commonwealth." She smiled at him and he read intelligence in her blue eyes. "Losing you would have hurt your brother. He would have greatly mourned your passing."

Peter looked down at the lacquered table and the brilliantly colored dragon coiled across it. "I very nearly got a lot of people killed. Had I used a gun and tried to shoot one single person, I would be on trial for attempted murder. I threatened millions, but because of my station and the intervention of good people like Kai and you, I go unpunished."

Omi's face remained impassive, but her voice was not unsympathetic. "Is not punishment the solution to which we resort when rehabilitation is impossible?"

"Yes, yes, I suppose it is." Peter sighed and his shoulders slumped. "I am not certain rehabilitation is possible for a crime the magnitude of mine."

"I believe your analogy has contributed to a misunderstanding. In the Combine, attempted murder is a charge leveled when the perpetrator *intended* to cause death but failed in the attempt." Omi turned her cup around and drank again. "In your case, because your intent was not murder and because you did no one any harm in your attempt, your crime is not attempted murder. It is, perhaps, reckless disregard for life or negligence, but not attempted murder."

The recollection that those were the charges leveled

against his lance for his actions on Lyons made Peter blush. "Even in assigning guilt I arrogate myself." He used a swallow of tea to make his stomach feel as warm as his face. "Lady Omi, I already owe you a debt I can never repay because of your loaning the *Taizai* to Kai."

Omi allowed a look of puzzlement to cross her face. "Whatever do you mean, Duke Peter? The *Taizai* is here to serve as my transportation. It has gone nowhere."

Yes, and Kai says his computer man will erase all traces of ships going in and out from the planetary computers. "Then the debt comes from my forcing you to keep a secret from my brother. I owe you and Kai both for that one."

Omi shook her head serenely. "Your brother needs know only the important details of your life. Those things without consequence are, by their very nature, beneath mention."

"How can you do that? How can you say that?" Peter looked up at her, confusion twisting around his heart. "You and Kai both care for my brother a great deal—more than I have in the past, apparently—yet you dismiss mentioning all this to Victor as if it were nothing."

"I cannot speak for Kai, but I weigh the alternatives. If I tell Victor, it will cause him untold pain and, perhaps, might make him initiate the war that has so recently been averted." Omi met Peter's stare for a moment, then glanced away. "The pain of concealing something from your brother is much less than the pain of making him order troops to death. And, as you know your brother, you also know that he would go into battle at the head of his troops. Causing his death would be the greatest pain of all."

Peter nodded. "Where do you find the strength?"

Omi reached out and touched the center of his chest, then modestly withdrew her hand. "It resides in the heart. You find it when you are comfortable with yourself."

"That is much the same thing Kai said." Peter shook his head. "Though I have no place asking this, I require of you two favors."

"It would be my honor to be of assistance to you, if I am able."

"When you leave here, you will stop to recharge at a world called Zaniah. There is a monastery there for MechWarriors. It is called Saint Marinus House."

Omi nodded. "Morgan Kell spent twelve years there."

"He did. They take MechWarriors in and help them deal with problems. I think, for too long, that I have been Peter Steiner-Davion, the son who is not Victor, the son who will never have the chance to inherit what his father and mother created." Peter smiled slightly. "For the first time in my life I can say that without feeling some anger inside. I think, at Saint Marinus House, they can help me discover who I am and how I can be myself."

Omi smiled openly, then blushed. "Forgive me, Peter, but the spiritual quest you seek is the kind of thing most revered in our traditions. You honor me by letting me start you out on your course."

"The second thing I need from you, Omi, is for you to tell Victor to leave me there until I decide to come out of my own volition. Only Victor, Kai, and you will know where I have gone. Tell Victor I must do this because if I don't I will die. I hope he will understand."

Omi nodded. "I know your brother well, Peter. He will agree. He will not like it, but he will respect your decision. And he will look forward to your return."

Peter smiled and the constriction around his heart ebbed away. "How can I repay you?"

"Promise me this, Duke Peter." She raised her cup in a salute. "When you discover who Peter Steiner-Davion really is, you will one day introduce him to me as a friend."

Nancy Bao Lee paused in the doorway of Tormano's office, able to make out only the silhouette of his head against the top of his chair. "Are you well, my lord?"

Tormano replied while facing the window and keeping his back to her. "Yes, I believe I am. It is something of a shock, of course, to find myself so ably handled by the younger generation. There is much of his father in Kai, and his mother, too. Candace always was and still is a steel-hearted woman. I should have expected nothing less of a man who suckled at her breast."

"So, you are ruined?" she asked quietly as she entered the room. She stopped behind him and pressed her hands down on the tense muscles of his neck and shoulders. "Will you submit to your exile?"

"Ruined? No, not really." Tormano pointed to the window and the world beyond it as she kneaded his muscles. "He has taken from me my property, but he cannot take my connections. There are many people out there who respect me for my name and my bloodline. There are yet others who wish to use me the way Hanse Davion did. They will rally behind me to oppose Sun-Tzu. With that sort of backing I will endure no more time on my estate than Napoleon did on Elba, and there will be no Waterloo for me when I return."

"Exactly what I expected to hear you say, my lord." Nancy turned and twisted around to the right to pull a silk handkerchief from one pocket. She draped it over the pistol, brought the gun up and pressed it to Tormano's right temple.

Just as she was pulling the trigger, Tormano's right hand grabbed her wrist and, as he leaned forward, he dragged her over his shoulder and smashed her heavily into the ground. Stamping down, he shattered her right wrist, then backhanded her across the face.

"A Maskirovka agent trained before Romano settled her arse in the throne would have known better than to assume I would have offered Kai a loaded pistol," she heard him scream through her pain. "I am not a fool. Sitting here in the dark I determined that only one person could have revealed my true plan to Sun-Tzu and have enough reliability to prompt him to issue orders that would stop my little war before it got started."

"My arm, my lord, you have broken it!" She fought against panic and the wave of nausea rippling through her. "Have you gone mad?"

"Oh, very good, Ms. Lee, very good. You can deny your ties to Sun-Tzu." Tormano scooped up the pistol she had dropped, popped the empty clip from it and jammed a new one home. He pulled the slide back and let it snap forward, chambering a round. "Don't worry, my dear, I am not going to shoot you. You have amused me."

The Mandrinn laughed aloud. "To think of the irony of it. When I contemplated slipping you into my nephew's bed, I told you there was a family tradition involved. Little did I suspect Sun-Tzu was trying to do the same thing to me. He's clever that one—cleverer by half than his mother and sister combined. Must be he takes after his father."

Fire shone in Tormano's eyes. "You're free to go, Ms. Lee. I'm sure the Maskirovka station chief here in Solaris

City will take you in. I will have you escorted there, and I will have you killed if I ever see you again. Is that clear?"

Nancy nodded, pulling her feet in toward her stomach. "Yes, Mandrinn."

"Good. Take this message to Sun-Tzu for me." Tormano's smile became cruel. "Tell him I may no longer be the threat to his realm that I once was, but make sure he understands that is only because Kai is now an even greater one."

38

Victor Davion studied the communiqué and nodded. "I can live with Katherine's wording on this, I think." He took one last glance at it just to make certain his sister's last iteration of the message had not changed it in some subtle way, twisting it to her advantage.

"DATELINE: Tharkad," it began. "Archon Prince Victor Ian Steiner-Davion has announced his intention to shift the seat of power in the Federated Commonwealth. Where Tharkad and New Avalon previously served as co-capitals, each for six months out of the year, now the seat of power will rest on New Avalon alone. Citing the fact that the Federated Commonwealth has been ruled from Tharkad since his mother's death, the Archon Prince said he would spend the next year ruling from New Avalon, then resume the biannual shift between New Avalon and Tharkad.

"Duchess Katrina Steiner-Davion will act as Regent in Archon Prince Victor's absence. 'I have the utmost confidence in my sister and her ability to handle affairs of state both great and small. Leaving Tharkad in her hands will free me to deal with the grave concerns that threaten the Federated Commonwealth as a whole.'

"Through a spokesperson at the Winter Palace, Duchess Katrina said she was 'delighted' to be of service to her brother, for whom she has 'the greatest of respect and trust.'"

He nodded to the clerk from the Public Affairs Secretariat. "This will stand. See to its distribution."

"As you wish, Highness." The man bowed and exited Victor's office. The guards stationed outside closed the door, leaving Victor alone with Alex Mallory and Curaitis.

The prince smiled at both men. "Alex, I know why Curaitis doesn't like that communiqué, but I sense it leaves you uneasy as well. Your thoughts?"

The white-haired man shrugged stiffly. "I agree that your departure for New Avalon will help reduce tensions in the Skye. Ryan's death has slowed the momentum of the rebellion."

"Cut off the head of a snake and the body dies."

"Yes, Curaitis, quite true." Mallory frowned. "And Katherine has positioned herself as a conciliator in this matter, so making her Regent here is logical and doubtless valuable. Still and all, the move seems like a retreat to me and that does not leave a good taste in my mouth."

Victor smiled. "I appreciate your honesty. There are some things I think you should know that might make my strategy clear."

Mallory held up a hand. "Beware, Highness, of telling me secrets of state. I do truly intend to resign my position when we return to New Avalon. I will stay with you as long as it takes to find a replacement, but the time of my generation has passed. I fear I do not advise you as well as another might."

The Intelligence Secretary looked over at Curaitis. "Forgive me, but I cannot recommend you to take my place, despite the close working relationship you have with the prince."

Curaitis shook his head. "No matter, I would not take the job."

Mallory sighed as if the admission had lifted a weight from his shoulders. "Would that Kai Allard-Liao were to follow in his father's footsteps and advise you the way his father and grandfather did for your father. You must trust implicitly the person who has your ear."

Victor nodded. "I have someone in mind who will fill that bill, if you will consent to train him and consult with him."

"Of course, Highness. Who?"

Victor walked over to the bookcase built into the north

wall of his office. Reaching up under the trim, he hit a switch and half the bookcase slid forward and then to the left. "What you will see is a state secret, Alex, but one I trust you to keep."

A fair-haired man a good head taller than Victor emerged from the passage and nodded to the prince. He scratched at his blond beard, then stepped forward and offered his hand to the older man. "Secretary Mallory? I am Jerrard Cranston."

Mallory took his hand and shook it, but refused to release it. He pulled the man closer, then withdrew his hand from the other's grasp as if he had been burned. "No! This is not possible!"

"Why not?" Victor closed the passage. "Kai Allard-Liao was presumed dead on Alyina, yet he returned from the grave. Why should I deny that luxury to Galen Cox?"

Mallory's jaw dropped open. "But why the deception? Your sister is in mourning. She should be told."

"*That* is not possible."

"You must. To conceal the truth from her is monstrous!" Mallory shivered. "Your father never would have done anything like this."

"My father was never faced with the same problem." Victor started to ask Curaitis to explain everything, but he knew the taciturn security man would omit details that prompted full understanding. "Alex, Galen's survival is part of a process. Let me lay it out for you and then you decide if I am *being* a monster, or shielding my friend from one."

"Please, Highness, explain."

"On the eighteenth of April we received a priority message from Solaris that said Sven Newmark, Ryan's aide, had contacted Sergei Chou on Solaris, directing him to engage an assassin to kill Galen. We would have known sooner, but we had technical difficulties with our intelligence-gathering, as well you know. I immediately dispatched Curaitis to Solaris with the intention of intercepting the assassins, faking Galen's death to prevent further attacks on him, and giving Ryan enough rope to hang himself for my mother's murder. As you know, the man who slew my mother operated from Solaris, and Chou was the man who negotiated the deal to kill my mother. Newmark supplied a link between Ryan and Chou."

Victor looked at Galen. "Galen had not been informed of the plan to fake his death until Curaitis met him in the penthouse suite at the hotel to spirit him away right before they blew the building."

Curaitis half-closed his eyes. "We arranged for a troop of scouts to meet with Katherine so she would be out of the suite when the bomb went off."

Galen nodded solemnly. "When I met Curaitis, I surprised him with the news that Katri ... Katherine and I had become very close. He and I agreed that she would have to believe me dead for the time it took to get her back to Tharkad, primarily so she would seem truly distraught for the media here on her arrival. Had we known then what we know now, we would have known she could have—hell, she did—act the part on her own."

Mallory frowned. "I don't understand."

"We are getting a bit ahead of things." Victor clasped his hands together and cupped the back of his neck. "To make everything look normal in the given situation—which was that Katherine could easily have been the target of the bomb—Curaitis evacuated her *and* had the hotel swept for evidence, all of which was bagged and loaded on the DropShip. During the trip back here, one of the agents who had been guarding Katherine in the hotel lobby—a man who did not know the bomb was *ours*—mentioned to a lab tech that one of Ryan's aides had given Katrina a note, which she had discarded. He had noticed the man, David Hanau, because he'd seemed so nervous and the note had angered Katrina. The agent thought it might have been something special, perhaps a way to lure her back up to her room.

"The agent and the lab tech found the bag that had been taken from the trash basket in the lobby and went through it. They sprayed the invitation with a chemical solution, looking for fingerprints, then examined it under an ultraviolet light source. What they found, I understand, was the residue of a message written in a novelty ink that vanishes after contact with air."

Curaitis nodded. "It's called Lover's Secret and comes in a variety of packages, including a number of different scents. The message is written, sprayed with a scent fixative, then sealed in an envelope. After the envelope is opened, the fixative evaporates and the message fades. It is not intended for long correspondence."

Galen shook his head. "In this case the scent was Daffodil D'Amore and the message read 'Galen is target. Run.' "

The old man looked stunned. "She knew you were a target and didn't say anything?"

Galen shuddered, his wordless answer eloquent enough for everyone.

"Curaitis sent me a message from the DropShip as it came in, explaining the situation. We decided, at that point, to keep Katherine in the dark about Galen until or unless she spoke up about her knowledge that he was a target. I assumed, and a psychology consultant concurs, that she would have talked about her prior knowledge as part of the grieving process, first to accept guilt, then to work through it. She did not."

"At Prince Victor's suggestion, I did a check on David Hanau and found reasonable evidence to suggest he has been in Katherine's private employ for a number of years. It would appear, as indicated by his method of getting a covert message to her, that he is an amateur spy. As Ryan's aide, his intelligence had to be good, and we have retrospectively documented other unsuccessful attempts by Hanau to get messages to Katherine after the point when we know Newmark engaged the assassin to kill Galen."

Mallory looked from Galen to Curaitis and then to Victor. "So your sister did not warn Galen that he was a target." Mallory cupped his chin with his left hand. "There's something else, isn't there?"

Victor nodded. "Chou had a number of different methods for getting paid. In Ryan's case, Chou used computer thieves to loot a bank account for the correct amount of money. Other clients would pay with high-odds tickets on 'Mech battles there on Solaris. His most ingenious method, however, was buying up worthless properties for little more than the property taxes owed on them, and having a corporation buy those properties from him at an unbelievably inflated price."

Curaitis summed up the investigation succinctly. "We can trace no money from Ryan to Chou at the time the assassin was engaged to kill Archon Melissa. We do have a land-sale deal that ultimately involves a corporation, whose head was awarded a title and a land grant at Katherine's suggestion."

Victor flushed with mortification. "The land this corporation bought for twenty million has been set aside for reclamation and rehabilitation into a riparian habitat, which means the corporation got a tax deduction for the full amount. In effect, the Federated Commonwealth paid for my mother's assassination."

Mallory slumped back into his chair. "Ryan engaged the assassin and your sister paid for him?"

"Yes, but we can't prove it, not a bit of it." Victor shrugged. "If I were to accuse her with no solid evidence, everyone would think it merely an attempt to discredit her. She is so much more popular than I am that such a move could make the rebellion explode. She has already distanced herself from me and from Ryan in her statement from Solaris, and she could easily rally his forces to herself."

The Intelligence Secretary frowned. "If you suspect her of complicity in your mother's assassination, how can you leave her here on the throne?"

Victor exhaled slowly and forced his hands to unknot. "Had I a choice, Alex, I would stick her away in the deepest hole on the furthest planet in the Federated Commonwealth. That *is* an option, yes, but not a very viable one right now. Katherine has successfully positioned herself as the grieving princess of the Federated Commonwealth. Condolence messages have been flooding this place from all over the Inner Sphere. She is well loved, and any move against her would be a disaster."

The prince shrugged briefly, then slitted his eyes. "Katherine, while treacherous, still has her uses and I mean to take advantage of them. An incredible number of these condolence messages have come from the Isle of Skye. With Ryan's death, the rebel coalition is tearing itself apart while the rest of the population is mourning Galen's death right along with Katherine. This gives her incredible influence there and the rebellion is collapsing because of it."

Alex frowned. "But you're allowing Katherine to put herself in Ryan's position. This gives her a base from which to oppose you."

"True, but her coalition is based on peace and nonviolence. She can't shift that around to a war footing and still maintain her support. By giving her a peace-loving constituency, I'm pinning her down and limiting her options." Victor said. "At least, I hope that's what I am doing."

Galen folded his arms. "Letting Katherine sit on the Archon's throne also buys us some time to see how much backing she's been able to gather up to this point. Until we uncovered Hanau, we had no idea she was running her own network of agents. While seated on the throne as Regent she might become complacent and sloppy, giving us an edge against her."

Alex nodded slowly. "What I hear you saying is that you're going to give her a meter because you think she'll overextend herself going for a kilometer. You will forgive me if I am not reassured by that."

"There *are* other problems with which I have to deal." The prince turned and faced the window that looked out over the snowy capital city. "Aside from the fact that I don't want to start a civil war, the rest of the Federated Commonwealth needs me. I expect, with Kai taking over Free Capella from his uncle, that Sun-Tzu will step up his activities against the Sarna March. I want to be there to deal with him, so he will think twice about adventurism. Moreover, I *must* be there so the rest of the Federated Commonwealth won't think I've abandoned it."

Galen smiled. "And military exercises that warn Sun-Tzu off from being foolish also allow us to pull units out of this half of the Federated Commonwealth. It blunts Katherine's ability to do anything overtly military."

"But denuding the Lyran portion of the FedCom could prompt Thomas Marik to strike along the border," Alex objected, then seemed to think better of it. "Then again, with troops in the Sarna March, you could do much more damage to him than he could to you."

Victor nodded without turning around. "My thoughts exactly. So the situation is this: Katherine remains here to clean up the mess Ryan bequeathed us. We can't act against her without solid evidence, and we don't have it. Revealing her treachery concerning Galen would only be seen as a dirty trick by me, so we'll save it for a time when we can have the desired effect. We have no choice, and as long as we have a viper in our midst, we might as well let it deal with vermin."

"I don't like it, but there it is, my friends," Victor said as he turned to face them. "I have a nation to govern. Dealing with my sister must wait because my duty to my people cannot."

39

Solaris City, Solaris VII
Tamarind March, Federated Commonwealth
29 April 3056

Upon leaving his uncle's—actually it was *his* now—palace, Kai directed Fuh Teng's grandnephew Tsen to drive the hovercar through Solaris. He told himself it was so he would have time to think, but then he did everything he could to avoid it. He called out instructions to his chauffeur to turn this way and that. When that failed to keep introspection at bay, he turned and stared out the window, leaving the driver to choose his own aimless course through the streets.

Kai let himself be distracted by the sights and sounds of the city. He had lived here for nearly three years, yet it seemed as though he had never really seen it till now. The bright, garish lights hid none of the squalor, just dressed it up. The legion of people on the streets, from prostitutes and pimps to gawking tourists and seething, neo-Puritanical Wildmon sect missionaries, supplied an improbable cast for the dramas of Solaris. The images and the noises through which his vehicle slid silently made everything seem invention instead of reality.

Solaris is a world for those who cannot handle reality. Kai sank back into the leather upholstery of the aircar. *Solaris is a world for those who refuse to handle reality.*

It occurred to him that he was avoiding going home not because he wanted time to think, but because he was afraid. It struck him funny. Here he was, Kai Allard-Liao, the Champion of Solaris, the man who had killed Clanners and defeated Elementals in single combat, and no one would guess what it was that had his stomach tied in knots.

A woman, a child—who would believe it? Kai shook his head. *How can I fear facing them, when billions of others face and conquer that same fear?*

"Take me home, please, Tsen."

"Yes, my lord." Tsen spun the wheel once to the right, then slid the car into the driveway to Kai's home. "Here we are."

Kai looked up. "I didn't necessarily mean that quickly, Tsen."

"I can drive in circles some more, if you wish, my lord."

"No, that's fine. I'll get out now." He pulled the door open and climbed out of the vehicle. Closing the door, he mounted the steps up to the building's front door while Tsen drove off to park the aircar in the garage down the street. Kai dug into his pocket for the cardkey to the door, but Keith Smith opened it for him from inside.

"Welcome home, Kai."

"Keith? I hardly expected to see you here." Kai shook his hand. "Is there a problem?"

The computer expert shook his head. "Not really. After you left the office to see your uncle, a ComStar representative arrived with the news that permission had been granted for a Star of Jade Falcon Elementals commanded by Star Colonel Taman Malthus to come to Solaris. The holodisk is on your desk, and the order was backdated to the beginning of March."

Kai laughed aloud. "ComStar certainly knows how to cover themselves."

Keith nodded. "Tell me one thing."

"Yes?"

"If I looked at my JumpShip pattern projections back, say, to around the beginning of March, would I see a pattern that started near Jade Falcon space and ended in the village of Joppo here on Solaris?"

Kai rested his left hand on Keith's shoulder. "Without your work, I couldn't have gotten them here. I hoped permission would come through so they could have watched the title defense from my box, but the bureaucracy is too slow for that. About the same time the Falcons reached Equatus, a message I prerecorded explaining who they were and what they were doing was forwarded to the ComStar Precentor here on Solaris. I think presenting ComStar with a *fait accompli* prompted their permission, and even that took two days.

"I didn't want to keep you in the dark, my friend, but if you didn't know, ComStar couldn't hold you responsible. As I am an officer of the St. Ives government and the Falcons are here on a 'diplomatic' mission, well, ComStar can be upset with me, but there is very little they can do about it."

"Thanks for protecting me." Keith again shook Kai's hand. "I have to go. Larry actually got a date with that model he met at your uncle's reception. Kristina and I are doubling up with them to attend the opening of a Kessler show over in Silesia. I'm already late."

"Have fun, Keith, and thanks for what you did to rescue my son."

"He's a beautiful kid, Kai. You're damned lucky." Keith headed out the door. "I'm just glad I was able to help."

Kai latched the door behind his aide, but only got as far as the middle of the marble foyer before Taman Malthus appeared through the archway leading from the west wing. The unarmored Elemental stepped forward and swallowed Kai's right hand in his huge fist. "Kai Allard-Liao, I welcome you on your return."

"Thank you, Taman Malthus." Kai shook the Jade Falcon's hand. "I owe you a debt I cannot repay."

The blue-eyed Elemental shook his head. "You and I, we fought, we became allies, and we took a planet away from ComStar. Between us there is no account of favors. You honored me by entrusting your offspring to my men and me. If we were to compare debts, then I would owe you, for I have been far too long without fighting."

Kai smiled, then rose on his tiptoes to look around and behind Malthus. "Surely you are not alone here. Where are the rest of your men?"

"Most have returned to Joppo to pack our gear. With ComStar's permission secured, we will come to the city for a time." Taman pointed toward the ceiling with an index finger. "Locke and Slane are upstairs safeguarding your son against further predations by Tormano."

Kai sighed heavily. "I don't think we have to worry about him. If the option were open to me I'd try to send him away with you and get him placed in a bandit-hunting Solahma unit. As it is, I will pension him off and keep him under control."

"For what he did, we would have him and his offspring slain." Malthus' eyes grew cold. "Your son may be a freebirth, but he possesses your genetic heritage. Denying that to humanity would have been an unforgivable crime, and one for which your uncle's line should wither and die."

"Yours is undisputably a cleaner solution than what I have arranged, but it is not one open to me. My uncle was ambitious and frustrated and felt forced to act." Kai frowned. "Were that a capital crime in the Inner Sphere, every world would be a charnel house."

"And the harvest of one ambition crop would merely leave room for another to grow up in its place."

Kai smiled up at the big man. "You have learned a lot about the Inner Sphere."

Taman scratched at his closely cropped blond hair. "Joppo's only amusement comes from watching holovid dramas. The *Immortal Warrior* series is obviously art, however unrealistic, but the rest of the programs merely speak to the human condition."

Interesting perspective you have there. "You said my boy is upstairs?"

"He will make you proud, Kai. He is brave and strong." Malthus smiled. "And my calling him a freebirth was not meant as disrespect. The Clans would have matched you and his mother and bred a grand sibko of warriors."

Kai started to respond, when he caught a sudden motion out of the corner of his eye. Thinking the other Elementals were coming down the stairs he turned in their direction with a smile on his face.

Deirdre Lear awoke with a start, for the moment disoriented and unable to place her surroundings. Lights blazed in the room, including the lamps on the tables at either end of the couch where she lay. Sitting up, she looked to her right and saw David huddled beneath a blue blanket on a day-bed. Behind him stood two Elementals, alert and awake, their expressions slightly bemused.

She heard voices come up the stairs and through the open doorway, first the bass boom of Taman Malthus, then another, quieter voice. She recognized none of the words, but the tone and rhythm of the sounds pinpointed its author for her. She combed her fingers through her hair and tugged at the hem of her blouse, then ran past David's bed to the doorway.

She paused at the top of the stairs, then descended, freezing when he looked up at her. "Kai?"

"Deirdre?" He looked tired, but the smile spreading across his face banished all signs of fatigue. She saw the same light play through his eyes that had attracted her to him from the first, and he moved to the foot of the stairs with the grace she remembered from Alyina. "God, Deirdre, it has been too long."

Her heart began to pound in her chest and she felt her face flush. She continued down the stairs, faster than was decorous but not so fast as to be dangerous. She flung her arms around his neck and hung on tightly. His arms enfolded her, crushing her to him, and the fears lingering from her time at the estate crumbled away to nothing.

She slipped her hands down to his chest, then pushed gently back on his shoulders. He released her slowly and let his hands still touch her arms as they each stepped back. Deirdre looked up into his gray eyes, then looked down and away.

"I've been stupid," they each told the other in unison.

Kai threw his head back and laughed, and Deirdre luxuriated in a sound she had missed since Alyina. She could tell by his voice that he had not changed much from their time together. He looked more confident and sounded it too, yet the tentative gentleness of his hands as they slipped down into hers reminded her of his thoughtful caution.

Her "Kai" drowned out his softer "Deirdre," and he bowed his head to acknowledge her the victor in the exchange. "Kai, I have to explain some things to you. I was very confused, *unbelievably* confused until not long ago. About you and about me. I made some judgements that I shouldn't have, and I'm sorry."

Kai reached out and lifted her chin with his right hand. "Deirdre, it doesn't matter. The past is the past."

"It does matter, Kai, please." She led him over to a padded bench beneath a mirror on the east wall. Only as they sat down did she catch a fleeting glimpse of Taman's heel disappearing upstairs. "I misjudged you. By the time I returned

to Odell, you had already started on your rise to the top here on Solaris. I thought you had chosen to come here to spite me. My father's death here, on this world, at your father's hands was what kept us apart when we first met and I thought you were sending me a message."

She tucked a lock of black hair behind her right ear. "When I had David, my stepfather urged me to contact you, but by then you had become big news. The media played up how you were so much like your father, and that ate away at me. I built you into the worst stereotype of a fighter I could imagine, making you into a boozing, womanizing ogre whose only true pleasure came from crippling and killing your foes. I wanted nothing to do with you and I wanted to shield David from you.

"I wanted to believe the worst and, because of that, I missed all the signs that you hadn't really changed. Granted there was much I didn't know until I had a conversation with Keith today and learned about the reforms you've instituted, but my decision to blind myself to anything good about you meant I wouldn't have picked up any clue to your activities. Then, when I was on Zurich at a clinic that's funded by Cenotaph Charities, I chose to believe you merely gave money away because you had so much wealth you wanted to flaunt it. The charitable act of giving clothes to children became transformed, in my mind, to blatant self-promotion on your part."

She gave his hands a squeeze. "I realized how blind I'd been when your uncle held us hostage. I knew that act was evil and could only benefit him if it somehow limited your actions. As you were acting in opposition to him, well, you obviously were not being evil. If you were the monster I had imagined, you would have abandoned us."

Kai paled and a tremor ran through his hands. "I did."

"No. Keith wouldn't tell me where you'd gone or what you'd done, but if it involved Lady Omi Kurita surreptitiously taking up residence in your home, it must have been very important. And *that* not withstanding, Keith told me all you had done to prevent your uncle from knowing you had defied him. As you had done in the past, you set aside your personal concerns for the welfare of others."

Deirdre hesitated a moment and a tear rolled down one

cheek. Kai brushed it away from her face. "You don't have to do this, Deirdre, you don't have to beat yourself up."

"But I do, Kai, as much to chasten myself as to apologize to you." She looked up and met his unwavering gaze. "You see, I had turned you into a monster not because of anything you had done, but because I believed you had used what I'd said to prompt and justify your trip here. I was angry with you for perverting and betraying what we had known on Alyina, and for failing to live up to the potential I feared would consume me."

Kai laughed deliciously, brought her hands up to his face and kissed them. "You were right to be angry with me. I did betray you and certainly did not deserve to be the father of your son."

She frowned. "But the charities, the contract you handed out, what you did here to oppose your uncle. Those are all things of which you can be proud."

"I suppose you're right."

Deirdre raised an eyebrow. "I think I must have missed something."

"As did I, Doctor . . ." Kai looked at her and couldn't help but smile. "You see, when you sent me away on Alyina, you said it was because I had a military mindset. Taman and the other Elementals had finally convinced me that I was a damned good warrior, and your words made it a majority opinion. With that in mind, and damned little else, I'm ashamed to admit, I headed toward Solaris. I did get sidetracked to attend Hanse Davion's funeral and to visit my father's grave, but I never lost sight of my target.

"You see, all my life my father had been the greatest warrior I'd ever known. I got it into my head that if I came to Solaris and duplicated his success, then I would also prove myself a great warrior. I would have validated your view of me, which I wanted to do because it meant that you had really seen the true me. Bits and pieces of Clan philosophy got mixed up in there so that after defeating all this world had to offer, I saw myself as paying homage to my father. With each victory my stature grew, and so did his. That was why I called my stable Cenotaph, because I saw it as a memorial to him. By helping other people who had been on Alyina or in the war, I expanded that to memorializing those who had died fighting the Clans."

Kai swallowed hard. "What I didn't realize until I faced someone recently and had his dreams of glory collide with my hopes for peace, is that I mocked my father, not glorified him. The single strongest message I took away from him came from when he fought and killed your father. He told me that killing a man should never be easy, and I vowed that I would never violate that dictum. I had enough killing in the war and I thought I honored my father by winning here through skill, not mayhem.

"What I missed was a far greater lesson. When I asked him once why he left Solaris at the moment when he had become its Champion, he told me it was because the real world needed him. Far away from here I realized that I had been hiding from the real world. All the charities, all the reforms, all the things I had done were sops to my conscience, bribes so I could remain here and stave off my destiny."

Deirdre pulled his hands to her and kissed them. "But those programs helped people. They are a true window to your soul. On Alyina you told me that you were willing to accept the responsibilities of a warrior, terrible though they are, so others who could not bear them would not have to try. You've done that, here, and done it very well."

"Yes, Deirdre, yes, but I have not accepted *all* the responsibilities I can. When I returned here and determined how I had to deal with my uncle, I did so without remorse. A warrior would have killed him, but I found a way to neutralize him without causing his death. I have Victor Davion's trust—an asset squandered here—and I must make myself available to him. I have responsibilities to my family and to the people my mother rules. In taking over the Free Capella movement from my uncle, I recognize my responsibilities for the dreams of many people who wish to see the Capellan Confederation united once again."

Kai smiled. "Granted, I will reshape Free Capella, focus it and direct it toward preserving our culture and making Capellans stronger as a people, but I can and will guide it. At least, I think I can. I hope I can."

Kai's heart swelled as Deirdre smiled. "You can and will—and will do it wonderfully."

He looked down, refusing to meet her eyes. "And then there is the greatest responsibility of all, but I don't think it's one I can manage . . ." Kai's head came up. "At least, not alone. Would you . . . ?"

She pressed her left hand to his lips, stopping his words. "No more talking."

"But."

"No." Deirdre slipped from the bench and stood, then pulled him to his feet. "Come with me, Kai Allard-Liao, there is something very important I must do." She gave him a smile that erased the distance four years had put between them. "It's time I introduce you to your son."

Postscript

While writing this book I attended a science fiction convention (Wolfcon) at which an auction was held in memory of Curtis Scott, a game designer and convention organizer. Curtis had been killed in a traffic accident a month earlier, leaving behind his wife Mary and son Phillip, age five. I entered the right to appear as a character in this novel as one of the items to be auctioned. Keith Smith and Larry Acuff quickly outstripped the other bidders. Keith won the role and because Larry was willing to kick in an additional amount of money, Keith and I agreed to give him a part in the book, too.

A scholarship fund for Phillip Scott has been set up to take care of his education. Contributions may be sent to Phillip Anthony Scott Scholarship Fund, c/o Phyllis Lewis, Software Institute, Carnegie-Mellon University, Pittsburgh, PA 15213.

CRUSADER

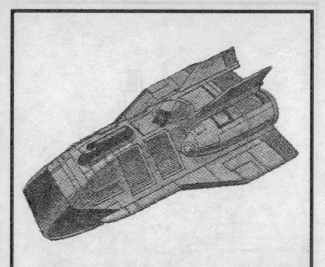

LEOPARD CLASS DROPSHIP

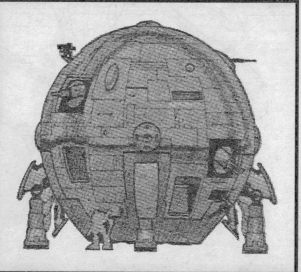

UNION CLASS DROPSHIP

LOCUST

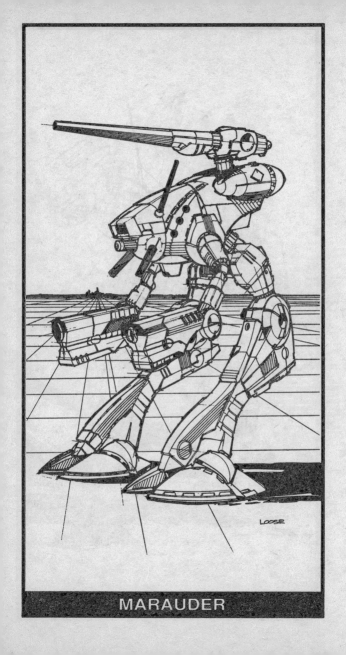

MARAUDER

PHOENIX HAWK

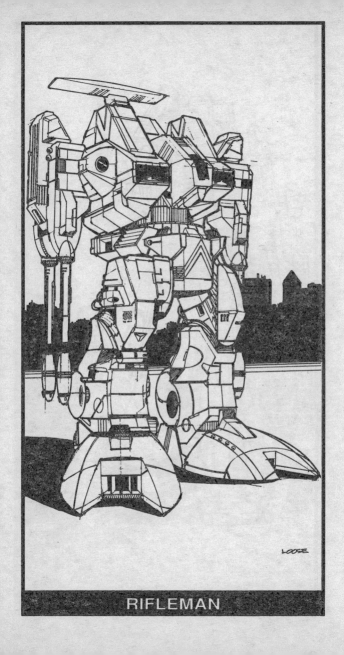

RIFLEMAN

SHADOW HAWK

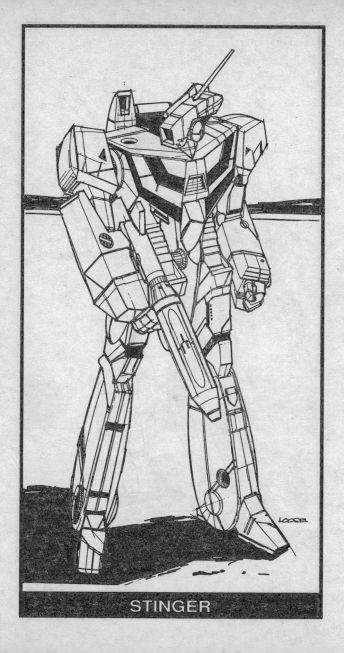

STINGER

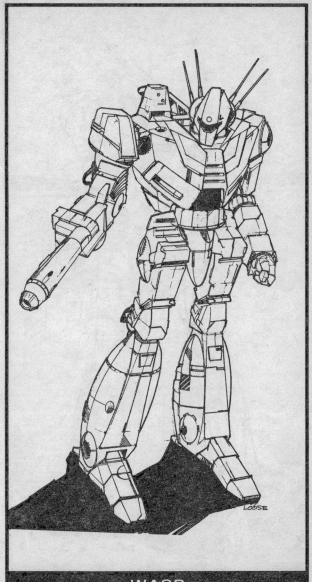

WASP

WOLVERINE